THE BUILDER'S SWORD

THE LEGENDARY BUILDER BOOK #1

J. A. CIPRIANO

Copyright © 2017 by J. A. Cipriano

All rights reserved.

No part of this book may be reproduced in any form or by any electronic or mechanical means, including information storage and retrieval systems, without written permission from the author, except for the use of brief quotations in a book review.

WANT TO GET THIS FREE?

Sign up here. If you do, I'll send you my short story, *Alone in the Dark*, for free.

Visit me on Facebook or on the web at JACipriano.com for all the latest updates.

ALSO BY J. A. CIPRIANO

∼

<u>World of Ruul</u>

Soulstone: Awakening

Soulstone: The Skeleton King

∼

<u>Elements of Wrath Online</u>

Ring of Promise

∼

<u>Kingdom of Heaven</u>

The Skull Throne

∼

<u>The Thrice Cursed Mage</u>

Cursed

Marked

Burned

Seized

Claimed

Hellbound

~

The Half-Demon Warlock

Pound of Flesh

Flesh and Blood

Blood and Treasure

~

The Lillim Callina Chronicles

Wardbreaker

Kill it with Magic

The Hatter is Mad

Fairy Tale

Pursuit

Hardboiled

Mind Games

Fatal Ties

~

Clans of Shadow

Heart of Gold

Feet of Clay

Fists of Iron

~

The Spellslinger Chronicles

Throne to the Wolves

Prince of Blood and Thunder

~

Found Magic

May Contain Magic

The Magic Within

Magic for Hire

~

Witching on a Starship

Maverick

Planet Breaker

1

I took a deep breath, trying to calm myself down. My heart was hammering so hard in my chest, I was sure the people at the bus stop could hear it. Ignoring their nasty looks as best I could, I stepped off the bus, pulled my coat around me, and made my way past them.

I was in the bad part of town. Dilapidated buildings hugged the horizon, their boarded-up windows a testament to the job loss that had taken place after the manufacturing shop in the company town had moved overseas.

Still, I didn't have time to think about it, not if I wanted to secure my prize, anyway. After my stop at the bank to pull every penny I had saved out of my savings account, I could practically feel the weight of my life savings drawing all eyes to me. It would only take one thug to push me down and steal it away at knife point.

I glanced around the parking lot, trying to see if anyone was waiting to accost me, but thankfully, the coast looked clear. Barely resisting the urge to stick my hand in my pocket and check my wad of cash again, I hurried across the cracked asphalt toward my destination, Angel's Pawnshop. It was a huge building, having slowly taken over the strip mall where it resided. The plastered-over, yellowed signs of a pet shop, comic book store, and an accountant was still there.

Actually, when I'd first found the place, it'd been because I'd seen the sign for the comic shop and gotten off the bus to scope it out. I loved comics, old ones especially, but I'd never had the kind of cash for the hobby. I was forever wishing I had a Spider-Man #121 (the issue where Gwen Stacy died) or a Hulk #181 (the first appearance of Wolverine), but alas at their current price tag, I'd have to skip paying rent for a month or two to have that kind of scratch. At least if I wanted to own more than the cover, anyway.

As I stepped onto the cracked concrete in front of the massive neon purple building, I took a look up and down the streets. Unlike most strip malls, I didn't see any of the homeless that were *everywhere* in the city. While I'd been mugged a few times when I'd missed the bus and been forced to walk home from work, I'd never worried about it here. Sure, I didn't have my life savings in my pocket then, but this was one of the reasons I'd risked it.

Angel's Pawnshop was one of the safest places to do business in the entire city, and I'd heard that was because Merle, the owner, had paid a military contractor to clean up his little slice of heaven. They'd rounded up all the homeless and dumped them at the McDonald's a few blocks away. Then they'd patrolled it long enough to make the muggers think twice before coming back because no one wanted to risk bringing valuables or getting large sums of cash when they could get robbed. Made sense given their sort of clientele.

I took a deep breath and stared at the barred glass doors in front of me. A red open sign glowed to my right, and even though I knew it was hopeless, I tried to look inside, anyway. Unfortunately, the motley collection of eighties and nineties movie posters made it impossible to see even the barest glimpses inside. I'd heard that the main reason the windows were blocked out was that Merle sometimes bargained for less than reputable items, but I'd never seen anything strange inside.

Truth be told, the place was like a wonderland of old knickknacks that someone somewhere had found valuable. And while they hadn't had any comics I'd wanted that day, they'd had something else, something I coveted a lot more than comics.

"No time like the present," I muttered to myself and ran a hand through my shaggy brown hair, brushing it out of my eyes. I knew it wouldn't help much because I needed a haircut, but thanks to the twin cowlicks at the back of my head, I always had to get my hair cut really short. Since it was winter, the idea of freezing my ears off wasn't exactly appealing. And don't even get me started on hats. They made me look ridiculous.

I pushed open the doors, eliciting a loud screech from the buzzer by the door. As I stepped into the store, the wash of heat inside hit me. It'd been chilly outside, with the first hint of rain barely clinging to the clouds in the sky. Inside was different, and as I glanced from old records stacked next to a crate full of musical instruments, I almost pulled off my jacket.

Instead, I rubbed the back of my neck with one hand and tried to find Merle. He wasn't behind the counter, but I knew he'd seen me thanks to the huge television mounted on the wall behind it. My mug was plastered on it as I stood there fidgeting, and without thinking, I tried to smooth out my hair since it was sticking straight up. It was no use, and I quickly gave up.

Moving quickly, I made my way past a rack full of blenders and toward the stuffed animals in the back left corner of the store. My footsteps seemed to echo on the cement floor as the fluorescent lighting blazed overhead. I dug my hand into my pocket, and as I felt the wad of bills with my fingertips, my beating heart eased its pace a tad. I had enough to buy my prize. Things were going to be okay.

Stepping out from between the racks at the back of the store, I found myself staring at a glass case filled with watches. I wasn't sure if they were real or not, but I also didn't care because I was staring at the pegboard just beyond the case where the swords were kept.

Excitement filled me as my gaze roamed over the board, trying to find the one I'd set my eyes on when I'd first come in here six months ago. It had been rusted to hell, but something about the blade had spoken to me. I wasn't sure why since it was nearly black with tarnish, and the hilt was rather simple.

Still, the moment I'd laid eyes upon it, I'd known I needed to own it. I'd felt the pull of the weapon with every ounce of my being. There was just one problem. It'd cost so much money, I couldn't buy it. Hell, even with working doubles and barely eating, I'd still had to sell nearly everything I'd owned to buy the weapon.

Only, I couldn't find it on the rack. Where was it? I took a step forward, knees shaking and smacked my palms on the glass case as I leaned forward for a better look. It wasn't there. The spot where it'd been hung empty. How could that be?

"Looking for something, Arthur?" Merle asked, his deep English voice washing over me a moment before I felt his huge, rough hand slap onto my shoulder. The feel of his touch shocked me from my sudden panic, and as I turned to look at the wizened pawnbroker, I let out a small squeak.

His sapphire blue eyes burned into me from beneath the brim of his camouflage baseball cap. He took a step back from me and ran a hand down his long white wizard beard as he studied me.

"Um... yeah." I swallowed hard. I turned and

pointed to the empty space. "You had a sword there…"

His eyes shifted from me to the spot and back again, and I could have sworn he looked a bit confused. "You mean the one you called about this morning and said you'd pick up after work and to put in the back?" His words held a hint of amusement.

Embarrassment washed over my cheeks as I looked down at my beat-up sneakers like they were the most interesting thing in the world. "Yes, that one… sorry, just nervous I guess. Have you sold it?"

"Arthur, you're the only person who has so much as looked at that sword in the whole time I've owned it." He put a hand on my shoulder. "I wrapped it up this morning." He gestured back toward the front counter. "I've had it up there since you called, and I'll be happy to sell it to you." He leaned in close. "Assuming you have the cash."

"I do," I said, shoving my hand in my pocket and pulling out the wad. Everything I had in the world. "Please."

He looked at my cash for a moment before nodding. "I do believe we can make a deal."

2

Rain drenched the parking lot as I stepped out of Angel's Pawnshop, the sword safely tucked beneath my arm. It was wrapped in brown butcher's paper and was about five feet long, making me stand out like a sore thumb.

I glanced around just to make sure no one was watching me. While I was pretty sure no one would mug me for a rusty old sword, I'd just spent my life savings on it. The last thing I wanted was for some thug with his pants around his ankles to stab me and take it because he thought it would make him feel cool.

"Fuck!" I cried as I spied my bus shutting its doors. Had I been in the pawn shop that long? A quick glance at my watch had me cursing myself for being late. I'd spent over an hour inside, and if I didn't catch this bus, I'd be stuck waiting at the stop in the rain for the next thirty minutes.

I waved my arms, trying to signal the bus to stop as it pulled away from the curb. My new sword cut through the air as I flailed, the rain drenching the paper and making it stick to the weapon that made me worried it'd tear through. That was the last thing I needed. If the bus saw me chasing after it with a sword, who knew what would happen?

Thunder boomed overhead as I sprinted across the lot, splashing through puddles with reckless abandon. I was already soaked to the skin despite my jacket's relatively good defense against the rain. Lightning arced through the sky as I hit the edge of the parking lot and cried out.

"Stop!" my cry was drowned out by the crackle of thunder, and the brake lights flashed as the bus began to pull away.

"No," I huffed, my chest heaving from the effort as I leaped the small array of wildflowers that separated the pawn shop parking lot from the sidewalk. My sneakers hit the puddle-laden sidewalk with a squelch. Water flew in every direction as I waved my hands again.

More lightning arched through the sky as the

brake lights on the bus flashed. I hit the curb a second later. My hand snaked out to rap on the side of the bus as the doors opened to reveal a svelte black lady with blonde cornrows. She took one look at me through the open doors and sighed.

"Come on, get in," she said, smacking the steering wheel with one hand. "You're making me late." Thunder boomed again. "I was gonna leave you, truth be told, but the storm made me feel bad."

"Thanks, I appreciate it." I nodded to her, flashing my bus pass at the scanner as I stepped inside.

"Everyone's got to do one good thing a day." She took one look at me and shrugged. "You're mine."

I wasn't quite sure how to respond to that, so I just nodded as I made my way past her toward the back of the bus. I flopped down on an empty seat beside the door and looked around. The bus was mostly empty, containing only a younger Asian man in a rain-soaked shirt with his jacket over his lap, and a lady who was either a nurse or a dental assistant judging by the scrubs. Both of them looked frazzled, which wasn't surprising given the late hour, and neither paid me any attention.

The nurse just kept looking through her phone, and the guy fiddled with his jacket like he felt like he should be doing something but wasn't sure what. I could relate. I was never sure of what I should be doing.

Granted, I was glad I had a job at the local Seven Eleven, but I was pretty sure I hadn't been put on this planet just to serve Slurpees. I mean, it wasn't like I thought I was destined for greatness or anything, but well, never mind.

I'd originally taken the job because I'd been able to study during the downtime easily enough but somewhere along the way, I'd run out of money to actually pay for books and what not. With my parents gone and my closest relative nearly sixteen hours away, I'd been forced to drop out.

I still had delusions of becoming a software engineer one day and had even worked my way through most of MIT's coursework, but so far, I hadn't gotten so much as a nibble from any of the local companies. Though that was probably because there were no jobs and I was way too much of a pussy to go find one somewhere else. I'd grown up in this stupid city and felt a little responsible for it even though the businesses who'd run it into the ground clearly hadn't.

While I wasn't quite sure what held me here, I did have a job and it afforded me time. I lived in a relatively roach free studio and owned a computer with a burgeoning Steam account. It was more than easy to waste away and not think things would ever get too bad.

Besides, I had a sword now and what a sword it was. It was a little weird, to be honest. I could tell it was worth something and just needed a little TLC, but at the same time I couldn't figure out why. It reminded me of one of those ancient longswords, but I'd seen tons of them at shows and while cool, I doubted this one was authentic. If it had been, it wouldn't be in a pawn shop. It'd be in a museum somewhere. Still, something about it had drawn my eye though I couldn't say why since Merle hadn't cleaned it for fear of ruining the value. I just knew I had to have it.

I spared a peek down at the sword but couldn't see the weapon through the paper. Part of me wanted to unwrap it a little but I was too worried the bus driver might see the weapon and flip out. She'd already done me a solid by waiting for me and I didn't want to betray that trust. Besides, there were two other people here and call me crazy, but I did not want the skinny white nurse to flip out and accuse me of something. That'd cause a whole thing, and I'd no doubt lose my sword.

Instead, as the rain swept streets of my dying city slid by through the windows, I tried to placate myself by running my fingers along the weapon. I could feel the strength of the steel even through the paper, and as my fingers trailed down toward the hilt of the weapon, I could feel my blood pound in my ears. Everything in me wanted to tear the paper off and grab hold of the weapon, to use it to drive my enemies before me until I heard the lamentations of their women.

I shook my head. That was an odd thought. I didn't really have any enemies. Okay, my boss at the Seven Eleven was sort of a dick, and that dumb stripper who always came in to buy condoms at 3 AM was annoying as hell, but enemies? Hardly.

I pulled my hand away from the weapon and leaned back so my head was against the window. I could hear the rain pelting the bus from outside. It beat a crescendo against the thin steel, and as we approached my stop, I began to dread having to go out into the night. It was almost a block between my apartment building and the bus stop, and I knew that by the time I reached my place, I'd be soaked.

If I'd been smart, I'd have taken my umbrella with me, but I'd foolishly trusted the weatherman this morning because I hadn't wanted to carry the umbrella. Now, I'd pay for it.

"Nothing for it," I grumbled as I turned my eyes back toward the blonde nurse. She was frowning at her phone, and it made her look sort of cute in a run-down sort of way. Part of me wanted to talk to her just to pass the time, but if I knew one thing, it was that I did not know how to talk to girls, even casually. I'd say hello, and it'd be awkward, and then she'd be awkward back, and it'd just be a big awkward thing.

I'd probably have better luck with the guy, but truth be told, I didn't want to talk to him since well, he was a guy.

I sighed again and turned my eyes toward the streets outside and watched them pass by while counting the seconds to my stop.

3

Twenty minutes later, I was standing inside my apartment. I flipped on the lights and stepped inside, sloughing off my rain soaked jacket to the floor. It hit the cheap laminate with a plop as I took a step forward and pulled off my sneakers, tossing them next to the door to dry. My socks squished on the floor as I moved toward the kitchen space and set the sword down on the table I'd rescued from the Marie Calendar's when it had replaced a bunch of furniture a few years back.

I dropped into one of the brown wooden chairs I'd gotten from the thrift store and pulled off my wet socks. I stared at them for a moment before hopping to my feet and padding over to my room. I opened the door and wondered if it'd make the rest of my dirty clothes wet if I threw them in the hamper. I settled for dropping them on the lid to dry.

Turning toward my closet, I made my way there and slid open the tiny door. The few button ups and polos I had were hanging on the rack next to a red sweat-shirt I'd gotten as a giveaway for a radio contest instead of concert tickets.

Squatting down, I reached in and pulled out a brown tackle box with a red handle at the top. I'd gotten it at a garage sale to store all my sword cleaning equipment. Hoisting the box by the handle, I slid the closet door shut and glanced at the wall to my left. I'd rearranged all the swords on the wall around earlier to make room for my new purchase, and now my wall looked empty. Now my collection of katanas hung along the left of the wall, while my replica movie swords where on the right, leaving room in the center for my new purchase.

"You'll have a new friend soon enough," I said, nodding to the wall as I made my way back into the main room of the studio. Moving back to my table, I set down my tackle box. I flipped the orange tabs and opened the lid to reveal an assortment of fine grit sandpaper, gun oil, Scotch Brite pads, and a roll of aluminum foil. I grabbed the box opener from inside and turned toward my sword. I carefully cut away the tape along one edge and opened the paper.

I settled the sword in the center of it so I wouldn't get oil on my table, and stared at it for a moment. She wasn't much to look at, but to me she was beautiful. I ran my fingers along the contours of the hilt and down to the pommel where a cloudy piece of marble sat. The prongs holding it in place looked almost like flames, but they were so dirty, I couldn't quite make out the design.

Deciding to start there, I grabbed the oil from the tackle box and a rag from the packet I'd purchased at Walmart. I dabbed some oil onto the rag and moved to the prongs. I began rubbing at them, and as I did, years of age and dirt seemed to come away. In only a few moments, the gem was gleaming, and I'd worked enough dirt away to see that it had a deep sapphire core with veins that spiraled out along the surface.

The prongs were definitely flames, and as I cleaned the first one as best I could, I found that the way the light hit the marble ball in the pommel caused them to practically glow with blue flame. Satisfied with my one clean prong, I took a step back and admired it. There was a lot more to clean, and I knew I had weeks of work ahead of me. That was fine, though. If I could spend my life taking care of my swords, I would.

Unfortunately, I had to be at work in six hours, and I hadn't slept yet. I needed to do sleep if I was going to be able to work tomorrow, but at the same time, the sword beckoned me to work on her more.

I complied, putting more oil on the rag as I moved toward the blade. I'd give it a quick wipe down, and put it away for later. I began to rub the blade with the rag, and as I moved toward the hilt, I found strange ridges under my fingers. Pulling the rag away, I realized there was something etched into the blade, but it was so caked over with rust and debris that I couldn't tell what.

I began working in earnest then. I took my time with the rag before swapping it out for aluminum foil in the hopes of getting rid of some of the rust. As I began to clear it away, I realized it was a set of geometric symbols.

"Weird," I said, picking up the sword to look at it closer, only as I did, the blade slipped from my oily hands.

Like a dumb ass, I reached out to try to grab it before it fell. My left hand wrapped around the blade as it fell away and hit the floor, slicing my flesh open and spilling my blood down the length of the weapon.

"Fuck!" I cried out in pain, pulling my hand back and cradling it to my chest. Pain rippled through my hand from the wound, and I could practically feel the blood rushing straight from my heart out into the wound.

I took a step backward toward the kitchen to wash out the wound and look at it, all thoughts of the sword forgotten. Only before I could make it more than two steps, the smell of burning plastic hit my nose.

I spun on my heel to find the sword wreathed in blue flame and burning through the linoleum. The blood I'd spilled onto the weapon boiled and spat as the symbols I'd worked so hard to clean glowed with sapphire light.

"What the hell?" I cried, stumbling backward as I tried to figure out what to do.

"Good guess," the sword said, right before blood red smoke began to pour from the tip. The symbols emblazoned across the blade flashed once more, nearly blinding me as I turned away, one arm up to block the glare. Spots danced across my eyes.

As the glow faded, I turned back toward the sword and found myself staring at a Victoria's

Secret model. She was dressed in a black bikini and had black and red bat wings sprouting from her back. She looked me up and down, her bottom teeth scraping along her top lip in a slow, sensual movement.

"So," she said huskily as she offered me the sword hilt first. "What's your wish?" She grinned, displaying a mouthful of perfect, white teeth. "Master."

4

"Whoa, what's going on?" I said, taking a step backward and bumping into the counter that separated the kitchen from the front entry. As my back pressed into the cheap ceramic tile, the demon girl stood there watching me, her eyes full of hunger.

Her face screwed up in confusion as she stood there looking at me for a moment. Then she glanced down at herself for a second before turning her gaze back to me.

"Does my appearance not please you?" she asked, taking a step toward me and held the sword out once more. "If it doesn't…" she bit her lip again and swallowed. "I could try changing it." She reached up then and tucked one of her long raven locks nervously behind her ear with her free hand. "It's been a long time since I've been summoned so maybe tastes have changed?"

"No, um… that's not what I meant," I said, shaking my head as she stood there, lavender eyes searching my face for answers. The only problem was that I was so confused I had none to give her. I'd been cleaning the sword I'd bought one moment, and the next I was face to face with a living, breathing wet dream.

"What do you mean then?" She swept an arm down her body. "Just tell me what you require, and I will do it for you." She smiled, a strangely fragile thing like she was worried she'd displeased me in some way.

"Look, lady, I'm sure you're very nice and all," I paused as her smile started to slip, "and you're totally my type, any guy's type really, so that's not what this is about." I started to say more, but she looked up at me.

"You think I'm pretty?" she asked, a small, demure smile spreading across her full red lips. "You have no idea how happy that makes me."

"Um… what?" I took another deep breath. I know, this is where you're thinking what is wrong with me, and you know fucking what? I was asking myself the same damned thing. I was a Seven Eleven Slurpee monkey for Christ's sake. I was not prepared for a pretty girl to be looking at me like I was her whole world, and honestly, I didn't know what to make of it.

"It pleases me that you find me attractive." She took a step forward, moving so close that I could feel the heat wafting off her body. Her scent hit me next, a mixture of lavender and sage and that weird, inexplicable girl smell.

"Great, okay," I said as she reached out and touched my shoulder with her long, lavender-nailed fingers. "Just give me a second, okay?" I wormed away from her. I needed to focus on what was going on, and her closeness wasn't making it easy.

"Okay," she said, nodding to me as I moved into the kitchen, happy to have the counter between us. I just needed a minute to think, to get a grip on what was going on. I know. I know, I should have just leaped on her or whatever, but at the same time, what if she wanted to eat my soul? Oh my God, what if she was a succubus?

"Let's just take a step backward okay." I gestured at her with one hand as I edged toward my fridge. "There's plenty of time for whatever this is."

"Not as much as you'd think," she said,

nodding, "but I will comply with your command, Master."

"Okay, stop that." I shook my head at her. "My name is Arthur… Arthur Curie."

She looked at me for a long time. Not only that, but she didn't make a single Aquaman joke. Kind of nice, actually.

"I am pleased to meet you, Arthur Curie." She nodded at me. "Is that what you would like me to call you?"

"Yes, well, just Arthur," I said, opening the refrigerator for lack of anything better to do. As soon as I turned away from her, I felt the weight of her gaze between my shoulders. "Would you like something to drink?"

"Are you offering me one, Just Arthur?" she asked, curiosity filling her voice in a way that made me think she'd never been offered a drink before.

"Not Just Arthur. Just Arthur." I smacked my head with my hand. "Do you follow?"

"Yes. What am I supposed to follow?" she asked.

"No. That's not what I was trying to say." I sighed. "My name is Arthur. Don't address me as Just Arthur. Address me as Arthur."

"Okay. I shall call you Arthur," she replied, and

I felt the presence of her near me. I turned and found her hovering only inches away. She'd somehow folded up her bat wings, so they'd melded into the flesh of her back, arms, and legs like an iridescent black and red tattoo.

"So, okay, um back to the original question. Would you like a drink?" I gestured at the dismal contents of my refrigerator. I had a few cans of Natural Ice, a bottle of green Gatorade, and a half gallon of milk of questionable age.

"I would like a drink." She nodded. "Which would you like me to have?" She peered over my shoulder into the fridge and scrunched up her nose. "I am unfamiliar with these beverages."

"Um… how about a beer?" I said, swiping the two closest cans and shutting the door. The movement left us practically pressed against each other. Only, it didn't seem to bother her. Evidently, personal space wasn't a thing with her.

"Okay," she said, taking the offered can and looking at me. "How do I drink this?" She went to tap the lid, but because she was holding the glowing sword, she sort of just wound up gesturing at it with the pommel.

"Here," I said, popping the top on my beer. I took the closed one from her before handing her the opened one. "You drink that one." I opened my own and sort of clinked it against her can. "Drink up."

"Thank you," she said and took a sip. Her eyes narrowed. "This is alcoholic." She raised one slender eyebrow at me. "Are you trying to get me drunk, Arthur?"

I practically spat out my beer and had to work to swallow it. As it painfully slid down my throat, I tried my best to look innocent. "Um… no," I said, shaking my head at her. "I wouldn't… I mean…"

"It's okay," she said, and then laughed. The sound could have summoned wildlife, and as it hit me, something deep inside me stirred, making me like her in a way I couldn't quite explain. "But you do not need to ply me with alcohol. I will do whatever you command, Ma—Arthur."

"Okay, why do you keep saying that?" I asked, glancing at the sword. "I was just cleaning the sword, and I cut myself." Horror shot through me as I remembered the wound, and as my eyes flicked to my hand, I realized I was no longer cut. Blood still covered my skin, but I couldn't feel the wound anymore. As I wiped away the blood, I found no trace of it. How the hell?

"You summoned me from the border to the

Place Where Darkness Treads." She held up the sword, but we were so close together, she just wound up blushing before taking a step back. She touched the beer can to the symbols emblazoned on the blade. "These are the summoning symbols which you have activated. As such, I have appeared to fulfill your request." She nodded at me as if that explained everything perfectly.

I took a deep breath, trying to process what she'd just said. Evidently, when I'd cut myself on the sword, it had summoned her from somewhere to grant my wishes…

"So, you're like a genie?" I asked, raising an eyebrow at her. "Like with a magic sword instead of a lamp?"

"I do know some Djinn, but I am not related to them."

"Okay, that's good to know, I guess." I looked her up and down once more. "What are you?"

"I am a succubus," she said like that was the most reasonable thing in the world. "My name is Gwen, and I am here to fulfill all your desires." She smiled shyly at me. "Am I doing a good job so far?"

"Yes, I'd rate this interaction a ten out of ten." I nodded, trying to process that. I sort of knew about succubae from games and whatnot, but not enough to be reasonably sure I wasn't about to get screwed. Pun intended.

"What would make it one hundred out of ten?" she asked, and the fervor in her voice surprised me. "I do want you to be pleased. After all, you are exchanging your immortal soul for this."

"Wait, hold up." I made a time out gesture with my hands. "Say that again?"

She looked at me in confusion. "You activated the sword, agreeing to trade your immortal soul for a wish. I am here to honor that wish." She looked at the sword and tapped one of the symbols with her index finger. "It's written right here."

"I… um… I can't read that." I looked down at my shoes. "I was cleaning the sword and cut myself." I held up my hand. "I'm sorry, there's been some kind of misunderstanding."

"How can this be possible?" She glared at me for a moment before her face softened. She gestured at my apartment. "Well, you know the deal now. Surely you want something? Fame, money?" She sidled closer, practically pressing her body against mine. "Women?" She smiled at me.

"Look, that all sounds very nice, but I kind of want to keep my soul." I crossed my arms over my chest. "Sorry."

Anger flashed across her face, and for a second, I thought she might reach out and throttle me. I clenched my hands into fists, ready to defend myself against the demoness even though it'd probably be futile.

"You don't understand," she hissed, all nicety gone. "I *need* your soul." She looked up at the ceiling. "Every day the Darkness encroaches, and without souls, we cannot fight back." She looked at me. "Please, my brethren are counting on me."

"The Darkness?" I asked, confused. "I thought you were the Darkness." I gestured lamely at her. "You're a succubus from Hell, right?"

"Yes, but I do not live in the Darkness. I live at the border. Me and mine, anyway." She touched her chest with one finger. "It is our duty to keep the Darkness at bay, and we are losing." She tried to smile at me as she offered me the sword once more. "Please, Arthur. You're my only hope."

"I doubt that, Princess Leia," I said as she pushed the weapon into my hand. She responded, but I couldn't hear her because the moment my fingers wrapped around the blade, everything changed.

It's hard to explain really, but I suddenly saw green orbs hovering over everything in my apartment, including her. They pulsated in time to the glow on the sword's symbols.

"Um… what's with the glowing orbs?" I asked, looking at her and pointing to the orb above her head.

"What?" she asked, eyes widening in shock. As she spoke, the orb above her head flared, displaying a menu straight out of a video game.

Name: Gwen
Experience: 5,500
Health: 99/99
Mana: 89/89
Primary Power: Wishing
Secondary Power: Fire
Strength: 52/100
Agility: 47/100
Charisma: 65/100
Intelligence: 36/100
Special: 53/100
Perk: Leader of Lustnor

"Um… I can see all your Stats?" I asked, equally confused. "Wait, why do you have Stats?"

"It can't be possible…" she whispered, looking at me strangely.

"No, it is. I can see them in the menu." I reached out to show her, and as I did, my finger hovered over the Strength Stat. A blue glow surrounded the word, and then an additional popup cycled open to the side of the main menu.

Strength: This Stat represents Physical Power. It determines how strong the user is and how hard she hits.

Current Level: 50/100. Experience Cost to increase Strength is current level plus one. (51)

"What are you seeing?" she asked, waving a hand in front of me. "Your eyes are all distant."

"You really can't see the menu?" I asked, turning my gaze back to her. As I did, the menus disappeared back into the glowing green ball.

"No," she said, looking at the sword in my hand. The way she said it made me worried I'd done something wrong, only I couldn't figure out what. "You shouldn't be able to either." She took a deep breath.

"Okay," I said, nodding my head. "That I agree with." I gestured at my apartment. "But I can see the same type of menus everywhere in the room now."

"What happens if you put Clarent down?" she asked.

"Let's find out," I said, putting the sword on the table. All the menus vanished. "Yeah, they all disappeared." I picked up the sword again, and they all returned. "Back again. Definitely something with the sword."

"Clarent is definitely speaking through you." She smiled at me, glee filling her from head to toe. "You must be him. The Legendary Builder. He who will defeat the Darkness and bring peace to Heaven and Hell." She sprang at me then, wrapping her arms around me and hugging me with bone-crushing force. "Please, you have to come with me back to my home. We haven't a moment to lose. The border kingdoms have fallen, and now there is little to stand between my town and the Darkness. Please, you must come!"

"Wait a second," I said, but before I could say anymore her hand whipped out. Her lavender fingers cut a tear through the actual void of reality, causing a broken, blackened land to be visible through the rent in space and time.

"We don't have a second to spare," she said, grabbing me by the wrist and dragging me through the void.

5

The sulfurous air of the place hit me like a kick in the stomach, and I doubled over, gasping for air that didn't tear my throat to shreds. Tears filled my eyes as I sank to my knees in the warm black sand trying desperately to breathe air thick and heavy with caustic fumes.

"What's wrong, Arthur?" Gwen, the Succubus said as she knelt down beside me and put a hand on my shoulder. "We need to hurry. You can test the soil later."

"I. Can't. Breathe," I managed to squeak even though every word was like chewing a mouthful of broken glass.

She peered at me for a second and then understanding dawned across her pretty face. She bit her lip and nodded once. "Oh, I'm so sorry, Builder. Let me help you." She gripped my shoulder, causing her nails to dig into my flesh. Crimson light enveloped her arm before rippling off and surrounding my body.

I screamed as a wave of pure, unadulterated heat swarmed over me. Glowing energy cascaded over me, throwing sparks into the air as I collapsed face first into the sand. Only, as I lay there, I suddenly realized I could breathe, and what's more, I didn't hurt anymore.

Hell, I felt better than I ever had.

"Is that better?" Gwen asked, offering me her hand like she wanted to help me to my feet.

"Yes, actually," I said, taking her hand. She hauled me to my feet like I was weightless. "What did you do?" I gestured at myself. "You know, other than drag me to Hell without my shoes." I scrunched my toes in the warm sand before looking at the sky overhead. It was filled with dark, angry clouds.

"Oops," she said, looking down at my feet. "Sorry, I guess I should have let you gather a few things." Her gaze flitted past me toward where the rift in space and time was already closing. "I can take you back in a couple weeks, and you can get stuff then." She nodded. "It's not ideal, but I can't open a portal very often. I'll need to recharge."

"You mean I'm stuck here?" I exclaimed, surprise filling me.

"Yes, but I'll bring you back as soon as you help us get rid of the darkness. I promise." She looked at her feet. "Okay?"

As she spoke, I glanced at her Stat window and saw that her Mana level had fallen from eighty-nine to nine. Did that mean doing the portal spell had cost eighty Mana? As I thought about it, another realization hit me. That meant it took several days for her to recover her Mana. Even if I bitched at her about dragging me to Hell, she really wouldn't be able to bring me back. Damn.

"It's okay," I said, swallowing my anger before turning my gaze to the horizon and spying a town. "Do they have shoes and stuff?" I pointed toward the town.

She glanced over her shoulder and snorted. "No, well, maybe, but not for your kind." She shrugged. "Doesn't hurt to check though."

"My kind?" I asked as she reached out and took my hand, entwining her fingers in mine.

"Yeah." She looked at me and fluttered her lashes. "You're a man. Everyone in Hell is female."

She sighed. "It was rumored that the Builder would be male, so the Darkness unleashed a plague on our people that killed all the males. It's part of why they are winning since we can't replenish our troops through mating."

"Wait, is this gonna be a whole thing where everyone tries to gang rape me?" I asked, stopping. While the idea of becoming the designated master for a bunch of succubae was strangely appealing, I was pretty sure that'd end with me dead from complete exhaustion.

"Probably not," she mused, licking her lips. "You wouldn't be able to impregnate a demon, and we have ways of getting pleasure that do not require you. Still…" She touched her chin. "I wouldn't be surprised if you get offers."

"Got it, Hell lesbians. That's um… cool?" I shrugged, strangely disappointed.

"I'm not a lesbian," she said, shaking her head. "Trust me." She licked her lips again. "I could give you a night you won't forget." She bit her lip. "Was that too forward of me?"

"It's about the right amount of forward," I said because her words had a very noticeable effect on me. I just wasn't sure if she'd noticed. Probably better that way since I wasn't quite sure how I felt about it. "So, why did you bring me to Hell again? You keep calling me the Builder, but I'll be honest, I have no idea what that is."

"The legends say that a man will come, and he will wield Clarent. He will use the sword's power to remake the world and allow us the power to stop the Darkness." She spun on her heels and pointed into the distance. The clouds were so dark there it seemed like I was looking into a swirling black hole of the void. Lightning crackled in the skies and green fire burned across the entirety of the ground. Even from here, I could feel the cold, relentless hunger of the place.

"That's the Darkness?" I asked, shivering despite the heat as I glanced at the sword in my hand. Even if it was named after the one King Arthur had pulled from the stone, it didn't seem nearly adequate to do the job. "How the hell can I stop that?"

"With your sword, Arthur." She squeezed my hand. "I believe in you. Even if you do not, I do. Trust me when I say that we have been waiting an eternity for you."

"Yeah, okay," I said looking at my sword. The glow had faded, and now it just looked like a rusty piece of junk again. Well, except for the spots I'd cleaned. Otherwise, it didn't seem special. I guess it didn't matter since I could still see the glowing green orb above Gwen's head.

Only, unlike how it had been in my house, I couldn't see any more orbs. I thought it might be because we were too far away, but as we approached the towering gates of the town, I saw claw marks had scarred the wood, and there were places where the boards had broken away completely, leaving jagged openings that reminded me of a gap-toothed monster. The walls themselves were only shoulder high, and from the claw marks at the top, I was guessing they had gotten scaled more than once.

One thing that was certain is that even that close, there were no orbs for me look at.

I turned my attention to the two guards stationed outside the gates. They were both wearing armor that reminded me of the costume Wonder Woman had worn in the movie. Hell, everything about the two women screamed Amazon. The left one was a bigger lady with charcoal colored skin. She had close-cropped black hair and eyes that blazed with scarlet flames. She held a huge spear in one hand and a shield in the other.

The other guard was slimmer, built less like a

linebacker and more like a swimmer than her counterpart. She had pale blue skin, hair like rippling green seaweed, and glowing sapphire eyes. Instead of a shield and spear, she had twin short swords in sheaths at her waist and a small, circular shield on her back.

As we approached, they both turned to regard us and instantly dropped their heads, casting their gaze at Gwen's feet.

"Lady Gwen, it is good of you to return," the bigger one said, and as she spoke, a green orb appeared over her head. "We worried you might not return in time."

"It is good to be back, Sheila," Gwen said, nodding to the woman. "Be at ease, both of you." She gestured at me. "I have found the Builder. All our problems will be over soon."

"He's the Builder?" the slimmer one asked, looking me over in the same way most girls had always looked me over. "I expected someone… well, taller."

"You always think everyone should be taller, Agatha," Sheila said, rolling her eyes at the other guard. "I think you're just fine, and if anyone says different, you tell 'em, they can see me about it." She smiled from ear to ear. "I got your back."

"Um, thanks," I said, nodding to her as I tried to take that in. While I was glad Sheila seemed to think I was okay, I was well aware I did not look the part of a legendary warrior. Still, the sword seemed to have chosen me, and just because I didn't have tons of muscles, didn't mean I wasn't the right man for the job, and dammit, I'd prove it. To be honest, I wasn't even sure why I wanted to prove it, but Agatha's words sort of brought me back to my entire life. No one ever thought I was good enough. This time, things would be different.

I swung my eyes back to Agatha. A green orb now hovered above her head, and what's more, now one hung above the gate. It was a bit larger than the ones over my compatriot's heads.

"What's wrong?" Gwen asked, looking at me as Agatha moved to open the gates while Sheila stood guard, looking at the horizon with eagle-eyed intensity.

"Oh, um, menus just popped up for the two guards, and there's a bigger one for the gate." I pointed at them before I realized only I could see them. "They weren't there a minute ago."

"Odd," Gwen said, glancing from me to the sword and back to the town. "I wonder why that is, Arthur?"

"I guess we'll figure it out as we go," I said, shrugging. "Wish this sword came with an owner's manual."

As I spoke, a glowing green orb appeared above the tip of the sword. My eyes flicked to it, and as they did, it opened.

Clarent
Type: Longsword
Durability: 18/2,700
Damage: 1D20
Enchantments: none
Ability: Distribution – Can be used by the Builder to distribute Experience.

I stared at the menu for a moment before looking over at Gwen. "Give me a second." I didn't hear her response as I pulled my hand from hers and flicked open the Ability Menu.

As I did, an Ability window popped up in front of me with the word *Distribution*. I pointed at it, causing more text to appear.

Distribution: This Ability can be used to change the Stats of a person, creature, or structure under one's control. It allows the user to distribute unspent Experience points as well as redistribute Experience points that have already been spent. Note: Stats cannot be lowered below their initial levels.

"But that doesn't make any sense. They don't

work for you. They work for me... oh." Gwen scowled at me as understanding flashed across her face. "What I control must belong to you now." She harrumphed. "That hardly seems fair."

"Sorry," I said, sheepishly as I thought about what she said. "The sword lets me distribute the Stats of people under my power, so I'm guessing that since I summoned you, and you started calling me master, I gained control of you in its eyes." I flicked my hand toward Agatha and Sheila. "I'm guessing they became part of the package?"

Gwen sighed. "It will be as it will be. If giving you my people and territory will stave off the Darkness, it is hardly a price to bicker about. Just please remember these are real people. Do not spend their lives needlessly."

"I would never do that," I said, turning to look at Agatha and Sheila. Both of them were staring at me with a strange mixture of horror, resentment, and curiosity. To be honest, I wasn't sure which of those emotions scared me the most.

"Good," Gwen said before nodding to the gates. "Now, let us make haste and get inside. I want to show you the rest of the town before—"

The rest of her words were cut off by a crack of thunder. Strokes of lightning tore the sky asunder amidst peals of thunder, and the fiery planes exploded outward in a shockwave of force that threw me to the ground. As I hit the dirt, the gates swung shut, and both the guards moved forward, weapons in their hands.

A trumpet blast erupted from the sky as Darkness burst forth from the crackling flames and came straight at us.

6

The Darkness rushing toward us coalesced into a half-dozen lizard-like creatures that made me think of Sobek from Egyptian lore with their huge alligator faces. They all stood between twelve and fifteen feet tall with rippling muscles and large sweeping crocodile tails snaking out the back. Burnished black armor covered their bodies as they rushed forward with curved sickle swords resembling an Egyptian khopesh in each hand.

"Darkness scouts!" Sheila cried, charging forward, spear held high. She shouted something else in a language I didn't understand, and a swirl of scarlet flame sprouted up from the ground around her, rippling up her huge body and causing her shield and spear to become wreathed in flame.

Lightning crackled overhead as she hit the lead scout with her charge. She smashed it down with her shield, throwing it to the dirt.

The rest of the creatures ignored her completely, rushing by her and coming straight toward us.

"You watch the Builder," Agatha said, glancing at Gwen before moving to meet the charge.

"Will do," Gwen said and I watched fire sprout to life in her hands. Agatha smashed into the next closest lizardmen, her swords blurring through the air, and while she stopped the charge of the two creatures closest to her with a series of sword cuts, the other three came running toward us.

Their eyes were pure Darkness and, oddly enough, they weren't even looking at us. They sprinted past Gwen and me without so much as a sideways glance which was odd because Gwen's hands were blazing like she was the Human Torch. Instead, they smashed into the wall.

Shimmers every color of the rainbow exploded above the gates, causing iridescent symbols to fill the air. As the creatures tried to leap the wall, more symbols came to life, flaring with energy and flinging them backward.

They lay there, shaking themselves off while

Sheila and Agatha struggled with their own monsters.

"This isn't going to work," I muttered, glancing from the enemies to the guards and back again.

"Why not?" Gwen asked. It looked like she wasn't sure if she wanted to blast the lizard scouts or stay here and wait it out. Probably because she worried she'd draw them to us.

"Well, if this was a game, you'd want the monsters focused on Sheila." I pointed at the burly guard as she beat the lizardman every which way. "Then while the monsters were attacking her, you'd want Agatha to pick them off with her quick attacks."

"But this isn't a game," Gwen said, shaking her head as determination set in. "This is real life."

"Fair enough," I said because she was right after all. After all, I was a stranger in a strange land. "So, what do you want to do?"

"I don't want to attack them. If they come closer, I will, but the priority is to keep you safe until you can make us strong enough to stop them. That won't work if they come over here and kill you." Gwen sighed, and as she did, her words resonated with me. I could change their Stats.

I glanced back toward Sheila, as she finally

finished off her lizardman by skewering it through the mouth with her spear. As the point burst out the back of the creature's skull in a spray of black ichor, I opened her menu.

Name: Sheila
Experience: 3,700
Health: 112/127
Mana: 80/91
Primary Power: Fighter - Defense
Secondary Power: None selected
Strength: 76/100
Agility: 51/100
Charisma: 9/100
Intelligence: 23/100
Special: 68/100
Perk: Trained at the Royal Guard's Academy.

As I stared at Sheila's Stats, her powers struck me as odd because unlike Gwen, who had the powers of Wishing and Fire, Sheila had only one, and it was labeled Fighter - Defense.

I had no idea what that meant, so I waved my hand over the Primary Power box.

Fighter - Defense: User has the Ability to learn defensive related fighter trees. None have currently been selected.

Sure enough, a list of powers filled my screen.

They scrolled down so long that I couldn't really make heads or tails of them.

"Um, Gwen, what's a Magical Power or Skill people use defensively?" I asked, glancing at the succubus as she watched the lizardmen continue to throw themselves at the wall. Each time they hit the barrier, concentric lines of force would ripple across it. I wasn't sure how much damage it could take, but I didn't want to find out. If those things got inside, who knew what would happen?

"What?" she asked, turning to look at me. "Uh, I'm not sure." She shrugged. "I know some of the castle guards in the Royal Centre have an Ability called Defensive Aegis, but I don't really know what it does. I'm told it's formidable, why?"

"I have a stupid Idea," I said, turning back to the Ability Menu and thinking about the Ability. As I did, the Ability Menu began to scroll along until it highlighted Defensive Aegis.

Defensive Aegis: This Ability allows the user to temporarily double the Health of all friendlies within a one-hundred meter range. Ability causes all enemy units to focus fire on the user for thirty seconds unless resisted with an Intelligence check.

Requirements: Special: 50+, Strength: 50+, Charisma: 10+

Cost: 1500 Experience

"Perfect," I whispered, selecting the Ability. As I did, another menu opened displaying a message that hovered in front of my face in glowing text.

Requirements not met. Charisma Stat too low. Would you like to upgrade? Cost of Stat upgrade: 10 Experience.

I took a quick glance at Sheila's total Experience. She had more than enough to purchase the Ability and the Stat upgrade. I quickly confirmed my choices, and the sword in my hand flared with sapphire light.

More light wrapped around Sheila as she sprinted toward the two lizardmen fighting Agatha. As it did, she stopped in her tracks and looked over at me.

"What'd you do?" she asked, confusion filling her voice. "How... I mean..."

"I'll explain later!" I called back, causing Gwen to look over at me. Before she could say anything, Sheila planted her spear in the soft earth and raised her shield high.

"Defensive Aegis!" she cried, causing a ripple of scarlet energy to explode out of her in a wave that crashed across the entire battlefield.

As it hit the lizardmen, they all went glassy-eyed. They stood there, trying to shake their heads before screeching like their gods had been affronted. Then they broke off all their attacks and sprinted toward Sheila, mouths agape.

The loss of concentration allowed Agatha to plant her short swords in the back of one of the creature's skewering it. As the tips of her blades burst through its chest and it collapsed to the ground, its partner, along with the three who had been attacking the gate, ran for Sheila.

"Gwen, burn them down!" I said, pointing my sword at the monsters.

"But what if we attract them?" she asked, shaking her head at me. "I can't risk it."

"As long as you kill them in the next thirty seconds, it won't matter." I nodded to her. "Trust me."

"But…" she started to say, but I cut her off by waving Clarent in front of her.

"Listen, who has the magic sword?" I asked before pointing my blade back at the monsters. "Now attack!"

She did as she was told, lobbing fireballs at the creatures. Her blasts hit one, knocking it to the ground and allowing Agatha to catch it. The guard leaped through the air and came down on its back, driving her swords down through its skull like she was Link in Legend of Zelda.

As it went still beneath her, the others reached Sheila, and the big woman smacked one in the chin with her spear, knocking it flat on its ass. Its two friends regarded her angrily as she dropped down behind her shield in a defensive stance, completely oblivious to everyone else.

Gwen threw another fireball. This one struck the left lizardman, sending it stumbling forward toward Sheila. The guard wasted no time, stepping forward and driving her spear through the creature's throat. As gore splattered across the battlefield, its friend attacked.

Its curved khopesh arced through the air, slicing into Sheila, but if the blow bothered her, it didn't show. Instead, she shoved it backward with her shield as its compatriot started to rise.

"I'm too tired to throw more fire," Gwen said as Agatha flung one of her swords. It sailed through the air and cracked the lizardman Sheila had knocked down earlier in the side of the head. As the creature fell to the ground, Agatha launched herself into the air.

Completely oblivious to her, the lizardman reared back to attack Sheila, only it never got the chance because its head was reduced to a fond memory by the force of Agatha's attack. As its body tumbled to the ground, the big guard turned and drove her spear through the prone lizardman, finishing off the final creature.

"We did it! Thanks for the help, Builder," Sheila said, wiping the sweat from her forehead with the back of one hand. As she spoke, the bodies of the lizardmen burst into green flame before dissolving in an instant, leaving behind only small, fist-sized spheres of glowing emerald.

"What's that?" I asked, pointing to the six spheres as Gwen turned to look at me.

"Did you teach Sheila Defensive Aegis?" she asked, and the intensity of her gaze was astounding.

"Yeah. I saw she had an open Ability slot, so I spent her Experience to buy it." I smirked. "She's also more charming since I had to spend some Experience to raise her Charisma to ten."

"Good, maybe she'll chew with her mouth closed," Agatha said with a snort as she picked up her fallen sword and sheathed it.

"What other things can you upgrade?" Gwen asked as the two guards began picking up all the glowing emerald spheres.

"I'm not sure." I shrugged. "Stats and Abilities,

it seems, but I don't know enough about the system to make good choices. I need to do some more research. I could just upgrade their base Stats, but it'd cost Experience, and then we might not be able to buy a really good Ability."

"That sounds really complicated," Sheila said as she came over and offered the spheres to Gwen. "I'm glad you have to figure it out while I just have to punch stuff." She grinned at me. "Though if you ever wanna go a few rounds, you look me up. You look like you could use a good workout."

"I'll keep that in mind," I said as Gwen took the glowing orbs and shoved them in a pouch that was hanging off a belt at her waist. I hadn't even noticed it before. "So, what are those?"

"Dark Blood," Gwen said, holding one out to me, and as I stared at the glowing orb, a window popped open next to it.

Dark Blood

Material: Gemstone

Grade: D

Contains the essence of a fallen warrior of Darkness.

"Um, what's it do?" I asked, gesturing at it with one hand. "The menu isn't giving me any ideas."

"Menus?" Gwen shook her head and waved off the question. "It's a crafting material. You can use them to empower different objects, usually weapons and armor, but typically we sell them to make repairs and what not. It's our only way of making money out here."

"Are they worth a lot?" I asked, glancing at the two guards. "It didn't seem like the two of you had much trouble with the lizardmen."

"Sometimes." Gwen shrugged. "They went down a lot easier than normal thanks to what you did to Sheila."

"Oh," I said, glancing at the two guards and feeling strangely satisfied. I'd already made a difference, and I'd been here only a few minutes. Imagine what I could do once I better understood what we were up against. "Well, I'll be happy to help some more once I figure out what's what."

"Great. I look forward to it," Agatha said, smiling at me. "If this doesn't prove you're the Legendary Builder, I don't know what does. I've never seen anyone do what you just did."

7

"So, when you said this was a town, you were, uh, exaggerating things," I said as we made our way through Lustnor. Ever since Agatha had declared me the Legendary Builder, I'd started to feel more responsible than ever before. As I looked at the place, I couldn't help but think we might be better off leaving the place and going elsewhere.

The roads, if you could call them that, were more potholes than anything else. Actually, that wasn't quite true because that would imply they had been paved, which they had not been. No, instead, the path appeared to have been made by people walking in the same general way, their traffic alone having eventually packed down some of the soil.

"It is a town," Gwen affirmed, glaring at me.

"Well, sort of." She sighed and gestured toward the empty trio of buildings to our right. "We have space for a bank, a general store, and even a haberdashery."

"Yeah, but they're all empty," I said, glancing around the town. There was a set of what looked like thatch houses to the left, and I could see people milling about over there, and by people, I meant women of varying age from small girls to old ladies. "If the Darkness is as close as you say, there should be way more guards here."

"We aren't able to recruit anyone here. There's not enough money in the town's coffers to purchase more." Gwen looked up at the cloudy sky and watched the lightning crackle for a moment. "We don't have enough people for commerce, and even if we did, we don't have any way of supporting more than we have." She gave me a sad smile. "We were always more of a waystation between the front lines and Royal Centre but because the front lines fell a few days ago, we're all that stands between the Darkness and the main city now. If we leave, they'll be at the doorstep of the Royal Centre in no time. So even though we should evacuate, the moment we did, we'd be executed for abandoning our post."

"Well that's heavy," I replied, feeling even more

responsible than before. If we couldn't leave, we'd just have to make this place a fortress. I just wasn't sure how. "But if the situation is so dire, why are those people here?" I waved a hand toward the demons by the thatch houses. "They don't seem like they're guards or tradesfolk."

"The Stained? Yeah, there's a few, but we tolerate them because they're like canaries. As long as they're here, we're safe enough." Gwen shrugged, gaze barely registering the demons she'd called the Stained.

"Um… why did you call them the Stained?" I asked, confused.

"They have been exiled from the Royal Centre and can no longer enter its walls. Their faces bear a mark to indicate their crimes. Some have tried to burn them off, but it shows up even through scar tissue. It truly is a stain that can never be removed." She took a deep breath, focusing on the group now. "They come in when a border town falls and stay until the next one falls. They come to towns like this because we tolerate them for the most part. As I said, having them here is a warning sign."

"Why not imprison them? Hell, why not execute them?" I shook my head. "This punishment doesn't make any sense."

"According to the Heads of the Guilds, imprisonment and death are both escapes and, therefore, are inadequate punishments. There is no greater punishment than to live with your disgrace, to see your shame every time you gaze at your own face, to learn to hate your own visage as much as everyone else who happens upon you, to know that you will never be anything beyond the stain of your crime on society. That's what the Heads say, at least."

I sensed she was holding something back. "Do you not agree?"

She took a deep breath before elaborating, "I think the Heads of the Guilds are not so naïve as to discount the possibility that they may one day have need of the Stained. They are, after all, still bodies capable of aiding in the battle against the Darkness."

"Doesn't it cost a lot to take care of them? Do they have skills that make them useful?" I asked, raising an eyebrow at her. "That seems like a drain on your resources, to be honest."

"It would be, but we actually get a bit of money from the Royal Centre depending on how many we have. They'd rather pay us to deal with them so they don't have camps of Stained in the forests beyond their walls. That, combined with the Dark Blood we're able to harvest from attacks makes up most of our economy." She tried to smile at me, but sort of failed and looked at her feet. "That's why we don't have a cobbler to make you shoes."

"What do you have?" I asked, rubbing my face with my hand. This situation seemed hopeless. Not only was there no economy of any kind, but there were no people. So far, in addition to Gwen and the two guards, I'd seen maybe a dozen peasants. That did not bode well because even if I upgraded them all, what good would that do against an entire horizon of Darkness?

"We have a blacksmith," Gwen said so quickly, I thought she might be trying to hide something.

"Why didn't you say so earlier?" I asked suspiciously as we turned a corner, and the blacksmith's shop came into view. "Oh."

It was a squat building about the size of the empty general store, and I could see black smoke pouring out a chimney. It had doors and windows, but they were open and more black smoke billowed out from them. In front of it stood a woman with pink hair clad in overalls.

She had her back to us and was busy cursing up a storm and flailing at the smoke with her hat. "Goddamned forge is on goddamned fire again. I don't know how I'm expected to work in these conditions. It's a goddamned outrage." She threw her hat onto the ground and jumped on it in frustration.

"And that's Samantha, but everyone calls her Sam." Gwen looked sheepishly at me. "She's from the Royal Guild of the Blacksmiths. They usually rotate in every few months, but I guess she pissed someone off because she's been here for three terms, and her contract has already been renewed for another three…"

"Okay," I said, sighing. "So, we have a blacklisted smith. Still, that doesn't mean she's not a badass."

"Do you see the same shop I do?" Gwen asked, looking at me and waving a hand toward it. "There's smoke pouring out of it."

It was a fair point, but since I didn't know anything about blacksmiths, I just hoped it was good smoke.

"I can hear you," Sam snarled whirling to look at us. She had one finger raised like she'd been about to do some serious pointing in our general direction, but before she could, her eyes widened, and her mouth fell open.

It was good because it took me a minute to catch my breath. Sam was a fucking knockout. She had one of those bodies I'd seen in rap videos. Her unblemished skin was white as snow, and she had one of those innocent, pixie faces that made her look barely a day over eighteen.

Her pink eyes sparkled as she looked me up and down. "Who in the blue hell are you?"

"I'm Arthur." I nodded to her. "Arthur Curie."

"You don't seem very tall," Sam said, taking a step forward and seizing my chin in her hands. "Hmm, he has good teeth." She shrugged. "So, plusses and minuses."

"He's also the Legendary Builder," Gwen said offhandedly before gesturing at the sword in my hand. "He's literally holding Clarent."

"It must be defective then," she said, releasing me and looking down at the sword. "His teeth aren't that good."

"I'm not a horse," I said, starting to get annoyed. Who did this chick think she was?

"Quiet," Sam said, glaring at me. "The women are talking." She harrumphed and turned to regard Gwen. "My shop is on fire because the piece of shit forge you have keeps spewing fire onto the walls."

She crossed her arms over her chest. "Use your fire magic and fix it."

"You could be a little nicer," I said. "You'll find you get what you want more often."

"This isn't your problem, Arthur. It's hers." Sam glared at me for a second before turning her ire to Gwen. "What's taking so long, Gwen?"

"Sometimes, I think I understand why you're here," Gwen said, moving past the woman and toward the blacksmith. She raised one palm, and as she did, the smoke buffeted a bit. "Give me a few minutes," she added over her shoulder before stepping into the smoking building.

"So, what can the Builder do?" Sam asked, and when I didn't respond to her, she raised an eyebrow. "Do you not speak English?"

"Oh, am I allowed to talk now?" I replied in a mocking voice. "I feel like you should apologize to me, but I don't think you have it in you, so let's try this again." I held out my hand to her. "I'm Arthur, pleased to meet you."

She stared at my hand like it was made of dog shit before sighing so hard it would have made a teenager ask for tips. "I'm Samantha, sixth level blacksmith of the Royal Guild of the Blacksmiths."

She took my hand, and I found her flesh was strangely cool.

"Sixth? Is that a Rank?" I asked as she squeezed my hand hard enough for it to hurt before relinquishing it.

"Yes. First Rank is the best, tenth is the worst. I was a third Rank before I got sent out here…" She shook her head. "I'm not telling the story."

"It's cool," I said, shrugging. "We all have pasts with things we don't want to discuss."

"That's very understanding of you," Sam said, watching me closely like it was a trick. Then she settled her hands on her hips. "So, what can the Builder do?"

"I can see your Stats and upgrade them if you have the necessary Experience," I replied matter-of-factly.

"I don't know what that means," she said, looking from me to the sword, but I had a feeling she knew more than she claimed. "Say can I see that?"

"Um… I don't really think—"

"I won't steal it," she said, making a grab for it that put her well within my personal space. As her hands closed around the hilt, I tried to push her away, but soon found she was way, way stronger than me. "If you resist, it will just get harder."

"Yeah, no kidding," I said as she pulled Clarent from my grip and held it in front of her. As soon as she did, the glow clinging to the symbols died away. Even still, she looked at it closely before her long black tongue snaked out and wrapped around the blade like a giraffe teasing leaves off a branch.

"What are you doing?" I cried, making a grab for the weapon, but she turned her back to me.

"Checking the sword," she said, smacking her lips. "Do I taste gun oil?" She shook her head. "Don't you know that messing with antiques ruins the value?"

"It's my sword." I crossed my arms over my chest. I knew that it did which was why Merle hadn't cleaned it, but at the same time, it had been really dirty, and I hadn't done anything that'd leave a mark...

"That it is, Builder," she replied, offering me the weapon. "Thanks for letting me look at it." She almost sounded sincere.

"Did that hurt?" I asked, taking the weapon from her. Once again it began to glow, and this time a green orb appeared above Sam's head.

"What?" she asked before glaring at me.

"What do you mean, 'did that hurt?'" Her eyes began to burn and black-feathered wings sprouted from her back, rippling out from her flesh to stand out against the shop. "If this is where you say 'when you fell from Heaven,' I will set you on fire."

I raised a hand defensively. "Oh, is that funny because you're a demon?" I asked realizing that I needed to explain myself before things got out of hand. Shaking my head, I quickly followed up, "No, I was gonna make a snide remark about you saying thank you, but that's way better. I'm gonna totally use that."

"I wouldn't. It's sort of a sore subject around here," Gwen quipped.

Sam ran a hand through her hair and elaborated with a strained voice, "None of us even knows how we got here. The war that split Heaven and Hell was before our time. That makes it even more annoying to be put upon about it."

"Point taken," I said as her wings flapped. "Now put those away."

"You're not the boss of me," she said, but she complied, furling her wings back into her flesh.

"He is, actually," Gwen said, coming out of the building. "I suppose, technically I am, but since he's the Builder, I've abdicated my power to him so he can help us."

"So, what does that mean for us? That you handed us off to him?" Her voice colored with irritation, almost anger. "You should have asked me how I felt about that before selling me like a common whore," Sam said, glaring at Gwen.

The succubus wiped some soot from her shoulder. "Oh, I was unaware this was a democracy." She pulled out an invisible stack of papers and began looking through it. "Hmm, that's strange. In the contract, it just says I'm the boss, and I can do what I want. Odd." She held out the invisible papers. "You want to look, Sam? Maybe you can find the clause where I give two handfuls of warm shit what you think?"

If looks could kill, Sam would have murdered Gwen, but instead, the blacksmith just sighed. "I'll be in my shop," she muttered before stomping off like a chastised school girl.

"So, as I was saying, we have a ton to work with." Gwen gestured at the retreating blacksmith. "Lots of potential."

8

"Okay, well, I guess the first thing is to go through all the Stained and see if any of them have any useful Skills," I said to Gwen as Sam stormed off and slammed the door to her shop even though it was still smoky as Hell inside.

"Makes sense," Gwen replied with a shrug. "I survey them all when they come in, and I don't recall anything of mention." She touched my shoulder with one slender finger. "But maybe you can see something I can't."

"Here's to hoping," I said, nodding to her. "Then we need to look at these buildings and go on a recruitment drive." I sighed as I glanced back at the smithy. "Damn, I forgot to scope out Sam while we were talking. We should probably do that first." I shot a glance at Gwen and winked. "I trust your assessment of the Stained for now."

"Aww thanks," she said, nodding to me. "Tell you what, you go bother Sam and I'll round up the Stained and bring them here. That way we can be more efficient." She smacked her hands together. "You know, the relentless elimination of waste and all that."

I shook my head at her. "You sound like my old boss. He was way into that Kaizen crap, made me read a whole bunch of books on the subject by Taiichi Ohno on how to make stuff more efficient by following the Toyota Way." I rubbed my chin. "Maybe that would actually work..."

"I have no idea what you mean by that." Gwen stared at me for a few moments. "Well, while you noodle on that, I'll go do my thing. Papers to push, Stained to round up and all that." She turned on her heel and strode away, giving me a spectacular view of her ass, but I was way too much of a gentleman to look... for long.

When I did finally tear my eyes away from the succubus, I wiped my face with my hand. I couldn't think about her like that. For one, she was a succubus, and if I knew anything, sleeping with a succubus was probably a bad idea.

"Okay," I said, clapping my hands together and moving toward the shop. "Let's tame a shrew."

A loud crash echoed from inside as I knocked on the door of Sam's shop. When there was no response, probably because of the crash, I grabbed the tarnished bronze handle and twisted it. The door opened, hinges screeching in a way that let me know they'd probably never been oiled.

The inside of the shop was barely more than a large square covered in soot. Black stained every inch of the wood and stone interior. Several of the beams looked like they'd been chewed through with flames. It was a marvel that the whole structure hadn't just come tumbling down.

Sam stood in the corner, a huge, iron sledge-hammer-looking thing over one shoulder. She was staring at what looked like a black iron forge, only unlike the ones I'd seen in movies and the renaissance faire, this one looked like it'd been beaten to shit. Dings and cracks covered the exterior of the structure, and even though it wasn't lit, I could see what had happened. There was a large crack along one side toward the bed where the fire sat. If it was lit, that flame would penetrate outward through the stone buffer into the wooden wall just a few feet away.

It wouldn't have been a problem if the insulation for the forge was intact, but since it wasn't, the heat would flow outward until, well, I'd seen the results of that.

"I know you're there," Sam said, not looking at me. "Do you need something else, Arthur?"

"Yeah, actually," I said, moving closer. If my hunches were right, Sam was probably one of the most talented and crucial elements to this outpost. She was where I needed to start if I thought I could actually do anything helpful here. "I wanted to chat with you if you had time." I moved next to her and stared down at the forge. "I cannot believe you even work with this thing. You must be supremely talented to get anything done."

She looked sidelong at me. "I see what you're doing, but it won't work." Sam was friendlier away from Gwen, not quite a ball of fur, but friendlier.

"I'm not joshing you," I replied, gesturing at the forge. "This is cracked, which means heat will spill out. That means the forge won't get to proper temperature, so the metal inside won't get to the right temperature. Assuming you could even work with the metal like that, all sorts of imperfections will be introduced. That the stuff you make still works is a testament to your Skill."

"Oh." She stared at me for a moment. Thoughts swirled in her intelligent pink eyes as she looked me up and down. "Well, you're right. You want a prize or something?" She was more facetious than sarcastic. My presence must have had a softening influence on her. That's what I was going to tell myself anyway.

"Look," I said, holding up Clarent. "We both know this thing is jacked up beyond all repair, but it at least lets me see your Skill sheet. I just wanted to take a gander at it. Then maybe we can work on making this place awesome."

"You just asked if you could look at me in one of the most intimate ways possible." She pointed at me with her hammer. "It probably doesn't seem like it, but you're reducing me to ones and zeroes." She touched her hand to her chest. "I am more than the sum of my Stats."

"Oh, totally," I said, nodding to her. Sam definitely knew more than she had let on earlier. "But I still want to look. I'm sorry if that makes you uncomfortable, but it has to happen." I smiled at her. "Afterward, I'd love to chat with you about the state of things. Gwen seems great, but I'm willing to bet you might have some ideas on what's wrong with this, uh, place."

"I could see you about to say dump," she scoffed before rolling her eyes so hard I was surprised they didn't pop out of her skull. "Fiiiine." She nodded at me and spread her arms. "You can look, but you can't touch."

I nodded to her. "Thanks, I'll try to be quick."

Name: Samantha

Experience: 6,762

Health: 80/80

Mana: 149/149

Primary Power: Smithing

Secondary Power: None selected

Strength: 54/100

Agility: 26/100

Charisma: 20/100

Intelligence: 76/100

Special: 73/100

Perk: Rank 3 Blacksmith (Officially reduced to Rank 5)

"Whoa, you have a ton of unspent Experience," I said, shaking my head. "You must work really hard."

"I do work really hard. No one makes third Rank by being lazy. It's complete horseshit they reduced my Rank," Sam grumbled. "Besides, if I didn't work hard, we'd be totally screwed. For the last thousand years, Gwen has barely done anything to keep up the place. It's why we're in such a sad state now. Everyone who could afford to leave did as soon as the front lines fell. Now, it's so dangerous, it's impossible to leave. A few tried to make it, but most were slaughtered along the way and forced to return. So, for better or worse, I'm stuck here."

"So why were you here to begin with? Does it have something to do with why you got demoted?" I asked, taking in what she'd said. Gwen had said the town was poor, but maybe that's because she hadn't been doing a good job? Sam had also seemed to imply being here was a punishment, which was also interesting.

"Yes," she said, taking a deep breath. "As I said, I don't want to talk about it, but that's why I was forced to take a contract with Gwen. If I hadn't, it'd be some other border town. Hopefully, if I work a few more terms with Gwen, I'll be able to get back to my old rank and make some real money." As she spoke, I noticed that the Perk section of her menu was highlighted in red. I selected it and an additional dialog box opened.

Rank 3 Blacksmith: Able to use Skills and Abilities based on Rank 3 Skill. This will allow the blacksmith to produce Rank 3 items 70% of the time. There is a 15% chance of crafting a Rank 2 item. There is a 10% chance of crafting a Rank 4 item. There is a 5% chance of crafting a Rank 5 item.

Note: Demotion present. Items will be considered by official channels to have a maximum Rank of five. This does not affect their quality, only their resale and acceptance values.

"That demotion sucks," I said, looking up at Sam. "It says that you can make Rank three items, but some ass hat has made it so you can only sell them like they are Rank five."

"I'm aware. As I said, that's the *only* reason I'm still here," she said, shaking her head. "Why if I ever get my hands on Guildmistress Nina, I'll..." she trailed off into mumbling as I opened her Primary Power window.

Smithing: User has the Ability to learn smithing related trees. None have currently been selected.

Like with Sheila, Sam already had an Ability Tree that displayed a bunch of Skills. Some, like *Weapon Repair*, were already known.

Below the known Abilities were a list of Unknown Abilities, which included everything from smelting to engineering. I clicked on the smelting one for fun, and it opened into a huge Skill Tree with basic ore at the top and flowed through, allowing the user to craft different ores. None of them were particularly expensive, costing between fifty and a hundred Experience points each, but the cost of the tree itself was over a thousand.

"I think I have to purchase the Skill Tree itself, and then I'm allowed to buy the individual Skills inside." I looked up at Sam who was giving me a blank look.

"I don't really have any idea what you're talking about," Sam replied, staring intently at me. "Can you explain in words?"

"Oh, um, okay. Like, you have a bunch of accumulated Experience points, over six thousand actually. I can spend your Experience to buy Skill Trees. Like I just looked, and you don't know Smelting. So, I could spend some of your Experience and cause you to learn the Ability. Then I could spend more Experience to have you learn how to use different ores and make different metals." I shrugged weakly. "Does that make any sense?"

"Sort of," she replied and rubbed her chin thoughtfully. "What about things I already know how to do?"

"I'm not sure, let me look," I said, and I selected weapon repair. As I did, it opened a new window.

Weapon Repair
Skill: 7/10.
User can repair items with a maximum Skill requirement

of 7. The quality of repair will depend on the Rank of the item being repaired as well as the time spent on the repair.

Below that was an upgrade tab, and when I looked at it, another message appeared.

Do you want to upgrade Weapon Repair to Skill level 8? Base cost 4,000 Experience. This price can be reduced by attaining an overall Rank of 2 in Smithing.

"Um, yes, but it's expensive. I guess if you were Rank two, it'd cost less. How do you increase your Rank with the guild?" I asked, looking at her.

"Normally?" She blew out an exasperated breath. "You take a smithing test. The guild will give you a bunch of tasks, and you have to complete it by crafting Rank two items at least seventy percent of the time. Only, I'm not allowed to take the test because I've been demoted, so I have to retake the Rank four and three tests. I could pass them, but I don't have the cash for that." She sighed again. "It's why I signed on with a regiment to come out here. I get a fifty percent bonus by being out in the waystations because no one likes to be in them. It almost makes up for my pay as a Rank five smith."

"What's it cost to take the test?" I asked, raising an eyebrow at me. "Actually, how's money work here, anyway?"

"You really are fresh off the turnip truck, aren't you?" She laughed. "Our primary form of money is Blood Coin. Each test costs a thousand Blood Coins times the level, so the level four test will cost four thousand coins. To put that in perspective, I make fifty coins a month here."

"Wait," I said, making a time out gesture, "I don't even understand why you need money here. And Gwen talked about it too. There's a giant void of death coming toward us right now. You'd think there'd be more people here to fight."

"Hell hasn't worked that way since our queen left nearly ten millennia ago. Before, she was able to command everyone to do things that made sense, but when she suddenly left, there was a power vacuum to fill..." Sam shook her head.

"She left? To where? Wait. Who's in charge?" I asked, interrupting her.

Sam continued on as though I hadn't spoken. "Everything fell to the bureaucrats working for her, the guild leaders. They've done little more than consolidate their power under the guise of protecting us." Sam clenched her fists in frustration. "Now, you can't get anything done without chasing signatures from fifty people who don't want to help you. Stupid bureaucratic paperwork and red tape."

Hell seemed a lot like home. Maybe there was some truth to the whole *hell on earth* bit. "Sure, it sounds like a pain, but I'm still not clear why there aren't more demons fighting the Darkness on the frontlines, especially if the pay is better," I added sheepishly.

"Right, let me lay it out for you," Sam said, a little bit of annoyance directed toward me. "I took a contract to come here. My Guildmistress gets a certain percentage of the profit for my contract since I am part of her guild." She paused and stared at me until I nodded my understanding.

"My Guildmistress uses that profit to buy more contracts. As one of the original guild leaders from when the queen left, she's had *some* assistance from the other original guild leaders disbanding competing guilds. If you are a blacksmith, you work for her. Period. It's that simple." Anger at the system leaked into her voice as she spoke. "Since she owns almost all the blacksmiths, it's almost impossible for the regiments to secure a contract for a blacksmith without paying her ridiculous price and she has no reason to lower the price. It's a whole thing where the rich get richer and the poor get poorer."

"But there's an all-consuming Darkness out there. I get people wanting to be rich, but it could eat them." I pointed toward the horizon. "They should be helping."

"Part of it is denial. The Royal Centre doesn't think it will get to them anytime soon. After all, the front lines *just* fell, and they stood for millennia. They think towns like this one will last just as long, but they're wrong." She sighed and rubbed her chin between her thumb and forefinger. "But then again, someone seems to understand how dire the situation is. Outposts like this are the last barrier holding the Darkness away from the Royal Centre. If we fall, it'll only be a matter of time before the Darkness surrounds the Centre, wears down its walls, and consumes every last one of them." She furrowed her eyebrows and wrinkled her forehead in thought. "Besides, imagine their perspective. If they sent troops here, and those troops died, they wouldn't have people to protect them when the time comes. Everyone's largely treading water and trying not to think about it."

"So, we need to pay exorbitant prices to defend the city because they don't want to send their people somewhere they might get killed, even though they'll all die eventually?" I asked, sort of understanding, but not really. They were all just buying time when they could have been trying to stop the Darkness by working together.

"Yes, and it isn't easy to get that money unless you want to hire someone like me." She pointed to a bookshelf to her left where a Dark Blood orb sat. "Those sell for roughly twenty-five blood coins each. It would be more, but we can't refine them, so a refiner buys them cheap, does the process. A well-refined piece can sell for over a thousand Blood Coin."

"Seems we need to find a refiner," I said, an idea forming in my brain. If I could find someone who knew how to work with Dark Blood, I could upgrade them enough to make us rich. Then I could recruit more people.

"Good luck with that," she snorted. "Those hoity-toity bastards will never come out here, even if you had the coin."

"You never know," I said, shrugging. While there might be more puppeteers pulling strings in the Centre than I realized, I was going to have to make this work, or we were going to be screwed. "Okay, I'm gonna go check the Stained and see about getting that fixed." I gestured toward the forge. "Anything you want me to upgrade before I leave. I assume you know your, uh, class better than I do."

"Well, I'd love to be able to fix the forge myself," she said, shaking her head at it. "That'd make my job so much easier."

"Can you do that?" I asked, and before she could respond, I was already searching the Repair Tree she knew. Sure enough, there was a Skill for Forge Repair, and since it was just a single offshoot Skill based on the tree she already knew, it was only ten points.

"I know some smiths who can do repairs like that, but I never learned much about it beyond the basics." She shrugged. "I'm a sharp, pointy objects girl myself."

"Well, you can do it now," I said, learning the Skill for her. My sword glowed with soft blue light, and so did Sam. She stood there blinking at me for a minute.

"Holy shit, I can do it," she exclaimed excitedly as the glow faded. Then before I knew what was happening, she was hugging me. "Thanks. I'll get right to it!"

I nodded to her as she released me. She spun on her heel, already grabbing tools off the shelf as I glanced at her Skill window one last time and searched for the Skill to refine Dark Blood.

She couldn't learn it though, not without taking on the Alchemy Tree, and the cost for that was insane.

9

"Okay, I think I understand how the Skills work now," I told Gwen as I stepped out of Sam's shop. She was standing just a few feet away next to fifteen Stained of various ages. All of them were wearing clothes that probably should have just been burned, but I was guessing they didn't have anything else. We'd have to fix that.

"Hello, nice to see you too," Gwen said, turning to look at me and raising a slender eyebrow at me.

"Oh, yeah, sorry. Um, nice to see you again," I said, moving next to her and peering at the assembled women.

"So, what were you saying about Skills?" she asked, following me down the line as I moved to look at each one.

"Basically, there are these primary Skill trees that are opened up. Like for Sam, she had a whole tree opened because she was already trained. That's good because the Experience cost to buy a tree is really high. Once you know a primary Skill Tree though, buying the offshoots of that tree is pretty cheap."

"I'm not even slightly following what you're saying," Gwen said as I looked at the fifth Stained. She was a short girl with blue hair and eyes like the sun and a red mark in the shape of a cudgel on her left cheek. It was deep and penetrated her skin. It was a mark that would never wash away. She also had no discernable Skills.

"Basically, if you are a guard, it's easy to teach you to use swords, bows, whatever. Or even Skills based on those weapons. But if you have no training as a guard, it becomes incredibly difficult to teach someone those things because they don't know the basics." I pointed at the blue-haired girl. "For instance, if I wanted to teach Tonya here how to do Defensive Aegis, I'd have to teach her a Combat Tree, then a Shield Tree, and then the Skill. The Shield Tree is only a thousand Experience, and the Skill itself is fifteen hundred Experience. However, the basic Combat Tree? That's like five thousand Experience."

"Ah, well, what if Sheila trained her for a while first, would that make it cost less?" Gwen asked, staring at the girl in front of us. Tonya fidgeted uncomfortably under the scrutiny.

"More than likely, yes." I nodded. "The best thing to do would be to find people with the primary tree unlocked and then use Experience, assuming they have enough, to teach them what we want them to know." I shrugged. "I just did that with Sam. I taught her the Forge Repair Skill, and it was nearly free."

"Okay, I think I'm following," Gwen said as we moved to the next girls, but like the others, they had no useful Skills.

"Yeah, what I'm thinking is we need to find someone with the Alchemy Tree, then we can teach them refining." I sighed. "Because the cost to learn that tree is expensive, but the Refining Tree isn't so much."

"Makes sense." Gwen nodded, and a wicked gleam filled her eyes. "If we had an alchemist who knew refining, we could transmute all the Dark Blood into refined stuff and make a killing."

"Exactly. That's the best plan I think," I said,

looking toward the horizon. "Assuming we don't just leave the town. I know you said you could get executed but really, look around. Who is going to hunt you down?"

"It's really not an option to do that," Gwen said, her face turning serious. "I *need* you to help us here." She waved her hand at the town for emphasis. "I'll give you anything. Do you like gold? We have that here. I could give you some?" She took hold of my hand. "Please."

"Okay, okay," I said, pulling my hand away because her sudden begging was making me uncomfortable. Worse, all the Stained had gone downright panic-stricken at the process. Was I really that important?

"Thank you," Gwen said, breathing a sigh of relief. "We can work out the details of payment later." She gave me a wink. "Just please, help us."

"I will," I said, glad everyone wasn't looking so worried anymore. They had been really serious over what was only a passing observation and a smart one at that. "What's the big deal?"

"The big deal is that if I, along with all the people who work for me, are bound to this town, and if we break our contract and leave, we'll all grow weaker and weaker until we die." Gwen swallowed hard. "I've seen it happen before. It isn't pretty."

Well, that changed everything. While I didn't know Gwen that well, I certainly didn't want her, Sam, or any of the others to die. That meant we had to stay here, and if we had to stay here, we needed to fix this place up quick. If we didn't, we might die anyway. For that, we'd need money.

"Guess we need to find an alchemist then," I said, fixing Gwen in my gaze. "That's the first thing."

"We will likely need to go to the Royal Centre to find someone like that," Gwen said, giving me a sad smile. "I'll be surprised if anyone here has something like that, but even if we do, I doubt anyone will help us."

"You never know," I said, stopping as I stared at a mousy haired girl in front of me. She was a bit taller than the rest, and as I stared at her Stat sheet, I smiled. "Oh, that's neat."

Name: Taylor
Experience: 725
Health: 39/39
Mana: 41/141
Primary Power: None selected
Secondary Power: None selected

Strength: 12/100
Agility: 27/100
Charisma: 15/100
Intelligence: 33/100
Special: 8/100
Perk: Trained at the Royal Clothier's Academy.

"What is it," Taylor asked, twisting her hands in front of herself nervously and staring down at her feet.

"You were trained at the Royal Clothier's Academy," I said, smiling at her. "Why didn't you say anything earlier?"

"Oh…" Her frown deepened, and color spread across her cheeks. "I never finished my apprenticeship. I'm actually not allowed to say I'm trained there because of it."

"Who cares?" I said, putting my hands on my hips as I opened her primary Skill Tree. It was true, she didn't have any underlying Skills learned, but since she had the basic tree learned, I didn't care because now I could upgrade her Skills accordingly without having to buy the expensive basic tree.

"Um… the Guildmistress for one. If they find out I am claiming to be a clothier, they will do extraordinarily bad things to me." She swallowed. "I'd have continued, but I ran out of tuition money." She twisted her hands again. "I'd hoped to come to a border town for work, but then the town I was in got attacked." She looked like she was about to say more, but I turned to Gwen.

"I thought you said you interviewed everyone." I gestured at Taylor. "You should have brought her to me at the start."

"I didn't know," Gwen said, glaring at the girl. "She didn't tell me."

"That's true, I didn't." Taylor looked around sheepishly, but couldn't find a way to hide from Gwen's withering gaze. "I… um… got nervous. What if I messed up?"

I sighed and rubbed my face with my hand. "Look, it's okay to mess up. Why I'm a world class screw up. Anyway, let's get you settled." I looked around. "Um… pick one of the empty shops and make a list of what you need. We'll try to scrounge it up. Until then…" I glanced through her tree and had her learn the Clothing Repair Skills. "Let's get to work on stitching up some of these garments."

Taylor nodded and bit her lip. "I'll do my best. Thanks for trusting me."

"No problem," I said as she turned and made her way to the smallest shop on the left. "Say, Gwen, can you go help her get situated? I can finish up here, and that way by the time I'm done we'll have a better idea? You know, split the work?"

Gwen looked at me for a long moment before nodding. "Yeah, okay. I'll take care of it." She moved off to follow Taylor as I turned to the rest of the Stained.

"Anyone else have anything they want to tell me?" I asked, but none of them responded, so I carried along. Unfortunately, none of the others had any discernable Skills nor much Experience either.

"Too bad," I said as I rubbed my chin. "Still, I think I can work with this." I looked over the Stained for a few minutes before pulling two girls, Jesse and Jenny, aside.

"I want to check something," I told them. "Is that okay?"

They nodded in unison, and I smiled at the pair of them, trying to put them at ease. "Nothing bad," I said, waving my hand toward Sam's shop. "I'm going to see about making you apprentice blacksmiths. How's that sound?"

"You're going to give us jobs?" Jesse asked, completely flummoxed. "Why? We don't know anything about smithing."

"Yeah, I'm going to try to fix that." I turned to

the rest of the girls. "You all go see Sheila and Agatha at the gate and wait for me there."

"So, um, why did you pick us?" Jenny asked, following behind me as I turned and made my way back toward Sam's blacksmith shop.

"You two had the Stats most similar to Sam's own." I shrugged. "I was making an educated guess."

"Oh," they said, both looking at each other for a second and then they nodded like they'd had a whole unspoken conversation.

"Hey, Sam," I said, walking into the shop. The smith was busy at work on the forge and barely paused long enough to look over at me.

"What?" she asked, turning back to the forge. "I'm kind of busy here."

"I brought you some helpers," I said as I reopened Sam's Skill Tree. Sure enough, there was a whole tree dedicated to teaching, and better yet, she already knew some of it. It appeared that unlike some of the other trees, this one was automatically learned based upon Sam's own Skill level. The only thing that was low was the proficiency Skill at the top.

Teaching Proficiency
Skill: 2/10.

User can teach Skills up to a maximum level of 2. Increasing this Skill increases the speed with which knowledge is imparted as well as the maximum level of Skill that can be learned.

Like before there was an upgrade tab. This time the message was a bit different.

Do you want to upgrade Teaching Proficiency to Skill level 3? Base cost 300 Experience. This price can be reduced by attaining an overall Rank of 2 in Smithing.

"Well, that's neat. Evidently, since you're a high-level smith, I can make you a better teacher." I smirked, and before Sam could object, did the upgrade. Blue light surrounded her, and she glared at me.

"Did you just waste my Experience so I could teach those two no-nothings the difference between their asses and holes in the ground?" She put her hammer down and shifted her eyes to the two girls. "Never mind." She waved off her train of thought. "So, they're really mine to do as I wish?"

"Yep, well, within reason," I said, nodding to her, and she actually smiled at me.

"Excellent." She gestured at the two girls. "Come here and let me teach you a thing or two."

The pair of them looked at each other for a moment, nodded, and moved forward.

"Thanks," Jenny whispered as she passed by me.

"No, thank you. You're going to be doing the work," I said as I turned to go.

"If we can do anything to repay you, just let us know," Jesse added over her shoulder, right before Sam smacked her upside the head.

"You're here to learn, not to flirt," Sam growled. "Now, you go. You're much too distracting." She made a shooing gesture at me. "Go bother Gwen. Maybe take her in a backroom somewhere and keep her out of our hair for a while."

10

A few minutes later, I found myself at the gate. I'd stopped by the new clothing shop to see Gwen, but she'd shooed me away because her and Taylor were still busy setting up. Evidently, they'd found some old supplies somewhere and were still going through it to see what worked and what didn't.

"Hello," I said, as I approached the group of ladies waiting there. "Everything okay?"

"Yes," a few of them murmured, watching me with careful eyes.

"Good, I'm glad to hear it," I said, trying my best to be cheery. "Let me just speak with Agatha and Sheila for a moment, and I'll come back, and we'll do a whole spiel." A few of them nodded as I made my way to the gate and rapped on it with my knuckles. "Open up."

"On it," I heard Sheila say, and a few moments later I saw the gears on this side of the gate begin to move. The doors swung open enough for me to squeeze through before slamming shut. Now that I had watched it in action from both sides, I realized it was set up on springs that naturally made it close.

"So, what do you need, boss?" Agatha asked, her eyes flicking from me to the horizon and back again. "It's really not safe for you out here."

"I'll just be a minute," I said, opening her Skill Tree.

Name: Agatha
Experience: 4,300
Health: 131/131
Mana: 72/72
Primary Power: Fighter - Offensive
Secondary Power: None selected
Strength: 54/100
Agility: 77/100
Charisma: 11/100
Intelligence: 25/100
Special: 47/100
Perk: Trained at the Royal Guard's Academy.

Like Sheila, Agatha had no Abilities known, but that was something I could fix. Still, that wasn't what I was interested in at the moment. I scrolled to her Teaching Tree and was surprised to find it was already at four out of ten. Interesting.

"Say, Agatha, what's a Skill similar to Defensive Aegis but for offensive fighters like yourself?" I asked, as I moved to Sheila and checked her proficiency. It was also at four. That felt odd to me.

"Blinding Blade, probably," Agatha responded with a shrug. "Usually those teamed with a Defensive Aegis user, use that to increase their attacks to take advantage of the enemies leaving themselves open."

"Okay," I said, moving back to her Skill Tree and bringing up the Skill.

Blinding Blade: This Ability allows the user to temporarily double the speed of all attacks.

Requirements: Special: 50+, Agility: 50+, Charisma: 10+

Cost: 1500 Experience

"Hmm, you don't quite have the Stats for it," I mumbled, and was going to let the Ability slide away when I noticed a linked Ability.

Blinding Blade Omni: This Ability allows the user to

temporarily double the speed of all attacks for friendlies within ten yards.

Requirements: Special: 50+, Agility: 50+, Charisma: 10+, Blinding Blade

Cost: 600 Experience

"Does that mean I can't get it?" Agatha asked, and from the tone of her voice, I could tell she was a bit upset by it.

"Hang on a second," I said, selecting Blinding Blade.

Requirements not met. Special Stat too low. Would you like to upgrade? Cost of Stat upgrade: 147 Experience.

I made it so and then spent another 2100 Experience points for her to learn Blinding Blade and Blinding Blade Omni.

As blue light surrounded Agatha, I smiled at her. "I did you one better. Now the effect will be given to those around you."

"Great, I guess," Agatha said, confused. "But it's just her and me." She jutted a thumb at Sheila. "Seems like a waste of Experience to me."

"Yeah, I have a reason for that, but first I have a question. It seems you both have a high teaching Ability. It's strange because Sam didn't, and she was pretty high up in her profession Skill wise. Any idea why?"

The pair of guards looked at each other for a while.

"Not really..." Sheila started to say, but then stopped herself. "Maybe it's because of basic?"

"Must be," Agatha affirmed. "I can't think of another reason why."

"Basic?" I asked, raising an eyebrow at them. "Explain, please."

"Oh, well, in basic, we take turns teaching the lower skilled recruits. It's part of the Skill requirement to pass. You have to be able to teach certain stuff. The idea is that you learn something way better when you're forced to teach someone else how to do it." Sheila shrugged. "It's pretty typical in the guard profession since sometimes we need to teach people how to do things in siege situations. It hasn't come up here though."

"Well, it's about to," I said, nodding because that was absolutely perfect. "We have a dozen Stained I want you to train to be guards. Assuming they become somewhat proficient, that'd give us fourteen in total." I rubbed my chin in thought. "How about you pick the strongest three and train them, Sheila. Agatha, you take the rest and train them. Sound good?"

"Not really, but it'd be nice to have the help,"

Sheila said with a shrug. "Only, you'd probably know better who to give me."

"That's true." I nodded. "Well, Sheila, come inside with me for a second. We'll pick yours and then you can take them out here. Say, what about gear?"

"We won't have quite that much, but we will make do. We can get some wooden spears and the like for practice." Sheila smirked. "I'm actually kind of excited."

"I'm glad. Just make a list of what you need and get it to Gwen. I think we're going to make a trip to the Royal Centre," I said as we moved inside and looked at the assembled Stained. I picked the three with the highest Strength and sent them to Sheila. The guard nodded and took them off to a small, squat building a little way from the gate, which was where I presumed they kept their gear.

While Sheila was busy with that, I glanced through the open gate at Agatha who was busy holding it open. "These girls are yours. I expect them to be trained well."

"I'll do my best," Agatha said, looking them over. "I can't train them and hold the door though so Sheila and I will have to trade off…" Her eyes brightened. "Guess it's running then." She pointed toward the far wall a few hundred yards away. "Run there and back as quick as you can."

No one moved, and Agatha raised an eyebrow. "I'm sorry, was I unclear in some way? Move it, maggots!" she snarled.

The remaining girls took off, sprinting toward the far walls, only it was immediately obvious their clothing wouldn't work for this.

"I'll have them some proper clothing made," I said as I watched them go.

"That'd help, but for now, they can just strip down. Better to be half naked and alive, than dead because you can't kick in a dress." She grinned at me. "I'm sure you'll enjoy that, anyway."

She was right, I would, under normal circumstances anyway. These girls were my responsibility now, and the last thing I wanted was for them to think I was leering at them in their underwear.

"I'll make myself scarce," I replied, nodding to her as Sheila returned. Her three girls each held simple wooden shields and spears. They'd also been stripped down to their skivvies, and I looked away from them.

"Two sets of armor then," I said, and began to walk away when the clarion sounded and the skies above crackled with thunder.

Lizardmen poured from the horizon, at least three times as many as before, and as they approached I swallowed hard. We didn't have the forces for this. Not even close, and what's more, it had only been a couple hours.

"Fuck!" I cried as Sheila grabbed her spear and hustled back toward the gate. Agatha was already standing there, and I could practically feel her new power in the air as she stepped forward to defend.

As the first of the lizardmen reached her, she spun past it, driving her blades into the creature in a flurry of motion that split it from crotch to sternum. The creature struck the dirt as Sheila landed lithely on the ground, planting herself in front of the horde.

As the butt of her spear hit the ground, she activated Defensive Aegis. The green wave of energy spread out, drawing the lizardmen to her in droves. As they turned toward her, pulled by the spell, Agatha darted forward in a blur of speed, lopping off heads like a whirling dervish of death. Her hands and arms moved so fast she was practically a blur, and what's more Sheila was faster too. Every single time she lashed out with her spear, the air whistled.

In moments, what had seemed like an insurmountable force was lying dead on the ground. It was incredible, but as the sky above crackled, I still had the distinct impression we were on borrowed time. And not just that, from the way the horizon pulsed, I was pretty sure the waves were only going to get bigger and deadlier.

11

"I'm glad we made a list," Gwen said from beside me as we made our way down the road toward the Royal Centre, "but I don't think it's going to matter much." She held up her bag of Dark Blood. "There's no way we'll be able to buy even half of the stuff we need with what we've got on top of the recruitment we need to do." She rolled her eyes. "I love you, but your eyes are way bigger than your stomach in this case."

"We'll just have to do what we can," I said, glancing at the list. "I'd say getting the items to outfit our people are most important as far as supplies." I sighed and rubbed my face.

"I still think we need to focus on getting a miner and a lumberjack. If you could find a couple with their Abilities at reasonable levels, they could at least teach the Stained how to do those jobs." She smirked. "Stained are easy to find anyway. Once they hear you're actually turning them into skilled labor for breathing, well, they'll come in droves." Her smirk turned into a full-blown grin. "And the lazy ones won't come because they won't want to work. It's like a super win-win situation."

"I don't know if you're thinking about this altruistically enough," I said. The path around us was lined with trees, and with every step we took, I could feel the press of them. I wasn't sure what was out there, but it definitely wanted to eat us. "And, um, are you sure we're safe here?" I waved my hand at the forest anxiously.

"More or less since we're on a path." She shrugged. "You never know though. Could be an angry grizzly bear or something that wants to make a meal out of you."

"You guys have grizzly bears?" I asked, raising an eyebrow at her. "Aren't we in Hell?"

"Okay, so they're more like demonic mutant hell spawn, but I didn't want to frighten you." She shrugged and looked around. "Maybe we'd be better off flying though." She took a glance at Lustnor. "They don't come this close to town, usually, but at the same time I'm not sure the protection aura will extend much farther out."

"Is that the barrier I saw when the town got attacked by the lizardmen?" I asked, remembered the shimmering magical barrier that had covered the town.

"Yes. It projects an aura that makes the wild beasts keep their distance." She unfurled her wings then, and I'd forgotten how spectacular they were. They glimmered in the light of the lightning-filled sky like rubies.

"I don't know if you're aware of this," I said, nodding toward her huge wings. They seemed even bigger than they had before, giving her at least a twelve-foot wingspan. "But I don't have wings nor can I fly." I waved dumbly at the sky. "No yellow sun either, so Supermanning it up is out."

"I'll carry you," she said, moving closer and wrapping her arms around me. She hoisted me into the air and cradled me like a baby as though I weighed nothing. "See, you're light as a feather."

"You are making me feel decidedly unmanly," I said as her wings beat the air with enough force that we lifted from the ground. My heart leaped into my throat, and I wrapped my arms around her, clinging to her with my feeble strength. It made me glad my sword was in a sheath at my waist because if it hadn't been, I might have dropped it.

"Well, if you want to stay on the ground and get eaten to assuage your manhood, we can do that," she said as we rocketed forward so fast the air nearly peeled the flesh from my bones.

"I'm good," I murmured, but my voice was lost to the wind as we zoomed along. I tried to look around and gauge the scenery, but as we moved along the road, I found I could see nothing but forest. There were a couple mountains in the distance, but they were way too far for me to think we'd ever reach them.

"What's that?" I asked, pointing toward what looked like a small wagon on the road. From here it looked like there were several dog-like creatures circling it like wolves.

"Merchant's wagon." Gwen swallowed hard. "We best move on while they're distracted. They probably can't get us in the air, but I'd prefer not to find out."

"We can't just leave whoever is down there to the beasts. We have to help them," I said, squinting at the wagon. "Besides, if no one is there, we could really use whatever is in the wagon. Hell, just having the wagon would be awesome."

"How do you expect to fight off the three demon dogs?" she asked, pulling to a stop in midair. We were still a ways away, but now I could definitely make out the creatures.

They were huge, like donkey huge, and had rippling black flesh that looked to be covered in plates like an armadillo. A huge rhino horn jutted from a snout filled with hooked, dripping teeth. Their ears were pressed flat against their head as they circled the wagon, snapping at a tiny figure atop it.

From here, she looked like a goblin, and she was desperately trying to fight off the creatures with a giant spear but wasn't having much luck. They easily evaded her strikes and snapped back, and I knew it was only a matter of time before they either pulled her off the wagon or leaped atop it and ate her.

"Can't you blast them?" I asked, glancing at Gwen because I'd seen her use magic to stop the lizardmen earlier. "You know. Kill it with fire?"

"I don't have the energy for that," she said, and a quick glance at her Stats told me she was right. She only had three Mana.

"Jesus, why do you regenerate Mana so slow? It's ridiculous," I said, unsheathing Clarent.

"I don't know," she said, as I quickly scrolled through her Stats. Every single Skill Tree was the same. All the Regeneration Skills had been skipped in favor of Power Boosting Skills. She was like a huge single-shot cannon. She could do tons of damage, but because she hadn't gained any Regeneration Skills, she couldn't do it very often. Well, I could fix that.

"There!" I said, using forty-five-hundred Experience to learn every Regeneration Skill I could. The first one I'd found let her cut her regeneration time in half, and then had a spin-off that caused it to increase based on how low her Mana was. The lower it was, the faster she regenerated. I found a similar (and cheaper) one that only worked out of combat. Then I found another one that caused all regeneration effects to double.

She didn't have enough Experience to learn any of the others, so that would have to do. I accepted the changes. Blue light surrounded her, causing her Mana to surge up.

"What did you do?" she asked, shaking her head in confusion. "I feel way stronger than only a second ago.

"I min-maxed your Mana regeneration," I said,

pointing my sword at the demon dogs. "Now do your thing and turn them into hamburger."

"With pleasure," Gwen said, dropping down like a hawk. She settled onto the wagon next to the goblin, who let out a shriek.

"What are you two doing here?" the goblin squeaked in a "nails on a chalkboard" voice.

"Saving you," Gwen said, putting me down and summoning a huge handful of fire. She flung it at the closest dog. The fireball slammed into the creature, burning a hole straight through its torso before smashing into the ground beneath it. As the dirt turned to slag, the creature screamed, collapsing to the ground as the smell of burning flesh filled my nose.

I barely resisted the urge to gag as Gwen spun on her heel and lobbed another fireball at the next demon dog. This blast missed, but it was close enough that the creature yelped before taking off back into the forest with its compatriot chasing after.

"Wow, that was great," Gwen said. "Normally, I don't have the Strength to launch two fireballs with that much power." She flexed. "I bet I could do it again."

As she spoke, I saw the number fifty flash over

her head. I opened her window to see that she'd gained fifty Experience from the battle. Interesting. That meant our people could earn Experience via combat.

"Thanks for your help," the goblin said, grinning at me. She had a gold hoop through her nose and another couple on each ear and one through each eyebrow. She was short, maybe only three feet tall, but damn did she have back. It was like she was all booty and chest and not a lot else. I could tell, even though she was wearing a loose-fitting shirt and pants, that she had that much going on.

"You're welcome," I said as she jumped down from the wagon and moved to the dead demon dog. She pulled a small hatchet from her waist and then hacked off the horn.

"This will fetch a high price." She grinned and hopped back onto the wagon with ease. Then she plodded toward the far end which had a series of knobs and levers embedded into the steel.

"So, you should give that to us," I said as the goblin started the wagon with a rumble that caused flames to shoot out the back end as it began to lurch forward.

"Finders keepers," she said, turning to look at me as she rolled her multi-faceted silver eyes at me.

"But if you guys help me get all the way to Royal Centre, I'll gladly give it to you. Hell, I'll throw in fifty Blood Coins to boot." She smacked her thigh with one green hand. "Sound like a deal?"

As she spoke a red question mark appeared over her head, and without thinking, I gestured at it.

"Um, what are you doing?" the goblin asked as a message box appeared beside her in glowing red.

You have been offered a quest.

Objective: Escort Buffy to the Royal Centre.

Reward: 500 Experience per party member, 50 Blood Coins, 1 Demon Horn

Do you accept?

I considered what to do for a moment, but since we were already heading there, I accepted the quest, causing a red glow to surround my sword, Gwen, and the goblin.

"Whoa, what the fuck did you just do, pal?" Buffy exclaimed, smacking at the fading glow with her hands while the wagon puttered along.

"I accepted your quest," I replied, shrugging and turning to Gwen. "If we do this, you'll get a bunch of Experience and since we were going there, anyway …" I shrugged.

"I figured you were doing something like that," the succubus said before sitting down cross-legged on the roof of the wagon. "Wake me when we get there or if I need to roast some demons."

"What do you mean you accepted my quest? How did that make me glow?" Buffy said, glaring at me. "What the hell are you?" she looked me over then. "Wait..." she sniffed, causing her nostrils to flare. "You smell like a male." She swallowed hard and ran a hand through her brown hair, brushing it out of the way of her pointy ears. "Are you, um, male?"

"Yes, I'm male," I said, and I held up Clarent. "This is Clarent, and together we became the Builder of Legend!" As I said it, Gwen rolled her eyes at me.

"You shouldn't go around saying that to everyone," Gwen said before laying on her back and staring at the sky. "And especially not like that. It's sort of lame."

"Admittedly, it sounded better in my head," I said, shrugging at her before turning back to Buffy. "But, yeah, Builder of Legend. The sword lets me manipulate Stats of my party members and, evidently, accept quests."

"You can't be the Builder of Legend. There hasn't been one in over a thousand years," Buffy said, hitting a button next to her and pulling a lever.

Gears ground beneath the wagon and it lurched forward going faster. "Damn clutch is sticking."

"You don't have to believe me," I said, shrugging. "I'm not trying to win a contest or anything. It's not like I get a prize for you believing me."

"Prove it," she said, holding out one hand to me. It was covered in golden rings with sparkling gemstones. "Build me or whatever."

"You're not a party member of mine." I pointed toward the spot where the glowing menu orb would be. "You don't have a menu above your head."

"Well, I wanna join your party on a temporary basis," she said, narrowing her eyes at me. "How's that sound?" I could tell from the way she said it, she didn't believe me. Not that it mattered because as soon as she made the offer, a golden triangle appeared over her head.

I swiped at it, and a message box appeared.

Buffy has requested to join your party. Do you accept?

"Yeah, sure," I said, accepting her, and as I did, the normal blue orb appeared over her head. "So, what do you want me to change?"

"What can you change?" the goblin replied as I opened her Stat window.

Name: Buffy
Experience: 7,800

Health: 20/20
Mana: 141/141
Primary Power: Mercantilism
Secondary Power: None selected
Strength: 11/100
Agility: 9/100
Charisma: 77/100
Intelligence: 73/100
Special: 68/100
Perk: Rank 3 Merchant

"Hmm," I said, looking up at her. "This says you're a Rank three merchant. What's that mean?"

"How did you know that?" Buffy asked, alarm filling her eyes. "I didn't say anything about my Rank." She took a deep breath. "Are you some kind of mind reader? What number am I thinking of?"

"No," I said, it's just on your Character Sheet. Oh, never mind." I shook my head. "Can you just tell me?"

"While there's not an official merchant guild per se, we have a sort of ranking based on what we're allowed to buy and sell, and how much profit we're allowed to make. At the end of the year, if I've made too much, I'll be taxed harshly on the extra unless I buy myself another Rank." Buffy snorted. "It's basically formalized extortion by the high-ranking merchants to drive down competition."

"Sounds stupid," I said, opening her Mercantilism Power.

Mercantilism: User has the Ability to learn merchant related trees. None have currently been selected.

"It is stupid." She crossed her arms over her chest. "It's also exponential, so going from ten to nine is easy, but for me to go to Rank two? That's like nearly impossible without the Royal Centre's blessing. Hell, just to go from four to three cost me ten years of savings."

"Maybe you're just a terrible merchant?" I countered as I opened the tree and found a lot of trees sort of half-formed. It reminded me of those people I'd known throughout the years who dabbled in various get rich quick schemes but, for whatever reason, never stuck around long enough to make any of them really work. "Your Skill trees are all jacked up."

"Excuse me?" Buffy said, gritting her teeth. "I'm a great merchant." She fished a golden medallion out from her shirt and showed it to me. A giant three was emblazoned on it. "You don't get one of these without being awesome."

"Or, you know, pay a bunch of money," I said.

"Which I guess sort of works for you, but I'm guessing there's a bunch of rich nobles or something who have Rank one because they're rich."

"Being rich is the whole point," Buffy said with a snort as she turned her eyes to the road. "So, what's wrong with my Skills?"

"Well, I'm not an expert, but you have this one tree called Bartering," I said, pulling it up. "It has a Sweet Talk Skill that could have been leveled. Each Rank gives you an increased chance to sell or buy an item at a profit. You haven't even taken it. Then there are all the spin-offs related to it. I'd imagine you'd want almost every one of these Skills."

"My goods speak for themselves," Buffy harrumphed.

"Spoken like every bad salesman ever," I said, remembering how my boss had told me to sell more Slurpees even though it had been the dead of winter and ten inches of snow had been outside. When I'd complained, he'd sat with me for a day, selling Slurpees to everyone. The dude could sell ice to an Eskimo, which was probably why he owned the Seven Eleven, and I just worked there.

"I am not a bad salesman," Buffy said, glaring at me.

"Not anymore," I said as I spent around three

thousand Experience points to maximize Sweet Talk as well as a couple other Skills that seemed like they'd compound the effect. "Look, just see how well you do this time, and if you like it, we can work on your Skills more. In exchange, you'll come work for me. If not, I'll put everything back the way it was and send you along on your way."

"Whatever," Buffy grumbled, rolling her eyes. "Now, if you don't mind, I'd like to ride the rest of the way in silence."

"Okay," I said. I felt bad for making her upset but what was done was done. I wasn't exactly the most tactful person I knew by a longshot. My boss could probably have made Buffy happy during the exchange, but I knew one thing. My goods *would* speak for themselves.

12

"So, I had a thought," I said as we rode up toward Royal Centre. The path had long since changed from dirt to asphalt, and now there was a lot more traffic. We'd passed by everything from buggies similar to Buffy's to horse-drawn carriages. It seemed technology ran the entire gamut because I'd actually seen an airplane overhead at one point during the trip.

"What's your thought?" Gwen said, sitting up and stretching before yawning in an extremely attractive way. She glanced around. "Better make it quick because we'll be at the city gates in a few minutes."

"I don't know if the two of you have noticed, but I'm, well, male." I touched my chest with one finger. "The only male. In the whole realm."

"Yeah, get over yourself," Buffy snorted. "Bragging is so unattractive."

"You're missing my point." I sighed and shook my head. "I'm going to stand out like a sore thumb in a town full of women."

"Let me break this down for you, Arthur," Buffy said, rolling her eyes at me. "We're demons, not fucking nuns. We can go to earth and get a lil' something-something whenever we like. Sure, having you here for convenience is nice, but our entire purpose is to take souls and use them in our war with the Darkness." She flicked a hand toward Gwen. "How do you think *she* acquires most of her souls?" Buffy waggled her eyebrows a couple of times. "Eh, eh?"

"Yeah, fine, I just didn't want it to be a thing," I said, crossing my arms over my chest and looking up at the stormy sky.

Gwen touched my shoulder then. "Buffy makes a good point, but you are still the Builder of Legend. Even if most of the women here won't want to jump your bones, you will stand out because of who you are. Remember, you are important because of who you are and what you bring to the table, not for something as silly as gender." She winked at me. "But being nice to look at doesn't hurt your cause."

"Great, now he's going to have an even bigger head." Buffy rolled her eyes. "Both of them."

I'll be honest, Gwen's words made me feel a lot better. I knew I was the Builder and as such was here to help them fight the Darkness. I knew I'd come to the Royal Centre to help recruit workers for Lustnor so we could build up formidable defenses because Gwen and the others couldn't leave without risking execution.

At the same time, I'd never been around so many hot women, and crazily enough, they all talked to me. No, not just talked to me, but actually seemed to like what I had to say. It was strange and part of me had thought that maybe it was because I was the only guy here. Only, that wasn't why. Sure, maybe being the only guy helped, but at the end of the day, I was the fucking Builder of Legend. Me. And that meant something to these people and, more and more, to me too.

"Thanks," I said, nodding toward Gwen. "I'll try to do my best and ensure we'll win. Now onto the important business." I pointed toward the massive obsidian walls that appeared on the horizon as we crested the hill. "What the fuck is that?"

"Those are the Walls of Torment. It's said they are made of over a billion souls. At night, when the black wind blows across the valley, you can hear the cries of their torment for miles." Gwen shimmied a little bit. "It's simply marvelous."

"Yeah, okay," I said, staring up at the walls. They were so huge, they seemed to touch the sky. Part of me had sort of forgotten we were in Hell, and not just that, I'd almost forgotten Gwen was a demon. Sure, she was still dressed like Morrigan from Darkstalkers, but at the same time, I'd just kind of forgotten. I mean, Jesus, I was sitting here next to a goblin. My life had definitely taken a decidedly strange turn.

"So, what's the plan once we arrive?" Buffy said, glancing at me as we entered a line of cars, buggies, carriages, and other assorted vehicles along the right-hand side of the road. Up ahead, I could see several guards talking to the occupants before allowing them to enter, but it didn't seem like a big deal because the line was moving along fairly quickly.

"We'll go try to recruit what we need while you do your merchant thing?" I offered with a shrug.

"Also, sell these," Gwen added, handing the Dark Bloods we'd collected over to Buffy. "If

Arthur says you can sell for a high price, I trust him."

Buffy took the sack and looked inside before nodding approvingly. "I'd heard Lustnor was in a good position to get these but I didn't realize you'd collected so many. Your town must be rich."

"That's the accumulation of nearly six months of attacks, and we can never get near what they're worth." Gwen gritted her teeth. "I don't have anyone with high enough Rank to sell them for more."

"That's the kind of horseshit I'm talking about. Some jackass buys these for pennies on the dollar and then upcharges them a thousand percent." She shook her head. "Nice work if you can get it."

"You *can* get it. Sell them for a lot and come back with us. We can create a lucrative business," I said, smiling at her. "We could really use you."

"Don't go putting the cart before the horse, Builder." Buffy frowned. "Let me see what I can do." She glanced at the gold watch on her wrist. "Let's meet at Mac's Tavern at noon. So, four hours from now. We can talk more then, okay?"

"Okay, but there's one more thing," Gwen said as Buffy hit a button on the dash, causing a compartment to open next to her. She shoved the bag of Dark Bloods into it and hit the button again, causing it to close from view.

"What's that?" Buffy asked as Gwen offered her a piece of paper. "We need these supplies. Can you try to buy them for us?"

"I'll take a cut, but I think I can manage," Buffy said, taking the paper and looking it over. "Nothing particularly interesting."

"A cut?" Gwen asked, wariness filling her face. "How much?"

"Look, my cut plus what I pay will be *way* less than what you pay. You should consider it a gift," Buffy said as we rolled up to the front of the gate. She flashed her Merchant's badge at the guard as a slender woman with onyx hair walked up. She took one look at the badge and waved us through.

Quest Escort Buffy to the Royal Centre has been completed.

"Fair enough," Gwen said as numbers flashed above her head, indicating the Experience reward from the quest we'd just completed had been distributed. "As I said before, I trust you."

"Good," Buffy replied as the buggy rumbled through the gates.

The inside of the city was amazing. I found myself staring at a cross between a massive metropolitan city like Toronto or Chicago and a bazaar straight out of Aladdin. Massive skyscrapers filled the horizon, rivaling only the walls in size, while propped up in almost every space were food trucks, pop-up tents, and dudes with what looked like demonic camels laden with goods.

It was the damnedest sight I'd ever seen, and as I sat there, mouth agape like a slack-jawed yokel, Buffy began to laugh.

"Never seen the Royal Centre, eh?" She elbowed me in the side. "It always gets me too, and I've seen it so many times I've lost count."

"It smells like cinnamon," I said, shaking my head in disbelief before sucking in another lungful. "And sage and lemon, and damn I'm starving."

"That would probably be Voodoo Star," Gwen said, appreciatively. "They make the best donuts this side of Portland." She showed me a smile that was all perfect teeth and heart-stopping glory. "Come on, I'll buy you one. They make this cream-filled one in the shape of a penis that is simply out of this world."

"Oh, I'm jealous," Buffy said, pulling the buggy to a stop beside the road where people were unloading various wares. "Alas, no rest for the wicked." She cackled. "Now off with you, you're cramping my style."

"We'll see you at noon," Gwen said, taking my hand and pulling me off the cart while I tried to wrap my head around the donut in question. I wasn't sure if I could handle eating a penis-shaped donut, but at the same damned time, I'd pretty much eat a doorknob if it smelled as good as this shop did.

"Don't be late. Time is money," Buffy said with a wave before leaping down and approaching a bigger, darker skinned goblin with a grill that would put a rapper to shame.

"Anyway, the reason Voodoo Star is so good has to do with the dough. They use this brioche style dough that just makes it so cakey and delicious." Gwen licked her lips. "I can practically taste the cream melting on my tongue." She did that weird shimmy again as we approached a shop with a line practically around the block.

The smell of the donut shop was so intense it nearly knocked me on my ass. It smelled, and I kid you not, exactly like everything I'd ever wanted. I needed to have one of these donuts. No, all these donuts. Even that would not be enough.

"Are you sure we can spare the cash?" I asked,

glancing at Gwen as we began moving through the line. There were a burly couple of long-haired demons holding hands in front of us, and for some reason, the sight struck me as odd. In fact, lots of demons were holding hands. I wasn't one to judge, but I hadn't quite expected it.

"Donuts come out of a separate account," Gwen said, reaching into her top and pulling out a pair of blood red bills. She held them up to me. "I always keep a little extra cash to come here when I visit the Royal Centre. It's partially because they only take cash like a bunch of godforsaken heathens."

"Well, you know, credit card fees…" I muttered waving a hand because my old boss at the Seven Eleven always carried on about the "filthy bloodsucking" credit card companies.

"Pfft," Gwen blew a lock of hair out of her face. "Businesses do business." She waved a hand at her bikini-clad body. "Do I look like I have a lot of room to carry things?"

"Well, no," I said, feeling my face heat up. I looked away because it was then that I realized Gwen and I were still holding hands. Her skin was so warm I could practically feel it spreading out through my entire body.

"Exactly, so some consideration would be nice." She squeezed my fingers and leaned in close, so her breasts were touching my shoulder in a way that made my pants decidedly tighter. "Do you want an oyster?" She pointed past me toward the building I'd been looking at without seeing. It was filled with people and black, wrought-iron tables were strewn across the entire alleyway separating the oyster bar from Voodoo Star. "'Cause if you do, I'm your huckleberry." Her breath was warm on my neck as she spoke. "They do these vodka oyster shooters that are quite the aphrodisiac."

"Oh?" I said, swallowing as I tried to turn toward her, but we were so close together I couldn't really move. "I've never actually had an oyster."

"They're terrible, but I love them," Gwen said, her lips mere millimeters from mine as she spoke. "I can't even imagine the first guy who tried them. They had to crack open the shell and be like, 'hmm, well this looks like a bucket of snot, I bet it tastes great,' and here's the thing. They do taste great. A little bit of horseradish and some lemon. Mmm." She licked her lips as she did that shimmy again, causing her chest to rub against me.

"I, um, am not sure how to take that," I said, glancing back at the shop so my face wasn't quite as close to hers because if she kept looking at me that way, I might do something I'd regret.

"You take it hard and fast. That's the way I like it," she said. "If you go too slowly, you'll just be like 'what the fuck am I doing? This whole thing is disgusting? How did I let myself be talked into this?'" She shivered in disgust and somehow managed to press herself closer against my body. "The best thing is to do it so quickly, it's already done by the time you have regrets."

"Is that so?" I asked, turning back to her, and I found her staring at me in a way I couldn't discern. There was hunger and something else I couldn't identify.

"Yes." She licked her lips and stared at me for a long time. Her lips slowly parted, and she leaned in a little closer before pulling away suddenly. "Oh look, we're up!"

13

"Look, just try the tip. If you don't like it, that's fine, but you owe it to yourself to find out," Gwen said before flicking her tongue out to lick up the cream oozing from the tip of her eight-inch chocolate donut. I stared down at my own pastry. It was as thick as my wrist.

"Stop trying to pressure me," I said, weighing the thing. It had to have been at least a pound.

"Look, just open your mouth and stick it in. Don't overthink things." She opened her mouth and licked the length of the donut in one slow, sensuous movement before taking the entirety into her mouth. She sucked on it for a moment like she was trying to get every ounce of cream before pulling it out. "I really like how big and thick it is." She licked her lips, getting a bit of frosting that had dribbled down from the corner of her mouth. "The cream is my favorite. All hot and sticky."

"Does everyone eat them like that?" I said, opening my own mouth. There was no way I could get the tip inside, let alone the whole thing. It was way too big.

"It does take some practice." She squeezed the base to force more cream out before licking it again. "But you know the saying about eating an elephant. One bite at a time, right?" She smiled evilly at me before putting the donut into her mouth up to the hilt. She made eye contact with me as she slowly closed her mouth and chewed thoughtfully.

"Wow." I had a million very strange and equally conflicting thoughts running through my mind and couldn't quite articulate a better response.

She smiled at me, bits of donut flecking her teeth and lips. "It does take a bit of practice to get the whole thing in at once, but it's worth it." She looked at my still untouched donut. "But if you like, you can have the rest of mine, and I'll eat yours. It might make you less uncomfortable." She showed me her donut, and sure enough, it mostly just looked like a normal donut now.

"The things I do for my friends," I said, swapping my donut for hers. As I stared at my newly acquired donut, I felt ridiculous because it was a pastry. Still, now that she'd eaten some of it, the donut looked like a normal Bavarian cream.

"Stop being a baby and try it," she said, licking the chocolate off the length of my former donut. "It's really good." She winked at me. "And don't worry about this one. I've got big plans for him." She licked it again. "Big, big plans."

"Fine," I said and took a small bite. Flavors exploded in my mouth. Chocolate, vanilla, cinnamon. They all hit me at once, practically knocking me on my ass. My eyes opened, and I saw everything in my life had been insignificant before I'd found this donut. Hunger consumed me, taking over my entire being with the need to have more of it inside me.

Before I realized what I was doing, I'd crammed the entire donut in my mouth, and as it slid down my throat and into my belly, a strange sense of satisfaction overcame me.

"Best donut ever?" Gwen asked, offering me one hand as I sat there on the dirt beside the donut shop. Several other patrons were looking at me in the "How embarrassing" sort of way I'd gotten from chicks in high school, but I couldn't even focus on it because as I stared up at Gwen, I could tell she didn't feel that way at all. No, she was just happy I'd enjoyed the treat she'd bought me.

"Best. Donut. Ever," I responded, taking her hand and getting to my feet. "Now, um, I think we're supposed to do more than eat donuts."

"I know, it saddens me too." She brushed a lock of dark hair behind a perfect ear. "Royal Centre is such a food city, and I'm always here on business. It'd be nice to just come here and chill." She touched her belly. "But then I'd get fat."

"I don't think I'd ever think you were fat, so you shouldn't think that either." I smiled, and then before our conversation could move into dangerous territory, I glanced around the bustling streets. Vendors were everywhere, and I wasn't quite sure where to go. "But we should get a move on to the Guild house."

"Okay," Gwen said, nodding. "It's this way." She took a step forward, moving through the crowd toward the corner. I followed along behind her, careful not to get too far away and get cut off by strangers.

After a few minutes of walking, Gwen stopped in front of a large red brick building. It wasn't as tall as the skyscrapers all around us, but it was certainly wide and large, taking up nearly the entire city block. It made the place seem out of place because most of the shops we'd passed had gone up three levels. This one on the other hand was sprawling and single story.

"Is this it?" I asked, gesturing at the building. Red spruce trees decorated the front, casting a shadow across the doorway.

"Yeah, you can tell it's a government building because they waste so much space." Gwen snorted. "No one else would waste it like this. They'd go straight up and rent the rest out for profit, but what does the government care about that?" She grimaced. "They just raise taxes when they need more money."

"It doesn't seem like you guys like the government much. Buffy and Sam were both bent about it too." I shrugged. "After all, our government is kinda terrible back home too."

"You don't even know. We're demons from Hell. Trust me, ours is worse."

"Fair point. Guess I'll take your word for it." I glanced back toward the building and noted the black plaque above the huge stone doors. I couldn't read the language though. It was weird because everything else had seemed to be in English, but then again, what I knew about Hell couldn't fill a thimble.

"Let's get a move on. The longer we're out here, the less time we'll have to find people before we have to meet up with Buffy." She took my hand and moved forward, mounting the first red brick step and pulling me along like an errant toddler.

"Well, we could always make Buffy wait," I said as she pushed open the doors to reveal a hall made of polished marble. Gold filigree covered every inch of the place, and paintings displaying what looked like archangels getting ROFL stomped by the demonic version of Amazons filled my vision.

The hallway led straight to the back with more corridors forking off in every direction. More signs were displayed next to the arch for each corridor, but like the sign outside, I couldn't read it either.

"Say, what language is that?" I pointed at the signs. "I could read the stuff outside, so I'd just assumed everything was in my language."

"It's written normally, but you couldn't read it if you wanted to. Your human mind cannot comprehend it thanks to the wards on the place to keep out the unwelcome. That's why it looks like scribbles to you." She smiled at me. "You probably couldn't come in if you weren't with me, actually." She patted my head.

"Maybe you should have mentioned that before," I said, looking around. "Probably doesn't matter though." I turned to look at her. "So, what's first up?"

"Alchemist," she said, looking at her list. I had no idea where she'd kept it and part of me wanted to ask her about it. I didn't but only because I thought she might tell me to search her and then things would be awkward. "That's in hall 7B." She pointed to the left. "We're in hall A, so we need to go this way."

14

"You're out of your goddamned mind if you think I'm going to send any of my apprentices off with you," Saramana, the three-hundred-pound head of the Carpenter's Guild snapped before pointing at the exit. "Now, I'll bid you good day," she added with artificial formality.

"Look," I said, resisting the urge to shout at her as best as I could because this was the exact same result we'd gotten at every single guild house. No one wanted to work for us. It was really starting to piss me off. "Please. We just need one—"

"I said good day, *sir*." She crossed her arms over her rather large chest. "Please don't make a scene." She dropped her arms, and her hand danced toward the small bell on her desk that I knew from experience would summon a team of jackbooted thugs to escort us out. "I'd hate to have to call the guards to escort you out."

"You don't need to call the guards," Gwen said, scowling at the older woman. "I just don't understand why you're refusing. You haven't even heard us out."

"I don't have to explain myself to you," Saramana snorted and turned pointedly away from us before examining her nail-bitten fingers.

"This is bullshit," I said, barely able to keep my anger in check as I spun on my heel and exited the office.

"I just don't get it," Gwen fumed and stomped one foot on the tile. "I get that maybe we couldn't have afforded their people, but at the same time, they should have at least asked us about a budget."

"We should have brought Buffy. I bet that Sweet Talk Skill would have come in handy," I mused, trying to think of what we'd done wrong. We'd gone to the main desk and made the appropriate appointments and then waited for our number. Only, every time we got inside, we were shut down without so much as a backward glance. It was infuriating.

"That's not a bad idea," Gwen said before

grumbling. "As a head of a town, I can only call a meeting once a month. We'd have to come back next month."

"For one, that's bullshit and a waste of time, and for two, I don't want to waste a month. We need to start doing things now." I shook my head. "I saw the way that barrier buckled, and while Agatha and Sheila are better, we can't afford for things to keep being as they are. We need money, and that means we need an alchemist. Even if we become awesome at farming Dark Blood, it won't matter if we don't have one."

"Excuse me, sir," squeaked a voice to my left. "Are you who they say you are?"

"Eh?" I said, turning to glance at the demon who emerged from the hallway we were passing. She was tall and thin with blue skin, yellow eyes, and red hair. It would have made me think of the comic book version of Mystique from X-men where her skin was flawless and smooth. She was dressed in a simple brown tunic and pants, with heavy leather work boots, and her hair had been put into a tight ponytail.

"They say you're the Legendary Builder." She swallowed and took a step toward me. "Is it true?"

"Yeah, who is saying that?" I asked, glancing at

Gwen who just shrugged at me as we exited the Guild Hall.

"Is it really true?" She leaned in close to peer at me. "Really, really?" Her voice dripped with over-eagerness as she nearly skipped while trailing behind us.

"Yes, it is." I turned briefly and patted my still sheathed sword, so she could see. "You didn't answer my question though."

"Oh," she squeaked and took a step backward, flummoxed. "What question?"

"I asked who was saying that," I said, glancing around but finding the surrounding area empty. I stopped, faced her, and became a bit more insistent. "I haven't exactly heard anyone gabbing about it, and no one's been talking to me—"

"That's because a notice went out from the Heads of Guilds. It said that your power perverts the fruits of hard work and labor, and it warned us not to work with you." The smooth-skinned Mystique glanced back at the door, and then stepped closer, lowering her voice. "Can you really do what they say?"

"Why would what I do be a perversion? All I do is let people learn Skills they already have the knowhow to learn." I ignored her question and glanced demandingly at Gwen. "Are you following?" I wondered how much she knew, what she hadn't mentioned, and what she'd kept to herself.

"Unfortunately, yes." She blew out an angry breath. "Basically, they're worried you'll take away their monopolies."

As I mulled over what she'd said, I nearly went ballistic. So I was a threat to the bureaucracies. That's what this was about. The Darkness was literally eating away the horizon and killing towns and these people were more concerned about their pocketbooks? Seriously?

"So, you can do it?!" the blue demon squealed as her eyes traveled from Gwen to me, and then she reached out and took my hand, shaking it and pulling me closer to her so that only I could hear her. "I want to join you, sir, um, Builder."

"Wait, what?" I asked, her words displacing my anger and leaving me to sort them out.

Maribelle has requested to join your party. Do you accept?

"I'm a low-rank carpenter, but I want to be the best." She gestured back at the guild halls. "If I can be your main girl, I'll get better than that old hag. Then I can make lots of money and pay off my parents' debts. Even if I get blacklisted, it'll still be worth it because I'll be so much better than the guildies," she said so quickly that the words all sort of tumbled together and with a touch of spunk and bravado that surprised me. "They're ass hats to me, anyway. Well, the leaders. The rest are nice. But it's so cutthroat—"

"You're a carpenter?" I asked, accepting her request, which caused a blue orb to appear over her head.

"I am. Finished top of my class. I should actually be intermediate, but they won't let me take the tests. Say it's too soon, and I need to pay my dues, and well, that's not fair, so I thought I could go with you…" More words gushed out of her, but I was too busy looking at her Stats to hear them.

Name: Maribelle
Experience: 17,200
Health: 78/78
Mana: 121/121
Primary Power: Carpentry
Secondary Power: None selected
Strength: 35/100
Agility: 43/100
Charisma: 27/100
Intelligence: 53/100
Special: 66/100

Perk: Rank 10 Carpenter

"Holy crap," I exclaimed, unable to keep the shock from filling my voice. "You have a ton of Experience. That's insane. You could learn a ton of stuff." I stared at her Skill Trees totally flummoxed. "I like don't even know what to teach you because you only have the general tree, but you can learn so much."

"That's what I've been saying!" Maribelle said, glaring back at the closed door of the guild hall. "They won't let me learn stuff because they're just jealous of my skill."

"Normally when people say that, I think they're lying, but you're just not," I said, gesturing toward the menus before I realized she couldn't see me. "You have every basic Skill maxed. I bet you could frame an entire house in seconds."

"Not quite that quick, but yeah, everything they've taught me, I have the Rank lead in." She handed me a sheet of paper, and sure enough, it listed her name along with scores in various studies. I didn't quite understand what it meant, though, so I handed it off to Gwen.

"Well, that's not your concern now because you're definitely coming with us," I said, offering her my hand. "That is if you want to come with us?"

"I do, thank you so much. You won't regret this. I can't believe I'm going to work for the Builder of Legend. That's so awesome. I won't let you down." She let out a squee of delight as she violently shook my hand.

"I'm glad you're excited," I said, pulling my hand away perhaps a little too roughly. "Gwen can help you get settled back in town. She sort of runs the day to day. I just take care of the upgrades." Maribelle's shoulders sagged slightly, and Gwen let out a short chuckle.

"He's kind of dumb sometimes, but it's sort of charming." Gwen rolled her eyes and put a hand on Maribelle's shoulder. I felt like I was on the outside of an inside joke. "You said something very interesting, though."

"Oh, what's that?" she asked, smiling brightly at Gwen. It was like we'd just given Maribelle Christmas presents, only I was fairly sure she was totally going to get in trouble for coming with us. She *had* to know that, but at the same time, she obviously didn't care. Part of me wanted to ask her about it, but she was grown and could make her own decisions.

"We need an alchemist. *Any* alchemist. Do you know one who will come?" Gwen said, leaning in close to the girl.

"Um… not that I know…," Maribelle looked at her shoes like a guilty child hiding a secret she knew she was inevitably going to blurt out. "The guilds were pretty clear about not working with you. Normally, I'd get blacklisted for joining you…which for a carpenter is a big deal." She swallowed and leaned in close so only we could hear her. "But Guildmistress Saramana doesn't agree that we should be cutting you off… she thinks you might be the only thing that can keep the Darkness at bay … so she told me I could go with you." She flushed bright red then, sucked in a gulp of air, and let it out in a large whoosh. "You won't tell, right? If anyone finds out Saramana is *letting* me go, no, sending me, I probably will get blacklisted, if I'm lucky. Saramana's no fool. She'll deny any involvement, and I'll be branded a liar … maybe even … Stained …" Her voice dropped to an almost inaudible whisper with the last word.

"That explains a lot," I said, turning to look back at the closed door. Was that why Saramana had brushed us out so quickly? Because she wanted to send one of her best students with us but had to make it look like Maribelle was acting alone? I wasn't sure, but at the same time, I had a pretty good bet Saramana just wanted plausible deniability. Interesting. All the Heads of the Guilds weren't in agreement. Maybe, given some time, I could sway others to my cause.

Gwen grabbed Maribelle's wrist and pulled her away from the door. Her eyes said to follow and she led us further from the Guild Hall before ducking around a corner. Releasing Maribelle from her grip, Gwen leaned in close to Maribelle, nearly talking into her shock of red hair. "So, why don't you think we can find an Alchemist then? Does their guild leader not agree with Saramana?" Gwen asked, careful to keep her voice low. "I remember them being good friends."

"They are, but on this point, they disagree. Alchemists make a lot more money at low levels than all but the master carpenters. They'll want to stick to taking guild jobs because that's where the money is, and they especially want to keep others out of it." Maribelle shrugged.

"That's what I thought." Only, instead of sounding despondent, Gwen smiled devilishly and took a step back. "You talked about people who got blacklisted. Surely there's got to be a blacklisted alchemist somewhere."

Maribelle started to shake her head before stopping suddenly. "I may know someone, but she's—well—strange would be kind." She shoved her hands in her pockets. "But she's always at Mac's Tavern, so I guess you could see for yourself." Maribelle took an anxious step forward. "Most of the blacklisted hang out there actually, so if you don't care about guild status, it's not a bad place to go. Quality can be shoddy though."

"Isn't that the same tavern Buffy said to meet her at?" I asked, following behind Maribelle as she led the way.

"It is, and I bet I know why. She probably deals with the blacklisted. They probably pay a bit more and sell for a bit less," Gwen affirmed, stepping next to me. "We should have just gone there."

"Yeah, that would have saved us three hours," I grumbled.

15

"There's a fucking dragon's head over the door," I exclaimed, stopping dead in my tracks and pointing at the building. It was a short, squat structure made of emerald stone sandwiched between two skyscrapers. Only, instead of a door, a yawning green dragon's head sat gaping open.

"Yeah, they say that when old Mac killed the last green dragon living on the land where the Royal Centre stands, she put its head on a pike to ward off others." Gwen pointed at the huge silver spear that jutted through the brainpan of the dragon and out the other side. "It can't hurt you though, all the venom in those teeth has long since drained away."

"That is literally the last of my worries because

I just learned dragons are real," I said, swallowing back my sudden terror. Succubae, goblins, and demon dogs were one thing, but dragons? A whole different kettle of fish.

"Of course they're real," Maribelle clucked, glancing back at me as she stepped between the spear-like front fangs and approached the door embedded in the throat of the monster. "How else would we get Ember Flame?" she shook her head. "It's only the most valuable crafting material out there besides Angel Feathers."

"Angel Feathers aren't really rare," Gwen said dismissively. "You just go find an angel and pluck her like a chicken."

"Easier said than done," Maribelle said, knocking out a strange rhythm on the door. "And don't act like you've done it before. You may be with the Builder, but you wouldn't be running Lustnor if you could take down an angel. You'd be in Hog's Bend or Demon Fire, somewhere like that."

Gwen bristled as a slot in the door opened, and a single, immense bloodshot eye looked out.

"Password?" spoke a voice so deep, it made my stomach rumble.

"Satan's black balls," Maribelle said without even a hint of sheepishness.

The door swung open to reveal a girl with pale white skin, purple hair, and a single immense eye in the center of her face. It was weird because clad in her black pants and white tank top, she was banging, but that eye... that eye was a deal breaker.

"You may enter," she said, stepping aside and waving us in. "If you cause any trouble, there will be consequences."

Maribelle nodded to the cyclops before making her way inside. Gwen followed behind leaving me last in line, and as I passed through the door, the cyclops looked me over before snorting dismissively and sitting back on her stool by the door.

"Having two eyes is so disgusting," she muttered, shaking her head.

"Don't mind her," Gwen said, reaching back and giving my arm a squeeze. "I don't think you're hideous."

"She said disgusting, not hideous," I said, glancing back at the cyclops. As I did, she looked away and began whistling. As her head slowly drifted back toward me, she made another point of looking away and whistling louder.

"Yeah, don't be pedantic," Gwen said, releasing my arm. "Just take your compliment."

"Fine," I mumbled, turning back to the inside of the bar, and this time I got a good look at the place.

It was just one huge room. The walls were made of that same green material as the outside. It both glistened and glimmered in the light of the torches in the sconces. Heads of all sorts of beasts I couldn't identify were mounted around the room, and as I looked around, I nearly cried out once again.

"She seriously mounted a unicorn?" I asked, gesturing toward the head on the wall directly in front of the massive green bar.

"Have you ever hunted a unicorn?" Gwen asked me, eyebrow raised. "Because they're quite common in the Blood Hills. Nasty things. Eat all the crops."

"Only good unicorn is a dead unicorn," Maribelle affirmed.

"Oh, well, on Earth they're kind of cool." I stared at the three-foot long prong on the horse's skull.

"Hey there, boss. You're early!" Buffy called from our left, and I spun to find her sitting at a table beneath one of the establishments many ceiling fans with two other demons. One looked almost like how I pictured an angel with long blonde hair and deep sapphire eyes. She had a kind, cherub-like face and was wearing a white gown.

The other girl had a similar skin tone, but her hair was red and close-cropped, and instead of a dress, she was wearing a tight-fitting catsuit covered in pockets and sheaths.

"Is that okay?" I asked, waving toward her as I weaved past the high tops strewn across the bar's floor in a way that suggested the patrons regularly moved them around.

"It's fine," Buffy slurred, slamming one fist down on the table. The contents shook, and the redhead reached out and snatched a bottle before it could topple over.

"Your friend is drunk," the blonde said, looking at me. "You should probably take her home."

"I am not drunk," Buffy said, looking at me a touch unsteadily. "I'm just celebrating. I made three times my normal haul, and it's all thanks to you, Builder." She got to her feet and took a step toward me, stumbled, and fell into me. She gripped my shirt and pulled herself upright, looking up at me. "I don't know how I can ever repay you."

"With money. We had a deal, remember?" I said, looking down at the goblin. "I'm not sure how I was being unclear."

"Pfft, of course, you'd just want me for my mind," Buffy said, releasing her hold on me and turning toward the table. "I found you an alchemist by the way."

"I'm not an alchemist," the blonde said. "I do not have the right to practice as an alchemist and therefore cannot claim to be one."

"Cut the horseshit, Sally," Buffy said, moving back to the table and flopping heavily into the seat. "Can you or can you not refine Dark Blood?" She gestured for the three of us to sit.

"Well, yes, I was taught to do that at the academy, but as I told you before, my license was stripped." Sally looked at me and blushed as I sat down next to her. "Really, I can't help you. It's one hundred kinds of illegal."

"What's gonna happen, you get *more* blacklisted?" Buffy said, grabbing the bottle and taking a swig before wiping her mouth with the back of one hand. "As if."

"I'm hoping to get un-blacklisted," Sally said, shaking her head, and I realized in that moment, we might be able to get her to join us. She wanted to do it, she just needed to justify it to herself first. I'd seen it happen all the time back at work.

"That's never happened, ever," Buffy said, reaching across the table and taking Sally's hand. "You know that." Buffy smiled brightly and pointed at me. "He's the Builder of Fucking Legend. Really, seriously. He can make you awesome beyond all recompense. You just need to agree to work with him."

Sally looked at me, her sapphire eyes sweeping over me. "I don't believe you. It's not personal, but she's a very drunk goblin." Her eyes shifted to Gwen. "And she runs a crappy town." She nodded toward Maribelle. "And she's got apprentice stripes. Not exactly glowing recommendations."

"I can prove it," I said, meeting Sally's eyes. Once I showed her what I could do, she'd join up. I just knew it.

"Let's assume you can, or this conversation is stupid, but believe me when I say this, I won't take any job that doesn't also employ my friend, Crystal," Sally said, turning to look at Crystal. The two women nodded to each other, doing that whole silent communication thing I really needed to get a translator for.

"I'd be happy to take both of you," I said,

glancing at Gwen who made no outward facial expression. She did, however, squeeze my leg in a way I took to mean she trusted me.

"You don't even know what I do," Crystal said, eyeing me for a long moment. "I will not sleep with you."

"While that sounds like a great offer, I don't need you to sleep with me. I just want to make Lustnor the greatest town on the map so we can defeat the Darkness at the border. I need people to do that. You can be one of them." I gestured to Sally. "If she can really refine Dark Blood, I'm willing to bet you're just as bad ass."

"Not so much," Crystal said, putting her other hand on the table. Only it wasn't a hand at all. It was a hook. "I'm not good at either of my trades like this, unfortunately. I know a lot, but alas, I can't do much without both of my hands."

"Knowledge is power though," I said, nodding to her. "I still think we can work something out. I'm quite sure you'll make a valuable addition to our team."

"That settled," Sally said, turning to look at me. "Prove you are who you say you are."

"Okay," I said, offering her one hand while

gripping the hilt of Clarent with the other. "Would you like to join my party? Both of you?"

"What?" Sally asked, staring at me like I'd grown a separate head. "What in the blazes do you mean by that?"

"Just accept," Buffy said before putting her head in her arms. "It's his thing."

"Okay…" Sally looked me over one last time before huffing. "If you're lying, I will tear your still-beating heart from your chest."

"I'm not lying, just accept." I held my hand out.

"I accept," she said, taking my hand.

Sally has joined your party.

"Me too," Crystal said, waving her hook at me. "Um, do you want me to shake?"

Crystal has joined your party.

"It doesn't seem to be necessary." I turned my gaze onto the orb above Sally's head. It was time to show them the goods. "Now then, just give me a second."

Name: Sally
Experience: 7,700
Health: 36/36
Mana: 142/142
Primary Power: Healing
Secondary Power: Alchemy

Strength: 10/100
Agility: 26/100
Charisma: 25/100
Intelligence: 56/100
Special: 86/100
Perk: Rank 4 Alchemist (Currently Blacklisted)

"Whoa, why didn't you say you were a healer?" I asked, tearing my eyes away from her Stat trees. "That's really awesome."

"Um, how did you know that?" Sally asked, raising an eyebrow at me. "Did you see my signet?" She checked herself over before pulling a locket with a white pentagram emblazoned across it. "No…"

"I can see your Stats. It tells me things like that. I'm the Builder, remember?" I waved off the comment as I looked through her skills. She had an entire tree dedicated to Buffs, but had only learned the Haste Skill. That didn't seem useful, so I turned my attention to her healing tree. "Wow, you seem to be pretty adept at healing, but you can't regenerate limbs."

"Obviously," Sally replied, glaring at me. "Do you think that if I could, Crystal would be like that?"

"Oh, well, I can fix that for you. It'll cost five

thousand Experience, but you have enough. Want me to do that?" I looked at the Abilities to let her heal Crystal for a moment.

Limb Regeneration: This Ability allows the user to regenerate the limb of a friendly upon touch. Skill can be used once a day and requires Mana commiserate to the damage. For example, a finger will cost much less than an entire hand. This Power must be used within twelve hours of injury.

Requirements: Special: 50+, Intelligence: 40+
Cost: 4000 Experience

Restore Old Injury: This Ability allows the user to cause an old wound to reopen. It will then function as a fresh wound. Can only be used on a friendly target. Skill can be used once a day and requires Mana commiserate to the damage.

Requirements: Special: 75+, Intelligence: 55+
Cost: 1000 Experience

"I basically have to give you two Abilities. One to make her wound into a new wound, and another to heal said wound." I looked past her at Crystal. "This is going to hurt a lot, I'll bet."

"I don't care how much it hurts if it works." Crystal pulled the hook off, revealing the stub of her hand. "Let's try it."

"Sally, it's your Experience, and you may not be strong enough to heal that much damage at once.

You up for trying anyway?" I asked, and when she nodded, I confirmed the Abilities. Blue light enveloped her for a moment before fading away.

"That's it?" Crystal asked, turning to regard me. "Because my hand is still missing."

"I can't heal you," I said. "I just gave Sally the Ability to do it."

"Sally?" Crystal said as her friend turned toward her and put one hand on the old wound.

"I can do it," she said. Blue light sparks leaped from her fingers and enveloped the nub. As the magic seeded deep into Crystal's flesh, her skin turned raw and angry. Crystal bit off a scream as her wound reopened, spilling fresh blood on the table and causing some people to look at us and others to start to rise from their seats.

It felt like forever, but was only a second or two at best, then Crystal's hand grew out from the nub so quickly that I couldn't exactly see the where and when of it. Crystal's eyes got as wide as dinner plates as she slowly opened and closed her fingers.

"I can't believe you did it," Crystal said, looking at me with tears in her eyes.

"I didn't do it, Sally did," I said, smiling at the two of them. "And I can teach both of you to do much more if you decide to join."

16

The trip back to Lustnor from the Royal Centre was rather uneventful even though we were assaulted by demon dogs a couple times. This time, the tables had turned because Gwen, Sally, and Crystal made short work of the creatures.

What I wasn't prepared for, however, was to arrive back at the city and find two armed guards at the back gate. It had been previously unguarded since only Sheila and Agatha were trained, but now I found myself staring at two of the Stained clad in full guard armor.

"Well, this is new," I said as we pulled up in Buffy's buggy.

"Welcome back, my liege," the left woman, Polly, said in unison before nodding their heads at me. "Agatha sent us back here to guard the far gate. We had a couple demon dog attacks, and she wanted someone out here."

"Ah, well, good to know," I said, glancing at Gwen who seemed more shocked than me.

"Have demon dogs really been attacking the back gate?" she asked, leaping down from the buggy and landing lightly on the road beside the buggy. "That shouldn't be happening. The wards protecting the town should keep them away."

"Agatha thought you'd be concerned. She's prepared a full report," Polly replied while somehow managing to look both uncomfortable with Gwen's scrutiny and semi-confident.

"Okay. Please open the gates," Gwen said, before turning to look at the rest of us. "Let's get inside. I need to look into this. Usually, when demon dogs start attacking the town, it means the Darkness has taken another town and pushed into their habitat. There becomes more competition for resources, and they attack until the population is thinned."

"Good plan," I said as Polly opened the gates, allowing Buffy to move the buggy inside. Unlike the front gates, these weren't spring-loaded or as well made. We'd have to fix that.

I stared at the gates and walls as we made our way through, and I was struck by the absurdity of it. Wouldn't it be better to have our people inside the walls? Then they could fight without getting into harm's way.

"I have a question," I said, glancing at both Crystal and Maribelle. Both of them looked less than satisfied with the town, which was probably because it hadn't been built up at all.

"If it's about the buildings, I think we may need to knock them down and rebuild them from scratch. There's no saving this shoddy construction." Maribelle pointed to an abandoned shop to the left of Taylor's shop. "That doesn't look even close to up to code."

"Yeah, okay, whatever," I said, waving off her comment. "I was thinking about the walls. Would we be able to build some kind of platform so the guards could stand within the walls, and like attack with long poles or bows?"

"Possibly," Maribelle said, rubbing her chin as she turned back toward the gates. "Honestly though, those walls are wood anyway, and pretty shitty. We'd be better off using cement walls with a rebar skeleton and making them three times the height. Then we could even carve wards into the stone to make it stronger. Those," - she gestured offhandedly at the walls - "a good-sized bull demon would just run straight over it. What we should do is build a pit on the other side, so if they broke through with something like that, they'd fall into the pit. That's what I read they do in Rage Canyon, but they have a lot more bulls there. Are there bulls here?"

"No," Gwen said as she walked alongside the buggy. "I haven't seen one. We get big Dark Ones sometimes, but they've never broken through the warding."

"Ah, so maybe wood is good here then…" Maribelle turned back to me. "To answer your question, yes it can be done, but it's sort of like, I dunno, putting expensive windows in a shack next to a dump. People do it, but they're dumb, and it's dumb."

I shook my head at her. "I see your point. It doesn't make sense to spend time making something we can't really use."

"We probably don't have the materials for that anyway," Buffy said as she pulled her buggy into the spot Gwen had pointed out. "We're really limited in what we can do until we get set up properly. Then it'll be less of an issue." She pointed at the surrounding forest. "For instance, you have a lot of lumber to harvest, but I don't see anyone actually doing that, nor a mill for processing. That could be lucrative. Then we'd have another good avenue for trade, and besides, it'd clear out the trees closest, providing us with farmland, and giving us the ability to build things cheaper."

"That makes a lot of sense," I said, glancing at Gwen. "Any particular reason we haven't done that already?"

"We can't afford to get people to do it." She sighed and ran a hand through her hair. "It's the story with everything. Lots of potential, but you can't pay people in potential."

"That's true," I said, nodding to her. "Okay, how about you get everyone settled? I would love it if Sally could get started refining whatever Dark Blood the guards have gotten as soon as possible. Then maybe we can get to work on whatever. Is that okay with you, Sally?"

"Yeah, I can do that. I just need some floor space and to get the equipment we bought set up. I don't have the materials to refine very many, so I'll do what I can, but we'll have to sell some to do more." Sally shrugged. "Way of the world."

"I'll worry about the selling. That's my job,"

Buffy said, hopping down from the buggy. "You just do your thing, okay? I've got this."

"How about I go meet with Agatha and get the report and the Dark Blood they've gathered. I'll meet everyone at Sam's in say ten minutes?" Gwen offered, in a way that made it seem like she wasn't asking. "If someone could let Taylor know to be there, that'd be great."

"Okay, sounds good. I want to look at these buildings first, anyway. Maybe we can do some easy stuff to fix it up," Maribelle said as the group started to disperse.

As I watched them go, I took a step forward and put a hand on Crystal's shoulder. "Can I chat with you for a moment?"

The girl stiffened and looked at me. She nodded once and turned to face me, causing Sally to do the same. As both of them stood there, I sighed.

"Sally, you go do your thing," I smiled at the alchemist. "This is just gonna take a second."

"Um… I'd rather not." Sally fidgeted uncomfortably with her hands.

"It's okay," Crystal said, reaching out and squeezing Sally's hand. "I'll just be a minute." She put on a brave face. "I doubt this is where he asks for sex."

"I'm not asking for sex," I said, shaking my head at the two of them. I wasn't sure why every girl thought I wanted to proposition them for sex. Not my style.

"Okay," Sally said, still looking uncomfortable. They did that strange mental communication again before she finally relented and made her way toward the stores where Maribelle was using a measuring tape on one of the walls.

"What do you want to talk to me about?" Crystal said, turning her red eyes on me.

"I noticed you actually have two Skill trees available," I said, flicking my hand at the orb above her head to open her Stats window.

Name: Crystal
Experience: 3,300
Health: 91/91
Mana: 98/98
Primary Power: Fighter - Stealth
Secondary Power: Gathering
Strength: 23/100
Agility: 68/100
Charisma: 34/100
Intelligence: 36/100
Special: 62/100
Perk: Trained at the Royal Guard's Academy.

Perk: Rank 9 Herbalist.
Perk: Rank 10 Lumberjack.
Perk: Rank 10 Miner.

"I've never seen anyone with so many perks. You're an herbalist, a lumberjack, and a miner. That's in addition to having been trained at the Royal Guard's Academy." I smiled at her. "What gives?"

"There really is keeping no secrets from you is there." Crystal gave me a brittle smile and finger-combed her red hair out of her face.

"There are but not when it pertains to your Abilities. Unfortunately, those are an open book to me as long as I have my sword." I nodded to her as I looked through her Fighter - Stealth Tree. It seemed like most of the abilities were related to slowing and snaring opponents. "Please, tell me. I really want to know"

"Well, it's not that odd of a story. I trained at the academy. I was assigned stealth instead of offense or defense because of my nimble fingers." She waggled her long fingers at me. "Only when I lost my hand, I couldn't do most of the stuff they'd trained me, like picking locks or using a garrote. Well, not as easily anyway, so I was given a severance package and kicked out." She looked at her shoes. "Sally tried to support both of us, and that worked okay until she got blacklisted." Crystal waved off the comment. "So, I applied at the Gathering guild. They took me on as a favor, but I couldn't do the work well either. I can't use a pick or an axe with one hand very well. I did okay at herbalism since a lot of that is lore, but it's still hard to pick some of the herbs and mix things effectively." She gave me a weak smile. "Sorry, it's not a very glamorous story."

"It's pretty much the best story ever," I said, smiling at her as I reached out and put a hand on her shoulder. "I mean that. Honestly. You're seriously like the best person in the world right now."

"I appreciate the compliments, but I don't quite follow," she said, shaking her head at me. "What use do you have for that stuff? I'm no good at it." She showed me her hand. "Sure, I have my hand back, but I'm much better at fighting and the like than any of those things."

"Sure, but I can fix that," I said, gesturing at the forest. "We need to do the whole lumber thing. You know how to do that. It'll be easy enough to pull a couple of the worst guard recruits from Agatha and Sheila for you to use as lumberjacks."

"I can't really teach anyone. I don't know

how…" Crystal shook her head. "I'm sorry, what you're asking is beyond my Ability."

"I can see that, like the others, you're a Rank four teacher. That's plenty good enough, and as for the Skills, like I said, I can show you that." I opened the Lumberjack Skill Tree. "You have all the basic blocks learned, they're just not leveled."

"I, um…" she sighed. "Well, if you think it will work, I'll trust you. I did get my hand back after all." She bit her lip. "I just don't think it's possible."

"Well, not with that attitude," I said as I opened her Teaching Tree and looked it over again. That's when I found a Skill that nearly made me dance with joy.

Ivory Tower: This Ability allows the user to effectively teach a known Skill to another person, even if they have no real world Skill. It causes the Skill in question's level to double for the purposes of teaching.

Requirements: Intelligence 50+

Cost: 2,500 Experience

Requirements not met. Intelligence Stat too low. Would you like to upgrade? Cost of Stat upgrade: 609 Experience.

"Well, looks like we're in luck," I said, annoyed it would cost all her Experience, but there was nothing for it. That was the problem with not specializing, but at the same time, we might be able to train lots of people.

"How's that?" Crystal said, glancing around like she wanted to be anywhere but here.

"We have enough Experience to make it work," I said, selecting the Skills.

Blue light surrounded Crystal, and as it did, intelligence filled her eyes. She shook her head a couple times and blinked rapidly before meeting my gaze.

"Did you just make me smarter?" she asked, wide-eyed.

"A lot smarter actually. I dunno if it means anything to you, but I moved your Intelligence from thirty-six to fifty." I smiled at her. "How's it feel?"

"Different. I have all these thoughts rattling around in my head." She paused and looked up at the sky. "However, if I think about what you asked me before, I feel like I can make it work. I just feel like I'd be able to teach it better now."

"Great, we'll talk about it at the town meeting. Speaking of which, we'd better go, the last thing I want to do is make Gwen mad by being late."

"Yeah, I bet she's really into the whole whips and chains thing," Crystal added with a grin.

17

"So, as I was saying before, we still have a people problem," Gwen said, holding up the report she'd received from Agatha. "It's just sort of the opposite problem."

"Some of the people you gave me just aren't suited for guard work," Agatha affirmed, shrugging. "I think out of the dozen we got, maybe six at most will make the cut. Only four of those six will be worth half a damn." She dropped her hands in exasperation. "Back at the academy, we start with classes of over a hundred and only twenty-five percent or so make the cut to go to round two. The final tally is something like six percent of the original class actually graduates, and that's among the three major disciplines." She looked to Crystal.

"You were trained there, right? You can confirm what I'm saying."

"She's not wrong," Crystal said, looking at me and giving me a quick nod. "We have a much bigger basket of people. On top of that," she gestured past the gates, "we need all sorts of people to cut lumber, mine the ore around here, and find herbs. While some of the dropouts will make the cut for one of those jobs or even will work to help Taylor or Maribelle, we're still going to be short staffed."

"So, what we need is a bunch of people, I got that. We're all teachers and no students." I rubbed my chin as I looked at the assembled ladies. "Can't we just go on a recruitment drive? There seems like there are lots of refugees around. Can't we get them to come here?"

"Maybe," Maribelle said, meeting my eyes. "But maybe not. No one will come here who can learn a trade because they still want to get into a guild, and that won't happen because the guilds don't want to work with you. Besides, Lustnor isn't exactly safe. Not many refugees want to head *toward* a war zone."

"Yeah, but I'm not talking about getting that kind of people. I'm talking about Stained plain and simple, you know, poor huddled masses types with nowhere to go. The dregs. The overlooked. That's who I want." I turned my attention to Gwen. "You said you thought the increased demon dog attacks were caused by a town getting overrun. That means more Stained. And what about all the homeless we saw in the back quarter of Royal Centre? We could take them."

"Assuming we do that," Buffy said, raising her hand in the air like a kid in school, "we won't have the food to feed many more people. We have no food other than what we buy, and we can't afford a lot, especially if we need to set up a mill and apothecary. The stuff we have for Taylor is laughable, and while Sam's forge isn't bad—"

"It's utter shit," Sam interrupted.

"It needs an upgrade. That's in addition to axes, saws, and all the other stuff just to get the trees knocked down. Sam might be able to make that stuff, but we haven't the materials."

"Okay, so we need money." I glanced at Sally. "How's your refining process coming with the Dark Blood? I know you haven't had much time…"

"I was able to do one. Like with everything else, if I had better equipment and more time, I could do more, but this is what I got with what we have.

This is sort of an eighty-percent effort. I could increase the quality about twenty percent more, but it'd take probably twice as long as what I spent on this." She held out a glowing orb, only unlike before now the Dark Blood was faceted. Fire burned within, casting flames across the ground in front of us.

<u>Dark Blood</u>
Material: Gemstone
Grade: B
Contains the essence of a fallen warrior of Darkness. Has begun the refining process.

"It says it's a grade B Dark Blood now. Is that good?" I asked, turning my attention to Buffy.

"It's probably worth four times as much, which given what it cost to produce, probably doubles our profit on just selling them outright." Buffy shrugged. "Definitely worth doing, but I doubt we'll have enough for it to help significantly. We need a few big-ticket items, or this is going to take forever." She gestured at the horizon. "I'm okay with forever but who knows if the Darkness will be."

"Right, okay, hmm." I sighed. "Anyone have any ideas?"

"I think we just need to keep on, keeping on for a bit," Gwen said, putting a hand on my shoulder.

"We don't need to build Rome in a day. I'll go through the Stained once again with the rest of the girls and see if we can split them up based on what Skills they have. That might help some. Then we'll just slowly expand."

"I have an idea," Sam said, suddenly. Her eyes were fixed on the glowing Dark Blood. "What if we could turn out Blooded Blades?"

"Blooded Blades?" I asked, confusion filling my voice. "I have no idea what those are."

"If we could do it, we'd make a lot more money, but I don't think you have the Skill," Buffy said, hands raised palms out. "No offense or anything, but there's maybe three people in Royal Centre who can do that. And you'd need at least Grade A Dark Blood, if not Grade S."

"Can you make Grade A or S?" I asked, flipping my gaze to Sally, and before she answered her Skill sheet told me the answer.

Rank 4 Alchemist: Able to use Skills and Abilities based upon Rank 4 Skill. This will allow the alchemist to produce Grade B items 70% of the time. There is a 15% chance of crafting a Grade A item. There is a 10% chance of crafting a Grade C item. There is a 5% chance of crafting a Grade D item.

Refining (specific) – Dark Blood

Skill: 6/10.

User can refine Dark Blood with a maximum Skill requirement of 6. The quality of the refinement is based on time spent and a multiplier based on Skill level.

For every Skill level of the item greater than the alchemist, chance of success is decreased by 10%. For every Skill level lower than the alchemist, chance of success increases by 10%.

I turned my gaze to the upgrade tab.

Do you want to upgrade Refining – Dark Blood to Skill level 7? Base cost 2,000 Experience. This price can be reduced by attaining an overall Rank of 3 in Alchemy.

A quick glance at her Experience bar let me know she had three thousand Experience available. She'd had twenty-seven hundred left after I'd given her the healing Abilities, so she must have gained three hundred between then and now. That seemed like quick growth, but then again, I had no idea how the Experience gain actually worked.

Still, if she had a higher Rank, she'd have a better chance of crafting higher grade Dark Blood. That much was obvious. I just didn't know what the Skill level of Dark Blood actually was.

"Is Dark Blood difficult to work with?" I asked, before dismissing the question. "Guess it doesn't matter." I looked at Buffy. "What's the price difference between Grade A and Grade B Dark Blood?"

"Triple, maybe quadruple if you find the right guy," Buffy said, watching me carefully. "Are you thinking of upgrading her Skill?"

"Yes," I said, turning back to Sally. "Would that be okay? It is your Experience, after all."

"It sounds fine." She shrugged. "I have no idea what the options are, so if you think that's best, I trust you." She shot a fond look toward Crystal. "You've already given me more than I ever thought I'd have."

The way she said it made me feel pretty good, I'll be honest. I'd basically given her the power to fix her friend, and that was something no one else could have done.

"That still leaves the problem of Sam not being able to craft the weapons," Gwen said, shrugging. "But I guess more money is better than less money."

"One thing at a time," I said as I upgraded Sally's Skill level to seven and looked at the cost for the next level.

Do you want to upgrade Refining – Dark Blood to Skill level 8? Base cost 4,000 Experience. This price can be reduced by attaining an overall Rank of 3 in Alchemy.

"Well, that's out," I said, turning my eyes back to the main Alchemy Tree so I could figure out what base Stats affected the Skill Tree the most, but as I did, a new Ability popped up.

Artisan: User has a 3% chance to create an item of higher quality than normal.

Requirements: Special: 50+, Intelligence: 50+, Agility: 10+

Cost: 1500 Experience

"Well, it's better than nothing," I said as I scanned it further. At Rank ten the Skill would have a 30% chance of crafting better stuff, and it would affect every Skill, not just one. That was worth getting. I accepted it, and then dumped the rest of her Experience into Agility because it was her lowest Stat that also affected alchemy.

As the blue glow faded from Sally, I smiled at her. "I'll spend a few more minutes talking to Sam, but I think we go with Gwen's plans while Sally tries out her newfound Abilities. Is that okay with everyone?"

"We'll go interview the girls and see if we can find them more appropriate jobs," Gwen said, gesturing for the others to follow her.

As they all filed off, I turned my attention to Sam. "Now, let's see what we can do for you."

Sam rolled her eyes at me. "Let's get this over with. I wanna check on the two apprentices before they burn down my shop."

I scrolled through her tree until I found the Skill we were talking about.

Smithing (Specific) – Dark Weaponry: User has the Ability to infuse normal items with the energy contained within Dark Blood.

Requirements: Special: 75+, Intelligence: 75+, Agility: 50+

Cost: 7,000 Experience

"Holy crap that Skill is expensive. Worse, you can't even learn it because you don't have the Stats for it. I could raise your Stats but then we'd be short by," I glanced at her Experience, "nearly five hundred Experience."

"That doesn't seem like much," Sam said with a shrug. "If I was you, I'd do the Stat upgrade now, and then when I get enough, have me learn the Skill because the Stats will help the whole time."

"That was my thought too," I said, spending the nearly eleven hundred Experience to bring her Special to seventy-five and her Agility to fifty. "Glad we're on the same page."

"Whatever," she said as the glow faded from

around her. "I'm going to go do my job now unless—"

Her words were cut off by the sound of a massive explosion at the front gate. The barrier overhead shimmered like the sun as the shockwave threw me from my feet.

18

I arrived at the gate in time to see Agatha vault over the wall itself, huge black wings spread behind her like a giant bat. She landed on the ground in front of a massive creature I'd never seen before. It sort of looked like an eighteen-foot-tall eyeball with a mouth full of dagger-like fangs, skin the color of squid ink, and was covered in writhing tentacles with huge spiked eyeballs on the ends like morning stars. Fear surged through me. I had no idea what that thing was but it seemed more than capable of killing us all.

A quick glance behind me revealed Polly and the other guard, Michelle, running across the town toward the gate. While I couldn't see much of the fight from behind the wall, I could hear the sounds of the battle raging. Did that mean everyone else was out there already?

I wasn't sure, but as Gwen sprang into the air, huge wings beating the air at hummingbird speeds, I was fairly sure of it. Her hands were awash with flame. As she threw fireballs at the big beast, it ignored her, focused on someone on the other side of the gate.

Clambering up onto the wall so I could see, I sucked in a worried breath.

Sheila had at least half a dozen of the lizardmen on her. While she was doing a reasonable job of keeping them at bay, mostly because the rest of the guards were attacking them from behind, I knew she couldn't take all those monsters and the big guy who was lumbering after her.

It wouldn't have been a problem because she could have probably kept kiting it, except I could see more of the lizardmen rushing toward us from the Darkness. A second wave! Worse, it'd be on us in seconds. If that happened, we'd be as good as dead. As I pushed down my own fear, I tried to think of what to do.

As Polly and Michelle hopped the wall to join the fray, I caught sight of Sally and Crystal. Both were zooming through the air toward us, their wings flapping for all they were worth. Good. Sally could keep Sheila topped off.

"Crystal, you keep that big guy slowed down so he can't reach Sheila. Sally, you keep our tank at full Health," I said as they landed on the wall beside me.

They exchanged a quick glance with each other before turning their surprised eyes onto Sheila.

"How did you get someone with Defensive Aegis out here?" Sally asked before waving off the question. "Silly question. Okay, we're on it."

They jumped down from the wall and leaped into battle. Sally's hands glowed with golden light before a wave of energy enveloped Sheila. The wounds on her arms and legs vanished in a flare of power, and I watched as her Health returned to full. Perfect.

Crystal sprang into action, spurred on by Agatha's Blinding Blade technique. She darted forward, a palm full of what looked like caltrops in one hand. She flung them in front of the huge eye, and as they struck the ground, they began to glow with soft ethereal blue light. The creature, determined to catch Sheila, hovered right over them.

The traps exploded in a flare of light, sending

vines of blue smoke snapping upward to wrap around it and bind it into place.

Agatha seized on the chance, slamming her swords into the back of the creature, while Crystal produced a pair of old-fashioned pistols from beneath her cloak. She unloaded the two weapons into the back of the creature, blowing huge chunks of blackened flesh across the battlefield. The creature snarled, writhing in pain as it tried to break free of the caltrops.

I wasn't sure if the two of them could take it, but I was willing to bet we could keep it down and out until we dealt with the lizardmen.

"Agatha, Gwen! You two focus down the lizards. Everyone work together to take them down, burn them down one by one. Then we can focus down the eyeball," I said, and while Gwen spun in midair to throw her next fireball at the lizardmen on Sheila, Agatha didn't move.

"We need to take down the beholder before it breaks free. If it gets to Sheila, it can turn her to stone." She shook her head at me and plunged her blades into it. "Trust me, even if we can keep it bound up, Sheila's Defensive Aegis won't keep it focused on her for much longer. We need to take it down first."

"That's an excellent point," I murmured as the second wave of lizardmen hit the battlefield. They were swept up by Sheila's Defensive Aegis and moved to intercept her. Worse, we'd only downed a few of the lizardmen.

Sally let loose with another healing wave, bringing Sheila back up to full before turning toward Crystal and flicking her wrist out. A band of sapphire energy wrapped around Crystal and the girl's movements began to blur as she quickly reloaded and fired into the beholder.

"Sally, can you haste Gwen and Agatha as well?" I asked, glancing at the healer.

She nodded. "I can, but it will take a lot out of me."

"Do it anyway," I said, pissed I'd just spent all her Experience. If I hadn't I could have increased her Regeneration Rate.

Instead, I turned my attention toward Sheila because she was just going to have to make do. She'd gained a ton of Experience since I'd last looked and had almost six thousand Experience to call upon. That seemed insane. Had it all been from defending the gates?

I wasn't sure, but I didn't care. I dumped another three thousand Experience into her Defensive Aegis so it could hold threat for an additional minute. Then I used the rest to give her two additional Abilities: Skin of Steel which reduced incoming damage by fifty percent for thirty seconds, and Leeching Blows, which let her convert a portion of her damage into Health.

Turning my eyes to Agatha, I quickly saw that, like Sheila, she had a bunch of Experience to spare. I upgraded her Blinding Blade Ability a little, but then I saw the Skill Flash in the Pan. It would increase her chance of dealing a critical hit by ten percent. Since her attacks were based on speed, that would add up to a lot more damage over the course of a battle. There was just one problem. She didn't have the Stats.

I quickly dumped Experience into Agility, Special, and Strength to bring them up to the required levels of eighty, seventy-five, and seventy, and then had her learn Flash in the Pan.

As the blue light of my spell faded from around the women, the beholder broke free. It surged forward, more pissed off than ever. Gore leaked from its body. Only instead of pursuing Shelia, it shook itself, its skin undulating, and spun, lashing out at Crystal and Agatha. A blast of fire lit from its eyes, turning the dirt between them into slag.

"Told you!" Agatha cried, leaping to the left to avoid a blast of cold that turned the spot where the guard had been standing into a winter wonderland.

"Sorry," I said, glancing at Sheila. "Can you pull it back on you?"

"No!" the guard called right before a lizardman decked her in the chin, sending her spinning to the ground. As she struck the ground, more lizardmen attacked her.

"Fuck!" I cried as Gwen hit the ground beside Sheila, arms awash with fire. She plunged a flaming fist through the back of a lizardman's skull and grabbed hold of Sheila by the breastplate. With a Herculean effort, she flung the girl into the air.

Sheila's wings opened in midair. She hovered there as the lizards screamed and gnashed for a moment before whirling to attack the people nearest to them.

"Fuck, leaving the ground makes her lose agro on the monsters," I cursed, pissed off.

Gwen seemed fine, backpedaling as she blasted them with flames, but the other guards were much less skilled and their gear was inferior. A quick glance at their Health stats let me know we were fucked.

"You have to get them back on you, Sheila!" I

cried as Sally began throwing healing spells out left and right. Her chest was heaving, sweat dripping down her face, and I knew we didn't have long.

"Dammit!" I cursed right before Sheila taunted the beholder, causing the creature to spin and face her. Then it shot a lance of flame through the air that hit Sheila in the chest, knocking her backward to the ground. Steam rose from her body as the smell of charred flesh filled my nose.

"No!" Agatha screamed, leaping on the beholder's back and slamming her blades into the top of its skull. Their edges were covered with dark ichor, and as she continued to pound on it, Crystal threw a handful of powder into the monster's maw.

It hissed and spat, shaking itself as its skin turned a motley shade of green. The eyes on the ends of its tentacles began to water, and I realized she'd blinded it somehow.

"I'm out, boss," Sally said as she threw the last of her Power at Sheila. It was enough to get the guard on her feet but not much more.

"It's okay," I said, pissed at myself because it was my fault and we needed her healing now. "I shouldn't have made you waste the power hasting them."

"Defensive Aegis!" Sheila cried, slamming her

spear into the ground. Blood leaked from her lips, her armor was scorched and melted to her flesh, but as she cried out, a wave of power swept out like a crashing wave. Once again, the lizardmen turned their attention toward her and rushed forward. Only, now she had way less Health.

"Crystal, use your caltrops to slow them. They can't reach her until Sally recovers enough to heal her," I yelled, and the girl turned to me and nodded. "Everyone else, don't let them reach Sheila." I glanced at Agatha. "You keep DPSing the boss."

As Crystal raced forward, unloading her twin pistols as she went, she managed to take down two of the creatures closest to Sheila. Gwen was able to do the same, clearing a path for Sheila to backpedal away from the rest.

Crystal's hand shot out as she flung more caltrops to the ground between Sheila and the horde of lizardmen. The trap sprung, slowing all but three down. Those that remained stuck were quickly taken down by the guards Agatha and Sheila had trained, but the rest continued forward.

"Gwen, Crystal! Focus fire left to right!" They followed suit, unloading on the left lizardman and bringing it down as the other two reached Sheila.

Another bolt of fire split the air, sizzling by her and causing her to leap forward. Her shield slammed into the right creature, knocking it on its ass as the other lunged forward. Its blade sank into Sheila's arm, but she ignored it as she smashed her forehead into its snout. The sound of cracking bone filled the air as it staggered backward.

A barrage of bullets hit the lizardman on the side of the skull, turning its head into a fond memory, while a surge of fire from Gwen turned the one on the ground into toast. Just like that, all the lizards were down, leaving us with a very pissed off beholder.

Agatha was still pounding on it, but because the thing was all black, I couldn't tell how hurt it was.

"I'm nearly out of Mana," Gwen said, trying to call more fire and failing.

"Almost out of ammo too," Crystal called as the beholder finally succeeded in slamming one of the mace-like tentacles into Agatha.

The guard was flung to the ground but managed to somehow roll through it, coming up on her feet just in time to meet a bruising charge. The blow flung her backward across the sand.

The beholder howled in triumph, ignoring Crystal's shots as the bullets sank into its flesh. It raised its tentacles, aiming the flame and ice eyes at Agatha.

Before it could strike, Sheila was there in a blur of motion, her wings flapping with all their might. Her spear slammed downward into the thing's open mouth, piercing straight through the back of its throat and bursting out the back, splattering black goo everywhere. The tip of the spear sank into the dark earth as the beholder convulsed before collapsing to the ground in a twitching heap.

19

As I stood there staring at the corpse of the beholder, I realized how crazy my current situation was. Numbers were flashing above the heads of my girls, and the corpses of the other monsters had already dissolved into Dark Blood, but it was the twisted, oozing body of the lifeless beholder that really brought it home for me.

A few days ago, I'd been just a Seven Eleven Slurpee Monkey with delusions of landing an IT job in a burned-out husk of an industrial city. Now… Now, I was in charge of a town and all its inhabitants. It was crazy to think it had happened to me of all people. Not only that, but thanks to me, we were winning. We'd even taken down a beholder of all things.

It was crazy and unreal and, if I was being completely honest, a little bit frightening. Only, as I gripped the hilt of Clarent, I realized how lucky I truly was. I'd been given a chance no person had ever been given in the history of the universe.

I would defeat the Darkness if it was the last thing I did. Not because I was the chosen one or anything like that. No, I'd do it because deep down, I wanted to protect my girls. They'd fought hard and trusted me even when my decisions had been bad. I'd been so preoccupied with everything that had been going on and all that recruitment that I'd forgotten we were in the middle of a war zone and because of it, Sheila had nearly died.

That would not happen again.

I jumped down off the wall and moved toward the beholder as its body began to bubble and slough away into the ether. Each step I took caused my compatriots to look over at me, and while none approached as I knelt down by the fallen monster, I knew some of them wanted to. They didn't, and I was glad for it.

As the last of the beholder dissolved away, revealing a mass of Dark Blood the size of a football, I reached out and took it into my hand. It felt both hot and cold, and as I stood, lifting it into the air, Clarent began to glow with blue fire.

"We won," I said, turning toward my team. "Thanks to all of you, we won. I know it was tough, and we nearly lost, but we'll continue to stand. We'll continue to win. That is my promise." I turned to look at Sheila and moved toward her. "I should have never let you get as hurt as you did."

"What are you talking about?" Sheila asked, confusion playing across her face as she looked me over. "I've never seen any border town survive a beholder attack before. When they come, it's almost always the end of the line. Those creatures would take down the ward over the town in ten seconds flat if they could. The only reason it didn't was because of the Skills you gave me, gave to us." Sheila put a hand on my shoulder. "That we won and didn't lose anyone at all is a win so massive you don't even understand."

"Maybe," I said, turning to look at the crackling horizon of the Darkness, "but that's not good enough. We should have taken them down before they got to us, but we didn't." I shook my head. "And what if I wasn't here—"

"Then we'd all be dead right now," Gwen said, coming toward me. Agatha, Crystal, and Sally followed in her wake. They all nodded. "We'd all just be dead, and there'd be a smoking crater where Lustnor once stood. Only that didn't happen thanks to what you did here."

"Believe me when I say that I hear you. I just," I sighed, turning to look at our town with its too low walls and shoddy gate, "I just want you all to be safe." I handed the Dark Blood from the beholder to Sally. "We'll need to work on that but first thing's first. We need to get our asses in gear because I know what I'd be doing now if I was the Darkness."

"What's that?" Gwen asked as we all moved back toward the gates.

"I'd send ten beholders." I glanced over my shoulder as the lightning arced through the sky and the thunder boomed. "And something a lot worse than beholders along just to make sure." I smacked my hand against the pommel of Clarent. "We have to be ready for that."

"We will be ready for that," Gwen said, putting a hand on my shoulder as we stepped inside. "For now, we need everyone on the same page. Get some more people."

"Yeah, more people." I looked up at the sky for a second before shutting my eyes as I tried to ignore the punishing responsibility threatening to bury me.

If more people came, I'd be responsible for them too. Every person here was trusting in me to win, but worse, everyone who died would be my fault. I sighed, and for a second, I almost wished I was back home. Sure, it hadn't been much, but it had been safe. Only no one had counted on me. Now people did.

"Let me take care of some of the details. We still need to split up those we have appropriately." Gwen squeezed my shoulder. "Maybe you can just take a break for a few minutes. All this must be new to you." She leaned in and kissed me on the cheek, causing a rush of warmth and energy to sweep through my body. "Go on, you deserve it."

"No," I said, waving off the idea. "I'm going to go meet with Maribelle and Buffy. We need to do something about those walls."

"Okay," Gwen said, nodding to me, but as she turned to head back toward the assembled Stained-turned-guards, I stopped her. "Hmm?"

"I want long range people. Crystal seems to know a bit about that. Anyone who has the Skill for it becomes a priority, okay?"

"Understood," Gwen said, a glimmer of humor flashing through her eyes as she looked me over. "You're enjoying this, aren't you?" She gestured at me. "There's definitely some more 'oomph' to you than when I first met you." She licked her lips. "I like it."

With that, she spun on her heels and moved back to the assembled townspeople, leaving me to go on my merry way.

I wasn't sure how I felt about that. If by oomph she meant the weight of the world on my shoulders, then yeah, I was different. Now, I had a duty to my people, and I would succeed. She was right though. She could see to having the townsfolk associated accordingly. I'd leave her to that and see to the buildings.

A few minutes later, I found myself standing before both Maribelle and Buffy, which was convenient, if annoying because the two women were shouting at each other.

"Look, missy, we just don't have the funds for what you're proposing," Buffy snarled, whipping a hand back toward the building where she'd set up shop. It looked like it was seconds from completely collapsing under the weight of the weird pigeon-like birds settled atop the roof. "We're like seconds from being bankrupt as it is."

"You can't even be in that building. It's so not to code that it might actually turn into a black hole and absorb the town. You need to release the funds to fix it." Maribelle crossed her arms over her chest. "Unless you want to die."

"We all have to die sometime. Money is forever," Buffy said, taking a step forward and making a wringing motion with her hands. "It isn't like I have a magic money tree I can shake to make all our dreams come true."

"What's the problem?" I asked, stepping between the two girls and holding out my hands. "Because we just killed a fucking beholder at the gate, so unless whatever this is" - I gestured to them - "is that important, I think we can figure out a solution."

"The problem is that nearly every building here, even Sam's, is dangerously unstable. We need to tear them down to the frame, in some cases to the foundation, and completely rebuild them, or we risk people dying." As Buffy opened her mouth to interrupt, I held up a hand, silencing her. "And I'm not talking about stupid regulations, like you need at least four nails per foot of board, either. These are dangerously unsound problems." She moved forward and pushed on the corner of the building, causing it to sway dangerously. "That shouldn't happen."

"I agree," I said, turning to the goblin. "I can't imagine you think it's safe, so what's the problem?"

"The problem is we can't afford it." Buffy threw up her hands in exasperation and stomped her foot. "We just can't. I have some funds earmarked for the mill, but even if we take every penny I've earmarked for other important things, we cannot afford to remake even a single building, let alone that one."

"Okay," I said, turning to Maribelle. "And I'm assuming there are no quick fixes to the problem?"

"Not really," Maribelle said, shaking her head. "Maybe if I was more skilled, but I'm just not." She threw up her hands in frustration.

"Are you sure?" I gestured to the buildings, and as I did, I had a thought. "Um… why do we need them?"

"Well, we just um…" Maribelle frowned and looked at Buffy for help. "We need cover for the shops so the equipment and whatnot doesn't get ruined."

"Can we get a tent or something?" I asked, looking around for Taylor, but when I didn't see her in her shop, I figured she'd gone to Gwen for the selection. "Just for a short term solution?"

"I suppose we could erect tents or some such

thing," Buffy said, rubbing her chin. "It's a stop gap."

"We just need some time. Actually, that's what I need to talk to you two about anyway." I pointed to the gate. "That isn't good enough. As I said, we fought a beholder, and if I had to guess, the next attack will be worse. We need to get better." My shoulders slumped. "If not, we're fucked. Buildings up to code or not."

"What would you like us to do?" Maribelle said, looking at her feet embarrassed. "And sorry, I should have been more focused on defense."

"The hell you should have been," Buffy snorted before glaring at me. "We need money to do anything, and we have none. We won't be getting better stuff until we do that."

"There's the Dark Blood Sally will refine and all the lumber," I motioned toward the forest surrounding the town.

"And that will help, but it's not going to be enough. I'm guessing that getting the mill up to the point where we could actually use the lumber effectively will take almost every penny we'll make on this round of Dark Bloods. We either need a lot more of it or a lot better quality." Buffy rubbed her face with one hand. "Look, we need at least twice the funds we have to buy the materials for the walls…"

"The problem is we can't buy them. We'll have to make them." I turned to Maribelle. "What will it take to make the walls you talked about?"

"On average?" she mused before pulling out a piece of chalk from behind her ear. She moved toward a section of wall and began scribbling down notes. A few moments later, she took a step back and gestured at the scrawling on the wall. "That seems right, Buffy?"

"Unfortunately, yes," Buffy grumbled, "and if we did nothing else, we'd still only be able to afford ten percent of that."

I leaned in closer to examine the numbers, and as I did, they began to glow, resolving themselves into a strange menu beside each recipe.

Wood Wall (currently in use)

Durability: 1,000

Option: Can be crafted with a window frame or a door frame.

Cost: 10 Wood, 5 Thatch, 5 Fiber

Spiked Wood Wall

Durability: 500

Bonus: Can damage opponents who attack it.

Cost: 10 Wood, 5 Thatch, 5 Fiber, 5 Stone

Stone Wall
Durability: 5,000
Option: Can be crafted with a window frame or a door frame.
Cost: 10 Stone, 5 Wood, 5 Thatch
Reinforced Stone Wall
Durability: 10,000
Option: Can be crafted with a window frame or a door frame.
Bonus: Cannot be damaged by most weapons.
Cost: 10 Metal, 10 Stone, 5 Wood

"Interesting," I mused, turning back to the two of them. "Um, can you show me a piece of lumber?"

"Um," Maribelle said, looking at me quizzically. "They're just chunks of wood. Is this a Builder thing?" I nodded, and she shrugged. "We have some over here."

We made our way toward a pile of wooden boards in a heap, and as I stared at them, an icon appeared beside them like it had with the Dark Blood.

Lumber
Material: Wood
Grade: D
Boards made from common trees.

"Okay, I think I understand the problem in numbers now," I said, turning back to Buffy. "How many people can we support, by the way?"

"Maybe another fifteen. After that it gets dicey," she said, motioning to her building. "This is why I'm trying to get the trading post set up. If we can get trade coming here, we'll be richer."

"That's an excellent point, and I want you to focus on that and getting the mill ready. Tear down these buildings to use for materials and get some tents. Taylor can probably make what we need. As far as everything else?" I smiled. "I think I may have another idea."

20

I found Gwen just as she was dismissing the others to get back to work, and as she turned toward me, she smiled so brightly, my knees shook a little. Damn, I was going to have to get used to her looking at me, otherwise, well…

"Hey, Arthur," she called, waving at me. "I've got everyone rounded up and going to do their stuff." She bit her lip and gestured at Crystal as she led four women off toward the blacksmith's shop. "We're probably going to have wood long before we have a mill."

"Not a horrible problem to have," I said, shrugging. "Actually, I wanted to talk to you about that."

"About the mill?" She raised a perfect eyebrow. "I don't know how to make one or anything."

"Not that." I waved off her comment. "More

about the people problem. We just don't have enough, but I've been thinking about what you said."

"What I said?" she asked, looking at me carefully. "What did I say?"

"That the demon dogs are more hostile because of a town falling." I glanced toward the gate. "Sheila seems to think we'd be dead under normal circumstances."

"I'm not quite following," she said, taking a long look at me. "Can you go slower?" She smacked me lightly on the top of the head. "And you know, explain in words that make sense?"

"Yeah, I can," I said, sighing and looking at the sky to collect my thoughts. "Well, what if we weren't the only ones attacked? Hell, maybe people are getting attacked right now." I turned my gaze to the horizon. "Maybe there are towns that need our help."

"We can barely help ourselves right now, Arthur. We need to focus on us," she said, and as she reached out to touch my arm, I shook her away.

"The best way to catch flies is with honey, not vinegar, and what we need are people. If we can ride in on white horses and save the day, we can probably get them to come back with us." I nodded to her. "I just talked to Buffy and Maribelle. They both agree that if we can absorb other townships, even ones as bad as Lustnor, we'll get a huge head start. Especially if they have equipment we can use."

"So," she said, and the word had a lot more venom behind it than I expected, "you're saying Lustnor sucks?"

"That's really what you took away from my point?" I waved off the comment as she bristled in anger. "That's not what I meant. What I was trying to say was that I want Lustnor to be the greatest city ever, and to do that, we need lots of things we don't have." I rubbed my hands together. "We go out and offer the other towns worse off than us a chance to join up, and hey, you never know, right? Besides, maybe we can find some Stained from destroyed towns."

"We can't support that many people," she said, crossing her arms over her chest. "You might cause us all to starve."

"Just trust me," I said, gesturing at the town. "It's been what, a few hours and we're fighting off beholders. Imagine what we could do in a few weeks."

"It's the getting a few weeks that worries me,"

she said before throwing her hands in the air. "Fine, we'll do it. It's not a bad plan, per se."

"Great," I said, happy I'd swayed her to my way of thinking. Now I just had to make everything work out. "Buffy and Maribelle will be ready to go soon. I want to take Sheila and Crystal with us. Agatha can stay behind with the others."

"What if there's an attack while we're gone?" Gwen asked, looking concerned. "The few guards we have left aren't nearly good enough."

"I'll upgrade them to work for the interim. The last time it was only one beholder. I'll make sure they're skilled enough to take on a couple."

"I just don't like the idea of it." As she shook her head, a scream tore through the air from the back gate. Panic surged through me as I spun on my heel, and sprinted toward it. I wasn't sure what was going on, but as the sounds of battle filled my ears, I knew it wouldn't be good. Maybe Gwen was right. Maybe taking away our guards was foolish.

"Come on!" Gwen cried, grabbing me around the waist and leaping into the air. Her huge bat wings beat the air propelling us both forward and upward.

What I saw made my blood run cold. Our two gate guards, along with Crystal and her lumberjacks, were engaged in combat against a couple dozen demon dogs. More of the creatures were chasing a traveling caravan that was barreling toward us like a bat out of Hell.

I wasn't sure where they'd come from but one thing was for certain, we had to save them. Fast. If we didn't hurry, those dogs would tear the caravan to pieces.

"What's going on?" I cried as fire began to radiate from Gwen's free hand. "Where did all those people come from?"

"Those are the Stained. Somewhere nearby must have fallen if they're fleeing this way," Gwen said, flinging a fireball at the demon dogs. The blast hit one, knocking it aside, while Crystal and her contingent of lumberjacks engaged the demon dogs, picking them off as they nipped at the caravan.

"Great. We don't even need to go anywhere!" I said as Gwen set me down just inside the walled area before bursting into the melee. "Hey, open the gates and let these people in," I said, grabbing hold of one of the doors and shoving it open.

"But sir," Polly said, turning her eyes to me, "the dogs might get inside!"

I'd thought of that, but there wasn't another

option. If we left the Stained outside, they'd die. If a few dogs got inside our gates, we'd deal with them.

"Then keep them out," I hollered, putting my back into it as I shoved the doors open enough to allow the Stained to start pouring in. As they rushed by me in a terror-fueled mass, I turned my attention toward my team. "Get them inside!"

"On it!" Crystal called, unloading her revolvers into the nearest demon dog before pulling a small, thin rapier from the sheath on her belt and stabbing the next creature to death. She swung her arm in a motion that sent her lumberjacks running to help the Stained through.

To be honest, the problem wasn't those on foot so much as it was the pair of large lumbering wagons. There were a few women dressed like our guards surrounding the wagons, but since the wagons were being attacked by dozens of demon dogs, they were having a tough time.

"Gwen, focus on getting the wagons through!" I called before spinning on my heel and making my way toward the main gate. I reached it only a couple seconds later, my chest heaving with effort as I clambered back over it.

"Sheila!" I called breathlessly, causing the guard

to turn toward me. Her eyes had been fixed on the horizon while her weapons had been held in a white-knuckled grip.

"Yes?" she said as she along with the other guards turned quick, furtive gazes on me.

"I need you to go to the other gate and pull the demon dogs off the Stained!" I said, and when she nodded, I let myself fall back to the ground. I stood there for a moment, trying to catch my breath as Sheila's winged form rocketed through the air toward the other gate.

She landed on the other side before I had even started to move. Taking a deep breath, I willed myself into action, forcing myself to sprint back across the battlefield. I needn't have bothered.

I arrived just in time to see the first wagon move through the gate, and as I peered past it out onto the road, I saw that most of the demon dogs had been killed. Those that hadn't were running for cover.

As I watched the creatures go, Gwen landed on the ground next to me.

"Who do you think they are?" I asked.

"By my grandmother's golden tooth, Elizabeth, is that you?" Buffy called, sprinting toward us as a diminutive goblin on the last cart rumbled through the gate.

"Why I'll be a horse's ass," the goblin on the cart said, right before Buffy picked up a rock and flung it at her.

21

I watched in horror and confusion as the rock struck the goblin on the side of the head, sending her tumbling to the ground. As she crashed to the black earth, Buffy jumped on her, one fist raised to pound her face into putty.

"Stop!" I cried, grabbing Buffy by the back of her shirt and trying to haul her off. It was no use because, despite being much smaller than me, the goblin was practically immovable. Thankfully, she relented and stood up before glaring at me.

"That's Elizabeth, head of the damned Merchant's guild in Tricolm!" Buffy snarled with barely contained anger. "They won't let me trade there on account of the place not being big enough for the both of us." She said the last part in a sort of dumb, mocking voice.

"It's a moot point now," Elizabeth said from the ground. She wiped her mouth with one hand before pushing herself to a sitting position. "Tricolm just fell to ravagers." She got to her feet and brushed herself off.

"Ravagers?" Gwen asked, taking a deep breath. "That's…"

"Not possible, I know," Elizabeth said, glancing back at the caravan as the doors shut. There were three wagons in total and one buggy like Buffy's. There were maybe twenty or so people including five guards who looked like they hadn't slept in over a week.

"How could ravagers get into Tricolm?" Gwen asked, shaking her head.

"How about you help us with some food and drink in a nice safe spot, and we tell you about it? Then we'll be moving on. We have to get to Goldheim before they start missing this." She smacked the side of the buggy she'd been riding. "Not that it will matter much. Damned ravagers will be following us. We've got a day at most."

Her words chilled me because that wasn't a lot of time. Not by a longshot. Especially since I had no idea what a ravager was or how to deal with it.

Worse, from the look on everyone's faces, they didn't think we had a chance.

"What's a ravager?" I asked, worry threatening to leak into my voice. "Because let me just say they sound really bad."

"They are. A ravager is a twenty-foot tall monstrosity of tentacles and spikes. Its skin is practically impenetrable, and its legs are like tree trunks. It wanders through a battlefield grabbing things with its tentacles and shoving them into its immense maw." Gwen turned to look at me. "The only time I've even seen one die was when it tried to eat a guard who triggered her internal core, causing it to explode right as the creature swallowed her." She shook her head. "And we can't risk our people on a chance like that."

"Then I suggest you get a move on too because they are heading this way," Elizabeth said, shaking her head dismally. "There were two at Tricolm, and they're all after us. Me and mine were just there as an envoy from the merchant's guild and barely made it out of there. I'm not sure if there are other survivors."

"Just so we're clear," I said, glancing at Buffy who was still seething in rage, "you are leading a bunch of giant fucking monsters here to kill us?"

"That's about the size of it, yes," Elizabeth replied, taking a deep breath. Her nostrils flared, and then she stopped and looked at me. Her eyes filled with recognition and I got the impression she was seeing me for the first time. "Wait, you're him."

"I, er, what?" I asked, suddenly confused.

"The Legendary Builder. We've been looking for you since you left the Royal Centre. That's why I was in Tricolm because we'd heard you were in a border town." She rubbed her hands together. "I never expected to find you here though. Maybe Sword's Deep, but not here."

"What's wrong with Lustnor?" Gwen asked, taking a step forward.

"It's a craphole with no resources and no economy?" Elizabeth offered, shrugging. She turned to look at me. "Come with me to Goldheim, and not only will I make you rich beyond your wildest dreams, you'll be swimming in girls." She glanced at Gwen. "You can't stay here anyway, so your friends are welcome to come."

"No," I said, waving off the offer. "I'm not leaving. I made a promise to Gwen and this town to make it the best city. I will do that, *and* I will stop the Darkness. Even if it has ravagers."

"Newsflash, kid, they aren't called ravagers

because they're misunderstood and really need a hug," Elizabeth spat. "Nothing you have here will be able to stop them."

"That's what you think," I said, annoyed now. "Look, we'll get you whatever you want, and you can go, but anyone who stays will get a job and a profession." I touched my chest with one hand. "I am the Builder after all, and *I'm* staying."

"You don't want her help, anyway. My sister is a total bitch," Buffy snapped, already walking back toward her shop. Well, her sort of shop because it was mostly just sheets of canvas on legs.

"Your sister?" I asked right before Elizabeth grabbed Buffy's arm.

"You can't stay here, Buffy. If you do, you'll die," Elizabeth hissed before looking around. "It's not safe here on the border, there have been rumors of beholder attacks."

"We just killed one," Buffy said, shrugging off her sister. "And I believe in Arthur. If he says we can win, I believe him." She turned and looked at her sister. "He can do what he says. You'd be wise to stay here and have your people join him because, to be honest, he's going to win. You can either help now, or wish you did when you had the chance."

"Why Buffy, I'd almost think you like the meat

bag," Elizabeth said, glancing over her shoulder at me and giving me a once over. "Fine. Even though it seems silly, I'll stay. For now. Someone has to make sure you get out alive, after all."

"You're being wise. For once," Buffy said, heading toward her shop as Elizabeth came waltzing back.

"Would you mind if my people join you, Builder? You'll find us well worth the trouble," she nodded toward the wagon. "And besides, we have an extractor."

"An extractor?" Gwen asked, shock in her voice. "How?"

"Tricolm bought it but they aren't there anymore, so I guess it's ownerless." With that, Elizabeth smacked the buggy's side, causing it to open up like a flower until all the panels were laying in the dirt. Sitting there in the middle was a machine that sort of reminded me of a mech only with saw blade arms, pick arms, scythe arms and normal grabbing arms.

"What's that do?" I asked, taking a tentative step closer.

"Why it's the greatest in harvesting technology. It slices, it dices, why it even takes out the trash. The Extractor XD-17 can do it all." Elizabeth gestured triumphantly at it. "And it can be yours as long as you take care of me and mine." She held out a hand to me. "Deal?"

"Deal," I said, taking her hand and shaking it. As I did, blue orbs appeared over all the women Elizabeth had brought with her. "Guess we need to get things moving."

22

"A sculptor, eh?" I said as I looked over Annabeth. She was a shorter girl with long black hair, almond eyes, and tan skin. "How does one become a sculptor?"

Everyone else had been sent along already, and the extractor was busy chewing up the landscape like it had slept with its wife. Agatha had taken the five new guards on a hunting party to both look for more Stained and see if they could find some game to kill. We'd also dragged in the bodies of the demon dogs, and since one of the Stained had been a cook, she was busy preparing them for a meal. I was both concerned and excited by the prospect.

That just left the sculptor.

"It's easy," she said, showing me her teeth. "You

just punch statues for a month to build your endurance and toughness until you get a quest. One thing leads to another, and well..." She waved a hand. "Anyway, that's not important." She looked around before meeting my eyes. There was a surprising amount of both rage and resignation in them. "What would you have me do?"

"I'm not sure, to be honest," I said, pulling up her Character Sheet. "What would you like to do?"

Name: Annabeth
Experience: 25,773
Health: 75/75
Mana: 153/153
Primary Power: Sculpting
Secondary Power: None selected
Strength: 10/100
Agility: 65/100
Charisma: 28/100
Intelligence: 56/100
Special: 97/100
Perk: Rank 2 Sculptor

"Holy cow!" I exclaimed, looking from her to her Skill sheet and back again. "You're Special is really high, and you're Rank two!"

"Yes." She nodded. "I have not yet taken the

master level test. I believe I would pass, but the time commitment is too much."

Rank 2 Sculptor: Able to use Skills and Abilities based upon Rank two Skill. This will allow the sculptor to produce Grade A items 80% of the time. There is a 10% chance of crafting a Grade S item. There is a 10% chance of crafting a Grade B item.

"How the hell did you wind up out here in the boonies?" I asked, raising an eyebrow at her. She was clothed in simple yet sturdy garments, the kind which was likely expensive, but only because they were durable and comfortable.

"I often venture into the wilderness to pursue my craft. One must sculpt new and difficult things to improve one's Skill. Being out in the wilderness helps with that. I saw the group leaving, and I offered to help them as I'm good with a knife." She held up a small sculpting blade emblazoned with runes. "But alas, I could not hope to defeat the ravagers on my own, so I was forced to flee." She pointed the knife at me. "Now I belong to you. So, I ask again, what would you have me do?"

"Why do you keep asking me that like you expect me to tell you to blow me or something?" I asked, flicking through her Skill trees until I had a better idea of her powers. "I'm not going to do that."

"Oh?" she asked, raising a slender eyebrow at me. Then she flushed. "Of course. I am not your type." She gestured at her chest. "I'm not big enough here. I should not have presumed."

"What, no, you're fine. I just don't believe in ordering girls to sleep with me," I said, trying my best to reassure her. "In fact, it's the one thing I will absolutely not order you to do."

"Interesting," she said, still unconvinced, but I wasn't sure what by.

"Believe me when I say that I want you for your mind, Annabeth," I said, pointing at a Skill Tree I knew she couldn't see. It had two Skills I was supremely interested in.

Aura of Enhancement: This Ability allows the user to create a sculpture which gives a bonus to different attributes to all friendlies within a one-hundred-meter range.

Requirements: Special: 50+, Agility: 50+, Intelligence 50+

Cost: 1500 Experience

Aura of Detraction: This Ability allows the user to create a sculpture which gives a detriment to all enemies within a one-hundred-meter range.

Requirements: Special: 50+, Agility: 50+, Intelligence 50+

Cost: 1500 Experience

"I'm not sure what you're trying to show me," she said, following my finger as I had her learn both Abilities and then spent a few thousand Experience to increase the range of the Abilities and make them both more powerful.

Only as I was doing that, I saw I'd unlocked a third Ability.

Double-Bladed: This Ability allows the user to create a sculpture which has both an Enhancing and Detracting effect. Each of these effects will be based on the Skill of those Abilities.

Requirements: Special: 70+, Agility: 70+, Intelligence 70+

Cost: 1500 Experience

"How do you feel," I said after quickly upgrading her Stats and learning the new Ability. I turned my gaze back to her, having spent over half her accumulated Experience with a single goal in mind. Part of me felt bad, but at the same time we had ravagers coming, and we had to stop them.

"Strange," she said, touching a finger to her temple. "But not in a bad way. You changed me, didn't you?" She shut her eyes and took a deep breath. "I have so many more ideas now, I think…" Her eyes opened wide. "I know what you've done to me."

"Do you disapprove?" I asked, my smile threatening to slip off my face because she looked pissed.

"I do not know. I believe in hard work, and this feels like a shortcut, but at the same time, I want to try sculpting something. I think it will be helpful." She looked away toward the gate. "I will need a giant piece of stone. I will go find the appropriate piece, and then we will need to bring it into the center of the town."

"Sounds good," I said, and she nodded at me before making her way toward the back gate. I watched her go for a second before turning my attention toward the trading post. From there I could still see Buffy and Elizabeth arguing. I wasn't sure what about, but the sisters seemed to shout at each other so often, I knew visiting them now wouldn't help.

Instead, I turned my sights on Sam's shop and made my way toward it. As I knocked on the door before stepping inside, I found myself looking at her two helpers.

"Where's Sam?" I asked, and the closer girl who

was busy shuffling ore about the place looked over to me.

"She's with Sally in the refinery," she said before turning her attention back toward the rocks which were clearly more interesting than me.

"Okay, thanks," I said, turning to go.

"Oh, and the mill equipment Sam designed should be ready soon. Maybe end of tomorrow, if we're lucky," she added as I hit the door.

"Cool, thanks for the update," I said, moving down the road a bit toward the makeshift building, Sally used as an alchemist's shop. It wasn't nice, but it did have four wooden walls thanks to cobbling together the parts from the other buildings. Inside, I found both Sam and Sally staring at a huge piece of glowing ore.

"What's that?" I asked, taking a step toward them and causing both of them to look over at me.

"This is a grade A chunk of Dark Blood," Sally said, beaming at me. "But not only that, it's the one from the beholder. I did my best, trying to get it to S grade, but no luck. Still though, it's so huge, it could really sell for a lot."

"Size doesn't always matter," I said, opening up Sam's Character Sheet. "But I'm glad it's all working out."

"Well, if you aren't here to check up on me, why are you here?" Sally asked, moving toward the counter where a variety of Dark Bloods of different qualities sat ready for inspection. "I was able to get almost all of these to grade A. We even have a single grade S." She pointed to one on the end that was a bit smaller than the others. It glowed twice as brightly.

"I wanted to see if Sam has enough Skill to learn the Dark Weaponry technique yet," I said but was saddened to find she was still several hundred Experience short.

"And?" Sam asked, looking over at me.

"You haven't earned enough Experience yet. You best get back to work. We'll need that Skill if we want to fight the ravagers that are coming." I sighed. "I still don't know how we're going to fight them in a day or so."

"We have to be smart," Sally said, dusting herself off. "Maybe we can't beat them in a one-on-one fight, but maybe we can beat them a different way."

"What do you mean?" I asked.

In reply, she picked up one of the demon horns we'd collected from the demon dogs and held it out. "I think I might be able to make an explosive. We have a lot of the materials already, and we can use the shavings from the Dark Blood and some of these horns to make it super powerful."

"But you can't penetrate the hide of a ravager," Sam said. "You need a cannon or something to do it, and even then, it's iffy. Half the time the balls bounce right off."

"Which is why I'm proposing we blow them up from the inside." Sally smirked. "Skin may be the same thickness on both sides, but the gooey bits are still inside. I think if we can get them to swallow an explosive, we might be able to kill it."

"That's pretty genius," I said, nodding to her, "but how do we get them to swallow it?"

"Therein lies the rub," Sally said, looking down at her shoes. "I'm not sure. We could try just tossing it in their mouths, but that may not work, and we probably won't get many chances."

"Let me think," I said as I idly flipped through Sam's Skill trees to find something that would help. Unfortunately, everything cost too much or didn't seem useful. "You know, everything has a weak spot. We just need to figure out what it is." I nodded to myself as I stared at a particular set of Skills based on Tree I hadn't paid much attention to before. It seemed crazy, but the more I looked at it, the more

I thought it might work. Only having her learn the Control Tree would cost almost all her Experience and delay Dark weapons for a while. At the same time, it just might work. At least, if what I was reading about the helmets the tree could make did what I thought they did. "Let me go talk to Crystal, Sheila, and Agatha. I have a really bad idea."

23

"Your plan is crazy, and not in the cute, endearing kind of crazy we've come to know and love over the last couple days," Gwen said as I stood before her, Agatha, Sheila, and Crystal. All around the town workers were bustling to and fro, hurrying to gather materials to strengthen our defenses. Thankfully, Sam had been able to modify the extractor slightly so it could also process the raw material to turn them into usable building materials, and now Maribelle was hard at work getting our walls up to speed.

"Look, even if Maribelle and her crew get all the walls up, we will still get stomped flat by the ravagers when they show up. This is the only thing I can think of." I gestured toward the dark, crackling horizon. "We need to go in there and kill a few more beholders so we can harvest their Dark Blood."

"No one has ever ventured into the Darkness and come back," Gwen said, staring at me for a long time. "And I know you're the Builder, but if we lose you, we'll all die."

"You won't lose me, and we'll die, anyway." I turned from her slightly and looked at the three other women, trying to search their faces for clues and finding nothing. "Don't you guys think we can do it?"

"I honestly do not know," Sheila said, with a shrug. "I'm not sure what we'll find there. If it's just more lizardmen and a beholder, sure, we'll probably be okay. The four guards we got with the caravan are at least as good as Agatha and me minus the Special Abilities you gave us."

"What if we get attacked again while you're out hunting for beholders like a crazy person?" Gwen asked, this time with fear in her voice. "What then?"

"Polly and the others are more than capable of holding the town unless something much stronger than lizardmen shows up. They're good enough for standing there being bored. Besides, we just had an attack. We usually have some time in between," Agatha said off-handedly.

"And you'll be here, Gwen," I said, not making eye contact with her. "You're plenty strong enough to help them."

"What do you mean I'm not coming? Of course, I'm coming!" she snapped, marching toward me until we were practically nose to nose. "I have to come. I need to protect you."

"I'm going to have a full contingent of guards with me. And I need someone here to make sure all the work gets done. You're the only one who can do that." I touched her hand. "I need you to do this. You're the only one I can trust."

"I don't like it," Gwen said, shaking her head. "But if it's what you think is best, I'll trust you." She took a deep breath. "If you need me, you can summon me through the sword, okay? I'll come. No matter what, I'll come."

"We'll take care of him," Agatha said, putting a hand on Gwen's shoulder. "I promise. I'll die before I let anything happen to the Builder."

"I know," Gwen said, sighing as she stepped away from me and looked at the crackling sky. "That's sort of what I'm afraid of. I don't want to lose any of you."

"We're not going to lose anyone," I said, taking a deep breath before grabbing Gwen and hugging her. The succubus's body melted into mine as she wrapped her hands around me, and for a moment, I wanted to forget everything but the feel of her. "I promise."

"Don't make promises you can't keep," she said, pulling away from me and wiping her eyes with the back of one hand. "I still don't understand why you need to go."

"A real leader leads from the front. You said no one has done this before. That means I can't send them inside without going myself because if something happens, only I can give them the Skills they'll need." She nodded as I turned back to the three. "Let's get the others and head out, okay?"

"Sir," Crystal said, as the other two broke away to gather the four guards we'd gained from the merchant's caravan.

"Yes?" I said.

"We need to bring Sally. Look, I know she's valuable here and practically irreplaceable, but she's the only healer." Crystal swallowed. "I'd hate to wind up in a situation where we need her and don't have her because we left her behind."

"Me too. That's why I'm going to get her. I'll

meet you outside in a minute." I smiled, but she shook her head.

"Let me get her, okay?" She gave me a weak smile, and I nodded.

"Okay," I said. She took off for Sally's shop, leaving me to stand there by my lonesome. "I'll just wait here then."

Not that it mattered. Ten minutes later we were all ready to go. The dark border was only a half mile away, and as we approached it, the air began to feel hot and muggy. I rubbed my arms, trying to dismiss the feeling of creatures crawling across my flesh, only I couldn't. Every time I moved, more pinpricks prickled across my flesh.

"Well, this doesn't feel at all creepy," I mumbled to no one in particular. Sheila and Agatha stood in front of me while Crystal and Sally made up the rear. I had a pair of guards on either side of me, and before we'd left, I'd taken the opportunity to give the one with the most Experience as a defensive fighter Defending Aegis so she'd be able to trade threat with Sheila.

Her name was Romy, and she was a short girl with lime green hair and chalky skin. The others hadn't had enough accumulated Experience for me to do much with yet, unfortunately, since they were all fairly new to the whole guarding thing. Ah well.

Lightning crackled overhead, and as we moved closer, Clarent began to glow in my hand, throwing sparks of sapphire in every direction. Thunder boomed as we stepped closer to the darkened swell of shadow that made up the border. Inky stretches of pure black reached out like roots into the shores of Hell, and as I stepped foot on a tendril, I realized it felt sort of sticky. Like tar almost.

More lightning fractured the horizon, and the smell of sulfur hit my nose, bringing tears to my eyes.

As Sheila raised her shield and took a hesitant step forward, she glanced over her shoulder at me. "Last chance to go back, boss because in a second we'll be in."

"We have to do this. We need the beholder's blood." I steeled myself and took a step forward. Dark mist wrapped itself around me, and the thundering of hooves filled my ears.

"I love that you're one crazy son of a bitch, boss," Sheila said and strode forward. As she did, her body disappeared. It was crazy because one second she was there, and the next she was gone.

Agatha followed and soon disappeared. As she did, my eyes opened wide.

This wasn't a border. No, it was a giant portal. We were going to be stepping into a new realm.

"Fuck," I muttered, swallowing hard before raising my chin and stiffening my spine. Then I stepped through the portal into the Darkness, and my entire body was ripped into microscopic specs, doused with napalm, and tossed into the sun. And that was the fun part.

24

"You have got to be fucking kidding me," I exclaimed as I appeared on the other side. The girls were no longer with me, which while incredibly concerning because not only did I not know where they were, I didn't know where the fuck I was. And yes, that amount of cursing was most definitely required.

The landscape in front of me was filled with pink, yellow, and white flowers accented by several large rainbows. A pair of unicorns frolicked in the distance.

Before me stood a path lined with pink and yellow daisies, and as I looked at the golden bricks leading off through the green pastures, I grumbled in annoyance. Something had gone wrong, and I needed to get to my girls, only I wasn't sure how to manage that.

I turned in a slow circle, trying to find a way out, but behind me, I saw pretty much the same thing. Just the same path I currently stood on stretching off into infinity. Turning my gaze down to Clarent, I found myself looking at the symbols etched into the steel. Part of me wondered if I could really summon Gwen to my side but if I did, would both of us be trapped here?

I wasn't sure, but I couldn't risk it. Not when we had ravagers coming toward us, and besides, if I was totally honest with myself, the other girls I'd been with knew the plan. Assuming they'd actually made it through into the reaches of the Darkness, they'd be doing what I'd told them. If they weren't, well, they'd be here. I just had to find them either way.

Taking a deep breath, I made my way forward down the path. Clarent glowed softly in my hand. As I moved, I couldn't help but find myself admiring the place. It reminded me of those postcards of the green hills of Ireland, only with way more wildflowers.

As I followed the serpentine path past a mother deer and her young, I found myself staring at what looked like an insane tea party. A teddy bear with one eye sat in one chair while the one next to it was filled by a patchwork lop-eared rabbit. The third chair was empty and, like the previous two, didn't concern me.

No, it was the fourth chair that concerned me greatly. A woman with hair like freshly spilled blood and skin like alabaster looked up at me from the chair. She was dressed in gilded plate armor that gleamed in the sunlight, and her flat, jade eyes watched my every movement.

"Hello," she said, and her voice was a tornado in a trailer park. She raised a chipped white teapot. "Would you care for some tea?"

"Is it poisoned?" I asked before I could stop myself and my words made her lips quirk into an almost smile.

"I should hope not." She flicked her gaze to the teapot as if doubting her own words. "I'm not inclined to think that it is, anyway."

"Then sure," I said, moving toward her as she poured some tea in the china cup in front of the empty seat. "What's going on, by the way?"

"I'm offering you some tea," she said before sipping from my cup and swishing the liquid around in her mouth. "Doesn't taste like poison. Bit hot though." She put my cup down and gestured at the empty seat. "Sit. I won't take much of your time, Builder."

"Okay," I said, sighing as I decided to go with it. This wouldn't be the weirdest thing that had happened to me after all. "So, what's going on?"

"Drink your tea first. Then we can talk. We have all the time we need." She smiled, revealing a set of perfect teeth that glinted like opals in the sunlight. "I made it especially for you."

"Fine," I said, hoping to speed this along so I could get back to my girls. Who knew what was happening to them? I sipped the tea and was amazed at the rich flavor. The milk she'd added seemed to blend into the drink perfectly and was highlighted by a purposeful amount of honey.

"Pastry?" the woman held a tray filled with flakey goodness. As I stared at it, I realized I was famished. I couldn't remember eating anything aside from the donut a few days ago. Had I really not eaten in all this time?

Not wanting to be rude, I took a pastry that looked sort of like a croissant with raspberry jam oozing out from the ends. It looked delicious, and as I took a bite, I realized that its flavor more than delivered on the promise of its looks.

"Do you need more tea, Builder?" the woman pointed to the teapot. "I could get you some more? Or some water, would you like some water?"

"No, thank you," I said shaking my head. "Now, who are you, what's this place, and what is this all about?"

"I am Princess Nadine, Right Hand to the Empress, Bringer of the Shadow, Lady of the Blood Court, and Destroyer of Wills." She smiled, causing her eyes to twinkle in delight. "And I have come to offer you something, Builder." Her tongue flicked out, licking her blood-red lips as she spoke. "But first, I would like to make sure you are comfortable. Things will be easier that way." She leaned across the table then. "So, is there anything else you would like?"

"I'm good," I said, gripping the hilt of Clarent so tightly, it hurt. I didn't have time for this. If I was here, my girls could be in trouble. "Say your piece, your highness."

"Nadine is fine." She smiled again before sitting back in her chair and drumming the delicate red-nailed fingers of her right hand on the scarred wooden table. "And your name is?"

"Arthur," I said, taking a deep breath and urging myself to calm down. This woman looked like she could rip me limb from limb, and while part of me wanted to either fight or flee, I owed it to my girls to find out what she wanted. If I did, maybe I could use it to my advantage. After all, she had an impressive list of titles. Those had to mean something.

"Well, Arthur, here's the thing. My Empress desires the land that you protect with that sword of yours." She snorted. "I'm not quite sure what she sees in Hell, but alas, it is not my place to question, only to do. She has grown tired with our current rate of acquisition, so now I have come to take control of the border armies." She licked her lips. "Do you understand?"

"I understand, but I'm not sure why you're telling me this, Nadine," I said, meeting her eyes. It was like trying to stare down a black hole, and I felt the chill of her gaze all the way in my soul.

"I want you to leave. Just go back home and forget all about Hell. If you do, every desire you wish for will be granted." Her lips quirked into a sly smile. "And I do mean every wish. You could return to your land a god among men. You could have women, power, fame. Anything you want would be yours. You just need to leave." She gestured to our left, and a blue door of shimmering energy appeared. "Just walk through that door."

"And if I refuse?" I said, turning my gaze back to Nadine. It was strange because her offer wasn't even remotely tempting. Back home I was nothing but here? Here I was someone, and what's more, I was doing work I liked and protecting people I cared about. I couldn't just abandon them. Not for anything.

"Then my armies will kill you and put your head on a pike. We will carry it before our armies as we march across all of Heaven and Hell and take them for our own." She smiled. "But the choice is yours."

"I'll stop you long before it gets that far." I stood then, nodding to her as I gripped Clarent. "'Sides, you wouldn't make that argument if you weren't worried about me stopping you." I took a deep breath. "Send me back, Nadine."

"And if I do not?" she stood then though she didn't make any aggressive move toward me. "Will you attack me, then?" she shook her head. "You cannot defeat me. Now or ever. Not in this life or the next." She held out four fingers. "Do you know what this is, Arthur?"

"Four fingers?" I said, narrowing my eyes at her.

I was fairly certain she'd beat me in a fight, but that didn't mean I'd go down without even swinging.

"I have killed four Builders myself," she said, and her grin widened to Cheshire cat proportions. "Hundreds more have fallen since the time of man begun. You are not special. No. You are just the next in a long line of failures." She took a step toward me, trailing her fingers along the table and gouging up the wood. "Go through the blue door, Arthur. Save yourself. I'll even let you keep that pretty sword."

"You're lying," I said, shaking my head, but something about her words made me think she wasn't. No. Her tone was too cold and dispassionate, her eyes too calculating. And what's more, there was knowledge in them, dark, horrible knowledge. Most of all though? Most of all there was truth in everything she did. It radiated off of her, and that was enough to make my knees shake.

"I am not." She shrugged. "Do not believe me then." She flicked her hand, and a shimmering red door appeared. "Go find your friends as they wander the Graveyard of Statues. Bring them back to your pitiful town. It matters so little as to be without consequence." She leaned in close to me, the movement so swift I didn't even see her move until she was practically on top of me.

The smell of her hit my nose, the mingling scents of blood and sex, and as I took an involuntary step backward, she seized my arm. Warmth radiated through my flesh, washing over me like warm bathwater.

I took a deep breath, trying to ignore her scent. "Do you really think I'll abandon my friends just because you threaten me?"

"You'd be surprised how many have," she whispered, her words hot on my lips as she spoke. "Many have. Many have not." Her lips brushed against mine. "And neither choice has mattered one bit, Arthur. Not one bit." Her tongue flicked out then and tasted my lips. "But I always welcome the chance to be surprised."

She vanished so completely and suddenly that it took me a second to realize she was gone. I blinked, staring at my surroundings for a second before they began to melt like an army man in the sun.

"Make your choice, Arthur." Her words were a whisper on the wind as the two doors blazed in front of me. As I stared at them, I knew I could leave and go back to my life. I also knew Nadine would make good on her promise. I could ask for anything, and it would be mine.

I also knew that back home I was nothing, and I wanted to be something. And I had to earn that with blood, sweat, and tears. Not cowardice.

"You already knew what it would be," I said as the wildflowers melted into puddles of brightly colored wax and bloody rain began to pour from the sky, drenching me to the bones in the span of a second.

I waited a moment longer for a response, but when there was none, I stepped through the red door. If I said it hurt less than before, would you believe me?

25

Sheila was already talking to me as I appeared in the Graveyard of Statues that Nadine had spoken of, and I immediately knew why it was called that. It looked every bit like a weed-choked graveyard, only instead of markers, statues of warriors felled in gruesome ways littered the ground in ever expanding circles. They extended outward from an immense statue in the center, a woman who looked remarkably like sin itself.

She was clothed in scarlet chainmail that looked more like a macabre wedding dress than anything. She raised a bloody trident overhead while a severed head dangled from her other outstretched fist. Through all this, her face was serene like the goddess of death herself, just coming to bring about what was always inevitable.

"What do you want to do, boss?" Sheila repeated, and this time she glanced over her shoulder at me, her face expectant.

It was weird because I'd been with Nadine just a moment ago. Had they not noticed?

"Wait, you're not going to ask where I was?" I said, gripping Clarent a little tighter. Blue light trailed across the edge like a dying glow stick, but it was more than enough to beat back some of the shadows closest to us.

"What do you mean?" she replied, confusion spilling across her features. "We just stepped through the void and ended up here, wherever here is anyway."

I took a deep breath and was about to tell her where I'd been when I decided it wasn't worth wasting time on now. We could talk about it when we weren't in this godforsaken place. "Never mind." I pointed toward the statue in the center. "Who is that?"

"I have no idea," Sheila said, shaking her head at me. The other mumbled similar responses.

"Great," I said, taking a deep breath. I had a

pretty good idea who it was supposed to be. I was willing to bet it was the Empress herself. As that thought rattled around in my brain, I knew it to be true.

"All these people look like our warriors," Crystal said, taking a step toward the closest statue. It had so much detail that if it hadn't all been the same monochromatic gray stone, I'd have thought it was real. The woman in question had a sword and shield raised like she was bracing herself for a blow that never came. Her face was locked in stalwart determination. She looked brave, fearless.

"Could this be?" Sally said, moving beside Crystal and laying a hand on the statue.

As she did, the wind howled through the graveyard, kicking up blackened earth and rustling the dead brush. I shivered as the wind prickled my skin, but not from the chill of it. No, there was something about it that unnerved me. It spoke of death and the void. Of nothingness. Of what would be after the end of all things and what must have been before creation was spoken into being.

"Could it be what?" I asked, moving toward her.

"The Graveyard of Statues?" Sally swallowed as

she turned her eyes to me. "I'd heard about it, but not thought it real."

"I think you're right," I said, nodding to her, "but why does that matter?"

"It is said that those who enter the Graveyard of Statues never return. That they are cast into stone and forced to wait for eternity in suffering silence." Sally turned her eyes to me. "If that is where we are, we must flee. Quickly."

"How?" I said, turning in a slow circle. "I don't see a way back." I pointed past them toward where we come which was just miles and miles of statues spread out in ever extending arcs.

"Well, we'd better find one," Sheila said, tightening her grip on her spear. "I'd just assumed we'd be able to cross back through the border, but clearly…"

"Clearly, we shouldn't have assumed," I finished, nodding at the big guard. "Still, we didn't come here just to run away. We came here to kill us some beholders." I nodded to her. "Let's head toward the statue of the Empress. Maybe we can get a lay of the land then."

"Wait, why did you call her the Empress?" Sally said as we began to move forward, one slow step at a time. The guards surrounding me had their weapons ready in tense hands, and I knew the moment something happened, they'd be ready. I just hoped it wouldn't be poisoned darts to the face.

"No reason," I said, dismissing her question as we moved past a trio of statues that were standing back to back to back in a triangular formation like they were waiting to attack an unseen foe. In fact, that's how all the warriors were. None were cowering or afraid. No. All of them looked like they were ready for a battle that would never come. What's more, all of their equipment looked like it had been exceptional.

Even made from stone, it looked like it was more than a match for the best stuff Sam could make based on what I'd seen of her Skill Tree. No. Nearly everyone here was decked out in top tier stuff, and if I believed what Sally said, it hadn't mattered. These warriors had stepped into this void and been turned to stone.

A shiver went through me. What if I'd just led all my people to a horrible end?

No.

I shook off that thought. If it was true, Nadine would have never made me the offer. She may have said it hadn't mattered in the past, and maybe it hadn't, but the important point was that she'd made the offer. If she'd made the offer, it meant I could do something to stop all this, maybe even reverse the tides of war. It sounded like a longshot as we passed the statues, but at the same time, I knew it had to be true. Otherwise, I'd just be dead.

Which was also weird in and of itself. Why wasn't I dead? Why hadn't Nadine just killed me? She'd clearly been powerful, and I was just a guy with a cool sword. It was definitely something to figure out but not right now. No. I needed to focus on this place.

"I'm starting to think something turned all these warriors to stone," I said, looking around once more. "Only I don't see anything. Do you guys?"

"Hmm…" Crystal said, reaching into one of her pouches and pulling out a pair of lime-green sunglasses. She slipped them out before settling them on her face and looked around. "Fuck."

"What?" I asked, right before she flung her hand out, throwing a handful of caltrops across the ground to our left.

"Run! Now!" she cried, shoving me forward and to the right. As she did, the caltrops exploded into scintillating shards as the vines ripped up, ensnaring a once invisible beholder and dragging it to the earth. As it screamed and fought against the trap, Crystal shoved me behind Sheila. "Keep him safe."

Sheila nodded as Agatha burst forward, her wings beating the air to give her more height and speed. She landed atop the creature in one lithe movement and jammed her two swords into its flesh. It screamed in protest as the effects of Blinding Blade rippled out of the guard, causing everyone else to speed up.

Crystal unloaded her guns into the thing's screaming maw, the bullets punching into the tender bits inside its gullet. It roared, sending blasts of flame and ice crashing into the statues around us. Instead of blowing the statues to smithereens, the magic seemed to slough off of them.

"Crystal, are there more coming?" I asked as Sally whipped her hand out, hasting Agatha as the guard continued to pound away at the beholder, causing it to focus on trying to throw her off like a bucking bronco. With the caltrops holding it in place, it couldn't get all the force it needed to upend Agatha.

"Yes, but none are that close." She pointed into the distance. "There's three more that way and five more way down to our left."

"That's a lot," I said, swallowing hard as I

turned my gaze to Sally. "You think your bombs will work?"

"Who's to say?" the healer said as she dug one out. It was a small contraption and had been made from bits of leftover Dark Blood woven into a Demon Horn. "But I'd rather find out before we're faced with five monsters.

"Everyone fan out. Crystal, your job is to make the beholders visible before they sneak up on us, okay?" I nodded to Sally. "Do your thing. Agatha, get off it before you get blown up."

"On it," she said, giving the beholder one last slash that severed its flaming eye before leaping to the ground beside me.

Her feet had barely touched the ground when the beholder roared, tearing free of Crystal's trap and flailing around. Dark ichor sprayed from the wounds Agatha had dealt, but I knew that while it looked hurt, beholders could take an incredible amount of punishment.

Sally stepped out then, one hand cocked backward, and as the monster caught sight of her, it roared. She flung the glowing horn directly into its open maw. The creature sputtered, tentacles lashing out right before the bomb exploded. Bits of black ichor flew in every direction as the back of the monster blew apart.

Its lifeless corpse collapsed to the ground and more green Experience numbers appeared over the heads of my party members. A quick glance at their Stat sheets confirmed it. Everyone had gained almost five hundred Experience from that one kill.

"Get the Dark Blood," I said, gesturing to the glowing mass hidden within the corpse of the creature. "Then let's rush the other three. Let's do the same thing. Caltrops and then dark grenades. With any luck, we can take them out quickly enough to not die."

"Assuming that's all that's here," Crystal said as she took a few steps forward and pulled the hunk of Dark Blood from the corpse of the creature. She shoved it into her satchel and began to make her way toward the three beholders in the distance. It made me glad they were in the opposite direction of the five she'd marked earlier. Fighting eight at once didn't seem fun, even if we had a plan.

This time the beholders didn't stand a chance. Crystal easily froze them in their tracks with her caltrops, and as they roared and struggled, she, Agatha, and Primrose, one of the newer guards we'd gotten, planted the explosives. Two minutes later we were covered in muck and showered with Experience.

"How many more do we have?" I asked, glancing at Sally. "Because we've been here all of five minutes, used four bombs," - I pointed to the spot where Crystal had thrown down caltrops, ostensibly to catch the other five -"and there's five more coming."

"We have nine left now. So, after that group, we'll have four." Sally shot me a concerned smile. "I didn't realize we'd be fighting so many."

"It's okay," I said, shaking my head as the caltrops exploded, grabbing the beholders out of invisibility and anchoring them to the ground. As they flailed and spat, we repeated the procedure with both Sally and Sheila joining in. Ten seconds later we were pocketing five more of the massive Dark Bloods. A good haul.

"Now we just need to get out of here," Sheila said, turning to look at me. "Preferably before something worse shows up."

"I agree," I said, turning to Crystal. "You see any way out of this place?"

"No," she said, turning in a slow arc. She stopped and stared at the statue of the Empress. It was only a few yards away, and our last encounter had brought us pretty close to it. Even from here, I could feel the dark, angry malevolence flowing out of the statue like it was a living, breathing thing.

"What is it?" Sally asked, laying a hand on Crystal's shoulder. Only as the girl opened her mouth to reply, hideous laughter exploded from the horizon as the sky rent itself asunder. Bloody rain began to fall, turning the ground beneath our feet to scarlet mud as Nadine stepped forth from the rent in space and time.

"There is no escape, Arthur. I told you that before." She smiled at me as scores of lizardmen stepped through the rift followed by half a dozen beholders. "There is only the cold kiss of death." Her grin widened. "Don't say I didn't warn you."

She had, and even though her words filled me with fear for me and mine, I shoved it down. There was no way I was going to let her kill all my people. I just needed to figure out a way to stop her. Fast.

"Princess Nadine?" Sheila said, awe filling her voice as the woman stood beside the statue of the Empress with an entire legion of monsters at her heel. "What are you doing?"

"You know who she is?" I asked, turning to look at Sheila. Only instead of responding, the big guard dropped into a bow... as did all my other people.

"Of course." Nadine shook her head, causing her crimson locks to flutter. Lightning crackled overhead. "I used to be the ruler of Hell." She waved her hand at the monstrous horde behind her. "Then I traded up."

26

"Go!" Nadine cried, flinging her hand out toward us. "Drive them before you so the Builder may hear the lamentation of his women!"

The horde surged forward at her command, coming down the hill like a wave of death and destruction. My guards, bless their hearts, readied themselves for the onslaught, wrapping themselves around Sally and me in a whole shoulder-to-shoulder thing that reminded me of the Spartans in 300. Only, since half of our girls didn't have shields, that made me think we were in a losing proposition, even if a swarm of beholders wasn't coming down the mountain toward us.

"What do you want us to do, Arthur?" Sally asked, one hand whipping out to haste Crystal. As the glow of the spell wrapped around the girl, she unloaded her pistols into the coming lizardmen. Two fell, brains blown out in sprays of ichor. As their bodies tumbled to the ground to be trampled by their friends, she pulled out her rapier.

It was the last stand, and we all knew it.

"Just give me a second," I said, frantically looking through their Skill trees for anything that could help us. My eyes fell across buffs and suchlike, but unfortunately, there wasn't anything vaguely like a portal to get the fuck out of dodge, and even if there was, they probably couldn't have afforded it.

Only... Nadine had somehow conjured a portal before, and what's more, she'd manipulated space and time. How was that possible?

I wasn't sure, but I ran out of time to think about it because the lizardmen slammed into us then. They swarmed around the wall of guards, attacking with fervor, but my girls, thanks to Sally's hastes, were able to fend them off. For now, anyway.

Once those beholders got here, we were fucked. Even if we managed to blow up four, there would still be two left, and that would be two too many.

Sprays of ichor and screams of defeat filled the air as my guards pushed the line of lizardmen backward. My eyes flitted past them toward the portal.

As I stared at it, I realized there was an icon above it. I opened it to reveal an unhelpful message.

Gateway Nexus: Graveyard of Statues.

Next to it was a little symbol, letting me know there was more information to be had. I quickly opened it to reveal the Tooltip.

A Gateway Nexus has been activated and can now be used to transport the user to their desired location, provided their desired location has its own Nexus. If their desired location does not have one, the user will be placed at the closest Nexus.

"That's it!" I cried, pointing to the portal beside Nadine. The princess bitch was busy watching her forces whittle us down bit by bit. "If we can get to the portal, we can get out of here. It's why she came to stop us from reaching it."

"Then we'll just have to get to it," Agatha said, her blades whipping out at blinding speed to fell two lizardmen. As their corpses fell to the ground, more took their place, and I realized we might actually win. The lizardmen really weren't going to be a problem because my people were strong enough to fend them off. Really it was the beholders. We had to stop them.

"Sally, I need you to get those bombs ready. As soon as those beholders come into view, I want you to blow them away. I know we won't have enough, so we'll have to kite the remaining two."

Sally nodded to me as I spoke. "Okay." She took a deep breath and readied two of our bombs. "I'll make it work." Her wings unfurled like she was going to leap into the air, only before she could, I reached out and stopped her.

"I'm an idiot," I said, shaking my head. "New plan." I turned to the group. "We make a run for the portal. Don't look back, just get to it and think about Lustnor as hard as you can. As long as you do, everything will be okay."

"What about you?" Sally asked, glancing at me. "You can't fly."

"I was hoping you'd carry me," I said, giving her a hopeful smile.

"Oh." she fidgeted for a second. "Okay."

She reached out, wrapping her arms around me and pressing her body against mine before leaping into the air. Her huge wings beat the air, and I immediately realized she was struggling to hold me aloft. She definitely wasn't strong enough for this. Damn.

"Break formation and get up here," I said as the beholders lumbering forward unleashed blasts of fire and ice at us. Sally managed to weave around them, but barely. Not that it mattered because a second later my girls were in the air.

"Let me have him. I'm both stronger and faster than you," Agatha said, ripping me from Sally's grip and throwing me over her shoulder like I weighed less than nothing.

"Go to the portal!" I cried as we surged forward en masse, doing our best to weave by the blasts of beholder fire.

The portal loomed ahead, and for a second I almost thought we'd reach it. Then Nadine unfurled her own wings. Massive wings at least ten feet in width caught the air. Scarlet scales glistened along them, catching what little light there was and flinging it to the ground like drops of blood.

Energy wrapped around her body as she leaped into the air, one hand outstretched. The lightning heeded her call, arcing from the clouds and into her hand. She grabbed hold of it like she was Zeus and flung it straight at us. Our formation broke as the girls flapped toward the portal with everything they had.

"You won't escape," Nadine snarled, bursting forward with so much speed she seemed to blur. Her fist crashed into Agatha's chin, snapping the girl's head backward. The guard's eyes went glassy, and her wings seemed to sort of collapse mid-flight. Before I knew it, we were falling. We slammed into the ground just shy of the portal as Sally and Crystal disappeared through it, even though it looked like they'd been trying to avoid doing so.

Pain exploded through me, making my vision go hazy as the lizardmen turned on their heel and charged back toward us. Even though the pain, I knew we could make it to the portal before them. The rest of the guards came rushing forward, but I knew they would reach us after the horde was upon us.

"Go!" I cried, grabbing Agatha's arm and trying desperately to lift her onto my shoulders. Damn, she was too heavy. I couldn't do it.

"Come on, Builder. Don't you want to play with me?" Nadine asked as she landed on the ground beside me and flung out one hand, stopping her army from moving to finish the job. She nodded to me, a sly smile on her lips. "I will give you this one chance to send your people home."

"What's the catch, Nadine?" I asked, gripping Clarent. Blue energy rippled across the blade, but I had no illusions. She was too fast and strong for me to fight. Whatever she was offering, I had to take it.

If I didn't, Agatha would never make the portal. The others might but not Agatha.

"The catch? Hmm," she touched her chin with one hand. Eyes glinting with mischief. "Why that's simple, Builder. You have to stay with me." She licked her lips. "I assure you that I can be quite fun. You won't get to experience that side of me, of course, but I assure you, I am. I just feel like you should know that." She cocked a wry grin at me. "Now choose. Tick tock."

That choice was a non-choice. I couldn't let my people sacrifice themselves in a battle we couldn't win. I could, however, sacrifice myself to save them.

"Leave," I said, looking at my guards. They were all shaking their heads at me.

"We can't! You're the Builder. You're more important than us!" Sheila said, taking a step forward, her muscles tensing like she was going to hurl her spear at Nadine.

"No. I'm just a man, and you're my responsibility. I led you here, and I'll make sure you get out of here. Now go. Take the blood back and carry out my plan. It's the *only* way to save everyone!" I cried, and as I spoke, power rumbled through my words, and Clarent flared in my hand. "Go! Please!"

The remaining guards nodded, sprinting toward

the portal. Sheila didn't move, standing there unmoving as they all disappeared one by one. Her eyes flicked from Agatha's unconscious body to me and back again. This time those eyes had something different in them as they settled on me.

"Sheila, you need to leave," I said, gesturing toward the portal.

"He's right. My patience will not extend much longer," Nadine added, flicking her nails casually at the guard. "Go."

"I'm going," Sheila said, pointing at Agatha. "I just need to take her too."

"Oh, very well," Nadine said, sighing loudly as Sheila jogged toward us.

As the burly guard reached out to take Agatha from me, she grabbed my arm and sprang backward. Her wings beat the air, moving us closer to the portal at breakneck speed.

"No!" I cried, and as I turned my gaze back to Nadine, I realized she wasn't coming toward us. Agatha had grabbed hold of the demoness, and not only that, she was glowing like a radioactive explosive. Sparks danced across her skin, and her eyes were white voids of power as she wrapped herself around Nadine.

"Good luck," she whispered as she exploded.

"Cute," Nadine said as heat, sound, and light swept out of Agatha, burying her in the center of a solar flare.

Energy leaped after us as we hit the portal, and I knew that if we'd been even a hair slower, we'd have been flash fried. Only it was a small consolation as I was torn limb from limb by the Gateway Nexus because I knew one thing. Agatha had just sacrificed herself for me.

27

"Agatha!" The cry was still on my lips as Sheila and I reappeared on the other side of the Gateway Nexus. We crashed to the ground on the forested edge of the Royal Centre. The rest of the girls were there, looking battered and bruised but not broken, not dead.

I shoved my way free of Sheila and turned toward the Gateway Nexus as it vanished into the ether, leaving no trace it had ever been there at all.

"Where's Agatha?" Sally asked, voice small and distant as her eyes flitted from me to Sheila.

"She triggered her core to give us the time to escape." Sheila took a deep breath.

Agatha had sacrificed herself to save me. Only, I knew I wasn't worthy. I was just some guy who had been playing hero, and what's more, my incompetence had caused one of my girls to die. No, not just die. Sacrifice herself for me.

"She shouldn't have," I said, wiping my eyes with the back of one hand. Clarent was still glowing in my hand, practically mocking me for not being able to stop Nadine. The sad thing was that I knew deep down she had let us get away. Despite Agatha's sacrifice, I'd watched Nadine not even bat an eye as the explosion engulfed her. That bitch was still alive, and for all I knew, she hadn't even been hurt.

The idea pissed me off. Part of me knew I shouldn't be here, that I should give up before more people got hurt but more of me wanted revenge. Nadine had taken someone from me and for that, she'd pay.

My hands clenched around Clarent's hilt as the memory of losing not just Agatha but my parents washed over me. It filled me to the brim with anger and sadness. Only this time was different. Unlike with my parents, I had someone I could fight. Someone I could make pay. I had Nadine, and I had the Empress.

"She was doing her duty," Sheila said, putting a comforting hand on my shoulder. "It probably doesn't mean much, but if our places had been reversed, I'd have made the same decision as her." Sheila met my eyes. They were filled with pain and rage, but also understanding I'd never seen before. "You are the Builder of Legend. You are the *most important* person I know." She smiled at me. "And I know you'll make her sacrifice worth it. I know you'll make Nadine pay and pay and pay."

"I will." I nodded because if there was one thing I was damned sure going to do, it was make Nadine pay. "I promise."

"Good," Sheila said, before looking around. "Now let's get to Lustnor. We have ravagers to kill." She offered me her hand. "I'd be honored if you'd let me carry you back."

"Okay," I said, taking a deep breath while making a promise to myself. I would avenge Agatha. Her sacrifice would not be in vain. It. Would. Not.

Sheila nodded and swept me up in her arms before leaping into the sky. The others followed suit, swarming around me to keep me in the center. As we flew, I found myself watching the Gateway Nexus and wondering why Nadine hadn't followed us. Was it because she couldn't? Or was she just toying with us? I wasn't sure, but either way, I was going to be prepared for it.

"So, tell me about Nadine," I said as the scenery below us flashed by us so quickly, I knew we'd make the entire trip in a matter of hours instead of a full day. That was good. We needed all the time we could get.

"Nadine was once the ruler of Hell. A few millennia ago, she led an army into the Darkness to try to drive it back." Sheila's eyes flicked to me, and she let out a slow breath. "The Builder went with her. None of them returned. We thought Nadine dead when the Darkness began to devour our land with increased fervor."

"Now we know the truth." I gritted my teeth. They'd lost, and what's more, that Builder had lost. I wasn't sure how or why but I knew one thing. I would not go back into the Darkness unprepared. No. Next time I went, it would be to win.

"I suppose so, but there's the truth, and then there's the truth." Sheila squeezed me a bit. "Nadine was one of the strongest of our kind. If she'd wanted us all dead, we would be dead. I did not know her to be a fool then, and I suspect she isn't now. No. She's definitely up to something, and I'd give my left tit to know what it is."

"We'll figure it out and stop it," I said, my eyes flicking back to the Nexus Gateway. "Still, one thing bugs me. Why couldn't she come through the gateway? You guys make it seem like this is the first time she's been seen in a few thousand years."

"I don't know." Sheila shook her head. "I've never even seen something like that before. The gateway, I mean."

"You've never seen one before?" I asked, considering the thought. It didn't make sense because the Tooltip I'd seen made me think they were probably all over. If we could figure out a way to access them, we'd be able to fast travel across Hell and maybe into the Darkness itself.

"No," Sheila shook her head, "but I'm not that old, barely five thousand. There was more magic in Nadine's time. More technology. More, well, oomph." She gestured back at Royal Centre. "That place may seem nice, but it's nothing like the ancient cities we've lost to the Darkness."

"Hmm…" I said, resolving to take a closer look at Sam's Skill trees when we got back. I remembered seeing an Engineering Tree and a few others that were too expensive. So expensive, in fact, that not only had the costs been astronomical, but I had to unlock other trees just to be able to unlock that one. Still, it might be worth checking out. Then again, if it wasn't technology, maybe it was magic?

I turned to look at Sally as she fluttered next to Crystal. The two of them were whispering to each other in hushed tones. "Sally, do you think the Nexus Gateway is magic, tech, or some combination?"

She looked over at me and shrugged. "I have no idea. I remember reading about them, but it's ancient, from a time when technology and magic were so far advanced compared to what we have now that they'd be indistinguishable to me." She gave me a brittle smile. "But I can try researching it."

"No, it's fine," I said, giving her Skill trees a quick glance through, but even though I spent the remainder of the journey looking, I didn't find anything in any of her magic trees even slightly related to Nexus Gateways.

28

When we landed, I was surprised to see the mill had been nearly constructed, and what's more, there was a giant statue in the center of town. It stood about fifteen feet tall and at least as wide. It was still roughly hewn, but the general shape of a massive dragon tearing itself from the earth was there.

A menu appeared above it, and a quick glance let me know that even in its unfinished state, it doubled the Health and Mana of all the people who called this town home. It made me wonder just how powerful it would be when Annabeth was done. Either way, I was already proud of her.

Those weren't the only changes, though because we had a bunch more Stained. The forested area that had once surrounded the town had been cleared back several meters, leaving a clear path around the walls. How had so much happened in the time we'd been gone? It had been a few hours at best.

"That's a lot of construction," I said as we landed inside the town.

"Finally," Gwen exclaimed, rushing toward me. She threw her arms around me, pulling me against her body as she hugged me with nearly bone-crushing force. "When you didn't come back after nearly a day, we got worried." She bit her lip and looked away from me then.

"Nearly a day?" I said, totally confused. "How is that possible? It took a couple hours to get back from the Royal Centre, but there's no way we were inside the Darkness for more than an hour or two tops." I looked to the others, and they nodded.

As Gwen's gaze swept across them, a strange look filled her features. "Where's Agatha?"

"She didn't make it," I said, swallowing hard as I tried to ignore the guilt welling up inside me. She had been my responsibility, and because of my arrogance, had died protecting me during a battle we should never have fought. "She died a noble death. It's not much, but it's something, I suppose." I sighed.

"I'd known her for a long time," Gwen said, swallowing hard. "They always tell you not to get attached, that people die, but, well, you never quite listen, huh?"

"I don't want to lose anyone else," I said, gritting my teeth as I turned to the others. "If we've lost that much time, we need to hurry. Sally, can you get with Sam and work on refining those bloods? We won't have long before the ravagers show up and then after that, I want to figure out a way to stomp a mud hole in Nadine."

"On it," Sally said, nodding furiously as she took off toward Sam's shop.

Crystal shot me a strange look and shrugged. "I guess I'll go find out what's going on with the lumberjacks."

As she left to go busy herself, the guards did as well, heading to the gates, probably to tell them what happened to Agatha. The pain of her loss hurt me bitterly, but I couldn't let that drag me down. No. I had to use it as fuel to save us all. We had ravagers to face and Nadine to bring to justice. I couldn't do either of those things by moping.

"What happened to Agatha?" Gwen said when we were alone. She put one delicate hand on my arm. "And what's this about Nadine?"

"When we ventured into the Darkness, we came across Princess Nadine. Sheila says it's the same Nadine who disappeared thousands of years ago." I waved off the train of thought. "Anyway, she blindsided us with a massive army. Agatha sacrificed herself so we could escape. She detonated somehow." I shook my head. "It's all my fault. If we hadn't ventured inside the Darkness, she'd still be here."

Gwen nodded and wiped her eyes with the back of one hand. "Agatha is a big girl. She made the choice she thought was right." She looked at me. "Did you get what we need to defeat the ravagers?"

"Yes, so it wasn't a total loss. More than enough actually. We have nine of them. We only needed four." I shrugged. "So at least one thing is coming up Millhouse."

"I don't follow," Gwen said, still looking at me. "What's a Millhouse?"

"It's a character from the Simpsons. Look, never mind." I took a deep breath. I needed to go check Sam's Skill trees for information about the Nexus Gateways, but I had a question to ask Gwen. Especially since she hadn't even flinched when I'd mentioned Princess Nadine. "I need to ask you something."

"Okay." She nodded to me and took my hand in hers. She was so warm, so safe feeling, that I immediately felt myself relax. "What do you want to ask me?"

"How did you find me?" I asked, meeting her eyes. They widened a bit before she looked away.

"What do you mean? I told you that the sword summoned me?" She gestured at where Clarent sat in the sheath at my waist. "Your blood activated the weapon and—"

"Yeah, I got that part, Gwen." I shook my head and pulled my hand from hers. Then I stared at the sky, trying to orient my thoughts. "It's just Nadine said she's killed four Builders. That there have been lots of Builders. So, if that's true, that means you wouldn't have been surprised to find I was the Builder. Only you were and that doesn't make any sense."

"Oh." She moved next to me. "I guess it's time to come clean." She gave me a look that reminded me of a kid getting caught with his hand in the cookie jar.

"That would be nice, yes." I met her eyes, and even though I knew I should be pissed at her for not telling me the whole truth, I wasn't sure it mattered.

Agatha was still dead, and me finding out now wouldn't change that.

Gwen blinked her long lashes a few times. "There have been many Builders over the years, yes." She nodded. "And even more potentials. What I meant to say is that few who have the potential to become the Builder ever actually do since it requires that sword." She gestured toward Clarent. "Most of them never find it, and conversely, normal humans can find Clarent. It's been coveted for ages. Sure, it will call to the Builder, call to its rightful wielder, but that doesn't mean they'll actually come into contact."

"So, I was just one of the potentials?" I asked, remembering when I'd first seen the sword. It'd been the most beautiful weapon I'd ever laid eyes on, and I'd known I needed to have it. Hadn't Merle told me that no one else had even looked at it?

"You were the only potential." She smiled at me. "There's only ever one at a time. If you died, there might be another or there might not." She took a deep breath. "There hasn't been one in over a thousand years."

"So, how did you find me?" I raised an eyebrow at her. "What you are saying makes it seem even less likely that you showed up just to give me a wish."

"I was already in your world searching for the blade. Like the Builder, it had been lost, though for only a few centuries." She touched her chest. "I belong to the Sacred Order. We are charged with protecting the blade. Do you want to know how I found you? I didn't. I found the sword. I felt its power." She shook her head. "I didn't know who you were then. I thought you were just some guy who accidentally spilled blood on the weapon. I figured I could give you a wish, take your soul and the blade, and head back. Only, that's not what happened." She grabbed my arm then. "You turned out to be the Builder. After almost a millennium, you showed back up." She swallowed hard. "You don't know what that means."

"I have a pretty good idea." Anger flared inside me. "It means I can manipulate the forces of Hell to fight against the Darkness. I also get why you didn't tell me the whole story, but still, you probably should have."

"I'm sorry, Arthur," Gwen said, leaning her head on my shoulder. "I didn't mean for this to happen. Trust me. I didn't actually expect to find you."

"So, why are you protecting the sword?" I asked, trying to wrap my mind around it. If I fell in battle, there might not be another Builder for a thousand years. No wonder Agatha had sacrificed herself to save me.

"Why do you think?" Gwen frowned. "We can't have the agents of the Darkness get a hold of it. If they did, they might destroy the blade or worse, corrupt it. For while Clarent has the power to uplift, it could also destroy. They cannot get their hands on that power."

"Then we won't let them get Clarent," I said, nodding because that made sense. Even if the Darkness could use the sword to bring about destruction, just having it might be enough to keep the next potential from turning into the Builder. It almost made the sword more valuable than me.

"Anything else you want to know?" Gwen asked, squeezing my arm once more. "Because if there isn't, I have some things I want to show you." She gestured toward the town. "The supplies Buffy requisitioned came in, and what's more, we've received some more Stained. They know about the ravagers, but they think you can protect them."

"Well, I don't want to prove them wrong." I nodded to her. "Are the preparations made?"

"Yes." She nodded. "Sam has most of the bugs worked out because she used the Dark Blood we got from the first beholder. Once Sally refines the others, we'll be good to go. Assuming, of course, your plan doesn't get us all eaten."

"Good," I said as she pulled me toward where the mill was under construction. Even from here, I could see several women working under the tutelage of Maribelle. The girl was a damned slave driver. "Oh, one more thing, Gwen."

"What's that?" the succubus said, stopping to look at me as she brushed her hair behind her ear.

"You didn't bat an eye when we talked about Nadine. The others seemed surprised, so why is that?" I asked, watching her closely.

She shrugged. "Everyone in the order knows Nadine is alive because we can still feel her through the sacred bond we share. She was one of us after all. We didn't know where she was or what she was doing, but we assumed she'd been corrupted. It was the only thing that made sense. You just gave me confirmation."

"That's the other thing. If there's a whole order, where are they?" I gestured at the town. "We could use the help."

"They are forbidden to come now that I have

found you. If I am corrupted, they will seek to kill me, but otherwise, they will stay away." She took a deep breath. "I alone from the order am responsible. In the past, we tried having more of the order around when a Builder was found, but it just led to more casualties. There are so few of us now that we can't risk it."

"Even though it might mean the end?" I asked as she finger-combed her hair again and shifted from foot to foot.

"That's the thing, Arthur." She pointed at Clarent. "As long as one of us finds you, we can always rebuild."

29

The ground rumbled again, letting me know the ravagers were getting closer. It had started an hour ago, and with each passing minute, the tremors seemed to grow. I wasn't sure when they'd arrive, but we were as ready as we were going to be since Sam had finished building the helmets, and we were pretty much betting the farm on them working. Our walls had been fortified, even though it'd cost us nearly every penny we had. Now they were nearly twenty feet tall.

We had even managed to make a few watch towers so we could attack over the sides if necessary. While I was fairly sure none of it would matter versus the giant ravagers, I wasn't sure what else would be coming along with them. They could be alone or with lizardmen, but it almost didn't matter. We'd need these defenses in the event we got sieged.

The only thing that worried me was the battlefront. Judging by the way the tremors were hitting the town, the ravagers weren't going to hit us at one of the gates. No, they'd hit us along the left wall, which was a problem because we wouldn't be able to deploy ground troops. Sure, my girls could fly, but I still didn't like it.

"Arthur, you have a minute?" Sam asked, coming toward me. She was covered in soot, and her clothing stuck to her body with sweat. Her hair was matted against her face, and as she wiped her eyes with the back of one hand, she succeeded only in smearing more grime around her face.

"Probably. If I just stay here watching everyone scurry around to prepare, I'll go insane," I replied, moving toward me. "What's up?"

"I want to show you something." She stopped and spun on her heel. She gestured for me to follow. "Come on."

"Am I going to·like this something?" I asked, jogging to catch up with her.

"I damned well hope so. If not, I wasted the last twelve hours or so." She shot me a look. "So, you had better tell me you like it even if it's a lie." Her pink eyes met mine, and there was a small tremor of uncertainty in them.

"I'm sure I'll like it," I said, shrugging. "I was more trying to make a joke. Guess it didn't work very well."

"Oh," she said, letting out a slow breath. "Okay then." She bit her lip nervously as we approached the entrance to her shop. "There's just one thing I need you to do first."

"What's that?" I asked as she fidgeted with her fingers before holding one hand out palm up.

"I need you to give me Clarent and wait outside." She let out a slow breath. "I know you probably don't want to, but it will only be for a few minutes, okay?"

"Um… I'm not sure I'm comfortable with that," I said, and she dropped her eyes to the floor.

"Please. I promise it'll be okay." Her hand shook a little. "Trust me. You always ask us to trust you, but this time, well, you need to trust me." She smiled at me then and reached out to brush the hair from my face. "Trust me, Arthur."

I took a deep breath and searched her face for any sign of duplicity, but finding none, I relented. Reaching to the sheath at my belt, I pulled out Clarent. The rusted blade glowed in my hand as I held it out to her. "How long do you need? I'm worthless without the weapon."

"Not true," she said, taking it from me. As she did, the orb above her head vanished. It was weird because I'd gotten so used to seeing the menus and whatnot everywhere that it was suddenly like finding myself blind. "The most important thing about you is in here." She touched my chest with one stubby finger. Then her face flushed and she took a step backward. Then another. "I'll, um, just be a second, okay?"

"Okay," I said as she disappeared inside the shop with the most valuable thing I owned. Without that sword, I was nothing. Still, while I didn't know why, I felt like I could trust her. Not just that. I had confidence in everyone around me. And what was a leader who couldn't rely on his people?

Another rumble shook the ground beneath my feet. As I turned my gaze toward the direction of it, I saw Sally approaching with Crystal in tow. They both had crossbows slung over their backs like many of the other guards. It was another thing Buffy and Elizabeth had managed to acquire. Only these bows had special arrow heads made of explosive Dark Blood. All the better to take out beholders with.

"Hey, Arthur." Sally waved to me. "I found

something about the Nexus Gateways you might be interested in."

"How?" I said, moving toward her. That's when I realized she had a book tucked up under one arm.

"I was looking back through one of my old alchemy books." She held it up to me and showed me a page written in a language I couldn't read. "I found this."

"I can't read that," I replied, gesturing at the book. "What's it say?"

"Oh." Sally stopped and glanced at the page. Her eyes flicked over the words a couple of times. "This is the section where it talks about Etheric Flame." She tapped a symbol I couldn't read because it was in that strange demonic language I'd seen in the Royal Centre.

"I don't know what Etheric Flame is," I said, smiling at her. "Can you pretend I'm dumb when you explain? It shouldn't be that hard."

"Oh, right. Of course." Sally shook her head. "Etheric Flame is a resource we get from dragons. It's incredibly rare." She pointed at a particularly strange squiggle on the page. "It says here that Etheric Flame is the primary ingredient for creating a Nexus Gateway. Of course, it doesn't say anything about actually crafting the gateway, but it's a start."

She shut the book and looked at me triumphantly. "Now that we know it exists, we can just get the recipe from the guild."

"Assuming they even have it." I rubbed my face with one hand. "And that might be difficult since you're blacklisted. Then there's the whole slaying the dragon thing."

"Where's your sense of adventure?" Crystal asked, speaking up suddenly. She rubbed her hands together. "Sure, the guild may not want us to have it but that doesn't mean we can't borrow it for an undetermined amount of time."

"You mean steal it," I said, looking at her.

She smiled. "I'll make you a deal, okay? You get the Etheric Flame, and I'll find a way to get those old hags to give us the recipe." She smacked her hands together. "I'd love for a chance to teach 'em a thing or two after blacklisting Sally anyway."

"Fair enough," I said, nodding to her. "At some point between dealing with Nadine and the ravagers, we'll go find us a dragon to slay and steal the recipe for Nexus Gateways."

"See, I told you he'd go for it," Sally said, smiling at Crystal.

"No, you didn't. I told you," Crystal replied as I turned back away from them. I had no place in that conversation, and I knew it. The important thing was that we had a plan. A bad plan, sure, but a plan nonetheless.

I could hear Sam still hammering away in her shop, and as I resolved to go check on her and Clarent, another rumble shook the ground so hard I fell on my ass. My eyes flicked to the horizon as a walking mountain of angry Darkness stepped forth from the trees.

Only that would imply the trees weren't like toothpicks before it. Which they were.

30

The ravagers themselves were still too far away for me to make out any distinct features, and judging by their slow, plodding pace, I knew we had a few minutes before they actually got here.

"Get to the battle stations!" I cried, scrambling to my feet and sprinting toward the wall. As I moved, Sally and Crystal each grabbed me under one arm and hoisted me up into the air. Their wings beat at the air as they dropped me off on one of the watch towers.

That's when I saw the horde coming. Lizardmen rushed forward out of the brush, tearing across the space where we'd cleared the trees. They'd be on the walls in seconds. While they weren't low enough for the creatures to easily climb, the top sections of the walls were made of little more than reinforced wood. Given enough effort, their claws would tear through it.

We just had to keep them from doing so.

"Don't deploy the ground forces yet," I said, turning toward Crystal. "Get the archers ready. Let's hope the practice we gave everyone works to our advantage."

Crystal nodded to me before leaping from the tower. Sally stood next to me, watching the horde advance while the archer next to me readied her bow, waiting for Crystal's command. A moment later, a bolt of fire lanced through the sky. It was followed by a wave of arrows as the archers assembled in each of the six guard towers unleashed their arrows.

The arrows cut into the lizardmen, slamming through their darkened flesh and spilling ichor across the battlefield. Dozens fell but it didn't seem to matter because there were so many of them, they simply trampled over their fallen comrades in their haste to reach us.

"Ready the firewall!" I snapped, turning to try to find Gwen. "Wait, where's Gwen?"

"I haven't seen her," Sally replied as the lizardmen hit the wall.

The sound of them slamming into the stone reverberated in my ears. The barrier overhead shimmered to life as the lizardmen tried to clamber up our defensive wall. As their claws gouged up into the wood, creating scalable footholds, I cursed.

"Never mind! Use the oil." I looked at Polly who was standing next to me. "Signal it!"

"Affirmative," she said, switching to a different arrow and firing it into the air. The blue sliver of metal arced upward before exploding like a bottle rocket that lit the sky. All at once, the team of girls on the ground grabbed hold of the two massive ropes lying at their feet. They pulled with everything they had, causing the barrels suspended above the walls to tip, spilling viscous oil down onto the lizardmen.

As it flowed over the walls, pushing them to the ground in a wave of inky darkness, I saw a fresh wave of arrows fly from the guard towers. Unlike the others, these were ablaze. The second they struck the coming horde, the oil burst into flame. The snap, crackle, and pop of the fire below swept outward on the back of the oil, turning the battlefield into a hellish landscape of flame and death.

The lizardmen kept coming through, running through the flames until they'd buried the fire beneath their bulk like sacrifice meant nothing to them.

"Damn. How many are there?" I wondered aloud as the first of the lizardmen reached out walls again. Once more we triggered the barrels, flushing them backward with burning death. No matter how many died, it didn't seem to matter to the oncoming hordes. We'd been fighting for all of two minutes and had already exhausted most of our oil. Worse, from the look of the tree line, more were still coming.

This time, as the wave of flame washed them away, beholders lumbered onto the battlefield. There were so many that it seemed like the entire tree line had come alive. No wonder towns had fallen. Hell, this force might be able to siege Royal Centre. Then again, that was probably the idea, Nadine had insinuated as much when we had our teatime chat, and as much as I hated those assholes for being self-serving douchebags, I knew that if we didn't stop this force here, many would die.

That couldn't happen. One way or another, this army had to fall.

"Sally, find Gwen now," I said, turning to the healer even though she had been supposed to stay next to me. "We have to be ready for her to lead the charge against the ravagers."

"On it," Sally said, leaping from the guard tower and disappearing into town. I watched her go for a second before looking at Polly.

"Polly, signal for the ground forces to be deployed." I pointed to the beholders. "The second they come into range, signal them as priority targets."

"Your wish is my command," the guard replied, grabbing another arrow from her pouch and firing it into the air in one smooth motion.

Like before it exploded, but this time, it threw off green sparks. As the sky lit up like an emerald dream, a war cry resounded from just inside the gates.

Sheila and her cohort took to the air as the lizardmen came in for a third wave. They slammed down along the length of the wall in a tight shield wall formation, and I was glad I'd been able to upgrade the guards once again because a second later they were fighting the horde.

They threw the lizardmen backward as the guards who had learned Blinding Blade activated the Ability. While the lizardmen crashed ceaselessly against my wall of guards, the archers focused on picking them off.

A blast of cold ripped through the air, turning the lizardmen in front of it into icy shards as the closest beholder made a beeline for the guards.

Without even needing to be told, Polly grabbed a red-tipped arrow. She lined up on the creature and fired. It smacked into the top of its head and exploded, spilling red flame down across its face and causing it to scream in agony. As its bellows reached my ears, another arrow caught it in the throat.

The creature staggered backward before exploding into a pile of goo as the bomb on the end went off.

The battle continued like that with the archers focused on picking off the beholders. One would shoot the marking arrow which would light the creature on fire and cause it to open its mouth, then the next archer would plug it with an explosive one. As the corpses of beholders began to litter the battlefield, I almost started to feel like we might actually win.

Then the sky above tore itself asunder, revealing a Nexus Gateway. Unlike the others, this one was the color of a day-old corpse.

"What's going on?" Polly whispered, bow ready to fire at the portal.

"I don't know," I said as the first of the ravagers broke through the tree line. Their huge, hulking bodies seemed to absorb all the light, so they were nothing but fifty story masses of inky blackness. Their every appendage seemed to be some amalgamation of teeth and tentacles. Huge black gills pulsed on the sides of their massive, bulbous heads.

As the ravagers fixed their eyes upon the town, Nadine stepped through the Nexus Gateway.

31

"Did you really think it'd be that easy?" she asked, her voice a honey-sweet song on the wind, only this wind carried with it blood and death. She smiled down at me from the skies, her huge wings unfurled. As lightning crackled above and the rent she'd torn in reality pulsed, she flicked a hand at our town.

"You forget, Arthur. I have seen what the Builder can do." She licked her lips. "Many times. I don't know how you plan to defend this hovel, but I know that you can." Her wings flapped as she flicked a hand at the Nexus Gateway, banishing it from existence.

"You haven't seen anything," I snarled, reaching for my sword. Only I didn't have it. Sam still had it. Damn. To be fair, I didn't know what I'd do with the weapon if I had it, but at the same time, I was powerless without it.

"Oh?" she raised a shapely eyebrow at me. "Well, color me interested. Show me what you have." She gestured at the ravagers. "Bring him to me. The others you can eat."

The creatures roared, and the sound nearly blew out my eardrums. Their scent, like day old garbage and Spam, hit my nose and made my eyes water. Still, I couldn't focus on that, I had to focus on the plan.

"Fire the signal," I told Polly, turning to her. The poor girl was shaking like a leaf, and as she looked at me, I snapped my fingers in front of her face. "Polly. Do you hear me?"

"Y-yes," she said, swallowing hard as she grabbed her bow. As she reached for an arrow, Nadine flapped her massive wings, lifting into the air.

"That won't hurt me," Nadine said as Polly fired the arrow up into the sky. It exploded into a golden crackle that leaped across the sky.

"It's not meant for you, bitch," I snapped, glaring at her as the sky lit up.

"You know, you keep calling me names. I'm not sure I approve," she said as Sheila's guards sprang into the air as one, scuttling back through the barrier as quickly as they could. "And that barrier won't help you."

Nadine extended her hand. Scarlet light began to ripple across her skin, and the sky shrieked in pain. Darkness blotted out the signal arrow Polly had shot. The ravagers moved forward, their relentless steps chewing up the battlefield.

A crackling orb of pulsing crimson energy erupted from her hand. Tendrils of power flickered along its edges before slamming into the barrier and exploding into sparks. A scream like the whole of the world had been torn to pieces filled my ears, driving me to my knees as the symbols on the barrier went absolutely nuclear. They glowed so brightly, I could feel the heat of them baking the sweat from my body.

Horrific guttural laughter filled my ears as the barrier shattered into a billion scintillating shards of ethereal light. As they rained down around me, the sky itself opened into a swirling tornado-like vortex. Lightning crashed, and thunder boomed, and blood once again began to rain from the sky, and through it all, the only thing I could focus on was Nadine's stupid laughing face.

Not the ravagers even though they were getting

closer. Not Sheila and her girls as they scrambled to get the backups because Gwen and Sally hadn't returned. Not even Polly who was screaming something at me I couldn't hear, couldn't understand.

No. I only saw Nadine and Agatha, and Agatha's death. She'd died so I could escape, so I could save this town, and I wouldn't let that sacrifice be in vain. Besides, I knew my girls could stop the ravagers. Or, at least, I had faith in them. Nadine on the other hand?

That bitch was mine.

I just needed my sword.

"Whoops, I think I broke it," Nadine pouted, her eyes meeting mine. "Sorry." Her teeth flashed. "I'm so clumsy."

Then the Right Hand to the Empress, the Bringer of the Shadow, the Lady of the Blood Court, the Destroyer of Wills came for me. She was so quick that I could have sworn the afterimage of her still floating halfway across the battlefield was still there as she appeared in front of me.

She was huge and imposing in a way that made her seem larger than she actually was. Power rippled off of her, burning the wooden floor beneath her feet as she met my eyes. Polly, bless her heart, attacked.

"No, you're not on the A-team. You don't get to play," Nadine said, snapping her fingers. Polly exploded into a fountain of gore that splattered across Nadine's flesh, the walls, and me. As bits of Polly dribbled down my face, and my vision went red from rage, Nadine grabbed me by the throat.

She hoisted me into the air like I was weightless and marched me to the back of the tower.

"You know what is always so unfortunate about the Builder?" she asked, leaning in close so her breath was hot on my neck. "He can never fly. Pity."

She released me, and I fell.

Sam caught me. Her huge pink wings twisted as we slammed into the ground. She cried out in pain as her wing shattered, the bones bursting through the thin membrane-like flesh.

"Well, that's no fun. He was supposed to pop when he hit the ground," Nadine mused from high above.

"Sam, are you okay?" I asked, trying to turn toward me, but before I could, she shoved Clarent into my hand.

"Take this," she hissed through clenched teeth. Her face had gone white from pain as I touched the weapon.

Only it looked different, felt different.

My eyes grew wide as I realized Clarent was no longer a rusted hunk of metal anymore. The steel gleamed, and the fire was brighter than ever before. Energy spilled from the pommel as the symbols blazed with sapphire flame.

"What'd you do?" I asked as Sheila's team engaged the first of the ravagers.

"I used some of the Dark Blood to enhance it. All that work with the Dark Blood gave me an idea." Sam smiled at me despite the pain. Then she touched my chest. As she did a spark of power flittered across my chest before wrapping around the sword.

It glowed with light, and as I stumbled backward away from her, energy crawled across my body. Power unlike anything I'd ever felt before filled me as Nadine jumped down from the guard tower.

"Interesting," she said, gaze flicking from me to Sam and back again. "I haven't seen that in almost…" She trailed off, her head cocked toward the sky for a moment. "No matter." Her eyes settled back on me as the energy coursing through me solidified into a set of sapphire armor.

Only it was more than that because, in addition

to feeling like a bad ass, I could see things differently. I saw the world through the eyes of the Builder, saw all the Skills of my people laid out before me, saw an endless array of tooltips, and I knew them all.

What's more, I saw Nadine for what she really was.

Someone I'd destroy.

32

Nadine grabbed me by the breastplate and flung me across the ground. I hit hard, and pain shot through me. My head went fuzzy and the tooltips and menus I'd seen before vanished into the ether. She stood there between Sam and me.

"Poor Builder," she said, holding one hand out in front of herself. Fire danced between her scarlet nails as she strode toward me like a bored goddess. "You came, you built, you died." She hurled the fireball at me as Sam crashed into Nadine, tackling her to the ground.

The fireball went astray, hitting the ground beside me, scorching the earth and throwing molten glass into the air. Sam had saved me, but at what cost?

I sucked in a breath as I scrambled to my feet. I wasn't a fighter, wasn't much of anything, but a few days ago I'd been less than that, and now? Now, I was the fucking Builder, and she wasn't hurting anyone else.

In the background, I saw Sheila and the others attacking the ravagers. Tentacles lashed through the air, trying to down the girls as they peppered it with arrows, and I knew I just needed to buy them time. I could do that.

Nadine flung Sam away, sending the girl sprawling across the dirt several yards away. As Sam tumbled like a broken mannequin, I lunged at Nadine with Clarent. The blade blazed in my hand, cutting through the air beside the dark princess as she lithely stepped by my awkward stab and slammed her palm into my chest.

The armor shattered into fragments of blue light as I flopped backward onto the ground. Pain exploded through me, and the taste of blood filled my mouth.

"You can't stop me," she said putting her foot on my chest and pressing down. I felt my ribs give, shattering as she continued to press onto my chest. "No one can."

Something exploded against the side of her

head, knocking her off of me, but I hurt too much to do anything but lay there. My chest was on fire, and as I tried to draw breath, I realized I couldn't. The urge to cough filled me, but I couldn't do that either.

I struggled frantically, trying to breathe as I clawed at my throat for air that wouldn't come. Soft light wrapped around me then. As it did, I felt the twisted wreckage of my chest pull itself back together. I felt my cells knitting themselves whole, felt the fragments being pulled from my flesh as wounds closed.

Crystal took another step forward and fired her crossbow at Nadine. The explosive bolt took her on the side, blowing her across the ground but not doing any real damage. As the girl dropped the empty weapon onto its sling and pulled her revolvers, I realized that Sally had healed me.

I got to my feet in time to see her flying toward me, a chant on her lips. Blue light wrapped around me and as it did, time seemed to slow. I could see the dust motes kicked up from the battle in the air, hear every minute movement around me, even bear witness to the individual particles of the smoke coming off Crystal's revolvers as she unloaded into Nadine.

The princess fell onto her back, a thin line of blood trailing from a split lip, but for all that damage she seemed unharmed.

"Which of you is going to die?" Nadine asked as Crystal frantically reloaded. The dark princess got to her feet and nodded at my two girls. "Only one. That way the other can live with the torment of loss." Nadine's smile went absolutely vicious. "Maybe I'll flip a coin?"

I shut my eyes, for a second, drawing in focus. That couldn't happen, but I also couldn't fight her. That much was obvious.

Crystal and Sally's Skill sheets opened in my mind's eye, and as I stared at them, I saw a new icon next to their names.

As I examined it, the icon opened a message box.

All Skill costs cut by 25%.

Was that from what Sam had done to me? I wasn't sure, but either way, I was going to take advantage of it. I flipped open their Stat trees, frantic to find something I could buy that would save them, but there was a big problem. They had no way of doing anything that seemed like it'd slow Nadine.

"Nah, coins aren't fun. I know a better way,"

Nadine said, and then her hand was around my throat. My concentration broke, and their Stat sheets vanished as she hoisted me into the air. Her other hand glowed with light, and I saw to my horror that both Crystal and Sally were bleeding on the ground.

"You choose, Builder," Nadine said, pointing at the two girls. "If you don't, I'll just kill both."

"No," I whispered, my hand dropped to Clarent, to the symbols emblazoned upon its steel. I reached out to them, trying to find Gwen. Only I couldn't.

"Don't stall. Choose." Nadine's tongue flicked out, and she dragged it across my cheek. "It's so much more fun that way."

"Take me," Crystal said, reaching out to me with one hand. "Please…"

"No," Sally said, shaking her head. "Me, please."

"I won't pick," I said, meeting Nadine's eyes.

"Pity. Their anguish would have been so much more fun." She raised her hand to smite them as I focused on Clarent's blazing symbols.

"Come on, Gwen," I whispered.

"If you're hoping for the succubus to come, well, let's just say, she's got other problems," Nadine smiled at me knowingly before flicking out her hand. Fire tore through the space between us, forming a huge wall of living, seething flame.

And in that flame, I saw Gwen. Saw her bound to the statue of the Empress in the Graveyard of Statues. Saw the beholders and lizardmen surrounding her.

"How?" I said, turning my gaze to Nadine as the image faded.

"My dear, sweet summer child. You know nothing." She flung me to the ground in front of Crystal and Sally. "Now choose. I won't give you the chance again."

I got slowly to my feet, turning my back to the two girls as I met Nadine's eyes. Clarent blazed in my hand, begging me to try to save them, to do something.

"Okay," I said, taking a deep breath as I nodded once. "I'll choose."

"Perfect," Nadine said right before the giant fist of a ravager slammed down on top of her, smashing her into the ground.

For one blissful moment, the battlefield was silent. Sheila sat astride the ravager's huge neck, the mind-controlled saddle firmly in place on it. The huge Dark Blood we'd gotten from the beholders embedded in the steel. Energy crackled along the saddle as Sheila looked down at me.

"Thought you could use a hand," Sheila said, right before the arm of the creature blew off. As fragments of black ichor rained down around us and the ravager stumbled backward, gore streaming from its torn limb, Nadine slowly dropped her mangled hand.

"You'll pay for this," she hissed, and as she tried to get to her feet, the other ravager, this one being ridden by Annabeth of all people came forward to attack. Only before it could get to Nadine, the dark princess's bones snapped back into place.

Annabeth's creature hit Nadine then, sending her flying through the air to crash to the ground on the other side of the wall. I didn't see the fetid Nexus Gateway open, so much as I felt it.

"She's getting away!" Sheila called as the Nexus Gateway closed, leaving us standing there in an empty battlefield beaten, but somehow victorious.

33

"I'm torn between saying, 'I can't believe that worked' and 'she'll be back,'" I said as Crystal helped me to my feet. Sally was already moving toward Sam, one hand held out to heal the unconscious blacksmith. White light wrapped around Sam before fading into her body. As the girl started to recover, Sally shot me a tentative thumb's up, letting me know Sam would be okay. Good. I wasn't sure I could handle another loss. Not after both Agatha and Polly.

"Yeah." Crystal nodded and squeezed my hand as a realization hit me. Gwen was still in the Graveyard of Statues.

"Dammit," I cried, spinning away from Crystal and looking up at Sheila and Annabeth where they sat astride their huge ravagers. The creatures' flesh undulated in the light, and in the time it took me to walk the ten or so feet to them, the arm Nadine had blown off of the creature had already regenerated.

"What's wrong?" Crystal asked, catching me with ease thanks to her long legs.

"Didn't you see the images Nadine showed me in the flames?" I asked, turning to look at her.

"No. All I saw was fire." She swallowed. "You didn't choose." She put her head against mine. "Why?"

"I couldn't make a decision like that. You're all my responsibility, and we've already lost too many. 'Sides, I knew Nadine wouldn't stand a chance once Sheila got Big Bertha over here to help. I just needed to buy her the time." I pulled away from Crystal. "Only, now I'm not sure what to do. In the fire, I saw Gwen bound to the statue of the Empress. We have to help her, I'm just not sure how."

"We could take the two ravagers into the Graveyard of Statues and get her," Crystal said, gesturing at the two massive creatures. "I bet they eat beholders for breakfast."

"And how would we get back? Last time Nadine opened the Nexus Gateway. Without a way to do it, we're screwed." I shook my head. "We might rescue her, but we won't be able to get back."

"Well, we had a deal, right?" Crystal said, meeting my eyes. "You slay the dragon, I'll figure out how to get the recipe." Her eyes flicked to the two ravagers. "Something tells me, the dragon isn't going to be the hard part of that scenario. Just saying."

"Here's what I don't understand though." I shook my head, dismissing the idea. "Let's assume we have the time to do that and can slay a dragon. I didn't see any Skills related to the Nexus Gateways in her Skill Tree." I sighed. "Look, I know what you guys read in the book, but if it was there, I'd have found it."

"Maybe," Crystal said with a shrug, "but what it sounds like is you want to give up on Gwen already." Crystal shrugged again, this time with exaggerated emphasis. "I thought you cared about her."

"That's not fair," I said, and she grabbed my arms, forcing me to look at her.

"Life isn't fair. Now be the goddamned Builder, rally your troops, and kill a goddamned dragon." She touched her chest with her thumb. "I'm on the recipe. I *will* figure it out."

"Figure what out?" Sally asked, walking over to me with Sam. The blacksmith still looked beat to all hell, but she didn't look broken anymore.

"How to make Nexus Gateways," I said, gesturing at the darkened horizon, "because we need one to rescue Gwen."

"Okay," Sally said, nodding her affirmation. "I feel like I missed the important part of the conversation, but I'm in."

"Me too," Sam said, looking at me for a long time, "after I fix your armor." She pointed at the spot where it'd been blown open. As I looked down at it, the armor surrounding the rest of my body evaporated into bits of blue light that absorbed back into Clarent. "Or not."

"You had me at dragon," Sheila called down from astride her ravager. She smacked the creature lightly. "Bertha here wouldn't mind snacking on one."

"I guess that settles it then," I said, taking a deep breath. If we needed Etheric Flame, there was only one place to get it. "We're going on a dragon hunt."

"There's only one problem," Annabeth said, leaping off her ravager and landing lightly on the ground beside me. Her ravager, to its credit, didn't move a muscle. Instead, it stood there, waiting for her command.

"What's that?" I asked, looking at the sculptor. She was covered in sweat, black ichor, and bits of plaster.

"Tom Tom and Bertha are slow. They'll never make it across the entirety of Hell to Dragon's Reach. We won't be able to take them."

"Did you seriously name the ravager Tom Tom of all things?" I asked, raising an eyebrow at her.

"It was that or Weed." She smirked. "You know, tough and hard to kill?"

"I guess, Tom Tom works better." I was more than happy to leave the naming of the ravagers to the girls as I turned to the huge creatures. A smile crossed my lips as I looked them over. They had the same menu orb above their heads that the rest of my people did.

"Glad you agree," Annabeth said. "Now if you don't mind, I'd love to finish my sculpture." With that, she walked off, leaving me staring at the giant creatures.

"Okay, let's get to work. First thing's first. Let's get a hold of all the Dark Blood and set to refining." I looked back toward the other side of town where all the noncombatants had stayed. "Someone get

Buffy too, we need supplies and to offload some of these Dark Bloods. Crystal, Sally, can you two handle that? Maybe grab a few of the guards to help with the gathering?"

"Sure," they said in unison before looking at each other and blushing. Then they nodded to me.

"What about me, boss?" Sheila said, joining me on the ground as the Sally moved toward the battlefield to collect Dark Bloods while Crystal went to find Buffy.

"Round up all the people who fought. Give them some food and rest. I wanna talk to them after." I took a breath. "We need to do something for Polly."

Sheila looked up at the platform where Nadine had killed Polly. "I'll take care of it."

"Thanks," I said, and as she turned to go, I looked back at Sam.

"What about me?" she asked, watching me carefully. "Whatever you need me to do, I will." She bit her lip. "I'm not good at running things, but I'll try if I need to do that."

"No," I said, waving off the comment as I opened her Tech Tree. She had almost twenty-one thousand Experience. "I need you to start working on the Dark Blood weapons."

For whatever reason, the bonus I'd gotten from her repair was still effective, so I used it to upgrade the Dark Blood Tree she'd opened, as well as give her the Dark Weapons and Dark Armor Skills. That done, a quick glance through her Skills left me staring at a new tree that definitely hadn't been there before.

Legendary Smithery: Able to use Skills and Abilities to improve Clarent. Cannot be improved via Experience.

There were a bunch of Skills underneath the tree, but they were all blanked out except the first row, which had two of the three Abilities visible.

Legendary Armor
Skill: 1/10.

User can restore Clarent's Ability to summon magical armor. This armor will appear when the user uses Clarent to summon it. Once summoned, the armor will give the user increased Abilities.

Legendary Skill
Skill: 4/10.

User can increase Clarent's Ability to spend Experience on friendly targets. Doing so will decrease the cost to learn an Ability by 25%.

"Holy crap," I said, taking my eyes off the Skills and turning them to Sam. "You have a whole Skill Tree based on Clarent now. You can make it stronger, and what's more, you've barely unlocked any of it."

"So how do I make you even more powerful?" Sam asked as I held the glowing blade out to her. "I had to use nearly all the Dark Bloods we found before just to fix it."

"Well, that won't be a problem," I said as she took the sword from me, causing all the menus to disappear once more, "because we have a ton of those now. Work on the weapons and armor for our people. After that? See if you can upgrade Clarent some more."

"I'll do my best," she said, handing the sword to me. "You should keep it until I'm ready to work on it, okay? Just in case."

"Okay," I said, taking it back from her. Once again, all the menu orbs reappeared. "Good luck."

"Thanks," she said, waving at me, and then she leaned in and kissed me on the cheek. "And thanks for giving me a chance. It's been a long time since someone has."

"You're welcome," I said as she turned and hustled away. I watched her go for a moment before turning my gaze back to the ravagers. Taking a deep breath, I began looking through their Skill trees.

34

"I don't know what to do," I said, throwing my hands up. Buffy and Annabeth were sitting next to me at the table as we ate. To be honest, I was getting really tired of eating grilled demon dog, but we had no other source of food. Well, that wasn't entirely true. Annabeth had started making grass porridge in order to deal with all our people, but I was a man, not a rabbit dammit.

"Maybe if you just lay the problem out for us, we can think of an answer?" Maribelle offered in that hopeful voice that made me feel like my annoyance was unjustified.

"We already know the problem," I said, pushing my plate away and rubbing my face with my hand. "The problem is that we have no way to make the ravagers move fast enough to actually get them to where dragons are located. If we had Nexus Gateways, it wouldn't be a problem, but we can't get those without killing dragons."

I gestured at the wall in frustration. The ravagers were just outside, and surprisingly, didn't have any discernible Abilities. Pretty much the only thing I could alter about them were their base Stats of Strength, Agility, Special, Intelligence, and Charisma, which might have been helpful if they weren't already capped.

In short, they were Xboxes. Great if you wanted to use them for whatever they were designed to do, but not so much when it came to customization.

"Well, the answer seems simple then," Annabeth said as she looked up from her bowl of porridge. "We just go to the dragon cave without them. Kill us enough dragons to open the Gateways and then bring them through." She shrugged. "Might be hard, but we only need to kill one, right? After that it's easy." She scraped her spoon along the bowl, making sure to get every last drop before shoving it into her mouth.

"We can't kill a dragon," I said, shaking my head. "It's a dragon."

"Well, not with that attitude." Annabeth

pointed her spoon at me. "A dragon is just a monster. You're supposed to be the Builder. Rally your troops and go kill a dragon." She rolled her eyes at me. "Or are you scared?"

"I am scared," I affirmed, "scared more people will die. How can I ask them to go after a dragon? I saw that head back in the Royal Centre. It could swallow one of us whole."

"Firstly, you're fighting a war with the Darkness that Consumes All Things." Annabeth leveled her gaze onto me. "People will die. Your job is to make those decisions. No, not just that. Your job is to win the war, and so you have to understand wars have casualties." She dropped her spoon into her bowl. "Secondly, you didn't beat the ravagers by hitting them until they were dead, did you?"

"Well, no, I—"

She cut me off. "So be the Builder. Use that brain of yours to figure out a way to get what we need." She pointed at the wall where the ravagers stood. "Be smarter than all the people who want to punch us to death. It's the only way we'll win."

I wanted to reply to that, to tell her I'd been trying to think of a way. Only I hadn't been able to. We couldn't brain box a dragon without first having Etheric Flame to power the brain box. Otherwise, we could have beaten them the same way as the ravagers.

"You know, I think Annabeth is right. We have been going about this the wrong way," Buffy said, finally speaking. She'd been sitting at the far end of the table with a far-off look in her eye. As we turned to look at her, she grinned nearly ear from ear.

"I'm guessing you have an idea?" I asked, watching her carefully.

I still wasn't quite sure if I could trust the goblin. Sure, she and her sister had requisitioned what we needed, and thanks to all the Dark Blood we'd gotten from the battle, our mill, blacksmith, tailor, and alchemy shops were better than ever. Unfortunately, we hadn't been unable to do much else on account of needing to spend ever more money on supplies to keep people fed, and part of me wondered if the reason was that she'd been siphoning off funds. It just seemed crazy that all our money was already gone, but then again, we'd needed a lot of stuff.

"I do." She leaned back in her chair and stared at the ceiling even though I'd asked her not to do that because she might fall and get hurt. "Look, there are two ways to get Etheric Flame. You either get it from a dragon or…?"

"I'm not following," I said, shaking my head. "Or what?"

"Or you get some from someone who has it already." She rocked forward and slapped her hands on the table.

"I'm pretty sure anyone who has Etheric Flame isn't going to just give it to us," I said, waving off her idea. "That's a non-plan."

"Oh, I didn't say anything about giving." Buffy grinned. "I'm more suggesting we make them an offer they can't refuse."

"Oh, and what would that be?" I asked, sighing. "We don't even know who has Etheric Flame."

"That's not true. I know a place that has some." She pointed to the map that had been tacked to the far wall. "Blade's End has some. They're on the border of dragon country. They're probably swimming in the stuff." Buffy smiled at me, and as she did, I realized she was right. Maybe we could just trade for some Etheric Flame. "You've got a mountain of Dark Blood that's waiting to be processed, and a smith who can make Dark Blood infused armor and weapons. Pretty sure you can think of something they'd want."

"And if that doesn't work?" I asked.

"It will, but if it doesn't, well, we can always requisition it for an indeterminate time until it can be rightfully returned." Buffy shrugged. "Either way, they'll give us the flame. I'm sure of it."

"So, if they don't want to sell us some, you want to steal it?" I asked, not sure I was hearing her correctly.

"Steal is such an ugly word," Buffy said, getting to her feet and coming toward me. "But yes. If you want Gwen back, then yeah, we'll steal it." She shrugged. "Do you have a problem with that?"

"I suppose not," I said, wishing I didn't have to turn into a thief just to save the world. The people in Royal Centre should have been helping us, not making us have to rob them.

"Good," Buffy said, nodding.

I rubbed my face with my hands before turning to look at Annabeth. "What do you think?"

"I agree with the goblin. If you don't think we can kill a dragon, we need to get it from someone who can." She got to her feet. "Let me know when you set out for Blade's End. I want to come." With that, she exited the room, leaving me all alone with the goblin.

"Guess everyone's too busy to hang out with

me." I sighed, turning my gaze back to my uneaten lunch. I knew I should be doing something, but at the same time, I didn't know what to do. Everyone else was working to make the town better, and now it was humming along.

"You can get busy too," Buffy said, winking at me as she made her way to the door, "but not with me. I've got a list of goods to put together for our trip to Blade's End." She gave me a small wave before leaving me all alone.

"How long will it take to be ready?" I called after her, but if she heard me, she didn't bother to respond. I sighed, trying to think of what to do with myself when Maribelle walked in.

"Great. I was worried I wouldn't catch you in time. I really have something I need your help with." She beamed at me as she came over and unceremoniously flopped down in one of the chairs. "You have a minute?"

"Um… sure," I said, turning my gaze from the door to Maribelle as she laid plans across the table. As I stood up to take a closer look at the diagrams, they resolved themselves into menus I actually understood. "What's all this?"

"These are the plans for the town," she said gesturing at it with one hand. "I need to know what you want me to do next." She bit her lip. "It really can't wait."

"Um, okay," I replied, shrugging as I looked over the papers she'd spread out once more. "What do we have here…?"

"Now that we have the mill, we're producing enough lumber to build some more buildings." She pointed to the plans again. "If we had those buildings, we could get them set up with equipment and maybe lure some more craftsmen from the Royal Centre or train our own. Either way, these are the ones I'd suggest next, given our current materials."

"What about enhancing the walls and building more towers?" I asked, waving a hand at the plans. "Won't doing this take away from that?"

"Yes and no," Maribelle mused. "I've already earmarked most of the material for that so it should be okay, but shit happens so, you know. We can't necessarily predict what we'll need. Still, I think we should be able to make three new buildings without any impact to the wall. We might get a fourth building done if the wall and guard towers go perfectly." She rolled her eyes at me. "And yes, that includes the new gate on the south side where the demon dogs keep attacking."

"Well, fine then." I shrugged. "Let's look at the

buildings." I turned my eyes onto the ones she'd suggested, and like before, her notes resolved into Stat windows.

"Well, these are the two I think we should definitely build." She moved her hand to indicate the note closest to me.

Barracks
Durability: 1,000
Use: Allows for the training of Fighters of various types. Increases Experience gain by ten percent.
Cost: 100 Thatch, 1,000 Lumber, 500 Cloth, 100 Brick

Archery Range
Durability: 1,000
Use: Allows for the training of archers. Increases Experience gain by ten percent.
Cost: 500 Thatch, 1,000 Lumber, 100 Cloth, 100 Brick

"Okay, those make sense to me," I said, nodding to Maribelle. "I think we should do them, but can you give me a quick overview of what we already have so I can decide?"

"I thought you might be interested in that so I already prepared it." She beamed at me, and I had the sudden urge to give her a cookie.

"Awesome," I said as she handed me another list. This one had all the buildings we currently had.

Blacksmith
Use: Allows for the creation of weapons, armor, tools, and other metal based items.

Tailor
Use: Allows for the creation of clothing and cloth based items. Creates 4 Cloth for every 1 Fiber processed.

Alchemist's Lab
Use: Allows for the creation of alchemy based items.

Trading Post
Use: Used to facilitate trade within a town. Grants a 10% bonus to all transactions with other towns.

Lumber Mill
Use: Used to refine Lumber. Creates 4 Lumber for every 1 Wood processed.

Kitchen
Use: Used to increase edible food production by 25%.

Town Hall
Use: The seat of government within a town. Towns cannot exist without a town hall. Also doubles as a dormitory and a bathhouse.

"That's kind of a lot to have already," I said, looking over at Maribelle. "You built all that so quickly?"

"What can I say, I like my job." Maribelle

shrugged and looked away from me, clearly embarrassed. "So, do you want to build the barracks and the archery range?"

"Probably but let's go through the rest of the buildings first. If we say we'll build those, what's next?" I asked, looking back over the notes.

"Well, there's support type buildings and food production based buildings. Which do you want to look at first?" Maribelle asked, pointing at two different sets of plans.

"Let's go with support buildings first," I said, rubbing my chin. "I know we need food production, but at the same time, maybe we'll better in the long run if we build those."

"Okay, here they are," Maribelle said, sliding a set of plans in front of me. "If I had my choice, I'd recommend the masonry. Of course, we'd need to find a mason…" She shrugged.

Apothecary

Durability: 1,000

Use: Allows for the creation of poisons, potions, herbal remedies, and the like.

Cost: 500 Thatch, 1,000 Lumber, 100 Cloth, 100 Brick

Rune Works

Durability: 1,000

Use: Allows the creation of wards which can be used to imbue items with magic.

Cost: 1,000 Thatch, 1,000 Lumber, 500 Cloth, 100 Brick

<u>Masonry</u>

Durability: 1,000

Use: Refines Stone. Creates 4 Bricks for every 1 Stone processed.

Cost: 100 Thatch, 1,000 Lumber, 500 Cloth, 100 Brick

"I can see why you'd want the masonry," I said, nodding to her. "We would need a mason, but I think we definitely do that one too. Maybe we can recruit one?"

"I'll put it on the list," Maribelle replied, scribbling something on the notepad next to her. "Here are the production based buildings. Keep in mind that you already chose three, so if you want another, we may not get to it."

"I think we'll still have the same problem we'll have with the masonry," I said as I glanced down the list. "If we build farms, dairies, or any of these other structures, we still don't have the skilled labor to run it." I shook my head. "As much as I hate to say it, I say we wait on doing any other infrastructure building until later. I'd hate to run into a farmer and not be able to build him a farm because we built a dairy instead."

"Okay," Maribelle said, nodding. "I guess you don't want to see the academic buildings either then?"

"Not particularly," I said, getting to my feet. "I need to go find Buffy now so we can figure out a way to buy Etheric Flame." I rubbed my temples. Part of me couldn't believe I'd just said those words aloud because they seemed ridiculous. "Can you take care of everything else?"

"I'm on it. You can count on me." She gave me a salute as I walked out the door.

Evidently, it hadn't taken long to get ready because, by the time I'd finished with Maribelle, Buffy was sitting atop her buggy waiting for me. It was laden down with supplies, refined Dark Blood, and even a couple of the enhanced weapons and pieces of armor Sam had made.

"I'm starting to think you may have planned this before you talked to me because it hasn't been that long, has it?" I asked as I turned my eyes from Buffy to the rest of the assembled women. Annabeth was seated on the buggy, but she was too busy fiddling with something to pay me any mind.

Sheila, Sally, and Crystal were there too, all watching me carefully.

"Perhaps," Buffy said, giving me a rueful smile. "Look, I know you want to go after Gwen so we sorted it out. The others will stay and keep the town going. Elizabeth will handle the day to day. It will be fine." She smacked the buggy. "We'll be there in less than two days with this."

"What if Gwen doesn't have two days?" I said, turning my gaze to the buggy as Annabeth set a small sculpture of a rearing deer on the front of the buggy like a stone hood ornament.

"Everything will be fine. Trust me," Buffy said, offering me her hand. "Besides, it's not like we have a better plan." When I didn't respond, she continued, "Now saddle up. We're burning daylight."

35

Thanks to the speed boost provided by Annabeth's hood ornament sculpture, we arrived in Blade's End after only a day of travel. Better still, thanks to our incredible speed, we were able to outrun most of the monsters, so we'd only had to stop and fight a couple of times.

Even still, I was nearly a wreck by the time we got there. What is Gwen had been killed? What if Nadine had come back and sacked the town? More what ifs burbled in my mind, and I frantically tried to keep a lid on them. I needed to focus on getting enough Etheric Flame to make the Nexus Gateway. Then I'd march on that stupid Graveyard of Statues with my pet ravagers and lay waste to everything, Nadine included.

Assuming, of course, she was dumb enough to show her face when I came a-knocking. Something told me she would. After all, she needed to prove herself after her last defeat. She wouldn't come behind my back to do that. Not now anyway. At least I hoped she wouldn't.

As we came up the bumpy road, I stared at the huge walls of the town. They were made from redwoods thicker than the ones I'd seen in the sequoias back in California and stretched nearly as tall. As we zoomed up the asphalt path toward the massive gate hewn straight into the wall, the smell of smoke hit my nose, and I had the growing feeling that something was wrong.

"Shouldn't there be guards outside?" I asked, gesturing at the gate as I looked around. The entire landscape looked like it'd been burned. Just a few minutes ago we'd been surrounded by more lush vegetation. Granted it had been vegetation with leaves like blue flame but vegetation nonetheless. Now everything was scorched earth.

"There should be," Buffy said, pulling up to a stop. "At least there always has been before."

"Sheila, can you fly up and check it out? I have a bad feeling about this," I said as I unsheathed

Clarent. Just in case my feeling was correct, I called upon the blade's power. Once again sapphire armor snapped into place around me like I was a medieval Iron Man.

"On it, boss," Sheila said before leaping into the air with so much force, the buggy came off its two left wheels. Her massive wings propelled her upward as the wheels smashed back into the asphalt hard enough to knock me on my side.

"See anything?" I called, getting to my feet as Sheila reached for the spear and shield on her back.

"Yeah, and you ain't gonna like it none." She turned her eyes on me. "There's a whole mess of lizardmen and beholders fighting with the villagers inside the town. The other end of the wall looks shattered." She gestured toward the far end of town where I couldn't see. "Looks like someone marched a ravager straight in here. There's a dead one and a whole mess of dead dragons to boot. Must have been a heck of a brawl."

"Really?" I asked, and as she nodded, I cursed. "Damn."

"What do you mean 'damn?'" Buffy asked, grabbing my arm. "This is our chance. Go in there and get the Etheric Flames from the dead dragons."

"No," I said, shaking my head. "We have to help them." I turned to Crystal and Sally. The two girls were already unfurling their wings. "You got any explosive bolts or bombs?"

"A few," Sally said, showing me a small sack with half a dozen bombs.

"I've got about ten arrows," Crystal added. "Am I gathering you want us on beholder duty?"

"Yeah," I said. They both nodded at me before springing into the air, but neither made any effort to move into the town yet.

"What about me, boss?" Sheila asked.

"In a second," I said, gesturing for her to come to me. "I wanna see the battlefield first. Sally, Crystal, you're on me."

"Affirmative." Sheila dropped down and grabbed me up like a baby. A moment later, we were high above the battlefield, and it was as Sheila had described.

About twenty or so beholders were working their way through the wide streets of the town. The guards inside were doing their best to fight them but every time they seemed to gain an advantage, the lizardmen would attack.

"Okay, I've got a plan. Can you take me to whoever is supposed to be the leader down in that cluster?" I asked, gazing across the battlefield. There was so much smoke, I couldn't make out anyone individually, but maybe Sheila would know.

"I think so. Let's get in closer. I wanna circle overhead first." As she spoke, I turned to look at Annabeth and Buffy.

"We'll be back in a bit. Stay safe."

Sheila took off, flying straight through over the gates. Smoke stung my eyes, and the acrid taste of soot filled my mouth as I tried to breathe and wound up sputtering. Then we were through it, and Sheila set me down behind a blockade of women dressed in armor every color of the rainbow.

Crystal and Sally landed next to me as a woman a bit taller than the others and dressed in gleaming red and green armor turned her yellow cat eyes on me. Stray locks of snow white hair tufted from beneath her helmet as she looked us all over.

"Who are you?" she asked in an accent I could only classify as Scandinavian. "Surely not the reinforcements from the Royal Centre. There's not nearly enough of you." She gestured at me. "And *he* isn't even a demon."

"We're from Lustnor actually," I said, bowing my head to her. "I'm the Builder of Legend. These are three of my best warriors. Sheila, Crystal, and Sally. We saw the smoke and came to help."

As she opened her mouth, I pointed past the line of armored warriors toward a beholder a few hundred feet away. "Sally and Crystal have a way of taking down beholders pretty easily, and Sheila knows Defending Aegis."

"Oh?" she said, turning her attention to Sheila. "Is that true?"

"Yes," Sheila said, meeting the woman's eyes. "I do."

"Excellent." The woman nodded. "I am Diana. This is my town. If you offer me assistance, I will gladly take it."

"As I said, that's why we came," I said, nodding to the battlefield as the glinting tower shields of the armored warriors knocked back the lizardmen before advancing a few feet.

"Good," Diana said, looking me up and down before turning her attention to Sheila. "Use Defending Aegis to draw the lizardmen away. My dragon warriors will protect you." She looked to Sally and Crystal. "When the beholders are vulnerable, take them down."

The three women nodded, and as Sheila used her Defending Aegis Skill to draw the lizardmen away from the beholders they'd been protecting, Sally cast haste on her and Crystal.

Crystal, for her part, unslung her crossbow, and as she did, I realized the problem. We could only take the beholders down by shooting them in the mouth. Otherwise, the explosive wouldn't do enough damage. It was why we'd been hitting them with fire arrows first. Only we didn't have any.

"Do you have any archers?" I asked Diana as the lizardmen slammed into her dragon warriors, only to be thrown backward again.

"Yes." She pointed to the rooftops, and I looked up to see more women on the rooftops, shooting into the horde.

"They need to hit the beholder with fire so it opens its mouth. That'll let Crystal finish it off," I said.

"If that is what you need, I will make it so." She gave three sharp whistles before pointing to one girl in particular. "Crystal, that is Leilani. She will assist you. She is my best archer."

"Okay," Crystal said, reaching out and squeezing Sally's hand before taking the satchel of bombs from her. "I'll be back."

With that she was off, flying toward the rooftop.

As she did, beholders filled the sky with fire and ice, but she somehow weaved past them all.

"Good luck," Sally whispered as I opened her Skill window. Thanks to the recent battles and all the travel, she had a bunch of Experience to spare so I quickly used some of it to improve her healing and haste Abilities. Not enough to drain more than a few thousand Experience but enough to give her a haste effect aura similar to Blinding Blade.

"Can you trigger Greater Haste, Sally? I think we'll need it."

"With pleasure," she said, twirling one hand in the air. A giant ethereal clock exploded into being overhead, the second and minute hands spinning at ludicrous speed. Then the entire thing shattered, raining down bits of energy across the line of dragon warriors. As it touched them, their bodies began to move even faster.

"You have someone with Greater Haste, another with Defensive Aegis, and a way of taking down beholders?" Diana asked, raising an eyebrow as the closest beholder exploded into bits of goo.

As its corpse crashed to the ground, the newly hasted dragon warriors took advantage of their increased speed to run roughshod over the lizardmen. It didn't hurt that they were focused on getting to Sheila and couldn't really get to her without reaching past the dragon warriors and opening themselves up.

"I'm the Builder of Legend." I offered her my hand. "Pleased to make your acquaintance."

She took my hand as another beholder fell. "It's almost unfair." She shook her head. "Wish you were here when we fought the ravagers. We wouldn't have had to sacrifice so many dragons."

"About that. Do you train them?" I asked, gesturing to the glittering armor. "Cause that's all made of dragon scale…"

"No." She spat. "Dragons cannot be trained. Little better than mindless beasts. We lured them into the path of the ravagers, and once they saw each other, well, the rest was history. Those that survived were quick to leave to lick their wounds and divide the spoils of those that had fallen."

"Hmm," I mused as more of the beholders fell. "Would you like me to teach you how to make the Beholder Killing Arrows?"

"Yes, but from the look on your face, I suspect you want something." She looked me up and down. "I suppose I can do as you ask. For my people. But not until this battle has ended."

"I wouldn't have it any other way," I said,

nodding to her as I turned to watch more of the lizardmen die beneath the dragon warrior's might. It wouldn't be long at all before only beholders were left, and they'd go down quick enough without lizardmen to protect them.

36

"Thank you for your help. I'm not sure we'd have been able to hold out much longer without it," Diana said as we walked through the burned-out husk of the town. Because most of her non-combatants had fled behind the barricades at the other end of town, there were surprisingly few casualties.

"You're welcome," I replied, kneeling down beside a downed lizardman and picking up the Dark Blood glimmering within his corpse. "Anyway, as I was saying earlier, having these are key." I held it up so it caught the light.

"I sort of get what you're saying about the explosive arrows being powered by Dark Blood," Diana replied, taking the Dark Blood from me and examining it. "But we at Blade's End have two problems with doing as you say. The first problem is we don't have an alchemist skilled enough to turn this," she hefted the Dark Blood, "into an explosive arrow. Hell, we don't even have an alchemist at all."

"What's the second problem?" I asked, turning from her and purposely making my way toward the dead dragons. Their scales glimmered in the sun, throwing a kaleidoscope of colors across the ground. As I approached, the tinny smell of their blood hit my nose, and I had to work not to gag. Their corpses left a decidedly more familiar smell behind in death, and it shocked me in a way the corpses of the Darkness creatures hadn't.

"The second problem is that attacks like this are rare." She gestured at the ravager's corpse. "That thing stepped out of a portal a few miles away. We were lucky our scouts saw it in time to lure the dragons down, and even then, it almost wasn't fast enough." She waved off her train of thought. "My point is simply that even if we rounded up all the Dark Blood here and used it to make arrows, we simply would run out before long."

"Why do you want the arrows then if you don't get attacked by the Darkness very often?" I asked, shaking my head in confusion. "They're not really effective on the ravagers because of their healing Abilities."

"I like to be prepared." She gave me a pointed look. "Besides, it's not your business why I want the arrows, only that I do, no?"

"You make an excellent point," I said, nodding to her. "What if I agree to supply you with arrows?"

"And what would you want for that?" she asked, and she gave me that same look she had on the battlefield. "You still haven't said why you came here."

"I need Etheric Flame," I said, laying my cards on the table even though Buffy would have had my head. Still, if she had wanted to be here, she could have. Instead, she was busy talking to the local merchants about supplies and trade.

"Why?" Diana asked, and there was a lot more curiosity in her voice than I expected.

"Does it matter?" I asked, smirking at her. "Doesn't it only matter that I want the Etheric Flame?"

"Ha, ha," she intoned, running a hand through her snow white hair, causing it to fall across her shoulders in a wave. "I suppose you make an excellent point so I will add more information." She looked toward the corpses of the dragon. "Every dragon possesses a single Etheric Flame, which makes it rare in that a dragon has to be killed in order for one to be obtained." She gestured at the slain creatures. "Normally we do not have a ravager to do that for us, making it quite rare."

"I expected it to be quite rare so if you're trying to drive up the price, I'm not sure why you don't just tell me what you want and go from there," I said, putting my hands on my hips.

"It is not a question of price," she waved her hand dismissively. "Despite being quite rare, it is largely worthless. Few know how to work with it, and even then it is usually the odd piece of jewelry or decoration. Nothing of note." Her eyes sparkled. "So tell me why you would venture here and offer me a way to kill beholders in exchange for it."

"I can use it to reopen the portal you saw. They're called Nexus Gateways. Etheric Flame is one of the key ingredients for controlling them. Once we have it working, we'll be able to control where we go. It will make travel between here and other towns instant." I took a deep breath. "I suspect that soon your Etheric Flame will be quite valuable."

"Interesting," Diana said, rubbing her chin. "I will agree to a trade. Arrows for Etheric Flame. The merchants can work out the details." She put a hand on her hip. "But you have to give me control of my Nexus Gateway or the deal is off." She looked up at the mountains framing the small valley where Blade's End sat. "We're quite remote and getting people and supplies here is difficult. If you can eliminate that by getting your Gateways working, I will gladly help you." She held out a hand to me. "Deal?"

"Deal." I took her hand. Her grip was surprisingly strong and firm.

"Excellent." She pulled her hand away. "So, when will the Nexus Gateway be completed?"

"Soon, I hope. We need to get the rest of the recipe, and then figure out how to create it." I pointed at the dragons. "Getting the Etheric Flame is step one."

"What if the rest of the ingredients are impossible to obtain?" she asked, arching an eyebrow at me.

"Then I will have traded you a bunch of arrows for something worthless." I shrugged. "I'm the real loser here."

"I somehow doubt that," Diana replied, turning away and moving back toward the main part of the town. "I will instruct the butchers to collect the

Etheric Flame. I hope that you succeed, Builder." She licked her lips. "I would love to see more of you."

"Thanks," I said as we approached the merchants. "I hope we succeed too."

She gave me a strange look for a moment before shaking her head, causing her hair to whip around her face. "Anyway, I have no desire to sit and squabble over prices with them." She gestured toward the merchants. "This is where I'll take my leave."

With that, she left me to the merchants, and as I walked up, I wondered if I could somehow avoid it too. I honestly didn't care what we paid as long as we got what we needed. Everything else was just a distraction. Besides, I really needed to talk to Sally and Annabeth. I had an idea I wanted to try.

"You're in luck, Arthur," Buffy called, waving at me before I could escape. "I think we've hammered out a good baseline. There are some details to go over if you have a minute…"

"Sure," I said, moving toward her, and if she caught my reluctance, it didn't show.

"Great, pull up a chair," she said, patting the empty space between her and the other goblin.

An hour later, I got bored with the whole thing.

There was a lot of nuance to the negotiations I wasn't aware of, but at the same time, it was all details, and Buffy definitely didn't need me for that.

As I sat there listening to a discussion about transport costs, Diana showed back up with a burlap sack.

"What's that?" I asked as she placed it on the table in front of me.

"Those are the Etheric Flames we collected from the dragons felled by the ravager. I wish to give them to you as a way of saying thank you for your help." She pursed her lips, and as she was about to say more, her goblins poke up.

"Lady Diana, if you have a moment, I'd love to speak to you about the infractions clause in the contract." The goblin pointed to a spot the two goblins had been arguing about for at least an hour.

"I can't right now, but I'm sure you've got my best interest. I'll leave you to it." She turned and ran off so quickly, I almost expected to see one of those cartoon smoke outlines around her.

As I watched her go, I decided I was done too. I had some Etheric Flame now, and every second I didn't talk to Sally about it would be a wasted second.

I wasn't quite sure how many we'd need to

complete a Nexus Gateway, but I felt like we were getting closer to it, and that was good. We'd already waste too much time here, and who knew how little time Gwen had. I was determined to save her, but I couldn't do it half-cocked. If I went in without a plan, we'd be trapped in the Graveyard of Statues forever. That wouldn't help anyone.

The only thing that gave me hope was that I could still feel her through Clarent. Not enough to know where she was or anything, but I could feel her life force still beating. It was weak, but it wasn't gone. That was good. If it vanished, I wasn't sure what I'd do, but taking a ravager into that graveyard to fuck up the Empress's statue would be first on my "to do" list.

"If you two will excuse me, I need to take these to Sally," I said, getting up from my seat. As I moved to the door, I put a hand on Buffy's shoulder. "Give 'em hell."

"Wouldn't have it any other way," Buffy said, smiling up at me and batting her eyes before turning back to the contract. "Now then, the weight limit in subsection 3A is completely unacceptable."

I left them and made my way toward where Sally had set up a temporary shop. Diana had gathered up a bunch of arrows from the archers and had them brought to the fletcher's building on the far end of the town. As I approached, I saw both Sally and Crystal working to create arrows. Perfect.

"Hey, Crystal," I said, walking up to them.

"Hey, Arthur," Crystal said, setting the arrow she'd been inspecting back into the pile beside Sally. "What's up?"

"I distinctly recall us having a deal," I said, holding up the burlap sack containing our six Etheric Flames. "I got my part done. Now it's your turn, eh?"

"Yeah, that." She took a deep breath. "I was thinking about that."

"You seem like you don't want to rob the alchemy guild anymore," I replied, part amused and part annoyed. I'd sort of expected this, but at the same time, we needed the recipe.

"I don't have a problem stealing it," she said, waving a hand. "But what if they don't have it? If they did, wouldn't they have already completed the gateways? I overheard Buffy talking to the other merchant earlier. The Etheric Flame is fairly worthless, and even if it was incredibly valuable, the government never cared about things like cost, so that's hardly a constraint." She pointed at my sword. "That makes me think the Alchemy Guild doesn't have it, and even if they *do* have it, the recipe could be buried in a tome in the library. In short, I don't know what to steal unless you want me to nick the whole library." She grinned then. "I'm always up to try that if you'd like."

"Those are excellent points," I said, rubbing my chin as I moved to sit next to them. "That's why I want to try something."

"What's that?" Sally asked, looking up at me as I pulled one of the Etheric Flame from the bag. This one was bright green like the dragon it'd come from, and reminded me of a sea anemone, complete with fluttering tentacles.

"I was thinking about Sam. See, she had a new Skill Tree pop up recently. I didn't see it before, and it was unlocked by working on Clarent." I patted my sword with my free hand. "I would be able to see if the Nexus Gateway Skill existed if you had it, obviously, but maybe you don't because you've never used Etheric Flame before." I turned my eyes to her Skill Tree. "You don't even have a Skill Tree related to its use at all."

"So, what would you have me do?" Sally asked, her eyes flicking to Crystal as the girl sat back down beside us. "I don't have any idea what to do with that." She gestured at the Etheric Flame in my hand. The tentacles were beginning to wrap around my fingers.

"The same thing I'm going to ask Annabeth to do with the one I have for her," I said, handing her the glowing, tentacle-ridden mass. "Anything. Do anything with it. I know you have some general Skills related to objects. Hell, try refining it. I'm willing to bet that if there is a tree related to it, working with the material will unlock it."

"And what if it doesn't work and I waste the flame?" Sally said, pulling the mass into her lap and staring at it. "I don't even know where to begin. It might be destroyed."

"That's the great thing about it," I said, getting to my feet. "It's worthless so I'm willing to let you try a few times before we go and steal the entire alchemist's library." I winked at Crystal. "Though maybe we can do that later for fun."

"I suppose that makes sense," Sally said, her eyes not leaving the Etheric Flame. "I'll see if I can refine it like how I do the Dark Bloods." She took a breath. "Better pass me a couple more."

"Okay," I said, opening the bag and removing a sapphire Etheric Flame. After a moment of thought, I simply handed the whole bag to her.

"You can have all of them. Pretty sure Annabeth will only need one, anyway."

"Why do you want Annabeth to carve one up?" Crystal asked as Sally took the bag from me and studied its contents.

"The highly technical answer is that the sculpture she used to increase the speed of the buggy was made from Dark Blood. It wound up boosting the power of the sculpture, making me think material matters. While she didn't get a tree or anything, I think that's because her Skills work differently. I am curious as to what bonus a sculpture made from Etheric Flame will have." I shrugged. "Maybe nothing. Or maybe something."

37

It took another hour for Buffy to finish up negotiations, and in the end, we walked away with almost fifty Etheric Flame with promises of more to come when we delivered the next batch of arrows. All in all, it felt like a good trade, provided we could actually get the Nexus Gateways to work.

I was still a bit concerned about that as I helped load the buggy with the Etheric Flame. Annabeth was sitting atop the buggy, working on another sculpture. She'd opted to make one similar to the Dark Blood one she'd made in the hopes it might further increase the buggy's speed. I was all for it, but at the same time, the boxes weren't going to lift themselves.

Worse, since Buffy was still signing forms and

Sally and Crystal were working on the arrows, Sheila and I were left to do the loading.

"These are heavier than they look," I said, hoisting a crate of supplies onto the back of the buggy. It was filled with green dragon scale, and I was hoping that Sam might be able to make something cool with it.

"Yeah, that's why almost no one wears it as armor," Sheila huffed as she put a crate of blue dragon scale next to my box. "I'm just glad that's the last one." She wiped her brow with the back of one hand before pulling her canteen from her belt and taking a long swig. "Want some?" she offered it to me.

"Thanks," I said, taking it and tipping it back for a drink. As I gulped it down, I realized it wasn't water. The liquid burned my throat like fire, and as my eyes began to water, I struggled to swallow it down. The substance stabbed at my insides the whole way down, and by the time I'd finished and weakly offered the canteen back to her, the big guard was laughing at me.

"Never had fire water before?" she asked, smacking her lips together. "Goes down easier with every sip." She winked at me and took another swig before offering it to me. "Trust me."

"Are you trying to get me drunk? That's like straight alcohol." I took the canteen and because I felt the need to prove myself, took another sip. It still burned but less so this time. Glancing down at the bottle just to ensure there wasn't actual flame inside, I gave it a small shake. No fire roiled out.

"Me? Get you drunk?" She patted me on the shoulder before taking the canteen from me. She took another swig. "Trust me. If I wanted you drunk, you'd be drunk." She capped the canteen and put it back on her belt. "Why I have some stuff back at Lustnor that will knock you on your ass after a single drop." She grinned wryly at me. "And let me just say there's absolutely no way to keep your clothes on once you've had succubian tequila." She leaned on the buggy. "Got some of that too. Been saving it for a special occasion, if you know what I mean." She waggled her eyebrows at me, giving me a very clear indication of exactly what she meant and making some very interesting thoughts run through my mind.

"Done!" Annabeth cried before I could respond, and even though my face was bright red (from the alcohol, I swear), I turned toward her.

"Done?" I said like the picture of suaveness. In fact, I was feeling mighty good. I took a deep breath that tasted of honey and chives as Annabeth appeared over the edge, brandishing something that looked exactly like an octopus riding a chariot pulled by dragons.

"I call it 'An octopus riding a chariot pulled by dragons,'" she said, offering it to me. The sculpture throbbed with an inner flame, and sparks of sapphire danced along its edges. She'd somehow preserved eight of the Etheric Flame's tentacles, appropriating them into the octopus's own. It was quite simply the most amazing thing I'd ever seen. As I stared at it, a tool tip resolved next to it.

An Octopus Riding a Chariot Pulled by Dragons
Class: Sculpture
Material: Etheric Flame - Blue
Grade: A
Contains the essence of a fallen blue dragon.
Use: Increases speed of transport by 100%. Increases water resistance by 25%. Can be combined with other effects. (Additive)

"This is pretty amazing, Annabeth," I said, climbing onto the buggy and moving toward the deer statue she'd placed earlier. As I placed the new sculpture next to it, I took a second to really look at the old one.

The Rearing Deer

Class: Sculpture
Material: Dark Blood
Grade: A
Contains the essence of a fallen warrior of Darkness.

Use: Increases speed of transport by 50%. Can be combined with other effects. (Additive)

"I know," she said, settling down next to me and staring at the new sculpture. "It could stand to be a bit more lifelike, but I was trying to be fast so we could go." She pointed at a spot on the chest of the dragon. "Took too much off there. A dragon with a build like that wouldn't have the muscle to fly." She rubbed her chin. "I'd like to try again if you could spare some."

"Maybe but not right now," I said, glancing back toward the crate where the Etheric Flame was stored. "I think we'll be back to Lustnor soon enough, and while I in no way consider your sculptures a waste, I don't want to risk not having enough for the Nexus Gateway."

She nodded to me, and as she did, I noticed a strange halo around the menu orb above her head. As she said something I didn't quite catch because I was opening her Skill Tree, a new message appeared.

New Skill Tree Unlocked. Prestige Tree- Sculpting with Feeling.

I quickly opened the tree and read the descriptor.

Sculpting with Feeling: User has the Ability to work with obscure resources to sculpt creations of higher Ability and value than normal. This Skill will also give a 10% bonus to all sculptures created with normal materials.

Looking closer at the tree, I saw the first Ability, Sculpting with Feeling, had been unlocked as well as three sub-Abilities. Specialty: Dark Blood, Specialty: Demon Horn, and Specialty: Etheric Flame. Both were Rank one out of ten. The rest of the Skill Tree was blacked out so I couldn't see the actual Skills, only spots for them.

"Oh my God," I whispered, swallowing hard as I turned my eyes back to Annabeth. "It worked. It fucking worked." I pumped my fist in the air before pulling her into a hug.

"The sculpture?" she whispered, eyes wide with confusion. "My sculptures always work."

"No," I said, releasing her as I sprang to my feet. I needed to find Sally now. "My idea. You had a new Skill Tree unlock." I took a deep breath. "That means that maybe Sally did too."

"Maybe Sally did what?" Sally asked, coming around the corner with Buffy, Crystal, and Diana.

"Maybe you have a new tree," I said, gesturing at Annabeth like she was exhibit A. "She got one by working with the Etheric Flame." I nearly jumped off the buggy in my haste to check, but before I could, Sheila grabbed my arm, halting me.

"Maybe we get on the road first," she whispered into my ear, "before you give away all your secrets."

I turned to look at her and then nodded. She was right. We should get out of here and on the road. After all, I'd have the whole trip back to examine Sally's Skills, assuming she had new ones.

"Actually, maybe we need to get on the road. We still have a lot to do back home and I'm worried we've been away too long," I said, turning my gaze to Diana. "Thank you for everything, Lady Diana. It means more to me than you know."

"A leader's work never ends, eh? Until we meet again," she replied, nodding knowingly to me. "Next time I'm around the border, I'll stop by and visit." With that, she turned on her heel and began walking away, leaving me alone with my women.

As if they'd read the haste in my words, they all climbed on board the buggy. Before I could say aardvark pizza, we were halfway down the road.

The scenery blurred by as the buggy zoomed across the asphalt like a bat out of Hell. It'd taken us about a day last time, but I was willing to bet we'd be back in less than twelve hours. Crazy.

"It's so much faster," Buffy said, her hands in a white-knuckled grip on the steering rods. "I like it."

"It's all in the materials," Annabeth said, looking at her sculptures ruefully. "I just hope that I can one day be good enough not to make such a mockery of them."

"Lady, have you ever seen me sculpt? I tried to make a platypus once, and it just wound up looking like an exhausted duck." Sheila shook her head. "You're awesome, and the false modesty is annoying."

The two of them quibbled a bit with Buffy chiming in as I turned to look at Sally. She sat cross-legged in front of her alchemy bowl. A pair of Etheric Flame, one red and one green, sat inside the bowl, glimmering with inner fire in a way they hadn't when I'd left her last.

"Any luck?" I said, making sure I paid attention to her even though I just wanted to open her Skill trees and look.

"Some," she whispered, gesturing at the bowl. "These didn't take very well, and even the ones that did are pretty bad. I guess they're maybe ten percent better than before." She made an offhand gesture to the sack sitting between her and Crystal. "The rest didn't even take, and I broke one into shards by accident." She made an apologetic face. "Sorry."

"It's okay. They were for you to try. I'm sure you'll get it. Besides, we have better equipment back in Lustnor. We can always try more there." I tried my best to look supportive even though I was upset. It wasn't her fault though.

"I know." She took a deep breath. "I just wanted it to work. I want to save Gwen." She took another breath, and I saw tears start to form around her eyes.

"I know, but you just need to do what you can. We'll save her." I put my hand on her shoulder. "Why don't you rest a bit?"

"I'd like to keep trying if that's okay," she said, looking down at the bowl.

"You know," Annabeth said, and as she spoke, I realized she was right next to me. I hadn't even heard her approach. "When I started working with it, I tried to carve it like I had the Dark Blood. Only I couldn't because it was innately different. Instead, I forced myself to see it as its own thing, but not only that, I tried to figure out how to enhance what it brought to the table already." She gestured toward her sculpture. "Hence the octopus."

"I'm trying to transmute it, not carve it into a pretty shape," Sally said, picking up the red Etheric Flame. The light of an arc of lightning caught it, sending gleaming flashes of scarlet across the buggy. "Wait." Her eyes widened as she stared at the Etheric Flame, and as another arc of lightning cracked, she smiled. "I've got it."

She dropped it into the bowl before fishing out the green Etheric Flame. She put the green one back into the sack before pulling a few pouches off of her belt. As she poured their contents into the bowl, a silvery liquid began to form. As it did, the Etheric Flame sucked it up like a sponge. Silver outlines flowed through the gemstone like veins drinking up ink. Then the color darkened to a deep burgundy color. Sally raised one hand over the dish and raised the other into the air.

Again, the sky rumbled. More lightning crackled through the air as she began to chant. Power began to flow from her hands, causing the dish to glow. Energy whipped off it in tendrils before striking the Etheric Flame like a Tesla coil.

Only with each strike, the gemstone began to glow brighter while the liquid within faded.

By the time all the liquid had been absorbed, the Etheric Flame was so bright I could barely look at it. Better still, the grade on the Tooltip attached to it had changed from D to A.

Etheric Flame - Red
Material: Gemstone
Grade: A
Contains the essence of a fallen red dragon. Has begun the refining process.

"Sweet!" I said, grabbing her hands and squeezing them. "You did it!"

"I almost can't believe it," she whispered, clearly spent. As she gave me a smile, eyes half-lidded from exhaustion, I saw the same halo appear above her menu orb that I'd seen on Annabeth's earlier.

New Skill Tree Unlocked. Prestige Tree- Equivalent Exchange

Equivalent Exchange: User has realized the one truth of alchemy. To obtain something of value, something of equal value must be sacrificed.

Unlike a normal Skill Tree, in addition to the specialties: Etheric Flame, Dark Blood, and Demon Horn, recipes were also listed under the Equivalent Exchange Tree and while they were all colored and usable, I had no idea what most of them were for. I did, however, understand the last one. Nexus Gateway Conduit. Barely able to contain myself, I opened the recipe.

Recipe: Nexus Gateway Conduit

Skill: 1/10.

User can fuse the necessary ingredients into a Nexus Gateway Conduit. Doing so will allow the Nexus Gateway to be opened at the user's will. All ingredients will be destroyed. 10% chance of success for every Rank in the Skill.

Ingredients: Etheric Flame - Red, Etheric Flame – Blue, Etheric Flame – Green, Prestigious Conduit (3), Prestigious Emitter (3)

Requirements: Special: 95+, Agility: 95+, Special: 95+

Since I didn't know what the Prestigious Conduit or Prestigious Emitter was, I opened their tooltips.

Prestigious Conduit

Material: Gemstone

Grade: S

Sculpted from Etheric Flame by a Prestigious Sculptor.

Prestigious Emitter

Material: Gemstone

Grade: S

Cast from Etheric Flame by a Prestigious Blacksmith.

"Okay…" I said, taking a deep breath as I stared at the box of Etheric Flame we'd gotten. It wasn't enough. Not nearly, given the requirements of the Nexus Gateway Conduit. "We're going to need a shitload more Etheric Flame because if this were a game, this is where I'd be buying gold from Chinese farmers."

38

Once we were back in town, Buffy went to find Elizabeth so they could work on getting ahold of more Etheric Flame. As for myself, my first thought was to seek out Sam, but I didn't. I'd been musing over the problem with the Nexus Conduit recipe for hours and I knew we didn't have time to grind out a billion of each item. Gwen's life force, while still there, wasn't infinite. There'd be a point where either she died, or Nadine came back. We had to be ready before that.

Besides, I didn't know how long it'd take to successfully craft the Nexus Gateway. While it might take one try, I'd once seen a coin break the odds by flipping heads twenty times in a row. I had no desire to spend months making the materials, to blow them up without success. That was just insanity.

Which was why I'd thought of an idea. I didn't know if it would work, but it damned sure couldn't hurt.

"Hey, Annabeth, got a second?" I asked as the sculptor got to her feet. She'd been working away on a piece of wood with her sculpting knife. As she turned toward me, I saw that it was a sparrow so lifelike, I almost couldn't tell it was made from wood.

"Of course," she said, taking a deep breath. "I assume you want me to start trying to craft the prestigious conduit." She looked at me. "I'm honestly not sure what to even make. Sally and I talked about it, but I don't quite know what it's supposed to look like."

"I think it's supposed to come from your heart," I said, nearly reaching out to touch her chest before stopping myself. That'd have been embarrassing. Instead, I dropped my hand to my side. As she watched it fall, she shook her head.

"That is non-advice." She shifted uncomfortably. "But I can still try."

"I'm glad, but I actually was thinking about it, and I had an idea come to me." I turned and pointed to the massive statue she'd carved in the center of town. The massive dragon tearing itself from the earth had finally been completed, and even though I'd seen real dragons, I found her sculpture more lifelike than they had been.

"What's your idea?" she asked, following my gaze toward the dragon sculpture. "I know, I need to fix it now that I've seen dragons. The shape of the scales is all wrong..."

"Forget that," I said, narrowing my eyes at her. "What I want you to do is craft sculptures to the..." I waved my hand uselessly. "I was gonna say gods, but that's not what I mean really." I looked at the ground, trying to think of the right word.

"Just tell me what the basis of your idea is. I'll come up with a suitable subject," she said, touching my shoulder lightly with one fingertip. "It will be better that way."

"Um... I want you to try to craft some sculptures that increase luck and alchemy. Hell, if they can increase sculpting too, that's a bonus." I gestured at the box of Etheric Flame. "Your prestige class, like Sally's, was unlocked because you've worked with rare materials so I want you to work an Etheric Flame, a Demon Horn, and a Dark Blood into each one too. They can be big or small, just make them as powerful and numerous as possible, okay?"

Her eyes widened in surprise as she absorbed my words. "That's a great idea." She nodded. "If I could do that, the sculptures I'd make would be better overall too." She nodded furiously, eyes glittering with excitement. "I'll do as you say. You'll have the best sculptures ever created."

"I'm sure I will," I said as she bounded off, leaving me standing there beside the buggy. I knew I still needed to see Sam, but before I did that, I had one more idea.

A few minutes later, I found Maribelle. She was standing near the lumber mill, surveying the lumber with a frown on her face.

"Is there a problem?" I asked, and she nearly leaped out of her skin at the sound of my voice.

"You scared the hell out of me," she said, one hand clasping her heart as she sucked in a few deep breaths. She tried to smile then. "Glad to see you're back. I've completed all the construction like you asked. We haven't found a mason though so that's out, unfortunately." Her smile turned upside down. "On the plus side, we can make a few more buildings, which will be good. We really need to work on the whole food production thing."

"Yeah, we can later. Do we have the stuff to build the Apothecary?" I glanced at the pile of lumber. "I can't quite remember what it required."

"Oh, that?" she rummaged around in her pockets for a minute before giving up. "Yes, we have the materials. I was trying to find my plans, but I left them with Elizabeth…"

"Great, can you start construction on it immediately?" I asked, looking around. "Then we can have a meeting about what to do for food production. This takes precedence though."

"Sure thing," she said, nodding furiously before looking around. "I laid out a few spots for new buildings so let me go find which will work best."

"Have fun," I said, and she waved at me before heading off. That done, I went to find Elizabeth and Buffy. It came as no surprise to me that the two of them were squabbling.

"Hey, you two," I said as I entered the door of the trading post.

Both girls turned to look at me before turning back to each other like they were going to continue their argument. Honestly, I wasn't sure if it was a goblin thing or a sister thing or some combination thereof, but right now, I didn't care.

"I need you to recruit an apothecary right now,"

I said, taking a step forward and pushing between them. "Is that clear?"

"An apothecary?" Elizabeth said, raising an eyebrow at me. "Why, that's all hogwash and snake oil."

"I want someone who can brew up luck potions. An apothecary can do that," I said, patting Clarent. "That I can make sure of."

"We could just buy luck potions," Buffy said, looking at me like I was crazy. "Though I'm not sure they actually work."

"That's why I want the actual apothecary because then I'll know. Maribelle is already starting construction on the shop." I moved to leave. "I know I can count on the two of you."

"Wait, we need to talk about food," Elizabeth said, running after me and grabbing my arm.

"We will in a few hours, okay? I promise." I smiled. "Actually, no, we won't. Get the apothecary, and we can talk about whatever you want."

"Are you seriously refusing to feed us until I find an apothecary?" Elizabeth asked, hands on her hips.

"I *am* feeding you," I said with a shrug because I was tired of hearing about farms. We had the money to buy food and didn't have the resources to grow it yet. She really needed to stop bringing it up. "So, don't be dramatic. Just find the apothecary." I turned my gaze to Buffy. "I'm going to see Sam. Come find me when it's done."

39

"Great, you're back," Sam said, not even bothering to look up as I entered her shop. She was hunched over a workbench I'd not seen before. Tools, as well as bits and pieces of metal, gemstones, and stone, were strewn about the surface. As I tried to get a closer look, I realized her two apprentices were nowhere to be found, and the forge had gone cold. That seemed a bit odd because, well, we needed to produce weapons and armor for the town and for trade.

"I am back," I said, taking another step closer. The smell of burning plastic hit my nose. "Whatcha working on?"

"A surprise," she said, turning to block her contraption from sight with her back. Her face was stained with soot, and she had grease in her hair. Her clothes were sweat-stained, and as she stared at me, pink eyes roaming over my body, I heard her stomach growl.

"Hungry?" I asked, raising an eyebrow at her.

"I hadn't noticed before now," she said, gesturing off-handedly at the table. "I was caught up in this idea I had. Guess I forgot about it." She wiped her forehead with the back of one hand, smearing grime across her flesh. "Sorry."

"Where are your apprentices?" I asked, looking around. "Why aren't they making stuff?"

"We ran out of materials. I sent them to talk to Elizabeth about it…" She looked toward the forge. "I don't remember when that was, exactly. I sort of forgot about it."

"What are you working on that has you so distracted?" I asked, taking a step closer, but as I tried to look over her shoulder at the work bench, she moved to block me, causing her body to press against mine.

"None of your business," she said, annoyance filling her words as she put her hands on my chest and pushed me lightly. I took a step back, respecting her wishes.

"Fair enough. Anyway, I need you to do me a

favor," I said, opening the sack in my hand to reveal a trifecta of Etheric Flame. The blue, green, and red gemstones gleamed in the light of her shop as she looked inside before turning her eyes to me.

"What am I supposed to do with those? Make you a broach?" She shook her head. "I don't normally work with materials like that." She pointed to the stack of Dark Blood in the corner. "Those aren't normal gemstones. When I use them, I extract the power from within and infuse it into the metal." She pointed at the bag. "Etheric Flame isn't forged the same way as Dark Blood. I've seen smiths try to use it that way and it doesn't work."

"Well, it's not the same." I shook my head. "Both Sally and Annabeth said it was a completely different substance that needed to be worked in its own way." I held the bag out to her. "You need to figure it out."

"Figure it out?" She gave me a hard look. "How am I supposed to figure out how to use a substance even the Master Blacksmith Allison cannot use? That's asking for too much."

"I believe in you." I smiled at her and reached out to brush a lock of hair from her face. "You're way better than her, anyway. She can't work on Clarent. You can." I patted the sword.

"That was different. All I did was infuse your sword with Dark Blood the same way I'd have done with anything. That's a known technique." She shook her head. "Your belief is misplaced."

"I need you to try anyway," I said, taking a deep breath. If she couldn't get it to work, she wouldn't be able to make the emitters. Without those, we wouldn't be able to open a Nexus Gateway after we rescued Gwen. That wasn't acceptable.

"I feel like you're being unreasonable," she huffed before finally reaching out and taking the bag. She pulled the green gemstone out, and the tentacles writhed around her fingers. "But if you really want me to do something with this, I guess I can mount it on some armor or something…" Her eyes searched my face. "Why is it so important?"

"We figured out how to make the Nexus Gateways open, and it requires an emitter which can only be cast by a blacksmith." I pulled out the notes I'd written and showed her the description of the item I'd copied down.

She took a look at it before turning her eyes to me. "Do you even know what casting is?"

"Um… not really," I said, somewhat embarrassed.

"I could explain it, but why don't you just look?

It will be faster." She waved a hand through the space above her head where the menu orb sat.

"Um... okay, give me a second." I opened the menu and found the Ability in the basic Blacksmith Tree.

Casting

Skill: 4/10.

User has the Ability to use the Casting technique in which liquid materials are poured into a mold. The contents are allowed to cool and solidify into a casting, which is then removed from the mold. Casting is often used to make shapes that would be too difficult to make via other methods.

"Wait, so all you have to do is melt these down and pour them into a mold?" I asked, turning my eyes from the Ability to the gemstone in her hand. "That doesn't seem too bad."

"In theory, yes. It's easy. I'm not very good at it, but I'm proficient enough at casting," she paused for a moment and stared at my eyes like she was trying to see into my brain and suck out the juices. "But you knew that."

"Okay, so you need to practice, or I can upgrade you. That's not a big deal," I said, moving to her Stat window and finding she had more than enough Experience for me to get her to Skill level seven or eight. She must have been busy while we were gone.

"Here's what's a big deal." She said hefting the Etheric Flame. "This is the heart of the flame from which dragons create their fire." She took a deep breath and blew her bangs out of her face. "How the fuck am I supposed to melt it?"

"Um, with fire?" I said, already seeing where she was going with this.

"How hot do you think dragon fire is?" she asked, shaking her head. "And let's just assume I *could* melt this stuff. Let's just say I figure it out because, honestly, I can probably figure it out. What mold am I supposed to make? What's the emitter look like?"

"I see your point," I said, nodding to her. It was the same question Annabeth had asked me, and I still didn't have an answer. What we really needed was our own Nexus Gateway Conduit so we could look at the damned thing. "Do you think the blacksmith's guild has the plans for it?"

"It's possible," Sam said, the fire in her eyes cooling a touch. "But if they did, I couldn't access it at my Rank."

"Feh, that's just a detail." I waved my hand.

"We need to know if they have the plans for the emitter, or better yet, a mold."

"I doubt they have a mold." Sam shook her head. "If they did, I guarantee Allison would have tried to cast one. Maybe she has, but that snobby bitch would have shown it off." She shook her head. "No, if the plans exist, it's definitely in their archives."

"That was the same problem we had with the recipe to begin with." I shook my head. "We're getting ahead of ourselves. What I want you to do is figure out a way to melt this stuff down and cast it into anything."

"Anything?" she asked, raising an eyebrow at me. "It doesn't matter?"

"No," I said, shaking my head. "See, here's the thing. For both Annabeth and Sally, once they made something with the material, it opened a new Skill Tree related to it. I think the same thing will happen for you. While Annabeth's didn't have the recipe for the conduit, Sally's did have the recipe for the Nexus Gateway Conduit. Maybe if you unlock yours, it will have the same thing?" I shrugged. "It's either that or go to the archive and root around for this side of forever." I gritted my teeth. "Call me crazy, but I don't think Gwen has that kind of time, and even if she did, Nadine will be back before too long."

"I guess it's as good a plan as any," she said, searching my face for a moment before dropping the Etheric Flame into the bag. "I'll try to figure out a way to melt this stuff."

"Good," I said, and as I turned to leave, I had a thought. The requirements for Sally to craft the item had been pretty high Stats wise, and while she'd had the Experience to do it thanks to the battle at Blade's End, I hadn't bothered yet. Only, what if those requirements were the same for Sam and Annabeth too?

I wasn't sure, but at the same time, it was worth a try. Besides, it wasn't like Sam didn't have the Experience to spare.

"You have smoke coming out of your ears," Sam said, watching me stand half turned toward the door. "What are you thinking?"

"I was just thinking that Sally had a really crazy Stat requirement to make the final item, but what if you need those Stats to make the emitter itself? It wouldn't surprise me all that much, to be honest." I smiled at her. "Care for an upgrade?"

"What's it cost?" she asked, raising an eyebrow at me. "Is it a lot?"

"Actually, not really. Stats don't seem to cost all that much, really. Still, you need a lot of Stats…" I did a quick bit of mental math based on her current Stats. "We need to raise your Special from seventy-five to ninety-five, your Intelligence from seventy-six to ninety-five, and your agility from fifty to ninety-five. It'll wind up costing six-thousand six-hundred-twenty-nine Experience." I gestured at her. "You have about eight thousand total, so…"

"Do it," she said, nodding at me. "It will pay off in the long run. Ever since the last upgrade, I've been able to make things I never thought I'd be able to."

"Okay," I said, adjusting her Stats. As the blue light flashed around her, new Intelligence sparkled in her eyes. She watched me for a few seconds before smiling at me.

"It's so weird to just feel smarter," she said, hand cinching down on the bag. "I'll figure this out. Come back in an hour."

"Let's make it two. I want you to eat something first." I smiled at her. "Your brain needs fuel, after all."

"I'll eat when I'm dead," she said, shooing me off.

"I don't think it works that way," I replied, but

she was already turned back to her bench, ignoring me.

I left, and after stopping by the kitchen to ensure someone actually brought Sam food, I went to find Annabeth. She was in the center of town, musing over a massive black stone with silver veins running through it.

"Well, that's certainly cool," I said as she walked around the six by ten-foot block. "Know what you're going to make, yet?"

"The stone has yet to speak to me," she said, turning to look at me. "Do you need something?"

"I wanted to upgrade your Stats a bit. I had an idea while talking to Sam. Basically, Sally requires really high Stats to craft the Nexus Conduit, so I want to upgrade yours to a similar level just in case. You have the Experience for it, so…" I trailed off because her gaze was boring into me.

"I would rather you didn't unless it's absolutely necessary." She shook her head. "Perhaps later, I will feel okay with it, but I was never that smart before. Now it's harder for me to concentrate on my work. I keep thinking of different things." She sighed. "It will be fine soon enough, but I fear if you do it now, I may never get anything done."

"What if I just increased your agility?" I asked.

I didn't want to upgrade her Stats if she didn't want me to but at the same time, I needed to ensure we actually were able to craft the Nexus Gateway Conduits. "Would that be okay?"

"No." She shook her head. "What you fail to understand is how comfortable I am with my hands. When you change things, I must spend time to adapt. Do you want me to spend that time now or craft the sculptures you asked for?"

"Fair enough," I said, sighing.

"Sorry," she said, bowing her head to me. "I know this is not what you expected me to say, but at the same time I believe this is the best course."

"I trust your judgment. I'll leave you to your work," I said, waving at her. "Good luck."

"Thank you," she said, and she watched me for a moment before turning back to her chunk of stone. She pulled out her knife, holding it loosely in one hand and slowly raised it to the block. Then, instead of doing anything, she dropped her hand and regarded the stone again.

Not wanting to spend time watching her carve, partially because I hated when people watched me do things, and partially because I needed to find something to do. Part of me wanted to check on Maribelle or Buffy and Elizabeth, but I knew not enough time had passed for anything appreciable to do. No, what I really needed to do was kill an hour.

Fortunately, I knew just the place to do that. I made my way toward the gate, and just like I'd thought, Sheila was going through training exercises with the guards who weren't actively watching the gate.

When she saw me, she gave me a nod. "All right, you maggots. Give me fifty more sword thrusts then take two laps." The crowd of women groaned, but Sheila ignored it as she came toward me. "Do you need something, boss?"

"I want to join your class, actually," I said, nodding toward the women. "I have Clarent, but honestly, I don't even know how to hold it. I'd love for you to teach me a bit."

"Are you sure?" she asked, looking me up and down. "Honestly, you're kind of scrawny. You'd make a terrible fighter."

"I still want to be able to defend myself a little," I said, shrugging. "And I don't actually have anything to do. Everyone's busy."

She stared at me for a long while. "It's your funeral." She jerked a thumb at the women. "Get in line."

40

An hour later I was tired, sore, and so sweaty I could smell myself. As I stood there, sucking down water like it was going out of style, part of me wanted to head to the bathhouse. I didn't, but only because I wanted to check on Sam first.

I ran a hand through my sweaty hair and grimaced. Even my hands hurt, and I knew that even though I'd worn training gloves like the other guards, I'd likely have blisters. Still, it had felt good to work off some steam. Besides, I couldn't be helpless forever.

Taking one last gulp of water, I made my way out of the training area and headed toward the blacksmith's shop. The first thing I noticed was the smoke pouring from the chimney. The next thing I noticed were the crates of dragon scale we'd brought back from Blade's End. They were stacked outside the shop, and Sam's two apprentices were busy going through them.

They waved at me as I approached before going back to work. I waved back before stepping inside. Like before, Sam was hunched over one of her work benches, but unlike before, she had several molds set out, each filled with glowing fragments.

She must have heard me come in because she turned to me, a mold filled with glowing crystal in one hand and an ear-to-ear smile on her face.

"I did it!" she exclaimed coming toward me and shaking the mold at me. "I was thinking about it, and I realized something important."

"What's that?" I asked as she grabbed me by the arm and practically dragged me toward the bench where various molds were laid out.

"I was thinking about casting, and I realized something. It doesn't always have to be molten metal. You can cast with other things. The key is that you have a mold." She shook the mold in her hand for emphasis. "And something liquid that will harden."

"Okay. I'm not sure I'm following, but you seem excited so explain it to me like I'm five."

She frowned at me. "Basically, I ground up one of the Etheric Flames and made a paste. Then I poured it into a mold." She pointed at the mold on the far end of the table. It sort of looked like a seashell, but I couldn't make out any other details. "Then the paste hardened and voila! I made this." She put the mold in her hand down and picked up a small red object. It glowed with internal fire, and while I could see impurities inside it, I still thought it looked pretty amazing. It reminded me of porcelain, except for that whole scarlet glow thing.

"You're amazing!" I said, taking the offered seashell. As I turned it over in my hand, I noticed more imperfections, but the detail was impeccable. I'd have never imagined it'd been cast.

"I know, but it's still nice to hear." Sam turned and grabbed up one of the molds. "So anyway, I made a few until I got most of the imperfections out. That's why there's so many of these sitting around." She gestured at the array of seashells and other knickknacks sitting on the bench. "I'm fairly good at it now. That's why I made this." She picked up another mold and showed it to me. From the outside, I couldn't tell what it was, but I could see flickers of green, red, and blue light within.

"What's that?" I asked, raising an eyebrow at

her as she broke open the mold to reveal an egg-shaped gemstone that was one-third green, one-third red, and one-third blue. Only the way they were intertwined together was sort of like a jigsaw puzzle, only more refined.

"Well, I wanted to make you something, and since I suck at making pancakes, I made you this," Sam said, holding the orb out to me. "Can I have your sword for a second?"

"Pancakes?" I asked, raising an eyebrow at her as I handed Clarent to her. She took it and placed it on her bench before beginning to carefully pry the orb out of the pommel.

"Pancakes make everyone happy." She gave me a weak smile. "I'm a terrible cook though, so this will have to do." With that, she finished prying the orb loose from the sword. It hit the bench with a thunk before rolling off the edge and striking the floor.

"I actually don't really eat carbs," I said with a shrug as the orb rolled toward me. I bent to pick it up as she fit the newly crafted Etheric Flame orb into Clarent. "I mean, I do, but not pancake carbs." I patted my stomach. "And when I do eat carbs, I pretty much just eat pizza."

"Well, I'll take you for pizza one day," she said, fitting the orb into place. "Would that be okay?"

"Sounds like a date," I replied, and her shoulders tensed for a second before relaxing.

"Great, I'd like that," she said, turning and offering me Clarent. "What do you think?"

Her cheeks were bright red, and instead of looking at me, she looked at her shoes while handing me the sword. I wasn't sure why she'd suddenly gotten embarrassed, but there was no reason for it. Her work was fantastic. Maybe she thought I didn't think so?

"It looks great! You're the best, Sam!" I said, taking the weapon from her and giving it a quick swing. I wasn't sure how, but it felt more powerful than before. What's more, I could feel heat coming off the pommel now.

"I'm glad you liked it. I didn't want to presume," she looked up at me and flashed me a quick smile.

"No, it's really great," I said, flipping the sword over so I could stare at the new orb. "It's truly splendid craftsmanship."

"Thanks," she swallowed and reached out to touch my wrist. As her fingers grazed my flesh, she met my eyes. "I'm glad you like it."

"I really do," I said, only as I went to see more, I noticed the halo around her menu orb like I'd seen with both Annabeth and Sally.

"Is there anything else I can do for you?" she asked, taking a step toward me as I opened her menu.

"Let me see, just give me a second, okay?" I replied as a new message flashed in the Tooltip box beside her head.

"Oh," she said, her smile slipping. "Okay."

New Skill Tree Unlocked. Prestige Tree- Elemental Crucible

"Booyah!" I cried, pumping my fist as I opened the Tooltip to see what the new tree entailed.

Elemental Crucible: User has the Ability to work with obscure resources in both casting and metalworking. This Skill will give a 10% bonus to all items created by the blacksmith.

After reading the message, I looked at the Abilities. Like with Annabeth's tree, most of the Abilities were blacked out, and similarly, only three sub-Abilities were unlocked. Specialty: Dark Blood, Specialty: Demon Horn, and Specialty: Etheric Flame. Both were Rank one out of ten.

There were no recipes at all. Damn.

"What's wrong?" Sam asked, and her voice held

a strange quality I couldn't discern. It was like she was hurt but also wanted to comfort me.

"There's no recipe in your Skill Tree, but you did unlock it." I took a deep breath. "I think you may have to figure out how to make the emitter on your own."

"Oh, yeah, okay," she said, taking a deep breath. "We do need to save Gwen and all…"

"What's wrong?" I asked, touching her shoulder as she moved to turn away from me. "You seem upset."

"I just, I dunno." She shook her head. "It's nothing, just me being silly. I'm glad you like your sword."

"Something is clearly wrong, Sam." I smiled. "I'm a dumb guy so if you won't just tell me, I'll never figure it out." I took a step closer to her and touched her arm. "Please, if I can help, I will."

Sam blew out a long breath. "I know we need to save Gwen and all." She turned to look at me, and her eyes were huge as she stared at me. She fidgeted slightly.

"We do, that's why—"

She cut me off by pressing her mouth to mine.

41

I awoke with a start, the last vestiges of a nightmare I couldn't remember sending my heart into a pounding flurry. I sat up, one hand gripping the blanket covering me, and looked around, trying to figure out where I was. I didn't even recognize the place.

As I sat there for a moment, trying to blink away the sleep, the sound of Sam sleeping next to me brought me back to reality. I took a deep breath, trying to calm myself but I couldn't.

You'd think it would have been easy to just lay back down and shut my eyes, especially since I had a super-hot naked chick in the bed with me, but I couldn't do that. No. I was wide awake now. Whatever had happened in my dream had scared me.

Worse, as I stared at Sam, I sort of felt like I'd

betrayed Gwen somehow. Granted, the two of us weren't anything, but I wasn't so dense as to think she didn't like me. What's more, even though she was a succubus, I really liked her back. How would she feel when she found out I'd slept with Sam? How was Sam going to feel about my feelings for Gwen?

Oh my god, I was in the Hell edition of Melrose Place. Worse, I didn't have time for that kind of drama. I had to get a handle on things. Had to find a way to get the recipes to craft the Emitter and Conduit for the Nexus Gateway Conduit so we could go save a woman who, for all practical purposes, might now hate me.

I rubbed my face with my hand and stared at the ceiling. I wasn't quite sure why I'd done what I'd done with Sam. I liked her a lot, and she was beautiful. At the same time though, she sort of worked for me. Granted, it'd been one hundred percent her choice, but still. Still.

Either way, I needed to get out and walk around. Some fresh air would do me good. Taking a deep breath, I pulled back the blankets and moved to climb out of bed. Only, before I could, I felt Sam's hand on my thigh.

"Where are you going?" she asked, sleep still

heavy in her voice. "I didn't peg you for the 'dine and dash' type. Can't you stay until morning?"

"I, erm," I said because I possessed a sparkling wit. "I just needed some air."

"Do you wanna talk about it?" She gave me a wry smile. "Wanna talk about us?" she added, sitting up so the blanket fell away to reveal her naked breasts. "That's a thing your kind does, right? Talk?"

"Wait, what's that supposed to mean?" I asked, raising an eyebrow at her. "Don't you want to talk about what we, uh, did?"

"You mean the sex?" She gave me a curious look. "If you want some pointers, I guess I can show you." She patted the bed next to her, and while I wasn't sure what I was doing wrong, I was definitely willing to let her tutor me. "Or we can have a more hands-on approach."

"Huh, no, that's not what I meant at all," I said and this time her face filled with confusion.

"What do you mean then? It seems like there's a problem." She let out a breath. "Was I not good enough? Did I do something you didn't like?" She ran a hand down her body. "We can try other things. I'm definitely open to suggestion."

"No, you were great. Everything was great. It's

just…" I sighed, not sure how to put my feelings into words. It seemed ten kinds of uncool to talk about Gwen to the girl I'd just slept with.

"Sorry, I'm not very good at the whole human thing." Sam scratched her cheek before dropping her hand onto her lap. "Can you explain it to me simply?" She gave me an apologetic smile.

"Human thing?" I asked, suddenly feeling stupid.

I'd sort of forgotten Sam wasn't human, and while I'd assumed she operated like a normal human female, it was possible she didn't. Actually, as I looked at the confusion plastered across every inch of her face, I realized that was entirely the problem. She had no idea what in the blue hell I was concerned about. Well, that was interesting…

"Well, you seem to have had some kind of problem with sex. You say it's not performance related, and I'm choosing to trust you on that because I would hope you would tell me what you do and don't like." She tapped her fingers against her bare thigh, drawing my eyes to them. She had a lot of muscle in those thighs, and she was even stronger than she looked. "So clearly it's something else. Only I don't know what that something else is because I'm not human." She touched her chest. "I'm a fallen angel."

"I'm worried that Gwen will be upset that we slept together," I blurted out. Then I willed myself not to flinch away and shut my eyes.

"Why would she care?" Sam snorted. "She's a succubus. They sleep with everyone. It's how they feed, and even if she wasn't a succubus, we're demons. While sex is important to us for pleasure and forming bonds and such, it's not like it means I own you or you own me." She shook her head. "It's not something I even considered for a second because Gwen would absolutely not care."

"Would you care?" I asked, gesturing at her. "Would you care if I slept with Gwen?"

"Not especially," she said, rubbing her chin. "The only reason I'd care is if you stopped sleeping with me because, I'll be honest, it was a lot of fun. Am I supposed to care? Would that make you happier?"

"Honestly? I have no idea." It was true too. I wasn't sure how I felt about what she'd just told me. It went against everything I knew about women, and again I had to tell myself that these weren't normal girls. These were demons.

"Well, come back to bed then. You can figure it out later." She bit her lip, slowly dragging her teeth over her bottom lip as she reached out and ran a hand down my stomach. "I want to show you a couple more things you can do with your tongue." She winked mischievously at me. "Then I can show you a couple more things I can do with mine. Sound good?"

42

When I next awoke it was after noon, and Sam was nowhere to be found. I sat up and tried to rub the sleep from my eyes. My stomach was rumbling, and I needed to hit the bathhouse with a fierceness. Then I had to find out what was going on with everyone.

I stretched, and as I went to get out of bed, I noticed a small tray sitting beside the bed. It had one of those metal chafing dishes on it with a small burner beneath, presumably to keep it warm. There was also a kettle next to it with its own burner. A note was taped to the top of the dish, and as I pulled it off and read it, I smiled.

Had to get to work. Let you sleep. You earned it.
Sam
PS. No, I didn't cook it. The chef did.

"Well, that was thoughtful," I said, swinging my legs over the edge of the bed. I knew part of me should have felt regret, but I just didn't. Sam had been okay with everything, and what's more, if she was telling the truth (which seemed likely), Gwen wouldn't care either. Hell, there might even be a threesome in my future. Wow, I really never thought I'd be that guy.

I pulled the lid off the platter and found myself staring at a whole mess of bacon and eggs. The kettle revealed itself to contain coffee, and there was a little cup filled with cream I hadn't seen at first glance. I hastily poured myself a cup of coffee and set to work on the eggs and bacon. I hadn't realized how hungry I was until I started eating, and it took me only a few minutes to clear my plate. After that, I got myself dressed and walked out of her room in the dormitory-like structure the girls slept in. Since it'd been there before I got to the town, I'd not really thought about it, but as I wandered toward the entrance, I wondered if it needed expanding. We'd taken a lot of people on, and I was fairly sure a bunch of them were probably sharing a room.

Still, first thing was first. I needed to find out how the apothecary was coming. With any luck, I'd find Elizabeth or Buffy, and they'd tell me one was here or at least on the way.

I quickly moved to my own room and changed my clothing, opting for a hasty shower of new deodorant before making my way outside. Only as I stepped through the doors, I nearly collided with Maribelle. My coffee cup slipped from my hand as I stumbled backward. It hit the ground with a crash that threw hot coffee and bits of broken ceramic in every direction. I stood there, my chest heaving from shock while Maribelle's face went bright pink.

"Oh no, I'm so sorry." Her head whipped around like a dervish as she looked from me to the coffee and back again in quick succession. "I'm such a klutz. Sorry." She pulled a dirty rag from her pocket and got down on her knees, frantically trying to sop up the mess.

"It's not a big deal," I said, getting down to help her. "I shouldn't have dropped it."

"I should have been watching where I was going," she said as she finished wiping up the mess while I grabbed a broom and dustpan from the janitor's closet. I scooped all the fragments into a pile on the dustpan before shoving them into a nearby trashcan.

"I'm so sorry. Want me to get you another

coffee?" she asked, shoving her hands in the pockets of her overalls.

"No, it's fine," I said, smiling at her. "I'm awake now, anyway. I was actually going to come look for you. Have a minute?"

"You were?" she asked, blushing harder at me in a way that made me why she was suddenly so flustered. She'd never been that way before. "I was actually coming to get you so I could show you something. What did you want to see me about?"

"I wanted to know how the apothecary was coming," I said with a shrug. "Is it finished?"

"Nearly. Maybe six more hours. A day tops." She shrugged and moved outside. "At this rate, it will be done long before Buffy gets through the mountain of red tape we just got wrapped with."

"What do you mean?" I asked, following her outside. She pointed at a building that was nearly complete.

"Oh, normal guild stuff. They don't want to allow transfer of someone here. Buffy is trying to find a blacklisted one, but they don't have any in Royal Centre. She's reaching out to other towns now." Maribelle sighed. "Same problem with the mason, I'm afraid. Now, that'd be helpful." She gave the sky an annoyed frown. "Ah well. If we didn't have setbacks, we'd actually get things done, eh? Couldn't have that."

"Yeah, I hear you," I said, mentally crossing off two items off my 'to do' list. That just left me to check on Annabeth and Sam, but I was fairly sure neither would have much to tell me. I'd still find them, but it was looking like another day with Sheila was in store for me while I waited for progress. I just hoped Gwen would live long enough. Part of me figured she would because otherwise, she'd be dead.

The more I thought about it, the more I wondered if she was just bait in a trap. If they killed her, I'd know, and then I might not come. So, if that was the case, it would be better if she was left alive.

"Anyway, guess I'll get back to work then," Maribelle said, waving to me before turning to head toward the building. "Got to keep the workers in line."

"Wait, what were you coming to see me about? I'm assuming it wasn't about the building?" I asked, and she stopped in her tracks.

She turned her eyes back to me, and her face was flushed again. "That's right, um, I do have something I want to show you, if, um, you have some time?"

"Unfortunately, time is the one thing I have none of and an abundance of. I feel like every day is hurry up and wait." I blew out a sigh. I needed to save Gwen, but there was just no way to do that quickly. "Anyway, yeah, I can spare some for you. Let's go."

"Okay," she squeaked, taking a hard left toward the back gate. "It's outside. Is that okay? A bit of a walk, really."

"That's fine," I said, patting my stomach. "I could use the exercise, anyway. Had a big breakfast."

"Glad you have lots of energy," she said as we exited town and began walking along the path. Ever since we'd taken to hunting the devil dogs and clearing away forest, there had been a lot fewer sightings so I wasn't really worried about them. They almost never came within a mile of the town.

A few minutes later, we were moving through the forest. I had my hand around Clarent but Maribelle didn't seem worried. Truthfully, I shouldn't have been either, but at the same time, I was in a forest in Hell.

"So, uh, where are we going?" I asked after another few minutes. The shadows were cast across the forest, but that wasn't what worried me. No, what worried me was the creepy as fuck cave we were heading toward. Its mouth gaped open like an old beast and moss clung to every nook and cranny.

"Inside. Don't worry. I checked it out earlier. It's perfectly safe." She held her hand out to me and the way she said it made me trust her. If she said it was safe, I was willing to believe her. Besides, I was more curious than ever. "If it makes you feel better, you can hold my hand."

"Do you want me to hold your hand?" I asked as we stepped up to the mouth of the cave. The air inside felt damp, but it carried with it a soft floral scent that reminded me of bouquets in spring time.

"I wouldn't be opposed to it. We are entering a cave." She gave me a weak smile and took my hand in hers.

"That we are," I said, taking a deep breath. "So what's inside?"

"It's better if I show you. Come on." She pulled me inside then, and I was surprised at how bright it was inside. Luminous moss clung to the rocks inside, causing it to glow like the inside of a rave. As we twisted through the tunnels well beyond the point where I got hopelessly lost, the air became thicker and heavier with the scent of flowers.

"Are we almost there?" I asked after another few

moments. I kicked my shoes a bit. "Because these boots aren't meant for this much walking."

"Actually, it's just around the bend," she said, pulling me around the corner. Only as I turned it, I didn't see anything at all because it was pitch black. Hell, I couldn't see my hand when I put it in front of my face.

Maribelle's fingers tightened on my hand, and I heard her shift in the darkness. She pressed something into my open hand. "Would you light the torch on the wall with the lighter?"

"Yeah, okay," I said, flicking the lighter open to reveal a tiny blue flame. It allowed me to see the wall next to me which did, in fact, contain a torch. I leaned in toward it and touched the lighter's flame to the bundle on top, causing it to burst to life. Not just that torch, but a bunch of them spaced along the entirety of the room at two-foot intervals.

Their flames all writhed with every color of the rainbow, and as I turned my gaze back toward Maribelle, I found myself staring at a cavern that was filled with gemstones. Not the cut and faceted ones, but natural ones that were embedded in the walls and ceiling. Millions and millions of them. Enough to make the dwarves from Snow White go absolutely berserk with greed.

Crazier still was that there were wreaths of flowers set over some of the particularly large gemstones. Was that what had been giving off the scent? I wasn't sure, but as I sucked in a breath, I realized it had to be true because it *really* smelled like flowers here.

"What is all this?" I asked as Maribelle pulled me forward into the center of the room where there was a small picnic basket set on a blanket.

"It's what I wanted to show you. Do you like it? I found it a few days ago when I was scouting for a particular type of wood." She smiled at me. "I added the flowers though."

"It's beautiful. Truly. Thank you for showing me." I nodded to her as she sat down on the blanket. She opened the basket's lid and pulled out a bottle and a small plate.

"I have some chocolate and wine too if you'd like to eat or drink." She offered me a small plate with a bit of chocolate. "I had it specially made."

"Um… sure," I said, taking the plate and looking at it for a moment. "What's this all about?"

Her face flushed a bit more. "Did I do something wrong?"

"Um… no?" I said, taking a bite of the chocolate. It was velvety and rich and rolled over my tongue in a way I hadn't ever experienced. I licked my lips. If I wasn't careful, I'd eat everything she'd brought before she had a chance to.

"Good." She nodded and poured a glass of wine. She offered it to me. "I wasn't sure what kind of wine you liked so I just got my favorite. It's not actually wine, more razzleberry punch with a kick. Hope that's okay."

"It's fine," I said, taking the cup from her. "I'm not actually that partial to wine, to be honest. Never could afford it, and Boone's Farm is so high school." I stuck out my tongue.

"I'm not familiar with that, but if you'd like, I'd be happy to get it for you. I want everything to be just right." She smiled at me. "Really."

"No, I absolutely do not want that. Promise." I took a sip of the punch and smiled. It definitely tasted alcoholic, but in that way all girly drinks did. The way that you'd suck down twelve of them without paying attention and be out of your mind drunk without realizing it.

"Good." She stared at me expectantly. "When would you like to begin?"

"I'm not following," I said, putting my cup and plate down. "Begin what?"

"Sex," she said. "I was told by Sheila that your

kind requires flowers, jewelry, candy, and alcohol to have sex." She gestured around us. "I have provided all those things for you, and you've told me they are acceptable." Her face dimmed slightly. "Unless it is me, do you not find me attractive?"

"Wait, what?" I asked, unable to believe my ears. "You want to have sex with me?"

"Yes." She nodded at me. "Sam told us what happened. We didn't realize you were willing to sleep with us." She fidgeted slightly. "Or do you not find me as attractive as Sam?" She cupped her breasts. "Are they too big? Do you prefer them smaller, like her?" When I didn't respond because I seriously could not believe this was happening to me, she looked down at her chest. "You do…" She looked back at me. "I promise it will be okay. I'll try really hard so…"

"Is this seriously happening?" I said, too stunned to do anything else but stare dumbly at her. "You really talked to Sam about it?"

"Yes, we all had a meeting after we found out this morning. Then we drew lots." She pulled out a small token and showed it to me. "I drew first chance. Only it seems I've done something wrong."

"You didn't do anything wrong. I'm just a little shocked and trust me, it's not you. You're beautiful." I took a deep breath as she reached out and touched my arm.

"Then what is the problem. If it isn't me, and it isn't this," - she swallowed hard - "why do you not want me?"

"It's not that. Like I said, I'm just not used to this." I shook my head, and as I did, she moved closer.

"How about we just try?" She leaned in toward me until our lips were nearly touching. "Would that be okay?"

"I suppose we can try if you really want to," I said, and her face lit up like a June sunrise.

"You won't regret it," she said, and as she leaned back and pulled off her shirt, I had a feeling she was right.

43

As we re-entered Lustnor, I couldn't help but feel a bit embarrassed. After all, Maribelle and I had essentially snuck off to have sex while everyone worked after I'd spent the day sleeping in. I felt like everyone was working but me, and that was no good. If I was to be a good leader, I needed to work harder than my girls did.

"What's wrong?" Maribelle asked as we approached the gate. "You've been quiet the entire walk back."

"Nothing really. I just feel like I'm doing a bad job." I shrugged.

She giggled and squeezed my fingers. "You did fine. Sure, you could use a bit more practice, but that thing you did with your tongue." She did a little shimmy, her eyes going half-lidded for a second. "That was amazing."

"Um, that's not—"

"Besides, I'm sure by the time you get back around to me, you'll be much better." She leaned in closer. "Unless you want to let me cut the line?" She waggled her eyebrows at me.

"That, um—"

"There you are!" Buffy cried, running toward me with a roll of papers in her hand. As we turned our eyes on her, the goblin hissed.

"Firstly, she needs to get back to work." She jabbed an accusing finger at Maribelle. "And not the kind of work she's been doing, either."

"Why, what's going on?" I asked as the goblin thrust a piece of paper and a pen in front of me.

"She's just mad because she drew the last spot," Maribelle said, sticking her tongue out at the goblin.

"No, for the thousandth time, I'm not." Buffy glared at the girl before turning her attention back to me. "I got you your stupid apothecary. That's the contract." She smacked the paper with the pen. "As soon as you sign it, I'll head to Royal Centre to pick her up." She glared at Maribelle again. "That's why you need to finish the building. Because if she gets here, and it's not done, we have to pay double, and since we're already paying double." She gestured at the contract. "Hopefully you see where I'm going with this."

"Can it be finished in time?" I asked, looking at Maribelle.

"Well, I'm quite good at working with wood, so…" She winked at me. "Yeah, I think it will be okay."

"Wipe that stupid grin off your face and get to work," Buffy snarled as she pointed back toward the building. It'd been framed up and had most of the roof and walls attached, but I could still see daylight through it. "You have at best four hours."

"I'd better get on it then," Maribelle said, giving me a light peck on the cheek before heading toward the building site.

"You sign this, now," Buffy said, shaking the papers at me.

"Oh, and Buffy, when it's your turn, ask him to do the thing with his tongue. It's… I can't even," Maribelle called over her shoulder.

Buffy's grip on the pen tightened to white-knuckled fury. "Go do your job!"

"Um… I'm starting to feel like a piece of meat here," I said, taking the pen from her before she could shatter it. I quickly signed the contract. I had no idea if the amounts were good, but I figured it was the best we could do because, well, Buffy.

"Do you know when I last got laid?" Buffy asked, turning her eyes on me. "Unlike Miss Huge Tits, I can't go out to the human world looking like this." She gestured at herself. "A thousand years, sir. I haven't been laid in a thousand years."

"I think you're plenty attractive," I said, shrugging. "I'm not sure I see the problem with you going to the human world."

"You don't need to lay it on me. You're already going to get some," she said, shaking her head as she took the contract and handed me another. "That's for the mason. Same deal as the apothecary, but that building is done."

"Um, okay," I said, taking the pen from her and signing my name.

"It better be better than okay," Buffy said, taking the contract from me. "And that thing with your tongue better be amazing too." She gestured at herself. "A thousand years."

With that she turned and stomped off, leaving me to stand there like an idiot.

I took a deep breath and looked around the compound. Women were everywhere, and as I turned my gaze on them, I saw them eyeing me hungrily. I took a deep breath and gulped. Gwen had said I wouldn't get gang-raped, but as I looked around, I wasn't so sure.

It was my fault though. I'd been the one to sleep with Sam, after all. I'd made my bed, and now I'd have to lie in it both figuratively and literally, which, to be fair, wasn't such a bad thing.

"I need to get some Gatorade," I mumbled, rubbing my chin. I wanted to check on Annabeth and Sam to see their progress since Buffy was well underway with the apothecary and mason. Then I'd go get a workout with Sheila and grab a shower. Beyond that, I wasn't sure what to do. My sword still pulsed with Gwen's life force, and I could have sworn it was even stronger than before. I couldn't say how that was possible, but it most definitely was.

Making my way through town was a little weird because everyone kept looking at me, but I tried my best to ignore it as I approached the spot Annabeth used as her "shop." Really it was just a big open area next to the fountain, and as I approached, I saw she'd completely remade the fountain. Before it'd been fairly standard looking, but now it was different.

A huge statue of Eitri and Brokkr, the dwarves who had fashioned Mjolnir. Brokkr was busy working the bellows, a fly busily attacking him, while Eitri worked the furnace. Instead of smoke coming out of the top of the furnace though, crystalline water poured out the top to cascade over the two brothers.

A soft glow surrounded it, and as I swiped over the bubble, my eyes widened in shock.

Mjolnir's Creation

Class: Sculpture

Material: Stone, Etheric Flame – Red, Dark Blood, Demon Horn

Grade: A

Contains the essence of a fallen blue dragon. Contains the essence of a fallen Darkness warrior. Contains the essence of a fallen demon.

Use: Increased blacksmithing, forging, and all related activities by 25%. Can be combined with other effects. (Additive)

"Do you like it?" Annabeth said, surprising me so much, I leapt forward, one hand going for the hilt of Clarent.

She gave me a strange look as I sat there, trying to keep my heart from beating its way out of my chest.

"Yes, it's amazing." I smirked. "Didn't know you guys followed Norse mythology."

"I didn't know you knew about it," she replied, a smile touching her lips. "But yes, I know about it. Complete hogwash, but still, for these purposes..." She shrugged. "I'm currently working on of the Sons of Ivaldi." She pointed toward a slab a few yards away. It was still roughly hewn, but even from here, I could see a trio of dwarves working to fashion a massive spear while a fourth dwarf watched.

"Is that supposed to be Dvalin?" I asked, pointing at the supervisor.

"Yes," Annabeth replied, nodding at me. "Again, your knowledge of Norse mythology surprises me."

"This must be the fashioning of Gungnir then." I smiled. "It's so cool."

"I'm glad you like them." She sighed. "I have another I'm going to do after this with Hephaestus." She sighed again. "The problem I'm having trouble with is finding ones that will enhance alchemy or sculpting." She shook her head. "Although the whole sculpting a sculpture to help with sculpting feels sort of masturbatory."

"Well, I have lots of ideas for alchemy. I'd be happy to share them with you." I shrugged.

"Wanna grab lunch with me, and we can talk about it? I just realized I'm starving."

"That would be acceptable. Only it can't take too long. I want to finish the Sons of Ivaldi by nightfall." She began walking toward the kitchen, forcing me to catch up to her.

"Yeah, I have some other things to attend to as well," I said catching up to her.

"Don't you mean girls to attend to?" she asked, arching one delicate eyebrow at me.

"Um… that's not what I meant at all. I actually do work too." I felt my face heat up.

"I was not trying to imply otherwise." She met my eyes then. "Did you know they actually had a drawing to decide the order they could sleep with you? I think Elizabeth even made a schedule." Annabeth clucked her tongue.

"Is that so?" I asked, wondering if I should find out if that was true. Part of me was a little horrified at the idea.

"It is." She shook her head. "Honestly, it's a little silly if you ask me." She waved a hand casually at the town. "I get the idea is to keep the peace or whatever, but I think that if you want to sleep with me, you'll do it." She stuck her tongue out. "Not because I had the winning chit."

"Is this your way of saying you're not on the schedule?" I asked, not really believing I was having this conversation.

She paused and looked me up and down. "I am not." With that, she stepped through the doorway. As I followed her inside, I spied a table in the corner. I tapped her shoulder and pointed. Annabeth nodded and, a moment later, we were seated. As the serving girl came by and took our orders, I settled my elbows on the table and looked around. It was busier than I'd expected. It was hard to believe we'd acquired so many workers.

"I think I may need to apologize," Annabeth said, breaking me out of my people watching.

"What for?" I asked, picking up my cup and taking a sip. It was just water, but I was so thirsty, I swore it was the best damned water I'd ever had. Before I realized what I was doing, I'd downed the whole glass.

"I didn't want to imply you were unfit to sleep with or anything." She refilled my glass from the pitcher. "My bed is open if you would like that, but I'm not participating in a drawing. That cheapens it to me."

"Um, good to know," I said, nearly choking on my water. Part of me agreed with her. It was one thing for them to want to sleep with me, but the whole thing sort of left my choices in the wind.

"Are you picturing me naked now?" she asked, a coy smile on her lips, and I realized I'd been staring at her without seeing her.

"No, um, sorry. I got distracted." I tried to smile. "Honestly, I'm worthless now though." I sighed and waved off my own comment.

"On that lovely note, perhaps we can discuss the sculptures." She sipped her water and looked back toward the door like she wanted to be anywhere but here. "I really do need to get back to work."

"Yeah, oh sorry." I smirked as the serving girl returned with our plates. I had a demon burger, and Annabeth had a salad covered in broiled demon. As she speared a mouthful, I wondered if that made her cannibalistic, but I figured it didn't because the only similarity between her and a demon dog was that they were mammals. Or whatever demonic creatures were called. Maybe they weren't mammals?

"Let's hear them." She chewed thoughtfully. "I'm sure they're very impressive." She paused. "That sounded sarcastic and condescending, but it wasn't."

"It's fine." I stared at my burger for a moment.

It smelled so good my mouth was watering, but I knew the second I took a bite, I wouldn't stop until I had licked the plate clean. "Anyway, I was thinking for alchemy we should do Nicolas Flamel and maybe even John Dee. They were both famous alchemists. I think Flamel was believed to have created a philosopher's stone."

"I'd been meaning to do a philosopher's stone but wasn't sure how to work it in." She swallowed her mouthful. "I'm not familiar with Dee or Flamel, but I'll look them up. If that is true, they'd be perfect." She pointed at me with her fork. "Any other ideas?"

"Well, there's always Full Metal Alchemist," I said, and she stared at me blankly.

"I have no idea what that is," she said, turning her gaze to her salad. "But then again I don't know who the other two are either. Would you explain it?"

"Full Metal Alchemist is a manga and anime that was pretty popular. It's about two brothers who do alchemy. It's really good." I nodded. "The statues are supposed to help with the whole je ne sais quoi of the art right, so they'd probably work."

"I didn't know you spoke French," she said,

licking some dressing from her lips. "A man of many talents, it'd seem."

"Not so much," I said, shrugging. "I'll have to think about sculpting. There's always like Michelangelo and Donatello. They were famous sculptors."

"I'd thought about that. I actually know a few I could do, but as I said, it seems silly." She speared another bit of lettuce. "Still, you're right. I'll get right on it." She took another bite before pointing her empty fork at me. "You better eat that before it gets cold."

"Right," I said, turning to my food. I picked up the burger and took a bite. Like always, it was just how I wanted it. The perfect amount of crunch on the bread with enough sauce to flavor but not make it soggy. Even the cheese was still melted, and the meat? Juicy and delicious.

44

Since Annabeth abandoned me after lunch, I made my way toward Sam's shop to check on her progress. As I pushed open the door, I found her standing over her bench. Her two apprentices were busy working at the forge and bellows, but as I stepped inside, they eyed me like hungry lions.

A flush crossed my face as I took a deep breath and pointedly turned away from them. I knew they'd made a schedule and had a drawing or whatever, but at the same time, I was a person. I should have some ability to choose who I wanted to sleep with, right? I felt like I should, anyway. I'd just have to talk to Elizabeth about that, even though the idea of doing so might hurt people's feelings.

Still, it was better than the alternative. I think.

"Hey, Sam," I said, moving toward her. "Any progress on the emitters?"

"Yes, actually," she said, glancing back at me over her shoulder and smiling. Was she wearing lipstick? Surely, not.

"Well, give me the scoop," I said, sliding up next to her and looking at the bench. Only instead of seeing gadgets and what not, I just saw a bunch of books, plans, and notes.

"Basically, I had an idea. We actually do use emitters for certain things like firebrands." She pointed toward the light on the ceiling. It was a thin wire that ran the length of the ceiling in a sort of crisscrossed pattern. It glowed with light, illuminating the room.

"Yeah, I've seen those from time to time, but I don't recall you having any. Didn't you use torches?" I asked because I wasn't sure. For all I knew, I was remembering wrong.

"I did, sort of. Mostly I used the big windows though." She pointed to the huge windows on the walls that let in the natural light. The place was weird because it didn't really have a traditional night or day. There was mostly just the same amount of ambient light at any time thanks to the churning sky overhead.

"So, let's take a step backward and start over." I smiled at her and pointed to the firebrands on the ceiling. "Those have emitters?"

"Yes, I actually made those as an experiment." She tapped her temple with her index finger. "I could never quite get it before, but I was working on it all morning. It just sort of clicked. Guess it's the new smarts." She took a deep breath. "Anyway, I figured I can just try to make emitters similar to those utilizing the Etheric Flame. That's why I've been practicing on them." She gestured to the table. "I researched everything I could find on them. Most of these books are from the archive, so I'll need to return them. I read everything they wouldn't let me take thanks to my Rank there, though, hence the notes." She waved a hand through the air like she was wiping something away. "Anyway, I'll be ready to try making the emitters for the gateway soon. So just let me know when you want me to start."

"I'm thinking two days, tops." I touched my sword, feeling bad Gwen would be trapped two more days, but there was nothing for it. If we couldn't get her and get back, we couldn't save her. Rushing in would just get everyone killed, and I wouldn't sacrifice everyone just to save her, no matter how much I liked her. That wasn't fair to everyone else.

"Okay, I'll be ready," she said, running a hand through her hair and combing it out of her face. "If that's all, I think I'd better get back to work. Buffy says these sell well, so I'm going to make as many as I can so we can buy more materials for me to practice. I'm trying to get really good at it."

"Alright, I'll leave you alone." I nodded to her before turning to the apprentices. "How are they doing?"

"They're doing better than expected. It actually helps a lot because I can show them how to do helpful tasks and not have to waste time on it myself."

"So, they do grunt work," I said, turning back to her.

"Everyone does grunt work for a while. It's how you learn." She shrugged. "Trust me, you gave me the smarts."

"Hey, I do trust you," I said. "I just wondered. Oh, what about the dragon scale?"

"We're making dragon scale shields and armor," Sam said, waving to the apprentices. "Well, they are, mostly. I'm just taking off the rough edges. It won't be quite as good as if I did it myself but it'll be close enough that me spending the extra time probably isn't worth it."

"All right," I said, turning to go. I was just happy they were working. The sooner we got better gear for our people, the sooner we'd be ready to go after Gwen because I really didn't want to finish the Nexus Gateway and then have to wait for our people to get weapons and armor made. "Keep up the good work, you two."

"We will," the apprentices said, both watching my every move. I wasn't sure if they were going to pounce on me, but I definitely did not want them to do that here. As fun as being with Maribelle had been, I was worn out and needed a shower.

Before they could say more, I was out the door and headed toward Sally's alchemist shop. I wanted to know how she'd progressed in her Etheric Flame Skill, and besides, if upgrading Sam had helped so much, I'd better just upgrade Sally too. Doing so would probably reap greater dividends.

A few minutes later, I was walking through her door. She sat in front of a giant bronze bowl that looked both new and used at the same time. A shelf full of Etheric Flame glittered behind her, and as I approached, she looked up. Her face was flecked with bits of silver dust from whatever she was working on so she glimmered in the light of her own firebrands. Sam wasn't kidding. She really had made a bunch of them.

"Hi, Arthur," she said, swallowing hard. "Did you need something?"

"Not really, I just wanted to see you," I said, moving to examine the shelf full of Etheric Flame. These looked much higher quality than the one she'd made while we'd been traveling, and as I glanced back at her, I opened her Skill Tree and saw her Specialty: Etheric Flame had been raised from one out of ten to six out of ten.

"What about?" Sally asked, turning to watch me as I picked up the brightest Etheric Flames she'd refined.

Etheric Flame - Red
Material: Gemstone
Grade: S
Contains the essence of a fallen red dragon. Has finished the refining process.

"Wow, you really have gotten good at this." I held up the Etheric Flame. "This is S grade."

"Thanks," she said, taking a deep breath. "I've gotten quite good at it, actually. I think I've gotten a few more S grade ones." She frowned. "It's hard because the difference between a S grade and an A grade isn't very much really, but there's a huge range of A grade." She pointed at two green ones sitting on a shelf, and one was clearly better than the other. "For instance, both of those are considered A."

I looked, and sure enough, they were both A grade. "Is it like comics and stuff? Where some flaws weigh more heavily than others?"

"Basically," she said, coming and pointing at the darker one. "This one is perfect but has bad luminosity, which drops it from S to A. Otherwise, it's absolutely perfect." Her finger moved to the other. "This one actually has internal fractures, but otherwise is perfect. That's what's dropping it." She looked back to me. "You almost need a really good one to start with to get S grade. A isn't super difficult, but S? S requires good stock to begin with."

"Hmm, is there a way to tell before we buy them? Maybe we can get rough ones that are more likely to become S grade?" I asked, moving down the shelf. Now that she'd explained it, I could see what she was talking about in a few of the others. Sometimes it was a small nick, other times it was a weird inner darkness.

"Not particularly," she said with a shrug. "Not that'd be worth it. The ultimate problem is that I can't sell these for squat. Even S grade is only worth a bit more than A. So, it's probably not worth the manual effort to sort them." She gave me an apologetic smile. "Mostly, I'm just practicing since I finished refining all the Dark Blood and Demon Horn. Granted the Demon Horn is so common, it really doesn't do much…"

"Do you know what Annabeth is using in her sculptures? What grade?" I asked, turning my gaze back to her.

"A grade mostly, but that's because we've been saving the S grades for the final construction of the Nexus Gateway Conduit. If you'd like, we can change it up?" She pointed to the shelf where I'd grabbed the S grade Etheric Flame. "That's all the S grade we have though."

"Just six?" I asked, surprised because there were almost a hundred on the shelf.

"Just six. As I said, it sort of depends a lot on the Etheric Flame itself. A few I messed up, but it's not that many. Maybe three." She flushed a little. "That was before though. I haven't messed any up in a while."

"Makes sense," I said, rubbing my chin. We had six of them, and we'd need at least three for each Nexus Gateway attempt. That would let us try twice, but since I was sure we'd need S grade for each of the components as well, that meant each one would require nine. Not good odds.

"Is something wrong?" she asked, looking at me nervously. "You seem worried."

"I was just thinking we need at least nine S-grade per attempt, and maybe more." I sighed. "How many more roughs do we have?"

"Another hundred or so. We should be okay." She gave me a weak smile. "If it's anything like the last batch, I'll get another six on the low end, maybe more."

"Not good odds, we may have to buy more." I stared at the shelf. "I'll go talk to Buffy."

"I don't think we can. I already had Buffy buy everything from Blade's End. It's on its way, but it's only about double what we have here." She nodded furiously then. "I'll work harder though. It'll be okay. I will make sure of it."

"I know you will, I'm not worried about that." I gave her a thumb's up.

"My firebrands are getting better too," she said, pointing at the ceiling. "I used the emitters from Sam and got Annabeth to make some conduits. It was actually Elizabeth's idea to try."

"Not Sam's?" I asked, somewhat surprised. "I thought she was making them."

"Well, it was sort of a group thing. I guess Sam can take credit." Sally flushed slightly. "She wanted the materials to make emitters, and when we asked her why, she explained her thought process. Then Elizabeth got it in her head to just make the whole thing so all of us could practice."

"Ah." I nodded. Sam had an idea, and Elizabeth had monetized it. *That* made perfect sense.

"Don't be upset with Sam about it," she said, shaking her head. "It really was mostly her idea."

"I'm not." I shook my head back at her. "Not even slightly. I love how well it worked out. Gives us a way to practice for profit. That's the best thing ever."

"I'm glad." Sally let out a relieved sound. "Really."

"There was just one more thing," I said, opening her Character Sheet.

"What's that?" Sally asked, not looking at me.

"I want to go ahead and upgrade your Stats. It may help with the refining. Is that okay?"

"Oh, yeah, sure. That would be great." She gave me a strange look.

"Awesome," I said, looking over her Stats. "Now let's see."

Name: Sally
Experience: 36,543
Strength: 10/100
Agility: 40/100
Charisma: 25/100
Intelligence: 56/100
Special: 86/100

"Okay, looks like it will take about seventy-five-hundred Experience to raise your Special, Intelligence, and Agility to ninety-five." I looked back at her. "You have about thirty-six thousand, so that's okay, right?"

"Of course," she said, and I made the change. As blue light surrounded her, she blinked at me a few times. "Wow, thanks." She gave me a mischievous grin. "I feel way smarter."

"Well, I nearly doubled your Intelligence, so that's not too surprising." I smiled at her. "Anyway, I'll leave you to it. I definitely need a shower." I sniffed at myself. "I stink."

"Not going to work out with Sheila today?" she asked, moving next to me.

"No, I'm too tired for that. I mostly just want to be clean." I tugged at my shirt, and it stuck to me.

"Ah, well do you mind if I walk with you? Crystal is there, and I want to ask her about something."

"Sure, let's go. You can let her know I'm waiting, that way she doesn't use all the hot water again," I said, moving out of the shop and heading toward the bathhouse. Like it normally was at this time of what passed for day in Hell, it was empty, but even still, I could hear one of the showers inside. That must have been Crystal. It was always a little weird because I had to wait until it was empty to go inside since it was communal.

"I'll go tell her," Sally said as we approached, and before I could say anything, she vanished into the building. I waited there, leaning against the wooden frame and wondered if it was worth it to have Maribelle build me my own shower. It seemed like a waste of resources, but at the same time, sometimes it was too hard for me to get one because of all the people.

A few moments later, Sally poked her head back out. "She's almost done, it'll just be a second." She moved out from the doorway. "Is that okay?"

"Yeah, that's fine." I smiled at her. "Thanks for checking."

"Of course," Sally said, moving toward me and

taking up the spot on the wall beside me. "I wanted to ask you something, anyway."

"What's that?" I said, raising an eyebrow at her. "Do you need some more materials or something?"

"No, it's more" She cleared her throat, "Well, here's the thing..." She shut her eyes for a long moment. "I guess I should just say it." As she squirmed, I started to get worried. Was there some kind of problem?

"That would be best, yes. Trust me, I'm pretty amenable." I tried to give her a disarming smile but it must not have worked because she looked back toward the entrance of the showers.

"Yeah, okay." She took a deep breath and turned to look at me. "Here's the thing. Crystal drew number fifteen in the, um, schedule." Sally looked away again, studying the wall like it was terribly interesting.

"Ah, I see. Are you okay with that?" I said, not sure quite how to take that. I'd always thought Crystal and Sally were a couple, so the fact that she'd taken a number was, well, I wasn't even sure.

"Not really, that's kind of the problem." She shook her head. "That's what I wanted to talk to you about."

"Oh? Well, if it's a problem," I said, reaching

out and touching her shoulder. "Honestly, I'm not even sure—"

"No, that isn't my problem. Not really." Sally waved off my train of thought. "My problem is I got number two, and we were wondering if maybe you'd be okay with sharing? Like maybe we could both go at the same time?"

"Did you just say what I think you said?" I asked. She'd just blown my mind.

"I think so?" she asked, blushing. "If it's not okay, I totally understand." She gave me a weak smile. "But would you think about it?"

"You're asking me if it's okay if we all three have sex at the same time?" I said, still a bit dumbstruck.

"Yes, but it's okay if you don't want to do that. I don't want you to feel pressured. I just sort of hoped…" She touched my arm. "It was probably wrong of me to ask. I'm sorry. Um… maybe I can make it up to you? You were going to shower right? I could wash your back."

"Just give me a second," I said, shutting my eyes for a second while I did a little mental cheer. This was really happening. Oh my god.

"I really wish I hadn't brought it up now," she

said, and when I opened my eyes, she wasn't looking at me. "If you want, I can give up my spot."

"No, look, what you just offered would be great," I said, nodding to her, "if it's what you two want."

"It is," she said, her face lighting up. She grabbed my hands in hers. "Thank you so much." Then she kissed me, pressing her lips against mine as she pulled me toward the shower door.

45

The next few days went by in a blur as we assembled the pieces for the Nexus Gateway Conduit. We'd wound up using Sam's idea and forging the emitter and the conduit itself like they were in the firebrand since despite our best efforts, we couldn't find another way. Hopefully, it would work. If it didn't, it wouldn't be for lack of trying. That would be for damned sure.

Still, even though Annabeth's statues were done and the apothecary had crafted potions to temporarily boost both luck and skill, I was worried. If it didn't work, Gwen would remain trapped in the Graveyard of Statues for even longer. The only thing that made me able to even tolerate that was that, somehow, she seemed to be gaining strength. With each day that passed, I'd felt the pulse of her power grow. I wasn't sure why, but it did make me feel better.

"I guess there's no time like the present," I said, turning my gaze to Sally. She was standing with Sam and Annabeth on her right and Crystal on her left. We were in the spot where Nadine had opened the gateway to escape. I wasn't sure if it mattered where it was, but since I knew one had been formed here, I figured it was better safe than sorry. After all, it had to be easier to reopen one instead of making another, right?

Then again, it wasn't like we were actually going to open a gateway here. No, we were going to craft the item and then siege the Graveyard of Statues. Once that was done, and we'd rescued Gwen, we would use it to escape. At least that was the plan.

"Okay," Sally said, taking a deep breath. "Let's go."

She raised her hands high overhead. As lightning lit up the sky and thunder boomed, she began to chant. I couldn't understand the words because they were in that weird demonic language I couldn't comprehend, but that didn't mean I couldn't feel the power in them.

It swelled up all around me, thrumming through the air like an electric storm. The hair on the back of my neck came to attention, and my heart hammered in my chest as the sky turned into a churning mass of darkness.

Lightning scoured the horizon as Sally brought her hands down in a decisive arc. Power tore from the sky and smashed into the spot in front of her where we had laid out the conduit, the emitter, and the Etheric Flame in a triangle. There was one set for each of the three colors, and as power coursed from the sky, I felt the ground beneath our feet heat up.

I turned my gaze downward as a tornado of swirling blue, green, and red sparks sprang to life in the center of the triangle. More power buffeted outward, and the wind howled, sweeping down through the town and throwing dust and debris in every direction. A chill wrapped around me as I stared at the glowing mass of objects. I couldn't tell if it was working, but as Sally channeled more power into the spell, I saw blood on her face.

My eyes widened as I realized it was coming from her nose, eyes, and ears to collect on her chin and spatter across the ground. A quick look at her Stats told me why. Her Health was dropping. Fast.

"Dammit," I said, grabbing Clarent and pulling it free of its sheath. I'd intended to use it to increase her Health or give her some innate regeneration Abilities, but as soon as the sword came free, it began to blaze with sapphire fire.

My eyes went wide as it began to pulse in time with the swirling vortex of color around the Nexus Gateway. Then a message popped up.

Do you wish to augment the process? Y/N.

I had no idea what that meant, but the word augment was glowing. After taking another look at Sally's Health, I swiped my hand over it.

Augmenting the process allows the Builder to sacrifice Health to increase the odds of success. In order to increase chances, 2% of the Builder's Health will be sacrificed to increase the chance of success by 1%. Health will continue to drain until success is achieved or the user dies. Do you wish to augment the process? Y/N

I stared at the message. Of course, I wanted to augment the process, but I didn't actually know how much Health I had nor if we were close enough to success for it to matter. For all I knew, I was at eighty percent Health, and we only had a twenty percent chance of success. After all, most of the people I worked with seemed to naturally fluctuate between about seventy-five percent and one hundred percent depending on if they were hungry, tired, or just plain beat up.

Still, I knew I could probably do about fifty percent without it really hurting me. That just left two questions. What would happen if I did it and would that be enough?

I wasn't sure, but I knew I had to try. We'd already done everything we could. We'd crafted the statues. We'd drank the potions. There was no other way. Sure, we could try again, but we'd only had enough materials to try this one time. We'd be starting over, and that was assuming we could even get enough Etheric Flame.

No. This had to work.

I took a deep breath and pointed my sword at the vortex.

"Yes," I whispered, and as I did, I felt blood trickle from my nose to be swept toward the vortex. Sheer, unadulterated agony stabbed into my brain, driving to my knees in the dirt. The sword in my hand glowed brighter. My heart hammered in my chest. An electric shock seemed to go through me then, causing my muscles to seize, and as Sam said something and Annabeth moved toward me, time seemed to slow down.

For one, glinting moment, I saw Gwen's face in the vortex, saw her still chained there, and as I stared at her, I saw her nose began to bleed. I saw her skin lose some of its luster. The sigils emblazoned across Clarent flared even brighter, and as I felt darkness starting to encroach upon me, I forced myself to give more.

The sword brightened as Gwen's face vanished into the dervish. Then I felt hands on my shoulders. Sam's and Annabeth's.

Crystal's were on Sally's shoulders, and as I watched the two girls, I realized Crystal was bleeding now. Her skin had gotten sallow.

I felt blood spatter across my back, and even though I barely had the strength to turn my head upward, I saw both Sam and Annabeth. Blood poured from their noses too.

That's when I heard people rushing toward us. Maribelle was next to me a second later, her hand outstretched toward the dervish. Then Buffy and Elizabeth. In the span of a second, it felt like the whole town was there, hands outstretched toward the spell. The dervish flared again, growing in size and intensity.

The buildings around us began to shake, and the ground grew damned near molten. Lightning split the sky and thunder boomed like gunshots in my ears. My vision went blurry then as I came right up to the edge of passing out.

Then the three sets of crafting materials at the corners of the triangle began to glow with star fire. Red for the blood we spilled. Green for the sacrifice in time, energy and materials we gave. And Blue. Blue for the magic we gave. That was when I understood and as that realization hit me like a thousand tons of rock, the entire world went black and empty.

46

A roar that shook the foundations of the building jolted me from sleep. The last thing I remembered was trying to create the Nexus Gateway Conduit, yet somehow I was in bed wearing only a white T-shirt.

"What's going on?" I cried, leaping from my bed and nearly falling on my face as I tripped over Clarent. The blade was still in its sheath attached to my pants which were themselves strewn on the floor. My hand went out, palming the wall for balance. My chest heaved as another roar nearly shattered my eardrums.

I wasn't sure what was going on. Had Nadine come to attack us while I was asleep? I wasn't sure, but I was going to find out. I pulled on my pants and sword belt on my way to the door before disappearing through it. I'd half expected to see people in the hallway, but it was deserted.

A trumpet blast of roars nearly made my heart leap into my throat, but I ignored them as I pulled Clarent free of its sheath and summoned my battle armor. I wasn't sure what I'd find, but I wanted to be prepared for the worst. As I burst through the doorway, I found myself staring at a trio of dragons so immense they made the ravagers seem small by comparison. They were decked out in glinting armor, complete with massive spiked helmets that glinted in the light of the stormy sky.

As I stared up at the green, red, and blue creatures, I whipped my head around looking for my people. Only they weren't here. Why was no one here?

I took a step forward as the dragons watched me. Their scales throwing sparkles of color across the ground as their eyes followed me. That's when I noticed the glowing menu orbs above their heads. How was that possible? Still, seeing them was a relief. It meant they weren't going to try to eat me. Probably anyway. Free will and all that.

Part of me wanted to flick through their Skills, but I wanted to find out where everyone was. Not that it mattered because a quick glance at the blue one's menu let me know they were exactly like the ravagers we had captured. Their Stats could not be altered, and they had no Special Abilities.

Satisfied, I made my way around them, trying to find someone, anyone, and as I did, I saw Diana walking toward me flanked by two other women decked out in dragon scale armor.

"Did they wake you?" Diana called, waving a hand at me as she approached. "Sorry about that."

"How, why?" I said, gesturing to the creatures, and as I did, I realized Diana and her two escorts had menu orbs over their heads too. When had that happened? Man, how long was I unconscious?

"Yeah, but it's okay." I took a deep breath as I sheathed Clarent. "I didn't realize you were here" - I tried to smile - "or that you brought friends."

"Buffy contacted me and asked if I could send soldiers for the siege." Diana nodded to her two warriors. "I was going to refuse, but she made me an offer I couldn't refuse." Diana patted the big blue one on the flank. "She gave us a way to tame the dragons." Diana smiled. "Flying on one is just incredible."

"I'd like to find out sometime," I said, trying to imagine what it'd be like. "How did Buffy let you tame dragons?"

"Your smith made something with all the Etheric Flame. Some kind of helmet." She pointed at the dragons' helmets, and I realized they looked awfully similar to the ones we had used to brain box the ravagers. Clever.

"I think I get it." I nodded to her. "Thank you for coming."

"You're welcome," Diana said, turning on her heel and gesturing to a new building I'd not seen before. "If you're awake, you should come to the banquet hall."

"Banquet hall?" I asked, raising an eyebrow at her.

"Yes," Diana said, pausing to give me a quizzical look. Then she gestured toward the building. "That's where everyone is right now. It's dinner time."

"Yeah, okay," I said, rubbing my head as I followed her. I really needed to get a handle on things, but something told me Diana wasn't the person to ask about it. Sure, she'd come to help save Gwen, and she'd brought dragons, but she wasn't one of mine. Not really anyway. Not yet.

A few moments later, we stepped into the banquet hall, and the room went absolutely silent. All eyes turned to me. What's more, there were more people than I remembered being in Lustnor. A huge contingent of them were dragon warriors, but there were more I didn't recognize.

As I stood there slack jawed, Buffy came over to me. "Act like you knew they were supposed to be here," Buffy hissed, voice low enough for only me to hear.

She grabbed my hand and led me toward a chair situated in the center of the massive table. Everyone was around it, and as I gave an unsteady beauty queen wave to the crowd, they went back to stuffing their faces. The noise level rose, and I saw Buffy give a little breath of relief.

"What in the blue hell is going on?" I asked as Buffy shoved me into the chair. The spot had been empty, but by the time we reached it, a meal had been laid out in front of it.

She slid into the empty one to my left. Elizabeth was seated in the chair on the right, but she was too busy chatting with Maribelle about cogs and boards to pay much attention to me beyond a relieved hello. It was weird because everyone looked at me, gave a polite wave, and then went back to what they were doing. It made me think they weren't all that happy to see me, but I had no idea why.

Actually, that wasn't true. They looked relieved

to see me, but at the same time, I'd have expected more commotion. Maybe I hadn't been asleep that long, after all.

"Don't look so surprised. You've only been asleep for a day," Buffy said, leaning toward me so her words were a warm breath in my ear. "During that time, we recruited people to come. Diana was easy enough, and once she came, we got some of the others. Most are mercenaries though. Expensive, but hopefully, they'll help. All in all, we have about a hundred people, plus the two ravagers and Diana's three dragons."

"You got all that ready in a day?" I asked, partially shocked at how quickly it had been done, and with how long I was asleep. That was the thing though. It didn't feel like I'd been asleep that long. For one, even as I stared at the food in front of me. Some kind of meaty stew and a side of vegetables, I didn't feel hungry.

"Well, Elizabeth helped." Buffy gestured toward her sister. "She's got the connections." She narrowed her eyes at me as I picked at the veggies with my fork. "You better eat up because now that you're up, we're going to head into battle. Who knows the next time you'll be able to eat?"

"I just don't feel hungry," I said, shoving a piece

of broccoli into my mouth and chewing it. As a kid, I'd always sort of liked broccoli because it was like being a dinosaur and eating mini trees, but admittedly, most of my adult life had been relatively broccoli free.

"That's probably because of Sally's magic. She was using it to keep you from dying while you recovered." Buffy took a deep breath. "Everyone is okay by the way."

I swallowed the piece of broccoli and looked around. Everyone was there. Sally, Crystal, Sheila. The whole gang. They were all laughing and having fun in an earnest, "last night before being shipped off" sort of way. I'd seen it before with my friends when they'd joined the military.

"I'm guessing we created the Nexus Gateway Conduit?" I asked, gesturing at the crowd. "Otherwise, I doubt everyone would be here."

"Yes. Sorry, I should have started with that." Buffy nodded to Sally across the table. "She has it. Once we're inside, we'll be able to activate it. The thing works really well. Gets us from here to Blade's End or Royal Centre pretty much instantly. If we had more, we could sell them for the town's weight in gold." She sighed. "Makes me almost sad we owe the next one to Diana."

"It is what it is," I said, nodding to her before standing up. I grabbed my goblet although I wasn't sure what was in it. I held it up, and the room got as silent as a tomb as all eyes focused on me. "Thanks everyone for coming."

I took a deep breath. "I know I'm not the smartest or strongest guy, but I promise I'll do everything I can to ensure victory over the Darkness." I raised my goblet a little higher. "But I'll be honest, victory won't be because of me. It will because of all of you and what you all bring to the table. For that, I thank you."

Applause broke out as I took a sip from my goblet. Razzleberry punch. Perfect.

47

As I stood at the border between the Darkness and Hell, I took a moment to look back at everyone who had come. While some of the noncombatants like Buffy and Maribelle had stayed behind in town, most everyone else was here. Sheila and Annabeth sat atop their ravagers. Diana's dragon warriors stood clustered around her and her dragon riders while the rest of the guards and mercenaries stood back in two distinct shield wall lines.

Behind them were the archers, all loaded with explosive and signaling arrows. I knew Sally and the other healers we'd managed to recruit were there too. I'd done what I could to shore up everyone's Stats and Abilities, but at the same time, I'd tried to leave them with enough Experience for contingencies.

I wasn't sure it'd be enough to take on the Darkness, but we had to try. If we didn't succeed, we'd lose Gwen, and what's more, the Darkness would continue eating all of Hell until there was nothing left. While Gwen had felt much stronger today than she had even a few days ago, something about her capture didn't feel right. It felt like we were walking into a trap. Last time we'd gone into the Darkness, Agatha had died, and that hadn't felt like this. Sure, we had the Nexus Gate Conduit now and could open them at will, but at the same time, I was worried.

There was a good chance not all of us would be coming back alive, and everyone who fell would be on my head. Sure, they'd chosen to be here whether out of loyalty, greed, or honor, but their deaths were still on my head, and as commander, it was my responsibility to bear.

And I would do it. I would lead a siege into the Darkness, and I would push it back or die trying. That was my promise to my people.

"Come on you apes, you want to live forever?" I cried, calling forth my armor. Clarent flared to life in my hand. As sapphire light enveloped me before solidifying into armor, the assembled troops shouted and stomped their feet.

Turning back to the Darkness, I stepped into the breach. Just like last time, it felt like my body was being torn apart, but unlike last time, it didn't feel like it took forever. I wasn't sure if that was because I was getting used to it or not, but as the Graveyard of Statues appeared before me, I felt a surge of confidence rush through me.

Beholders meandered around the Graveyard like last time, but aside from them, there wasn't anything much between us and the statue of the Empress at the top. While I couldn't see Gwen near it, I could feel her stronger than ever.

As the runes on Clarent began to blaze with blue light, the rest of my army appeared behind me. To be honest, I felt a little stupid being out in front, but I felt like I had to lead this way, at least when stepping into the Darkness itself. This was where my compromise with Sheila ended.

As she and Annabeth took the lead with their ravagers, I pointed my sword at the closest beholder. Already the creatures were coming toward us like I'd just chummed shark infested waters. The only problem, at least for them, was that they weren't the super predators anymore. We were.

"Archers, take out the beholders." As arrows flew through the air, dousing the massive creatures with fire before blowing them to pieces, I turned back toward the statue. "Sheila, let's take the Empress."

"Your wish is my command," Sheila replied, spurring her ravager forward. The big beasts began to move, each step sending a shockwave through the earth as they plodded forward. While I'd wanted them to avoid the statues as much as possible, after only a few moments, I knew that'd be impossible. The ravagers were so big, they crushed statues into piles of rubble with every step.

"Diana, take your dragons up and do a sweep of the area. I don't know what's on the other side of the hill, but I don't want any surprises."

She nodded to me from atop her massive red dragon before spurring it into the sky. As it soared upward, her two other riders followed suit, bursting into the darkening sky. Their scales glimmered even in the low light, and as they raced up toward the hill, all hell broke loose.

The ground beneath our feet fractured, spitting gobs of sulfuric smoke into the air. Winged black creatures descended from the sky while lizardmen pulled themselves from the shattered earth around us. Beholders came rumbling down the hill toward us, so numerous that I almost couldn't see through the wave.

To our right and left, spider-like creatures clamored over the horizon and made a beeline for the ravagers. Sprays of silky webbing shot from their mouths, latching onto the massive creatures in an attempt to pull them to the earth. I wasn't even sure what the spiders were exactly, but I knew that if they toppled the ravagers, we were screwed.

"Archers, engage the spiders. We can't lose the ravagers," I cried, and as arrows arced through the air like a wave of fire and brimstone, I turned my attention to Diana. I'd been about to ask her to lay down a wall of flame between the beholders and us, but as I saw her, I realized that was impossible.

She and her dragons were weaving through the air, engaged in aerial combat with the bat creatures. As they juked and dived in the air in some kind of prehistoric dogfight, I took a deep breath and focused. This was all a distraction, I knew it. We had to reach the Empress. That was where Gwen's power seemed to emanate from.

Annabeth's ravager fell, its legs bound up in white silk, and as the spiders surged toward it, I pointed my sword at the incoming spiders. "Guards, free the ravager!" As the first line moved forward to help while the second stayed behind to guard the archers, I saw Annabeth leap from the creature. Her sculpting knife whipped out as she hit the ground, severing the strands of silk clinging to her beast of burden.

Then the guards slammed into the spiders, spearing them with javelins and driving them back. Again, another distraction. This was a war of attrition, and if we let the enemy keep forcing us to react to them, to defend from them, we were hosed. Our only chance at victory was to claim our prize and flee before their full forces could come down on us like a hammer.

"Dragon warriors to me," I called, raising my sword into the air. Sapphire light blazed on it as the women moved to my side, encircling me with spear and shield. "We're taking that hill!"

A battle cry rang from their lips as we pulled forward. Sheila moved forward, ignoring the spiders and everything else as she continued upward, smashing through everything in her way. We followed after her, the dragon warriors battering through whatever lived or got out of Sheila's path of destruction.

Even still, it was slow going. Annabeth was back

up, but she was too focused on assisting the guards and keeping the archers alive to reach us, not with how slow her ravager was.

That was also our problem. While Sheila was good at clearing a path, she was taking so long that more enemies were coming. For every lizardman she killed, two more seemed to take its place, and it wasn't long before our movement upward turned into a hard slog through enemy lines.

Even still, we were only about a hundred meters from the Empress, and Gwen's life force felt stronger than ever. While we might be going slowly, we were making progress. Part of me wanted to rush forward, to bypass Sheila, but if we did that, the enemies wouldn't be blunted by her ravager. That was suicide since as good as the dragon warriors were, even they couldn't push through a wall of beholders ten deep. Sheila could.

The sky above crackled, and the ground shook again. More monsters surged from the sky, and as they did, I saw Diana coming toward me like a bat out of Hell. I didn't see her other two dragons, and she an entire sky full of monsters after her.

Her dragon's jaws seemed to unhinge as she let loose a volley of flame that scorched the earth between us and the statue, but as she pulled back up toward the top of the hill, she seemed to slam into an invisible wall. Electricity arced out from the space around the statue, turning her dragon crispy fried as she was thrown to the ground.

"Get to her!" I cried, sprinting forward through the path she'd just cleared for us. Already more enemies were coming, and without Diana and her dragons to help, the bats descended on Sheila. I instantly realized that while they posed no real danger to the ravagers, there was no way Sheila or Annabeth would be able to fight them off and help. We were on our own.

As we charged up the scorched path of death, I saw Diana at the crest of the hill. She was battered and bloody. Her face was a crimson mask, and as she made a move to stand, something flung her down the hill. She hit hard on her shoulder, and the snap of her collarbone was loud even over the din of the battle. She came rolling to a stop at my feet as Nadine took a step forward and smiled down at me.

"So, you've finally come, Builder. I wondered how long you'd take." Her blood-red hair glittered in the Darkness as she raised one hand high, causing the sky to crackle and split. "I have been waiting for this day for a long, long while." Her lips curled into a smile as more lightning than I'd ever seen in my entire life came arcing toward us.

I raised my sword to defend myself, wishing, hoping for some way to deflect the attack, and as I did, I felt the pommel of my sword flare. Green light exploded from it before rippling up through the blade and spreading out like an umbrella. The lightning slammed down into my makeshift shield, driving me to my knees in the dirt before sliding off the sides and hitting the ground beside us.

"Get Diana before it's too late," I said, rising to my feet. "I'll take care of Nadine."

"You'll take care of me?" she tittered as the dragon warriors moved to advance toward Diana. "How delusional you must be." She snapped her fingers, and the world erupted into flame that shot from the ground, turning the world molten. People screamed, and their cries were like daggers to my heart as geysers of magma shot from the earth.

"I'm not sure why you betrayed your people, Nadine, but I won't let you continue to hurt mine." I charged the dark princess. I had to stop her before she could do more, before she could hurt us more. If I didn't, we were screwed. We wouldn't rescue Gwen. We'd just die here.

"Pathetic," she said, and then she was gone.

Something hard slammed into my side, shattering my armor into shards. Pain unlike anything I'd ever felt before exploded through me as I tumbled across the battlefield like a broken mannequin. I wasn't quite sure if she'd broken my ribs, but from the way they hurt, it seemed likely.

Nadine stood next to where I'd been and pointed her bloody fist at me. "If you think I'm going to kill you quickly, you're wrong. No. I want you to suffer for the humiliation you caused me." Her face quirked into an amused smile. "I want to get my fingers all up in your gooey bits." She waggled her fingers at me. "But first, you need to learn what it means to lose."

With that, she spun on her heel and pointed at Diana and her dragon warriors. Before I could so much as shout a warning, the entire cadre of women exploded into bloody chunks.

48

"No!" I shrieked, my hand outstretched toward Nadine as pure, unbridled fury swept through me. My vision went red. I wanted to kill her. To rend her limb from limb. I. Would. Make. Her. Pay.

Scarlet flame spiraled off my sword as the Etheric Flame in the pommel flared to life. A comet of hellfire exploded from my outstretched hand, turning the ground beneath it to glass as it rocketed forward. The blast caught Nadine in her smug face, blasting her backward across the clearing before detonating like a nuclear blast. As a mushroom cloud of smoke filled the sky, and the shockwave threw monsters and soldiers backward, my chest heaved with pain. I could taste blood on my lips.

I wasn't sure what had happened, but I didn't

care. I was going to finish her. Even through the swirling flames in the distance, I could see someone moving. It probably shouldn't have been surprising because she'd been stomped on by a bazillion ton ravager and walked it off.

I took a step toward her, light still streaming from Clarent, and as I did, I realized that's what Nadine wanted because, at the end of the day, she was a distraction too. Albeit a violent psycho-bitch distraction but a distraction nonetheless. We had to save Gwen and get out of here. Every second we stayed to fight was a second too long, a second where more people died, and I was done with the Saving Private Ryan bullshit.

Turning, I ignored Nadine and sprinted for the statue at the edge of the hill. As I crested that hill, a thunderous shriek of pure insanity nearly stopped me in my tracks. My eardrums burst as the sky above ripped wide open to reveal something so massive and grotesque I could see little more than its head as it looked at me.

That single, unblinking, multifaceted eye fixed upon me, and it was all I could do to keep from going insane. Pain coursed through me and my vision tinged around the edges with blackness. Then it opened its maw and shrieked once more.

I felt myself wither, felt myself dying as Clarent slipped from my grip and hit the dirt beside me. Pain coursed through me, lighting upon every nerve as the fury of its gaze poured into me, ravaging me to the core. I coughed, blood spraying from my lips, and as the Darkness surrounding me threatened to swallow me whole, Sheila slammed into me.

The guard's massive bulk threw me sideways, out of the smoking crater where I'd been standing. Once again, the monster screamed. This time, its cry was met by a flurry of flaming arrows that poured into the void from our archers. Fire and explosions rocked it, causing it to pull back from the void long enough to reveal the squid-like mass of tentacles the thing called hair as it turned away from the void, retreating from our attack.

"Go!" Sheila cried, shoving Clarent into my hand before pushing me forward. I took half a step and nearly stumbled to the ground. My body was shot. Whatever that thing had done to me seemed to drain my power.

"I just need a second," I wheezed, and as I tried to suck in a breath that wasn't broken glass and barbed wire, Sheila grabbed me around the waist, hauling me into the air. Her feet pounded the earth as she sprinted up the hill with me in tow.

Only I knew it wouldn't matter. Distraction or not, Nadine stood between us and the top of the hill. Just beyond her, I could see the statue of the Empress, but not only that, I could see the altar behind it. Gwen lay bound on it, glowing sigils carved into her flesh. They burned with scarlet light, pulsing in time to the ones on Clarent.

"You won't be taking another step," Nadine said, whipping one hand toward Sheila and launching a bolt of scarlet electricity straight at her.

Only, instead of turning Sheila into a smudge on the ground, Nadine's attack slammed into an invisible wall just in front of the guard. As the blast dissipated into nothingness, the air in front of Sheila crackled into a gummy mess like safety glass.

That's when I realized Sally was behind us. She had one of her hands outstretched toward us while the other clasped Crystal's hand. Power surged forth from her, and the shattered air went back to normal to reveal Nadine standing there.

"Color me impressed," Nadine said, tapping her cheek with one finger. "You stopped one percent of my power." She smiled, the very picture of a Cheshire cat that enjoyed playing with its food. "Can you do it again? What if I get really serious?" She surged forward, practically blurring as haste magic wrapped around Sheila and me.

As the dark princess's fist shattered the shield, Sheila dropped me. I hit the dirt with a thud as the guard threw herself into Nadine, slamming her shoulder into Nadine's torso. The two of them crashed to the ground. As they did, Crystal's hand flew outward. Caltrops fell around both of them, wrapping the guard and Nadine up tight.

"We'll hold the line," Crystal said, pistols in hand as she began unloading them into Nadine's bound form. Energy crackled along her length as the magic binding her started to tear. I didn't have long, and worse, I didn't have time to stay and help. I had to stay on target.

"Thanks," I said, scrambling to my feet, trying my best to ignore the battle behind me. As I took one step after another, another volley of arrows entered the void, keeping the giant kaiju off of me. My people were holding the line. Now I just needed to make their sacrifice worth it.

As I reached the summit, the monstrous horde renewed its effort, surging toward the line of soldiers that had formed around the area to buy us time. Our ragtag group charged anyway, meeting the monsters' teeth, claws, and tentacles with swords, gunfire, magic, and huge fucking ravagers. They pounded through the enemies' lines, and through it all, I knew none of it mattered. We were so outnumbered, it nearly made me physically ill.

All they could do was buy me time at the expense of their lives. That, more than anything, was what I needed.

With that thought throbbing in my mind, I reached Gwen. Her eyes were shut, and the sigils still glowed. The statue of the Empress stared down at us, and even though I knew she wasn't real, I felt her gaze crawl over me like a swarm of oily bugs. Her eyes seemed to watch me as I raised Clarent and brought it down on the first of Gwen's bindings. It sliced through the chain with ease, shattering the bonds into etheric shards of fractured light and freeing her left arm. As I raised Clarent to do the same to her left leg, a lizardman came at me.

As its slavering jaws snapped at my face, I spun, swinging Clarent around like Sheila had taught me. My blade passed through its neck like a hot knife through butter, spilling ichor across the altar. An inhuman shriek erupted from that same altar, making me stumble backward, and as I did, Gwen's eyes fluttered open.

"Arthur?" she asked, confusion filling her voice. "Where am I? What's going on?"

"I'll tell you in a minute," I said, bringing Clarent down and freeing her left leg.

"Get off me, worm!" Nadine roared, a combination of agony and frustration tearing from her mouth.

A surge of power erupted from behind me, and as heat washed over me, Gwen screamed, "Duck!"

I dropped as burning wind rushed over me. Nadine's enraged fist passed over my head, and without thinking I lashed out with my elbow, driving it into her stomach. The force of the blow ran down my arm. It felt like I'd just tried to elbow a rushing locomotive. As pain rang through me, the dark princess smiled at me. She had a tiny cut on her lip but otherwise seemed unharmed. How was that possible? Where were Sally, Sheila, and Crystal?

"What did you do to my friends?" I cried as Nadine's murderous eyes met mine.

"They're dead," she said, like the lives of my girls were meaningless.

Rage flared up inside me, and before I could stop myself, I swung Clarent at her. The blade came at her in an upward arc meant to cleave her from crotch to throat.

And she stopped it.

Barehanded.

"You can't win," she said, tearing Clarent from my hand like she was ripping away a cobweb. She flung the sword away. "The Builder was never meant to be more than a tool," - she smiled - "and you're not even good at that."

"You killed my friends," I said, meeting her eyes as my sapphire armor evaporated into sparks, leaving me standing there before her defenseless. "You will pay for that."

"If I had a coin for every time I heard that, I'd be rich." She tittered. "Well, richer. I'm already rich." She grabbed my head and slammed me face first into the altar. My nose shattered into a spray of blood as my skull rebounded off the stone. My vision went blurry as she dropped me to the ground. I saw the broken sky again as she pushed me onto my back with her foot.

"Why don't you lick my boot like the pitiful worm you are?" She shoved her toe into my face. "Go on now. Give mommy a nice long lick."

"Why don't you give this a lick?" Crystal said, stepping from the shadows and slamming one of the explosive arrows into the side of Nadine's skull. The projectile exploded, blowing both women off the summit. My head twisted to watch Crystal fall, but only for a moment. I wasn't sure if she was still alive or if she would die any moment, but her sacrifice wouldn't be wasted.

I scrambled forward on my hands and knees, and as my hands wrapped around Clarent, I felt something grab my ankle.

"Where do you think you're going, Builder? My shoes aren't clean!" Nadine snarled, jerking me backward, and as she did, I spun. The force of her pulling on me combined with the strength of my thrust, and before I realized what had happened, I had driven Clarent clear through her abdomen. The blade jutted through her back, and for a moment, everything seemed to stop.

Her hands released me to go to the weapon in her gut, and as she stared down at it wide-eyed, she almost smiled. Tears began to fill her eyes as she sank to her knees in the sand beside me.

"Tell me, Builder. How does it feel?" she asked, turning her gaze upon me as her blood gushed through her fingers and onto the ground. "To penetrate me with your steel, is it everything you hoped it would be?" She smiled then, and it was the creepiest thing in the world because it was almost... relieved?

Only that didn't make sense.

"Here's where you're thinking it's over," Nadine tried to laugh, but only bloody bubbles left her lips as she threw her head backward and stared at the void above. "But it's only just beginning."

"What the fuck are you babbling about?" I asked, Clarent flaring inside her. The light along the blade pulsed, and the craziness receded from her eyes. For a split second, I saw something softer inside her, something that had been corrupted over the lips.

"There were always two." She coughed again. "Always two." She turned her eyes to the ground before toppling forward. One hand went out to arrest her fall, but all she served to do was drive Clarent deeper into her as she fell on top of me. "Maybe you're strong enough to stop it."

"Stop what?" I said, trying to work my way out from under her. Gwen was still on the altar. I needed to get to her, but something was definitely wrong with Nadine. I wasn't even sure why I cared, to be honest. After everything she had done, she deserved nothing but death. Still, from the way

Clarent was pulsing, I knew she was speaking the truth. I just didn't know what it meant.

"Always two," she whispered, one hand snaking up to grab my shoulder. She pulled herself up until we were nearly eye to eye, and it was strange because her vision had gone distant. "One to build," - she coughed, splattering my face with blood - "and one to destroy."

"One to destroy?" I asked, and she smiled then. "I don't understand."

"I know, but you will." Then Nadine kissed me, and my reality shattered. Literally.

49

I found myself standing on a battlefield similar to the one on which I'd been only a moment before. There were fewer statues though but the sky was still a swirling red mass of despair. As lightning cut across the horizon, I saw the giant squid-thing from the rent in space gazing down at us from above the statue.

At the very edge of the battlefield, Nadine stood beside an Asian man about my age. He had dark black hair pulled back into a samurai-style topknot. He couldn't have been much taller than five feet and was dressed in a strange blue kimono decorated with storm clouds. He had Clarent in one hand, and it blazed like the sun itself. His kimono shone with the same sapphire light my armor had, and his hands were wreathed in living flames.

Nadine turned to him, and the look on her face as she gazed upon him nearly broke my heart. I'd never had anyone ever look at me that way, not ever. There was so much love in it, the sight of it embarrassed me. She reached out, clasping his free hand in hers.

"We'll hold them while you drive into the center," she whispered, and her voice was calm and confident. "You must destroy the altar and free this domain from her grasp. Doing so will free our friends." She gestured at the statues. "That is worth any price."

"It will be done." The man smiled then as he turned to regard her with that same love. "On my honor." As he spoke, an army came through the void behind him. There were so many dragons and soldiers, it made my forces look like little more than a mote in God's eye.

"We can still leave," Nadine said, and for the first time, I heard the fear in her voice. "Run away together."

"I cannot." The man shook his head. "It would be like killing myself." He took a step forward. "Now let us find honor and glory."

He charged, and the world erupted into chaos. The scene scrambled into a pixilated mess, and as I stepped backward in shock, the shattered visage of reality morphed into a different scene.

Everyone was dead and dying and still more warriors surged from the Darkness. The man was on the hill, Nadine beside him as he slashed through a ravager like it was made of confetti. As the creature fell to the earth with a thud that shook the landscape, the beast from above howled.

"You have lost," the man said, moving toward the altar, sword blazing. He was so bright I could barely look at him, and as he brought Clarent down, the clang of the strike rang out like a clarion call.

That's when I realized it never struck. Another sword that swirled like a black hole held it away from the altar. With practiced ease, the wielder of that black blade knocked Clarent from the man's hand, stepping out from the shadows as the shining sword went spinning off the hill.

A writhing scar ran down the left side of his cheek where it looked like his cheek had been peeled away by a sword slash before being stapled back into place. His crisp white hair was cut close-cropped and his left eye burned with yellow fire.

"Who are you?" Nadine cried, moving to interpose herself between him and the Builder as he calmly lifted his own sword, laying it across his shoulder.

"You thought you would win, didn't you?" he said, and his voice was a black hole, sucking the life from the whole of the battlefield. Time seemed to slow down as he took a casual step forward, one hand extended toward the two of them. "I am Dred." His lips twisted into a smile.

"Dred?" the man asked, confusion filling his voice as he shot a furtive glance toward Clarent. It was only a few yards away. I knew that look, but so did Dred.

"Yes." He clucked his tongue, sword whipping out in a blur to point at Clarent. "If you go for the sword, I will kill your girl." He gestured toward Nadine. "I'd rather not, but I will."

"What do you want?" Nadine asked, unperturbed by his comment. I could tell she wanted to fight but something was wrong.

"To destroy." His grin widened. "Everything." He tapped his sword to his head. "That's what Excalibur wants." He pointed the swirling black blade at them. "To destroy everything. To turn the world into an endless void of nothing. I am its chosen." He smiled again. "Destroying is so much more fun after all." He swept his blade in an arc that caused the ground around them to turn molten, cutting them off from Clarent.

"Why would you aid the Darkness?" the man asked, confusion in his voice. Only there was more than that. There were worry and fear, sure, but more than that, there was failure. He knew he had lost.

"Here's the thing, boy. The Darkness was first." His blade came up, drawing all the color and light from the surroundings. "I am just returning the universe to how it should be, how it used to be." His blade came down, and as it did, Nadine threw herself in front of the man.

"Please, just let him go," she cried, tears streaming from her eyes. "If you do, I'll do anything."

"Anything?" he asked, blade hovering in midair. "Would you betray them all?" His hand swept across the battlefield. "Would you give it all up to save this miserable failure?"

"Yes," she said without hesitation, and the sky above boomed in response. Bloody rain began to fall, turning the battlefield to mush.

Dred turned his head heavenward. "It seems the Empress accepts your offer." His hand whipped out and a blast of Darkness tore through the space between them, rending open reality. Beyond the tear, I could see a feudal city straight out of the history books. "Send him away."

"You can't, Nadine. We must fight," he said, hands balling into fists. He took a step toward Dred, but before he could do more, Nadine grabbed him by the kimono, whirling him around to face her. Tears fell from her eyes, trailing down her cheeks as she brought him close.

"We cannot fight. I cannot lose you," she whispered, drawing him into a last kiss. Hunger and need flowed through her, and as I watched, I knew the truth of the gesture. She'd never see him again.

"We must," he said, pulling away from her.

"No." She shoved him backward, sending him through the portal. As his body exploded into a flash of light that transported him back to wherever he called home, the rent portal closed with another clarion call.

"I have held my end of the bargain up," Dred said, turning his gaze onto Nadine. "Now fulfill yours." He waved a hand at the remaining soldiers. "Kill them all."

And she did.

The scene resolved itself as Nadine's last shuddering breath escaped her throat, leaving her dead atop of me. Above the sky boomed, and the arrows flew. I wasn't sure how much time had passed, but it didn't seem long. Part of me still hated Nadine, but now? Now most of me just felt sorry for her.

She had sacrificed it all to save the Builder of her time. It had cost her everything, but he'd survived. As I replayed the memories I'd seen, I realized I thought she was wrong. I understood why she'd done it, but I knew the look on the man's face as he was pushed back to his reality. He had wanted to fight, and she had taken that away from him because of fear.

That was bullshit.

I pushed on her with all my strength, creating enough of a gap between us for me to wedge my knee under her. I shoved her off of me. As her lifeless body hit the ground next to me, I pulled Clarent free of her. It came away easily, blazing to life in my hand as I called upon its power to clothe me again. My armor reappeared, and with it, my extra strength and speed.

I sprinted forward as arrows pierced the sky and bats swooped down on my forces. I knew what I had to do. More than save Gwen, I had to destroy the altar. Doing so would free this land from the

Darkness. At least they'd thought it would and trying to do it had cost everything.

As I came to a stop beside the later, I saw Gwen. Her body was alight with magic as she flung fireballs with her free hand, desperate to keep back the horde of beholders surging up toward the statue.

"Gwen!" I cried, bringing Clarent down on her right arm's binding. As the bond shattered beneath my attack, she sat up, flinging a fireball past my ear to incinerate another bat.

"Arthur! Untie me, we have to get out of here!" she cried, pointing to the beholders. "Everyone else is too busy with that thing." She pointed, but I didn't need to look at the wannabe Cthulhu to know that's what she meant. Instead, I severed her last binding, freeing her.

She jumped off the altar, coming to my side. As she did, I shoved the Nexus Gateway Conduit into her hand.

"What's this?" she asked, confusion filling her voice as I turned back toward the altar.

"A portal home. Get everyone out of here, okay? I'll be right behind you. I have to do something first!" I moved toward the altar as she fumbled with the device. "Just hit the button on it, and it will work."

"You can't stay. You're too important!" She took a step toward me.

"Do as I say!" I snarled as the Darkness beyond the altar began to swirl, letting me know something was about to come through. I wasn't sure if it was Dred or something else, but I knew one thing. We were out of time, and I would not let Gwen become Nadine. "Go!"

She took a long look at me before nodding. Holding the device out in front of her, she hit the only button on the Nexus Gateway Conduit. A portal the size of a movie screen swirled to life in front of her, and as it did, my people instantly broke formation. They knew the drill. As soon as the portal opened, they were to shove everyone through.

I turned my attention back to the altar, Clarent blazing with blue fire as I raised it up to bring down on the altar. Darkness swirled all around me as the beast above turned its hideous gaze upon me. Power rippled through me, shattering my armor as I brought Clarent down with everything I had, driving the blade into the altar of Darkness.

The staccato clang of it filled my ears as the Altar fell in two. At first, nothing happened. Then, all at once, the sky began to swirl, sealing off the void from which the tentacle monster screamed at me with a loud pop. Sparks shot from the cleaved edges of the altar, and the Darkness spiraled around me dissipated into smoke. With a tortured shriek, the Nexus gateway behind me shattered. Blue light streamed across the whole of the sky as the sky changed from the torn mass of red to the familiar storms of Hell itself.

As that light spread out across the whole of the world, the Darkness warriors, beholders, and other creatures (including our own ravagers, unfortunately) dissipated into smoke.

"You think you've won, don't you?" a voice unlike any I'd ever heard rumbled. It was primordial and so evil that it made me want to jump into a black hole. The statue of the Empress glared at me with the same yellow eyes Dred had. "But you've really just lost." Hideous laughter filled my ears as the statue shattered into pink sparks that burst outward like a shockwave.

As the sparks touched the statues, the stone fell away, turning the warriors trapped within back into flesh and blood people. One by one they fell to their knees, finally freed from their endless purgatory.

"You did it," Gwen said, coming toward me, the

backdrop of Lustnor in the distance. She pointed behind me. "The Darkness has receded for miles!"

"Not far enough," I said, turning to see that while she was right, that was all it had done, pushed back like the shore at low tide. All that sacrifice for a few miles of territory. How many had we lost because of it? Too damned many.

"You should take your victories where you can," she said, laying a hand on my shoulder. "It is not often one stares into the abyss, and the abyss pulls back."

50

In the days that followed the battle for the statue, everything changed, and yet it stayed so much the same it was maddening.

We'd lost people. Good people, and that was my fault, plain and simple. I knew that we were at a war with an unceasing, uncompromising enemy, but that didn't stop each and every death from weighing me down. Buffy had told me that was good because I didn't want to be the kind of leader who could order troops into battle and not care whether they lived or died. With the way I felt, I wasn't sure if I believed her because the casualties had been high.

Sheila had lost both of her eyes and Crystal had lost an arm but Sally had managed to get them both back to normal. That had cost a lot of Experience, but she'd gladly ground it out. Not that it was hard since there were so many injured.

Blade's End had been left without a leader, but thanks to the Nexus Gateways and a little conniving by Buffy and Elizabeth, we were temporarily in charge of it. For the most part, they seemed okay with it, and not just because, thanks to Sam's casting technique, Etheric Flame and dragon taming had become lucrative.

We still had problems with the guilds of Royal Centre, but they were starting to come around. Not quickly because bureaucrats, but still coming around. After we'd freed all the warriors, some had gone home to their families, while others had settled with us.

Lustnor had expanded, and we even had farmers now. It was a good thing too because the food was getting expensive, and we couldn't send everything we needed to the front lines.

Hell was still being attacked by Darkness warriors, but not as often as before. Still, try as I might, I couldn't enjoy it. Something felt wrong.

Why hadn't Dred shown up? Why had the statue of the Empress felt so sure of her victory as she lost?

Neither of those made sense.

"If you keep worrying about it, you'll drive yourself insane," Gwen said, putting a hand on my shoulder as I stared out at the horizon. I wasn't sure what lay behind the Darkness, but it scared me. It would cost more people to take that bit of land back, and while the Graveyard of Statues had bolstered our ranks, I didn't think we had enough people to besiege the Darkness itself. More and more, I just felt like we got lucky.

"I'm the Builder of Legend. It's my job to worry." I took a deep breath and turned to look at her. She had a coy smile on her lips. "I have to be the one to fix all this."

"I know, and it's a big burden, but we're all here to help you." She smiled at me. "Thanks to you, we've recovered more ancient magic and technology than ever before. We know how to do things we thought myth and legend." She nodded at me. "If you did no more, this would be more than enough."

"For others, maybe but not for me." I could still see the look on Nadine's Builder's face as he tumbled back home. He would have fought until the last drop of blood had been spilled from his body. "It's not in me to give up, not while we aren't free."

"Are you thinking about Akimitsu again?" she asked, touching my shoulder. "His and Nadine's fates are not your fault."

"I know that," I said, taking a deep breath as I put my hand to Clarent, "and I know that Nadine was wrong but at the same time, it worries me."

"What worries you?" she asked, moving closer to me.

"How powerful Akimitsu was. Well, how strong all of them were. We could work for another century and not be as powerful as they were then, and the Darkness beat them without any effort." I gestured at our town. "What we have is not enough."

"We won. Yes, we will fight more, will drive the Darkness back until it is gone, but for now, we are in the eye of the storm. Let's relax a little." She quirked a smile at me. "Come on." She took my hand in hers and moved to drag me away. "You can put it anywhere."

I felt my face heat up, and as she winked at me, I thought I might be about to get one of my favorite things. "Stop trying to distract me. I'm serious."

"So am I," she said, fixing me with a stern look. "We should rest while we can. That Dred you spoke of will come. I know it, but he probably won't come today." She shook her head.

"What about what Nadine said about the destroyer?" I asked, shaking my head. "His sword, you should have felt it."

"Then train until you're stronger." Gwen pressed her body close to me. "Until we're all stronger." She leaned in until her lips were nearly to my ear. "I will not pull a Nadine and sacrifice everything for you because that is not your wish." She licked my ear lobe. "This you can trust."

Her words lifted a weight off my shoulder I knew I shouldn't have felt. I hadn't even realized I'd worried about something similar happening, but at the same time, now that she'd said it aloud, I knew that was what had been bothering me.

"Thank you," I said, smirking at her. "So, is that offer still good?"

"Which offer is that?" she asked, giving me a devilish smile.

"The one where I could put it—"

My words were cut off as a comet punched through the cloud cover overhead. Golden sparks trailed off the end as it hurtled toward us. As I watched the sky roil, golden light shone through, turning the ground all around us lush with life.

A moment later, the comet slammed into the ground just beyond the gates, sending a wave of gilded light outward as the shockwave threw me from my feet. I hit the ground hard, and as I did, I heard alarm bells going off.

Scrambling back to my feet, I climbed up on the wall, scaling the ladder in a moment to look out at what had come through.

A blonde woman wearing a snow-white gown with a golden belt stood there with a gilded mace in one hand and a glittering sword in the other. Her white, feathered wings were spread to their full expanse as she took a step forward. As she did, flowers sprouted in her wake. Her crystal blue eyes scanned the wall before looking up to find me.

"Builder," she called, and her voice was like honey and sage, threatening to wrap me up in the pure goodness of it. "I am Gabriella, Archangel. I require your assistance." She took a deep breath and leaped into the air, her wings easily holding her aloft as she came toward me until we were eye to eye. "You must help me."

"Wait a second. You're an angel?" I asked even though the statement seemed really dumb in retrospect.

"I am Gabriella, second to Michelle of the

archangels, and we require your assistance." She pierced me with her blue eyes, and I got the feeling she could see every speck of my soul. "Dred has breached our gates and will soon march upon the seat of Heaven's power. He has all the Empress's armies at his disposal." She reached out and touched my cheek then and warmth filtered through my skin, making me forget I'd ever worried before. "Please, you must assist us."

"Get back, angel!" Gwen snarled, stepping between us and pushing Gabriella's arm away. "I won't let you hurt him."

"I don't want to hurt him!" Gabriella snarled, her hand tightening on her mace.

"Stop, both of you," I said, taking a deep breath and pushing between them. I glared at Gwen. "You behave." As a look that let me know the offer was most decidedly off the table materialized on Gwen's face, I turned to Gabriella. "And you. Be nice to my friends."

"She is the spawn of the great deceiver." Gabriella crossed her arms indignantly over her chest. "I will do no such thing."

"Then I won't help you," I said, glaring at her. "You can just shove off back to Heaven and fight Dred on your own."

"You would really leave Heaven to the Darkness?" she asked, alarm filling her voice in a way that let me know this was not going as she'd expected.

"I would."

"You mustn't. You must help. If you do not come and stop Dred, he will come here next. Heaven will become a ravaged wasteland." She snorted at the town. "Maybe you're used to that, but once you see the splendor of Heaven, you will want to save it."

"Don't listen to that self-righteous bitch," Gwen sneered. "All that glitters isn't gold. That's for damned sure."

"Gwen, play nice." I smiled at her. "I got this."

"You've got this?" Gwen snarled at me while pointing a finger at Gabriella. "Do you even know what they are like?"

"Builder," Gabriella said, moving forward only to be buffeted back by the barrier surrounding the town. The sigils flared to life, keeping her from getting closer. She stared at it for a moment before sighing. "Please, you must come quickly. We are running short of time."

"Fine," I said, holding out a hand to Gabriella, "but only if you learn to be nicer to Gwen."

"You can't go, Arthur!" Gwen said, reaching for me. "She can't be trusted."

"It is you who can't be trusted!" Gabriella snapped back.

"Well, you both better get over it because she's coming." I took Gabriella's hand then, and the feel of her was like jumping into a swimming pool on a hot summer's day. "They're all coming."

THANK YOU FOR READING!

**Curious about what happens to
Arthur next?**
Find out in The Builder's Crown, coming soon!

AUTHOR'S NOTE

Dear reader, if you REALLY want to read my next Builder novel- I've got a bit of bad news for you.

Unfortunately, **Amazon will not tell you when the next comes out.**

You'll probably never know about my next books, and you'll be left wondering what happened to Arthur, Gwen, and the gang. That's rather terrible.

There is good news though! There are three ways you can find out when the next book is published:

1) You join my mailing list by clicking here.

2) You follow me on my Facebook page or join my Facebook Group. I always announce my new

books in both those places as well as interact with fans.

3) You follow me on Amazon. You can do this by going to the store page (or clicking this link) and clicking on the Follow button that is under the author picture on the left side.

If you follow me, Amazon will send you an email when I publish a book. You'll just have to make sure you check the emails they send.

Doing any of these, or all three for best results, will ensure you find out about my next book when it is published.

If you don't, Amazon will never tell you about my next release. Please take a few seconds to do one of these so that you'll be able to join Arthur, Gwen, and the gang on their next adventure.

Also, there are some Litrpg Facebook groups you could join if you are so inclined.

LitRPG

LitRPG Society

Made in the USA
Middletown, DE
31 July 2017